# WITH THE ENEMY

## JEN DENNIS

*Also by Jen Dennis*

The Underground
(Jordan Kennedy: Book One)

Published by Vivid Publishing
P.O. Box 948, Fremantle
Western Australia 6959
www.vividpublishing.com.au

National Library of Australia cataloguing-in-publication data:
Creator: Dennis, Jennifer, author.
Title:     With the enemy / Jen Dennis.
ISBN:     9781925442533 (paperback)
Series:    Dennis, Jennifer. Jordan Kennedy books ; Book two.
Subjects: Suspense fiction.
            Murder investigation--Fiction.
Dewey Number: A823.4

**This book is available in both print and ebook editions. To find out more about the book or contact the author, please visit: www.vividpublishing.com.au/withtheenemy**

*To all the dedicated individuals working in emergency services. Thank you.*

# Preface

I was unarmed.

Over the last few weeks I'd become accustomed to carrying a weapon, but now that I was without it, I felt more defenceless than ever. Death was inevitable, and I was the target tonight.

Or perhaps more accurately, I was like a sitting duck in an open field, just waiting for somebody to take the first shot. The odds were against me, but I would stand and fight regardless of the risks. Truthfully, I no longer cared if I lived or died, just as long as the woman I loved was safe. She was the one in the line of fire. She was the one in danger, and I was the one who put her in that position.

As I walked down the corridor, towards the room where she was being held captive, I thought about all that I could have done to avoid this situation. There had been many opportunities to survive this ordeal, but because of me, the chances were long gone.

The blood in my veins turned to ice as I reached for the door handle. I mentally tried to plan an escape route, but the chances of escaping unscathed seemed slim to none. I pulled the door handle down, but before I'd even opened the door an inch, somebody else grabbed me from behind, snaked an arm around my neck, and held me in a headlock.

I tried to scream, but the air could not reach my lungs. I tried to struggle free but my body was already too weak. I'd already accepted this is how I would die, but I wanted to see the woman I loved just one last time. It'd been so long since I'd gazed upon her hazel eyes.

I kept hoping that maybe my last wishes would be respected, but I think my life ended the second I heard a gun shot echo from inside the room, followed by her excruciating screams...

# 1

*Five weeks earlier. July 14th*

This was not how I'd pictured my life to be.

I was stuck in my car, caught in a never-ending stream of brake lights, knowing it would be some time before the traffic cleared.

I was also living far away from home, on the other side of the world. Yep—I was living in Australia, and although I'd lived here for almost a year on a working visa, this country was still foreign to me in every single way. I missed England. More than I'd like to admit.

To top it off? My dreams and aspirations were hanging by a thread. Five years ago, I thought I would be a top-selling recording artist by now, with at least five albums on the shelves. In reality, I wasn't good enough to even busk on the streets.

However, I had one thing in my life that made it worth it— Rochelle Hawthorn. My relationship with her was, without doubt, my greatest accomplishment. We'd been dating on and off for over a year—currently living together—and I guess I was at liberty to call her my girlfriend.

During my drive home from work that day, I called Rochelle, like I always did. After fiddling with my mobile and sticking in the earpiece, I waited for her to answer. Sometimes I'd wait forever for her to answer.

"Hello?" she said, as her voice never failed to put me at ease after a hectic day.

"Hey, it's me," I replied. "I'm about twenty minutes from home."

"Good, because dinner will be on the table in fifteen."

"And what are you cooking?"

Silence, followed by a snort of laughter.

"What, are you kidding?" she asked. "I ordered Chinese."

Typical. Life was so busy for the both of us, that the thought of cooking was quickly disregarded. Shit. I don't think I'd had a home cooked meal in over a week.

"Then can you do me a favour?" I asked. "Get the fire going. It's bloody freezing tonight."

"Already done, Jordan."

"Brilliant. See you soon. Love you," I said, just as I ended the call.

The traffic ahead began to move, but barely. I managed to pass through a roundabout and crawled along the road for a few metres, only to be once again stopped at a set of traffic lights. Glancing ahead, I could see at least seventeen cars in front of me. Even though I lived fairly close to work, when the traffic was heavy, some days it could take me almost up to an hour to get home.

I worked in a music shop. It was located in a tiny building in the heart of Castle Hill's industrial zone. The music shop—christened Jeff's Music—was located at the front of the building, in between a funeral insurance company and a laser hair removal clinic. Yeah, it was quite a bizarre location, but business was good. That's all that mattered to me.

I was working a healthy eight-hour shift five days a week. My main role was selling instruments—of course—but we specialised in guitars, and although I knew how to play one, my knowledge of different brands was minimal. In the beginning, I swear I had been hired out of pity, and then only a few weeks after starting my job at the store, I dropped out and disappeared for almost six months. I didn't even resign—I just vanished for a while. When I reapplied for the same job later that year, I couldn't believe my luck when I was rehired.

I guess I'd been given a second chance due to my exceptional knowledge and skills when it came to playing the keys. I also gave private piano lessons, but I only had two students. I guess kids didn't care so much about pianos anymore—guitars were cooler.

My girlfriend was working again too. Rochelle had returned to her position as a barmaid, but she was now working in an up-scale nightclub, rather than a rowdy pub. Although the money was good, Rochelle was ready for a career change. When she wasn't mixing drinks, she was studying part time at university, taking on a bachelor of applied fitness. Rochelle aspired to become a personal trainer, and I'd been encouraging her as best I could.

We'd moved in together too. Rochelle and I were currently renting a one-bedroom granny flat in Middle Dural. Our home was shabby, tiny and gritty, but we'd chosen to rent this place for two reasons; it was cheap and we were allowed pets.

I personally had never cared for pets, but Rochelle did. She especially loved dogs.

No, we didn't have a pup yet, but Rochelle dedicated her afternoons to checking out local pet shelters and adoption centres. She wanted a medium-sized female dog, and she wanted to name it some overly-clichéd pet name, like Roxy or Bella. I had no say in the matter, but then again, I didn't care either way.

After battling peak hour traffic, I came to the familiarity of the countryside, where the place I called my home was hidden behind vast lines of gumtrees, down a narrow dirt road.

As I pulled up beside the garden shed, I could see puffs of smoke escaping from the chimney, rising into the night sky. I locked my car and shuffled towards the front door. After fumbling with my keys for a minute or so, I unlocked the front door and stepped inside.

Our flat was—for lack of better words—trashed. Although we cleaned the place every goddamn weekend, there was never enough time during the week to maintain an immaculate home.

I wandered into the living area to find Rochelle cooped up at the tiny desk in the corner of the room. She was working on her laptop. Rochelle had heard me enter, but was so engrossed in her work that she gave me no acknowledgement.

"Hi," I said, as I remained standing from across the room. "You alright?"

She muttered one syllable that I translated into the word 'OK.' Although Rochelle was trying to hint to me she didn't want to be disturbed, I cautiously stepped across the room and closer to her. We'd made a pact last week to make more time for each other, but with life already so busy, we were struggling to keep our promise.

"Have you been home long?" I asked.

She didn't say a word. I don't think she even heard me.

"Dinner's on the bench, by the way," she finally replied, without even looking up from the screen. "Help yourself."

Although devouring a container of fried rice and chow mien was tempting, I took a step closer to my girlfriend and rested a hand on her shoulder.

"Come on," I said gently, "let's call it a night, yeah?"

"Can't. I need to get this done," she replied, still clacking away at the keys.

"What are you doing anyway?"

"I'm creating a fitness regime for a fifty-year-old woman suffering from arthritis in the knees."

"And why are you doing that?"

"For uni. It's an assignment due next week."

I bent down a little closer to Rochelle, maintaining my grip on her shoulder, and smiled.

"Then how about we make a little fitness regime for ourselves?" I whispered. "But we ought to do some research first, so let's go do a little practical test in the bedroom."

She cringed.

"I hate it when you try to be suggestive," said Rochelle. "You're just no good at it."

I knew it too, but that wouldn't stop me.

"I think you need to take a night off," I tried, but she wasn't listening anymore.

When Rochelle set her mind to something, she was stubborn. Although part of me wanted to persevere, and convince my girlfriend to spend some time with me, I reluctantly walked away and left her alone with her studies.

I dined alone that evening, in the bedroom, watching an episode of *The Simpsons* I'd seen over a dozen times before. After taking the garbage out to an almost-full bin, I showered, shaved and climbed into bed. I stayed awake until almost midnight, and when Rochelle finally decided to join me, she fell asleep almost immediately.

Even though I was lying beside the woman I loved more than anyone else in the world, I felt cold and isolated. Life had a habit of depriving you of the smallest pleasures, and all that was left was stress and anxiety. There was a time where I'd craved the mundane, but now that I was trapped in the same goddamn routine every day, I knew I needed an escape, because this was *definitely* not the life I'd originally mapped out.

# 2

I find it hard to make friends.

I figured it was because I'd always been a little socially awkward, but it was too damn late to change now. Nevertheless, in the short time I'd spent in Australia, I'd made at least one good friend. His name was Cosmo Rowland, a work-colleague, and a cool guy.

Cosmo and I worked very similar shifts at Jeff's Music, so we worked together most days. This combined with a shared love of music and song writing made it easy to maintain a friendship with him, although our tastes were at complete opposite ends of the spectrum. I liked power ballads, pop, and alternative music, while he was into hard rock, heavy metal and a new genre I'd never even heard of—screamo. I assumed it was a style of music that featured a lot of screaming.

Cosmo was roughly a year younger than me, but completely dedicated to music. He had his own band too, a death metal four-piece named 'Bleeding Black Bandits'. And, although he was the only person I could call a friend in this country, I hadn't been brave enough to attend any of his band's gigs.

Cosmo's interests could be summed up in just a few words—electric guitars, bodybuilding and tattoos. When he wasn't playing power chords or working out at the gym, Cosmo thoroughly enjoyed getting himself inked. In the eight months I'd worked with him, he seemed to have a new tattoo every few months. Cosmo's right arm was a sleeve of intricate images—dragons, skulls, bats and oddly enough he even had a boxing kangaroo at the top of his bicep. He reckoned he had a total of nineteen tattoos, but they all seemed to blend together so it looked like just one big tattoo to me.

Cosmo was pushing six foot, built like a machine, with hair slightly lighter than mine. He constantly wore black shirts with camo pants, black studded bracelets around both wrists, and his lip piercing never failed to intimidate (or disgust). Also, he had a tendency to swear just a little too casually—even when there was absolutely no need for it.

But despite his appearance, he was a good guy. In fact, I'd lost count of how many times he'd saved my arse at work. I seemed to struggle making sales to anyone under twenty-five. Sure, I was only twenty-seven years old myself, but I'd somehow lost touch with the younger generation. I swear that teenagers these days spoke a different form of English.

Today was no exception. I was trying to sell a Fender Squire to a teenage girl no older than sixteen, and as always, I was failing miserably.

"So, you've played guitar before?" I asked, already feeling my nerves take hold.

"No shit, Sherlock," she replied, rolling her eyes. "That's why I'm here."

"How long have you been playing for?"

She looked at me as if I'd asked the dumbest question possible.

"Like, six years."

"And do you play electric, or acoustic?"

The teen chewed her gum obnoxiously, crossed her arms and said,

"Acoustic, which is why I want an electric."

I nodded and then I asked the girl if she'd like to play the Fender to trial it, and once again she rolled her eyes and snatched the guitar off the hook. The teen sat on the floor—despite the fact there was a perfectly good chair right beside her—and began to strum.

For someone who had claimed she'd played guitar for six years, she didn't seem all that good. In fact, she seemed to be oblivious to the fact the guitar was still out of standard tuning.

"Yeah, I'll buy it," snorted the teen, after only playing it for approximately eight seconds.

"Sure," I said. "Will you be buying an amp too?"

"Why the hell would I need an amp?"

"Because it's an electric guitar."

"Meaning?"

"Meaning you should buy an amp so you can plug it in and play it."

A vexed expression crossed her eyes, and her stare was so fierce that I took a step back. Before I could explain myself, she exploded into rage.

"You trying to rip me off?"

"Of course not, I—"

"You are trying to rip me off!"

I raised both palms up as if trying to protect myself from a pending punch, but I had no reason to panic, because Cosmo Rowland stepped in and rescued the sale.

"There's a discount on Fender amps today," said Cosmo, his deep voice defusing the tension in a split second. "I think I can hook you up with a bargain."

At last, it seemed the teen was listening.

"What kind of bargain?" she asked, her tone softer and more reserved.

"I could get you the guitar, amp, lead, strap and a few picks for under four hundred."

"Is that a good deal?"

"You bet," he replied, smiling.

She returned the smile. I, on the other hand, slinked away from the sale before I ruined the deal. Cosmo and the teen chatted to each other for nearly fifteen minutes. The teen had already agreed to take the bargain package, but she and Cosmo were in a deep conversation about some kind of metal band I'd never even heard of before. Honestly, sometimes I wonder why I was ever hired (technically twice after I'd abruptly quit the first time around). I didn't truly belong here. I was just a square peg trying to fit in a round hole.

Cosmo successfully sealed the sale after a lengthy discussion about a band named Atreyu. The teen then began to leave the store, clutching her guitar under one arm, her new amp under the other, while staring dreamily at Cosmo.

Once she was gone, and it was just Cosmo and I behind the counter, I turned to him, arched an eyebrow and said,

"How did you do that?"

Cosmo knew exactly what I meant.

"Experience, man," he simply replied.

"No, it's more than that. You're just a sweet talker, Cosmo."

He smiled and shrugged his muscular shoulders. If there's one trait I envied that Cosmo had, it would be his ability to talk to women, regardless of age, race or personality. He could say one word and the ladies would swoon, and sometimes Cosmo took his talent for granted. He could have any woman he wanted, but that wasn't enough for Cosmo. He wanted lots of women. He seemed to have a different girlfriend every week, and although he appeared to like his badboy/heartbreaker/player status, I couldn't help but feel he was damaging his reputation.

Although I thought highly of Cosmo, he wasn't so well liked. I'd heard stories. He'd been labelled as a dirt bag, sex addict. I guess his long list of girlfriends, and constant trips to strip clubs at Kings Cross gave him that reputation, but he didn't seem to mind.

For the next twenty minutes, I restocked the box of *Family Guy* guitar picks—the Stewie ones usually sold out quite quickly—while Cosmo killed time by tuning all the display guitars. Soon enough, my shift ended. I finished earlier on Thursdays, so I clocked off, and collected my belongings.

"See you tomorrow, man," said Cosmo, barely looking up from the guitar strings.

"Yep," I called as I headed towards the exit. "Have a good night. Bye."

I stumbled outside into the cold July afternoon, and as I was walking to my car, my phone buzzed from inside my pocket. I fished it out, and checked the caller ID. Private number. Goddamn it, why is it that everyone had private numbers these days? Shaking my head to myself, I pressed the answer button, put the mobile to my ear and said,

"Hello?"

"Who is this?" asked a deep voice, belonging to a stranger.

"Jordan Kennedy," I replied, "but I ought to be asking you the same question."

The phone cut out. The caller hung up without more to say. It must've been a wrong number, so I put my phone away and thought nothing more of it as I made my way home.

# 3

By the time I arrived home, she was already gone.

Rochelle had left a note on the bench, explaining she'd been called into work a little earlier than usual, and that she'd see me tomorrow. Once again, I was alone for another night, but this time I'd have to fend for myself and cook dinner. Ordering something was a temptation. I was in the mood for pizza, but knowing better, I chucked a low-fat frozen meal into the microwave.

After dinner, I found myself doing the washing up. It hadn't been done in almost four days, and it had piled up so much that dirty dishes completely hid the granite kitchen benchtop. I even took the recycling out and did a quick vacuum around the lounge room too. Maybe I was secretly hoping Rochelle would reward me for my initiative, but then again, I had my doubts that she would even notice. Life had become all about work, with no play. Just the very thought brought my spirits down.

Now that I was alone, cold, and in need of someone to talk to—I called my little sister, Amy.

She lived in England with my parents, and despite the distance, we were close. Amy and I had been through a lot together, especially after what we'd endured last year. In fact, sometimes thinking about the past put my head into a spin. So, to keep it brief—five years ago my sister had faked her death in the London underground bombings, and lived under a new identity in Australia to hide a forbidden affair and an unexpected pregnancy—and of course, she'd managed to get herself into a big financial debt, complete with gun-wielding loan sharks. My sister was lucky to be alive, which is why I was relieved she was living back home, under my parents' watchful eye.

I was also an uncle. I had a four-year-old niece named Millie, and even though my sister was only a mere twenty-years-old herself, she was raising her daughter well. Millie had been through a lot in her short life too.

Just before nine o'clock that evening, I brought a chair over to the kitchen phone and took a seat. I picked up the receiver from its cradle, dialled in a seemingly endless string of numbers, and waited as the call went through. I waited forever. But at last, somebody picked up (after almost thirteen rings) and although I was only greeted with a simple hello, I recognised my sister's voice immediately.

"Good morning, Amy," I said, cheerfully.

"Jordan," she scolded. "Do you have any idea what time it is here?"

"Seven o'clock in the morning."

"Exactly. Do you think you could call at a more decent time?"

"Sure. How does two in the morning sound?"

Silence, followed by her aggravated sigh.

"Don't be a smartarse, Jordan."

I chuckled for a moment, and when the silence settled back in, Amy asked,

"How's Rochelle?"

"Fine," I said.

"Just fine?" she queried. "You could have made it a little more convincing."

If there was one trait I hated in Amy, it was the fact she never hesitated to be up front. She never sugar-coated what she needed to say—she was always direct.

"She's just a little busy these days, that's all," I explained.

"Which is why you've resorted to calling your little sister?" she questioned. "I know you don't want me to say it, but Jesus, you need to get yourself some friends."

"What, don't you like catching up with me?"

"Of course I do," said Amy, "but I still worry about your social life—or rather the lack of it."

My sister was the master of bluntness. Without question.

For the next half an hour or so, we spoke about our parents, Harry and Sharon. I hadn't seen them in over a year. Just thinking about my old house in Benfleet, Essex would make me feel homesick. Although I felt privileged to be living in Australia, the place I called home would always be England. After all, I'd spent the majority of my life there.

Amy then filled me in with her current dreams and ambitions. She was an aspiring actress, but let's face it—it's a damn hard industry to crack into. Knowing she needed a career to make an income, Amy was undertaking a course in graphic design. She was explaining her most recent project when the conversation came to an abrupt end.

"Look, Millie's up, and she has preschool today. I need to go."

"OK," I said, recognising the disappointment in my voice. "Speak soon."

Amy and I exchanged goodbyes, and without more to say, the line went dead.

I placed the receiver back into its cradle and sat back in my chair. This loneliness could not go on. I either needed to find something else to keep me occupied during the dull evenings, or I needed to confront Rochelle and demand that we spend more time together.

Our relationship had been through rough patches before— rougher than this—so to me it seemed that Rochelle and I could survive almost anything. That being said, I still couldn't take it for granted. She meant everything to me, and that was no overstatement. Without her, nothing else really seemed worth it.

# 4

*July 22ⁿᵈ*

The message alert caught me off guard.

I was sitting alone, on my lunch-break, eating a sandwich near the food court, when my mobile phone lit up in front of me, requesting that I accept a wireless download.

Although I was surrounded by hundreds of people inside a shopping centre, I was by myself. Who the hell would be requesting a wireless connection? As I took another bite from my chicken sub, I checked the request. Somebody dubbed 'Mal1976' was trying to send me a file, and without thinking much off it, I accepted the request. No, I wasn't sure who Mal1976 was, but my curiosity always got the better of me.

I continued to watch as the file transferred, and before I had the chance to inspect it, I received a slap across the back, which nearly made me choke on my sandwich.

"What the fuck are you doing?" asked Cosmo Rowland, as he sat opposite me.

I put my mobile away and simply said,

"Nothing."

Cosmo raised an eyebrow, and then grinned as he unwrapped his beef kebab.

"Were you watching porn?" he asked, making sure he spoke loud enough so that the strangers sitting at the tables surrounding us could hear.

"No, I wasn't," I snapped back, defensively.

"You sure about that?"

"Cosmo, unlike you, I'm not a sex obsessed rodent."

"Ah, don't be jealous just because I score more than you," he replied, still grinning.

We continued eating in silence for a few minutes. Lunch-breaks only lasted half an hour, so I tried to make the most of it.

However, Cosmo always tried to fill the gap with conversation, and the majority of the time it was about music, tattoos or women.

"I got a new girl," he announced as he unscrewed the cap on a bottle of Coke.

"A new one?" I asked, "but whatever happened to Susiana?"

"Dumped her. She was fuckin' boring."

"Then what's your new girlfriend's name?"

"Christine. She's hot."

"And where did you meet?"

"Kings Cross, outside an adult book store."

Go figure.

"And is she—nice?" I queried.

"Yeah. Great body, with an even better rack."

Although Cosmo was a good friend to me, we were undeniably different. Sometimes I craved to have an intellectual discussion, and although he was a smart bloke, he had very shallow interests. Even when I tried to talk seriously with Cosmo, he'd twist the conversation to make it light-hearted and irrelevant.

Then again, it's my fault for being the way I am. I enjoyed talking about current affairs, modern issues and the weather. Does that make me dull? Or an intellect? I wasn't sure, but I guess I didn't want to know either.

As I checked my watch, it was almost half past twelve, meaning I needed to be back at work and behind the counter within three minutes. I cleared the table, said goodbye to Cosmo and raced back to my car.

\*\*\*

My day had been dull and uneventful, just like any other day—at least that's what I had initially thought.

Cosmo had finished his shift earlier that day, so Jeff—the owner of Jeff's Music, of course—covered the rest of his shift. Technically speaking, Jeff was my boss, but he was even more laid back than Cosmo. I had to admit, even though working in a music store wasn't what I imagined I'd do for work, I couldn't have asked for a nicer work environment.

Just before five thirty, Jeff announced he had an appointment, and it'd be my responsibility to lock up the store. I nodded, and soon enough, he was gone.

The second it was time to close, I locked the main doors and pulled down the blinds. I loved being inside the music store alone. It was the only chance I had to play the most beautiful piano in the world. It was a Yamaha C series grand piano. It was located at the very back of the store, and it was usually covered up with a thick grey woollen blanket. According to Jeff, he'd had the piano in the store for almost six years, and no one had even shown an interest in buying it.

I had my eye on it though. Regardless of the price tag, I wanted it.

As I slinked to the back of the store, I pulled the wool cover off to reveal the masterpiece. I lifted the fallboard from the keys, and sat down on the stool. For a moment I just admired it. The only piano I'd ever owned was an old Broadwood upright piano that had belonged to my grandfather, and my ex-girlfriend currently had it in the corner of her lounge room across from the fireplace—if she had even bothered to keep it. Knowing Sophie Oakland, she'd probably disposed of it, along with any other memories of me.

I'd been bitter about our break-up for a long time, but now that I had Rochelle, it didn't seem to matter all that much anymore. She'd moved on. And so had I.

I rested my hands on the ivorite, and allowed my fingers to dance across the keys. And now that I was alone, I could sing too. As I played, I closed my eyes and let the performer within me break free.

I aspired to be somebody. I wanted to matter. I wanted to make my mark on the world, and I knew I could only do that through my music. Having a normal life wasn't appealing to me. I'd dreamt of big things, because I guess I felt like I had something to prove. For years I'd received no support or encouragement, but it had never been enough to diminish my determination. I was destined for a better life.

For almost forty minutes I forgot about the world, and performed for myself. However, midway through one of my original ballads, my mobile jittered inside my pocket. The atmosphere died. I was brought back to reality in an instant. Acting quickly, I pulled my phone from my pocket, to see that Rochelle was calling. I accepted the call and put the phone to my ear.

"Where are you?" she said, bluntly.

"At work, but I'll be home soon."

"Still?" she queried. "What's keeping you?"

"Something came up, but I'm leaving now," I said.

"Good. See you soon."

Our call ended, and I suppose my solo gig was over too. I closed the fallboard over the keys, replaced the woollen blanket, and stood up from the stool. I was about to put my mobile back inside my pocket, but it was then I remembered about the mysterious file I'd received during lunch today. I'd forgotten about it—until now.

I began searching through the files on my phone. I found a file entitled 'Justice' in my video folder. I opened the file, watching suspiciously, as the video began to play.

I watched as three figures came into focus. There were three men inside a darkened room. I tried to make out their faces, but the video quality was so poor that the men's features were lost. However, I could tell what they were wearing. One man wore a flashy suit and a tie, and stood with his arms crossed. Another man stood beside him, and as I squinted at the pixels, I noticed he was holding a gun—a pistol to be more specific. And the final man wore green shorts and a shirt, but he was lying on the ground in front of the other two men, clutching onto his arm, wailing in pain.

"You've had this coming for a while," said the man wearing the suit, as he uncrossed his arms and stepped closer to the cripple lying on the ground. "You knew it too."

"I-I did wha- what I had t- to do," replied the cripple.

"But you've taken lives," said the suit, "and you ended the life of a great friend."

"I never meant to kill him—"

"—Lies," hissed the suit. "For once in your life, be honest."

I watched intently, but I wished I'd looked away. The gun-toting man fired a bullet into the cripple's thigh. He screamed in agony. What the hell was this?

"You shot my friend dead, and for that, you must suffer the same fate," continued the suit, as he smiled down at the cripple.

"Please!" he screamed, now clutching his thigh, "I- let me ma-make it up t-to you."

"How? What can you possibly do to make it up to me?"

"I d-don't know," wailed the man, as the tears made his voice sound even weaker. "Just gi-give m- me a cha- chance. I d-don't deserve this."

The suit turned and looked at his gun-wielding associate, smiled, and said,

"End it here."

His accomplice nodded, and as I blinked, there was a sudden white flash and then an eruption of gunfire, along with deafening screams. My body convulsed as I watched, and the bullets seemed to penetrate the cripple's body, producing a spray of red mist with each hit.

My phone shook violently in my hand. What the hell was this? As much as I wanted to look away, I couldn't. Once the gunfire had ceased, the suit surveyed the dead body.

"Get rid of this scumbag," he said to the gunman, "then clean up this mess."

"And then what, Mal?"

"We'll find the other man involved, and then we'll kill him too."

The video ended. My hand trembled as I switched off my mobile and placed it into my pocket. I knew what I had seen. My mind tried to find an explanation, struggling to understand the logic behind downloading a video from a stranger. I found myself overwhelmed by thoughts. Who had sent me the video? Why had they sent me the video? And what the hell did it all mean?

I picked up my car keys from the counter and left the store without delay. I needed Rochelle. Maybe she could help me find the sense in all this.

# 5

I'd almost forgotten what fear felt like.

I'd been on an even keel for so long, that I didn't even feel human at times. My daily routine left me feeling like a robot, a conformist. I'd been craving a change for a while now. I wanted something to happen, but this brutal murder video is not what I'd had in mind.

I arrived home a little after seven o'clock that evening. I had expected to find Rochelle working on her assessments again, but she was in the kitchen. And she was cooking dinner.

"Hi," she said, without even looking up from the stove. "I made chicken soup for dinner. It's not a recipe I've tried before, but it looks pretty good."

I think I was only half listening, because I was more focused on showing Rochelle the video I'd been sent. I took out my mobile and stepped closer towards her, but before I had the chance to say anything at all, Rochelle had another announcement to make.

"I've found us a shelter puppy too," she said, smiling. "She's a German short-haired pointer. She's still young, but we can pick her up in two weeks—"

"—That's brilliant," I said, as I cut her off, "but there's something I need to show you."

Her eyes changed. Rochelle instantly knew something was amiss, so she turned off the stove and cautiously approached me. Before she could ask what was wrong, or even comfort me, I found the video on my phone and played it to her.

Rochelle watched silently as the pictures began to move on the screen. I, however, didn't care to watch it again. Once had been enough.

When the video had ended, I switched off my mobile and looked at Rochelle. She stared at me, puzzled. I ended the confusion and told her what happened.

"A stranger sent it to me today."

Her eyes met mine.

"So?" she asked, arching an eyebrow.

Silence. I struggled to register her question. The footage had left me feeling paranoid and terrified, but Rochelle had almost no reaction at all. I was beginning to think that maybe she didn't understand. Had she even seen what I had seen?

"Those men," I said, "they shot that man."

"And what, do you think it's real?"

"Well, yes."

Rochelle shook her head, and made a somewhat sympathetic smile.

"No—it's nothing more than old footage from a D grade movie, Jordan."

"How do you know?" I asked, my voice unnecessarily firm.

"Because it's damn obvious."

"But why would someone send it to me? Out of all people?"

"You're an easy target to scare," she said. "No offence, but it's true."

I thought about arguing with her, but I'd only lose. Although I'd grown stronger over time, a part of me still felt weak and power-less. My nerves seemed to be the biggest factor. I struggled to control them—they controlled me.

"Look, why don't you have a shower before dinner?" suggested Rochelle. "I'm sure it'll make you feel better."

I nodded, and slinked away into the bathroom. Even as I let the hot water rain over me, I couldn't let go of the film footage. It was weighing down on my conscience, dominating my thoughts. Call it intuition, but I could tell that something about the video wasn't quite right.

Somebody else would have to watch the footage. I needed a second opinion, and I knew just the right person to turn to.

# 6

"It's fake," said Cosmo, seconds after viewing the video. "It's pretty revolting, but it's about as real as Dirk Diggler's cock in *Boogie Nights.*"

I stared blankly. He rolled his eyes. Clearly, I had missed the sarcasm.

"But how can you be so sure it's not real?" I asked.

"Two reasons," replied Cosmo, "firstly, the acting is shit. It's so obvious that it's entirely staged. Secondly, if you watch carefully, a few bullets seem to ricochet off the injured dude's body after they hit him—and bullets don't bounce. Besides, if this was a real murder, why the fuck would they film it?"

"But none of them look at the screen. Maybe they didn't know they were being filmed—"

"—Doubt it, man. This is just someone's poor attempt at making a gangster flick."

I nodded, and put my mobile away, feeling slightly foolish. I had a habit of looking beyond the logical explanation. I had been so sure the video was legit, and I can't explain why, but part of me perhaps wanted it to be.

I returned behind the counter once more. Work had been slow today with only one customer all morning. There was plenty of work to be done, such as ordering in the new drum kits, or replacing the strings on old guitars—but with the shop completely empty, Cosmo and I took the time to socialise.

"So how's Rochelle doing?" asked Cosmo, picking up a guitar off the wall.

Cosmo had never met Rochelle, but I spoke about her so much at work that he felt like he knew her.

"She's alright," I replied, "but she's in her own world at the moment."

"In what way?"

"A little distant lately."

Cosmo made a small smile and sneered,

"I bet it's been ages since you last fucked her."

"That," I said firmly, "is none of your business."

"Really? Has it been *that* long? How are you coping, man?"

"Shut it, Cosmo."

His smile grew as he tuned up the guitar. For a few minutes, he played softly to himself, while I tried to tidy up the papers scattered across the counter.

"You should be spontaneous and take Rochelle somewhere this weekend," Cosmo said after sometime, "I reckon the best way to rekindle a romance is to get away for a bit."

"No offence, Cosmo, but why should I take relationship advice from you?"

"I know I'm not much of a romantic, but that doesn't mean I don't know how to be."

I thought about it for a moment, and daydreamed about the perfect getaway. I'd give anything to spend a weekend up at the coast. I loved it up there. Rochelle did too. However, before I could enjoy the thought, reality brought me back down again.

"She has work this weekend," I muttered, feeling disappointed.

"Fuck that, just get someone to fill in for her," said Cosmo. "It's not that hard to arrange."

"But Rochelle is stubborn. She won't want to take a weekend off."

"Then be sneaky, man. Don't tell her about it. In fact, it's quiet this afternoon, so you can leave now and take an early start to the weekend if you like."

I looked at the clock. 2pm. Rochelle would be at university right now, but she'd be home within an hour or so. I could dash home, pack the car, and the moment Rochelle arrived home we could drive up to the central coast and find a hotel to stay in.

"It's really OK if I go early?" I asked.

"Yeah," replied Cosmo, "go for it. See you Monday."

I thanked him, collected my belongings, and left the shop. As I unlocked my car, I could feel the happiness take me on a natural high. I'd wanted to get away from Sydney for such a long time, and this was the perfect opportunity.

I brought the engine to life, and reversed out of the car park, completely unaware that I was being watched.

\*\*\*

Behind tinted glass, Malcolm Lawson watched as his adversary drove away.

Jordan Kennedy had left from work early, but what for? His shift didn't end until later on. Mal was sure of it. Something had happened, and he intended to find out. They'd come too far to let their next victim fall through the cracks.

Acting quickly, Mal ordered his assistant and loyal friend, Isaac, to put the car into gear.

"And then what?" asked Isaac, his hands already resting on the wheel.

"Follow him," said Mal. "We'll attack later tonight, just as we planned."

# 7

I needed to move quickly, because Rochelle would be home soon.

I darted inside the house, packed a suitcase with our clothes, filling it with whatever I could find. My sense of direction had always been quite poor too, so I switched on the computer, logged onto the net and used *Google Maps* to figure out where the hell I needed to go.

Next, I called Rochelle's work and explained she wouldn't be in for the weekend. I didn't tell them why, but they never asked anyway.

She arrived just as I finished loading up the car. Rochelle parked alongside me, stepped out of her Ute, carrying uni folders under one arm and arched an eyebrow at me. I grinned, and beckoned her over.

"What?" she asked, without moving an inch.

"You're coming with me," I said, still smiling. "Come on, let's get into the car."

"Right now?"

"Yeah. Let's go."

She gave me an apprehensive stare.

"But where are we going, Jordan?"

"I'm being spontaneous."

"How long will we be gone for?" she asked. "You know I have to work this weekend."

I took a few steps closer to Rochelle, took the folders from her hands and said,

"All taken care of. You've got the whole weekend to spend with me."

She looked as though she wanted to smile, but Rochelle wasn't sure how to react. She deserved a break, but the guilt would bother her. She was so dedicated to her job that taking time off to enjoy life was difficult for her. Rochelle liked to be kept busy, either studying or working behind the bar. But she had earned a weekend away.

Stepping towards the car, I opened the passenger's side door and told her to hop in. Rochelle forced the doubts from her mind, and complied. Immediately I ran her folders inside, locked the front door and slid behind the wheel.

After reversing onto the road, we took off to start our private getaway.

***

Grey, ominous clouds hovered above the ocean, and stretched into the horizon.

The drive up to the coast had been peaceful, but the weather left a lot to be desired. It was going to rain. It was cold, and this was not the break I had first envisaged. Nevertheless, Rochelle seemed quite content.

We'd spoken about taking a holiday for months, but when it came to making plans, we'd both procrastinate. This spur of the moment weekend away was just what we needed.

As we continued to drive, I wound down the window. The fresh ocean breeze on my face made me feel so at peace, so alive. Killcare was my favourite place in Australia. I'd discovered it a little over a year ago. It was a fairly quiet place, very well hidden, but I'd give anything to move up here.

I pulled into the car park by the side of the beach. Instantly, Rochelle unbuckled her seat belt and jumped out of the car. I followed. She was heading towards the sand trail, and to the beach.

When she reached the bottom, Rochelle kicked off her shoes. I did likewise. The beach was completely empty. As I scanned my eyes from one headland to the next, I couldn't see a single person. We were alone.

For the longest time, Rochelle stared out into the ocean, not saying a word. I stood and waited, but I found myself mesmerised by the sound of the crashing waves, the howling wind, and the leaves in the trees gently rustling. Even in the dullest weather, this place was still undeniably beautiful.

"Let's go for a walk," said Rochelle, her fingertips gently caressing my shoulder.

I took her by the hand, and led the way. We didn't talk. I guess there was nothing to say anyway. As we walked, our footsteps covered up old ones, and the sand was so soft that our feet would almost completely sink in. We strolled closer to the ocean. The waves edged closer, and the tide was rising. Rochelle laughed as I tried to dodge a wave as it rippled closer to the shore. I laughed too, and then wrapped my arms around her, and tried to pull her closer to the waves. Rochelle squirmed, and tried to push me in front of her, which resulted in me tripping over her feet and crash landing onto my arse. I landed in wet sand too. The back of my trousers became drenched. Rochelle laughed hysterically, and began running away. I sprung to my feet and chased after her, chuckling too.

We dashed to the other end of the beach. Giggling and out of breath, we collapsed on a sand dune. I set myself down and closed my eyes. Rochelle rested next to me, placing her head on my chest. For a while, we laid in silence and stared up at the grey skies above. It was getting darker. There would be a downpour of rain at any minute now.

"Thank you," said Rochelle, as she stroked the side of my chest. "We needed this."

Before I could agree, her lips found mine.

An emotion I thought I'd lost, suddenly resurfaced. I wasn't sure how to describe it, but I liked it. It felt good. Even as Rochelle pulled away, I leaned closer. I felt my arms tighten around her body, as her hand slid to the back of my head.

The chill of a brutal winter's day didn't even seem to bother us anymore, because the warmth of her body next to mine was all I needed. I wasn't sure how long we laid together for, but it made up for all the times we'd let each other down. Right now, nothing else mattered.

After some time, I sat upright again and looked out to the ocean once more.

"You alright?" asked Rochelle, her hand resting on my leg.

"Yeah," I said. "But I think I have sand in my ear."

I'd killed the moment. As usual. Rochelle didn't seem to mind though, because she stood up, and then held out her hand to help me to my feet. We climbed down from the dune, still holding onto each other. The silence settled back in, but it was peaceful just standing together, watching as the waves violently crashed onto the shore.

It was then, that Rochelle locked eyes with me, and gently said,

"I think we should go for a quick swim."

"What? Right now?" I asked. "But the water is probably freezing cold."

She smiled.

"So? That's not going to stop me."

Without allowing the words to sink in, Rochelle peeled her shirt over her head, and tugged down her hipster jeans.

"Whoa—what are you doing?" I cried, praying she wouldn't go further.

But she did. Rochelle completely stripped down and dumped her clothes in the sand. As she stood naked in front of me, I felt a mixture of astonishment and embarrassment. Panicked by the very thought someone would see her, I urged her to cover up. She bit the corner of her tongue, leaned closer to me and whispered,

"You coming?"

Before I could answer, Rochelle turned her back on me and ran towards the ocean. She dived right in, and disappeared under the waves. I couldn't see her. I grew anxious. Just as I was preparing to rush in to find her, Rochelle appeared from behind the crashing waves, waving as I stood bewildered by the shore. She laughed. I didn't. I remained frozen, barely believing her utter madness.

"Well?" she called out to me. "What are you waiting for?"

"Get back here!" I cried. "Somebody will see you!"

"Then you ought to come too, so we'll both get sprung together."

"You're insane, Rochelle!"

"Come on!" she called back. "Join me!"

I scanned my eyes around the coast. It was still deserted. However, there were hundreds of houses overlooking the beach—filled with potential spectators. This was beyond my comfort zone, but I couldn't leave Rochelle.

"Jordan! Come on!"

It was then, that I felt the sudden urge to do something stupid, regardless of the consequences. I tried not to let my pride get in the way, as I unzipped my jacket, and buttoned down my checked shirt. I could hear Rochelle cheering for me in the distance. I couldn't help but feel a little self-conscious.

I didn't dare look behind me as I yanked off my cargo trousers and boxer shorts, dumping my gear in the sand next to Rochelle's clothes. I tried to cover up (with what was left of my dignity) and I shuffled towards the ocean completely undressed. I stepped into the icy water, cursing under my breath, questioning my idiotic decision.

The first wave hit, bringing the water to my waist. The chill of the ocean was the equivalent of being jabbed with a million ice-tipped arrows. My body began to shake.

"This is ridiculous!" I called out to Rochelle. "How did I let you talk me into this?"

She poked her tongue out at me. Although I feared we'd end up in hospital from hypothermia, I soldiered on and dived underneath the waves. I swam underneath the water as far as I could go, and when I couldn't hold my breath for any longer, I rose towards the surface. I took a breath. The air filled my lungs. I was far from the shore.

In fact, I'd swum further out than I realised, because I was even further out than Rochelle. She giggled, and beckoned me closer. I complied. I began swimming back to Rochelle, feeling more at ease by the second.

For a few moments, the two of us tread water, recognising our stupidity. But as we came closer together, a new kind of act of stupidity entered our heads. We moved a little nearer to the shore— just so we could stand. Immediately, Rochelle wrapped her arms around my neck and pulled my body next to hers. I closed my eyes, and kissed her tenderly. The feel of the fresh, pristine water gently cascading down her bare body was indescribable. Underneath the water, I felt her legs wrap around me, pulling me even closer.

"Jordan," she whispered, but I didn't know why.

It was in that moment, that I didn't care where I was, and what I was doing, as I grasped my hands behind Rochelle's slender back. I went hard. Without considering the consequences, or weighing up the risks, she allowed me to get inside her.

She gasped, taking me in. Rochelle then rested her hands over my shoulders, and I took control. Building up a rhythm, I carefully slid my hands down her back, to her legs, holding her a little tighter. We kissed, unaware that the current was slowly dragging us back to the shore.

She was breathing harder. I was thrusting faster.

The water rested just above our waists now, but neither of us seemed to care. I could feel her climaxing with me. Rochelle's grip around me tightened, so close to reaching her peak. Moments before I felt ready to explode—the heavens opened up and the rain began to pour. The crystal like droplets collided with the ocean, denting the rolling waves just before they crashed. The current had dragged us even nearer to the shore, the water just below my knees. Oncoming waves became an issue too, knocking us about as they forced their way past us. I maintained my balance though, and took no concern to the fact we were out in the open, exposed and vulnerable.

"Jordan," she said again, "perhaps we should find a place to stay?"

Still out of breath, I nodded. It would be getting dark soon, and the wind chill factor was beginning to take its toll. I gently released my grip from behind the back of her legs, and helped Rochelle plant her feet back onto the sand.

Coming back down to reality, the fear of being caught was once again regarded, so we dashed through the rain, back to the drenched, sandy pile of fabrics that used to be our clothes.

# 8

After dressing, Rochelle and I jumped into the car, and drove off to find accommodation.

Beyond the beach and just over the hill, was a quiet little place called Hardy's Bay. We drove along a narrow road and spotted a small billboard sign on the side of the road that read—Doyle's Haven, Bed & Breakfast. Immediately, I turned onto the driveway and parked the car. Seconds before Rochelle and I stepped out into the pouring rain, a bearded man burst through the front door, down the steps, and greeted us a little too eagerly, introducing himself as Bill.

"Got a free room?" I asked.

"You bet, mate," beamed Bill. "Would you like the top floor? King sized bed, with an ensuite and the view is a real beauty."

"Yeah. That'd be great. Thanks."

He nodded vigorously, and then insisted he take our bags indoors. We allowed him, following him inside to shield ourselves from the rain. Bill took us straight to our room, and since our dripping wet clothes had left a trail of water, he brought us fresh towels and left us to be. Rochelle and I were grateful. We wanted to be alone.

I made sure I locked the door, because we didn't want to be disturbed either. We entered the ensuite together, stripped down, and shared a hot shower. After screwing around again, we towelled off, moved towards the bed and screwed around some more.

Eventually, we rested. Night had fallen too, although I couldn't be sure of the time. Rochelle and I lay between the sheets, enjoying our time together. She had her eyes closed, breathing softly. I watched her. Rochelle had me mesmerised.

I reached out and stroked her hair, which was still a little damp. Rochelle usually straightened her hair too, but for once she was letting it dry naturally. Which was the way I preferred it—wavy, uncontrolled. Her make-up had washed off in the ocean too, but I liked it that way. Sure, I liked Rochelle with make-up, but I also appreciated her with a fresh face.

But she was perfect to me anyway. In my eyes, Rochelle was faultless.

"Love you," she said, finally opening her eyes.

"I love you too," I replied.

Rochelle rolled over in the sheets, closer towards me, and pressed her lips against mine. When we broke apart, she smiled at me and said,

"So, are you ready for round four?"

"Soon," I said. "But I want to have a quick shave first."

"No, don't. I like you with a bit of stubble."

"Then I'll just trim. Deal?"

Rochelle considered it for a moment, but finally agreed.

"OK," she replied, "but don't be long."

I planted a kiss on her forehead, sat upright, kicked my feet over the end of the bed, and slipped out of the sheets. I walked towards the ensuite. As I stepped inside, I gave Rochelle a quick wink just as I closed the door behind me.

At that moment, I wasn't aware it might be the last time I'd ever see her. If I'd known, I would have stayed. I would have protected her. I would have done anything to keep her safe—even if it killed me. But as I plugged my electric razor into the power point, I had no idea of what was to come. My fate was just around the corner. I hadn't heard the car pull up outside. I hadn't heard the door unlock, and I hadn't heard Rochelle's muffled screams.

***

Minutes after loading his gun, Malcolm Lawson arrived outside Doyle's Haven.

Usually Mal was not a nervous man, but his fate was on a knife-edge. He'd either succeed, and continuing living another day, or he'd fail, leading to his peril. Tonight, Mal prayed everything would go according to plan, but there were obstacles he'd need to overcome first.

Mal's good friend and associate—Isaac Fuller—pointed out Jordan Kennedy's car from across the road. The tracking device they'd planted under the tyre rim had not let them down. However, the car could not stay there. It would have to be moved, destroyed and dumped at a new location where no one would ever find it.

But first, there was a far more pressing matter to attend to.

Gazing up to the house, Mal noticed a light shinning through the window on the top floor. Jordan and his girlfriend were likely the only guests at the bed & breakfast. If they had signed any check-in books, they would also need to be destroyed. Mal didn't want to leave a single trace or clue behind. He could not afford a single error.

"How do you want to do this?" asked Isaac, changing the magazine in his own gun.

"With no mistakes," replied Mal. "Just follow me. OK?"

Isaac nodded, waited as Mal unbuckled his seatbelt, and stepped out of the car into the rainy evening. Their victims were completely unaware of what was to come.

Mal led the way and Isaac trailed behind. The two of them walked along the driveway, up the stairs and to the front door, when a bearded stranger opened up and stepped outside.

"Hi!" beamed the stranger. "I'm Bill. Looking for a place to stay?"

Mal didn't have the time to answer questions. He needed to stay focused. Without any hesitation at all, Mal jabbed the gun barrel into the man's skull, and he'd done it with enough force that the man stumbled backwards and slammed his head against the wall behind him, knocking him unconscious.

Isaac stared down at the stranger's still body, disapprovingly.

"Thought we weren't going to make a scene," mumbled Isaac.

"Then let's be quick," hissed Mal. "We don't have a second to waste."

***

Rochelle never saw it coming.

She was unprepared, defenceless, and vulnerable. While peacefully listening to the rain lash against the windows, Rochelle had closed her eyes, and waited alone between the sheets.

Growing restless, she had pulled the sheets up to her neck and lay on her side. Rochelle kept her eyes closed. The room was silent and still. Unfortunately, she never heard the bedroom door click open. Somebody from the other side had picked the lock, making an easy entry. The knob was turned, and the door was pried open.

Suddenly, Rochelle felt an uncertainty. Something was amiss. Call it a woman's intuition, but something was wrong. As she rolled her body, looking over her shoulder, she caught a glimpse of two strange men advancing towards her.

Before she could scream, one of the men jumped onto the bed, pinned her down, and shoved her face into the pillow. She squirmed, feeling the air rush out of her lungs. Breathing became harder. Seconds before Rochelle feared she may pass out, the man lifted her face from the pillow, and rested a gun barrel on her temple.

"Get up. Get dressed," hissed the man. "Don't say a word."

Fearing for her life, Rochelle complied. Meanwhile, the second man pulled out a gun from his jacket pocket, and opened up the ensuite door.

***

Just as I placed down my electric razor on the bathroom counter, I looked into the mirror to see an unfamiliar face over my shoulder.

I froze. A stranger was in the bathroom. The stranger had a gun. Before I could turn around, or cry out to Rochelle, I was attacked from behind. Something sliced into my skull. It had happened so quickly, that I barely even realised I'd fallen to the floor.

I crashed face first on the cold bathroom tiles, but within seconds, I felt blood trickle past my ear, and down the side of my face. I tried to stay conscious, but my body betrayed me. I closed my eyes and let the darkness take me.

# 9

*July 24th*

When I opened my eyes the following morning, I was dizzy and disorientated.

The back of my head was throbbing, my body was bruised and I was shivering. I couldn't even remember what had happened, or where I was. I tried to collect my thoughts, scanning my eyes around an unfamiliar room. I was lying on the floor, on top of a Persian carpet, wearing only my boxers.

What the hell had happened?

Through the pain, I tried to concentrate. I had no recollection of anything. My mind was blank. I was scared. As my anxiety began to build, I studied my surroundings. There was a moss green sofa at the back of the room, and the walls were hidden by towering book-shelves. There must've been hundreds of books. From where I was sitting, I could see the dust coating the spines.

There were no windows, but there was a narrow door at the other side of the room. I tried to get up from the floor, but I didn't have the strength. My body was battered and bruised. I began to panic. Why couldn't I recall what had happened? Why was I here? And where was Rochelle?

Her name. Rochelle's name unclogged my memory.

We'd taken the weekend off. Just the two of us. It had been a cold Friday afternoon, and I had taken her to the coast. We had been to the beach. We had screwed around. And then we found a place to stay. As I tried to piece the broken fragments of my mind back together, a memory resurfaced. There had been strangers. With guns.

Growing more anxious by the second, I began screaming out to Rochelle. Once again, I tried to move, but the pain was too much. I continued screaming. Sooner or later, somebody would hear my call.

And somebody did. Less than a minute later, the narrow door burst open, and a man stepped inside. At first, I didn't know who he was, but as my eyes focused, I realised it was the same man who had broken into the ensuite and whacked me across the back of the head.

The stranger was completely bald, and stood almost six foot. He had a goatee though, and judging by the colour of his facial hair, he was a redhead. The man was also dressed well, in a full suit with a navy blue tie.

"Where's Rochelle?" I asked, my voice sounding deeper than usual.

"She's fine," replied the man. "For now, at least."

"Where is she?" I shouted.

The man put a finger to his lips and hushed me.

"Be quiet," he said, sternly. "You'll know everything in due time."

"But who are you? Why am I here?"

The man made a small smile, and crossed his arms.

"Usually I never introduce myself to anybody," he began, "but under the circumstances, I'll happily tell you that my name is Isaac. Isaac Fuller."

"Why have I been brought here? What have I done?"

"Like I said, you'll find out in due time."

"What's that supposed to mean?"

Isaac's smile broadened, as he took a step closer to me and said,

"Mal is very eager to meet you, Mr. Kennedy."

The name triggered another memory. My mind flashed back to the video footage I had been sent just a few days ago. I recalled the dialogue. I remembered the name.

*"Get rid of this scumbag. Then clean up this mess."*
*"And then what, Mal?*
*"We'll find the other man involved, and then we'll kill him too."*

The footage had to have been real. It had been sent to me on purpose. Through the haze, there was clarity, but what I had learned didn't bring me peace. I was the other man. I was going to be killed. But what had I done? What had I been involved in?

"I'll be back shortly," said Isaac, turning his back on me as he headed towards the door.

"But where is Rochelle?" I cried. "I've done nothing wrong!"

"Yes, you have, Mr. Kennedy."

Before I could question the statement, or demand answers, Isaac closed the door on me.

\*\*\*

Isaac returned maybe three or four hours later, just like he said he would.

He had brought me clothes too. A suit—just like his—with a white collared shirt, navy blue tie and a silver Rolex, which looked genuine to me. Although I was not used to such upscale attire, I was grateful for it. Isaac threw the suit at me and demanded I put it on. I obeyed with no complaints.

Once dressed, I summoned the strength to stagger to my feet. The pain was still present, but my muscles were recovering quickly. Isaac instructed me to follow him. I complied. We exited through the narrow door, through an empty corridor and down the stairs.

As we walked, I tried to figure out where I had been taken, but my surroundings offered no clues. However, I was certain of two things. I was still in Australia, and I was in somebody else's home. That being said, I still didn't know why I had been brought here.

When we'd reached the bottom of the staircase, I was taken into another room, and judging by the beautifully decorated table that took up almost all the space in the room, I was in the dining area. The walls were scattered with enormous oil paintings of outback-Australian landscapes, and there was a unique candle sculpture in the centre of the table. And, as I looked to the end of the room, I spotted a man with his back turned to me. He was standing by the window, staring outside, clutching onto a manila folder.

"Take a seat, Mr. Kennedy," said the man, but didn't turn around to face me.

I pulled out a chair, and sat down at the table. I waited. The man asked Isaac to leave the room, and he obeyed. I was alone with the new stranger, feeling my fear rise.

"My name is Malcolm Lawson," said the man, still staring out the window. "But you can call me Mal. And although you've probably never heard of me, I've known about you for a long time, Mr. Kennedy."

This guy was trying to intimidate me, but my hunger for truth fuelled me with a newfound strength. I demanded answers.

"Where is Rochelle?" I asked, my voice almost flawlessly steady.

"She's fine, and we'll talk more about her later. First, we need to talk business," said Mal.

"What kind of business?"

"You're a smart man, Mr. Kennedy—I assume you know why you're here."

"No. I don't actually."

Finally, Mal turned around and faced me for the first time. He was reasonably young, maybe a few years older than I was. Mal was no taller than five foot four, and he seemed meek and powerless, but I knew all too well that looks could be deceiving.

"Is that so?" questioned Mal, a smile slowly expanding.

"The video," I began, "you sent it to my mobile. The footage was real, wasn't it?"

Mal chuckled, but there was no trace of genuine humour. He opened the folder he'd been holding onto, pulled something out, and stepped towards the table. A photo was placed in front of me. Immediately, my eyes were drawn to the image, but I wished I'd never looked. It was a photograph of the victim from the video. More specifically, it was a photograph of the victim's mangled body. This image had been captured just moments after his death, as I recognised the green clothes instantly. Bullet wounds were scattered around his torso, and his face, was non-existent. The shots to the head had erased his identity, and all that was left was a bloodied pulp.

My stomach churned and I looked away, feeling my hands shake on my knees.

"Looks real enough to me, doesn't it, Mr. Kennedy?"

"Yeah," I replied, feeling light-headed.

"And I must ask, how does it make you feel?"

"Disgusted. Revolted."

"What about relief? I know you loathed this man. Surely you wanted him dead too?"

I raised my head, feeling the confusion build from within.

"But I don't even know who he is."

Mal stared, uncomprehending.

"You don't?"

"No. Should I?"

"Yes, Mr. Kennedy, you should."

"Then do you want to clue me in?"

Mal flicked through the folder, and pulled something else out.

"How about I show you a photo of him before his death? Maybe that will unclog your memory."

He placed a second photo on the desk, and as I gazed upon it, something inside my head exploded and disintegrated into tiny fragments. I stared down at the photo, recognising a familiar face. I'd known him. I'd known him all too well. My brain was working overtime, trying to link it together, but then the memories of our past began to resurface. I'd hated the man in the photograph. I'd hated him with every piece of my soul.

And as I stared at the image, into his crystal blue eyes, his name spun around my mind like a carousel spinning out of control.

Eamon Bronson.

My enemy, after all we'd been through, was dead.

"Jesus fucking Christ," I heard myself say.

Mal watched me, both entertained and satisfied with my reaction.

The past began to resurface, and the unwanted memories returned. Eamon had been briefly married to my sister, Amy. He had been the man who had convinced my sister to run away to Australia with him to hide their forbidden affair. He had pressured Amy into decisions she never should have made, and for that, I had hated Eamon Bronson.

In fact, I could recall the last time I'd seen him. He'd been lying in a hospital bed, barely alive. From that day on, I knew I'd never see him again, but I never wanted him to die. Then again, maybe he deserved it. Eamon was a killer too. He tried to justify his actions by explaining his motivations were purely to protect the ones he loved, but it had never been a good enough reason for me.

Eamon had been sentenced to thirty years in prison with no parole for the murders of two high-profiled criminals. Although I hadn't considered it at the time, in the video I'd been sent, the victim had been wearing green shorts and a shirt, or more specifically, the victim—Eamon—had been wearing prison greens.

And Mal and Isaac were the other men in the video. Mal had been the one wearing the suit, and Isaac had been the one holding the gun. Although the footage was bad quality, and their features had been lost within the pixels, their voices had confirmed their identity.

My head was overloading with thoughts and questions, but I decided to condense it all into one simple word.

"Why?" I said.

I didn't need to elaborate. Mal knew what I wanted to know.

"Mr. Kennedy, can you recall a man named Bruno Samuel?"

"Yeah," I replied. "He was a hitman. Eamon killed him."

"That's right, but Bruno was more than just a killer. He was also an expert transmission hacker, and a master negotiator. Good man. Well respected. Bruno was a business partner and a friend of mine too. So when I heard he'd been murdered, naturally, I was enraged."

My head was spinning once again, and the surface below my feet felt ready to give way. I'd known Bruno Samuel, and he used to terrify me. He had been a heavy built giant with a passion for bloodlust. He killed for the money, but he also took pleasure in the task.

In that moment, I began to remember the dialogue from the video footage between Mal, and his dying victim, Eamon Bronson.

*"You've had this coming for a while. You knew it too."*
*"I-I did wha- what I had t- to do."*
*"But you've taken lives, and you ended the life of a great friend."*
*"I never meant to kill him—"*

It seemed so clear now, but at the time I had been too blind to see. I rested my hands on the table. After the initial shock, I had recovered.

"So killing Eamon was a pointless revenge plot?" I asked, feeling my confidence grow.

"Not quite," said Mal, and he took a seat at the table, next to me. "You see, I'm very good at what I do. I'm a personal tracker, and that's what I do to earn a crust. For instance, one year ago, I was asked to track you down—"

"—by who?"

"Beau and Linda O'Riley. Remember them?"

I did, but they were no longer in the picture.

"You and your family had run off to Noosa, Queensland," continued Mal. "You were all in hiding, because Eamon had murdered Bruno, and your debt was left unpaid. So, I was asked to track you down, and when Rochelle thoughtlessly used her credit card at a child care, the trail led me straight to you."

"And why is this relevant?"

"Because you need to know what I'm capable of. I can be dangerous, Mr. Kennedy."

My gaze met his, but I was not afraid.

"But why have I been dragged into this?" I asked, my voice regaining steadiness. "Eamon killed Bruno. I was not involved at all."

"But you were there that night. You drove the getaway car."

"How do you know that?"

Mal smiled, leaned a little closer and said,

"You can learn so much about a person, just by knowing their name."

In that moment, I wondered what else he knew. Did he have any leverage over me? Or was he merely trying to intimidate me? I tried not to show my anxiousness.

"So how did you get to Eamon?" I asked, placing my hands onto the table. "He was in a very secure prison."

"Killing somebody in prison is as easy as shooting fish in a barrel," explained Mal. "They're trapped, defenceless. Also, I have connections to that prison, so when I asked for a private meeting, they were more than happy to arrange it. And even when Eamon never returned from that meeting, there were no questions asked."

"Hang on, if it was a private meeting, then how come it was filmed?"

"I filmed it for you Mr. Kennedy. Once again, I wanted to show you what I'm capable of."

I said nothing. The dizzy, disorientated feeling had returned.

"But let me be honest with you," said Mal as he folded his fingers together, "in the beginning, this was all just a pointless revenge plot, but now it's something more than that."

"In what way?"

"Firstly, Eamon was in prison, and therefore useless to me, so I killed him. And to be completely honest, I had intended to kill you too. However, I see a use for you, and so if you help me complete an unfinished project, I will allow you to continue living."

I nodded, and waited for him to continue. At last, Mal opened up the manila folder and let the contents spill out across the table. I gazed upon dozens of different papers, but it all meant nothing to me. Mal picked up one particular document and slid it in front of me. I looked at it for a few moments, but I was still lost.

"What is it?" I finally asked.

"About three months before Bruno died, he signed on to complete a project no one else dared to do," began Mal, "and now that Bruno's gone, we have struggled to find a replacement..."

I listened intently, but I knew what was coming next.

"—So, Mr. Kennedy, if you're willing to step in and complete the project. I will spare you."

"And what would I have to do?" I asked.

Mal leaned back in his chair, too casually. He then placed both hands behind his head and smiled. I waited, trying my hardest to mask my fear.

"Mr. Kennedy, are you familiar with the name Nathan Burwell?"

"Think so. I'm sure I've heard of him."

"Good, because he's the multimillionaire owner and CEO of a major Australian broadcasting network," said Mal, "and the project Bruno had signed on to do involves Nathan Burwell. Basically, my theory is, everyone has skeletons in their closest. Everyone has a secret they hope to take to the grave. Nathan Burwell is no different from the rest of us, and so I want somebody to invade his life, and unearth what it is he wants to keep hidden."

"And let me take a guess, when you learn his darkest secrets, you'll blackmail him?"

"Exactly, Mr. Kennedy," he said, sounding impressed. "And your duty in this project will be to get the dirt on Nathan Burwell, by any means necessary."

"It doesn't sound that difficult," I said. "Finding a replacement should've been easy."

Mal chuckled, folded his arms and said,

"You truly are naïve."

"Why?"

"Dozens of people invested a lot of money into this project," explained Mal. "There will be state of the art technology available for you, along with powerful weapons. And why would you need it? Because it will be difficult. Nathan Burwell is a loved and respected man, but he is awfully paranoid too. He is surrounded by security almost all day, and when work is done, he retreats to a secure mansion. Revealing Nathan's secrets will not be an easy task."

My confidence crumbled again. I had a habit of simplifying every situation.

"But what if this guy is clean?" I asked. "What if he has no secrets?"

"Everyone has a past, Mr. Kennedy. You may need to dig deep, but you'll find something. After all, failure will not be tolerated."

"Are you trying to threaten me?"

"Yes," replied Mal. "I am."

Without warning, he pushed back his chair and stood up. He slid the manila folder over to me, dunked his hand into his jacket pocket, pulled out a set of keys, and tossed them on top of the folder. Mal then instructed me to pick them up and go.

"But what are these for?" I asked, staring at the folder and keys.

"Your temporary accommodation. You'll be staying in an apartment in Sydney, close to Nathan, and close to the network building," explained Mal, "and the folder will provide you with some background information about Nathan that may be helpful."

I stood from my chair, but I wasn't ready to go yet. Not until I had my girlfriend.

"Take me to Rochelle," I said.

Mal crossed his arms and smiled.

"You'll see her again once this project is complete, so I'll be holding onto Rochelle for a little while longer. Just think of it as the motivation you need to get the job done."

"No. It's not going to work like that," I said, my tone losing all of its civility. "I refuse to help you until you let her go. She will not be involved in this."

Mal took a stride towards me. His arms had unfolded. The smile was gone.

"She already is involved, Mr. Kennedy."

"No, she's not!" I shouted. "Let her go!"

"It's not just your life at stake, Rochelle's life is on the line too. So if you don't cooperate, I will not hesitate to put a bullet in her skull—"

"—Don't you dare fucking say that to me! You will not touch her!"

"I don't like your attitude."

I snapped. I hadn't even predicted it myself, but before I could comprehend my actions, my hands reached out and I clasped Mal by the collar. Before I could decide what to do next, Mal jerked his body back, before delivering a fierce head butt into my face.

As our skulls collided, pain tore through my flesh. I stumbled backwards, tasting blood in my mouth. I fell back onto the table. I tried to get up, but my head was pounding. The force of the head butt had split my lip open. I tried to focus on Mal. He was unhurt. I rolled over, and pushed myself up from the table. Mal called for Isaac, and he appeared within seconds.

"What's up?" asked Isaac, stepping into the dining room.

"Take Mr. Kennedy to the apartment," said Mal. "He's starting to piss me off."

I tried to raise my fist as an attempt to defend myself, but my actions were so delayed, that my hands were twisted behind my back before I could even blink. I yelled for Rochelle. Isaac jabbed me in the side of the rib and told me to shut my mouth, but I wouldn't listen. Even through the pain, I called out her name.

I was dragged from the dining room, with my hands still twisted behind my back. I tried to break free from his grip, but I was overpowered. He took me down another set of stairs and down to the bottom floor of the house. We walked down another narrow corridor, and it was then, that I heard her voice.

"Jordan!" screamed Rochelle.

I jerked my head around. The voice had come from the room at the very end of the corridor.

"Rochelle!" I shouted. "I'm here!"

"Jordan..." she called, her voice now just a desperate plea.

Once again, I tried to break free from Isaac's grip. Rochelle's cries had fuelled my determination, and I managed to slip away, but Isaac's retaliation was too quick. His arm lunged out and grabbed me by my shirt, before shoving me headfirst into a wall. I had taken my final hit for the day. Although I was drifting away into a state of unconsciousness, I could still hear Rochelle's voice as my world blacked out.

# 10

For the second time that day, I awoke in an unfamiliar environment.

However, this time I was fully dressed, and lying on a comfortable king sized bed. I rolled over, and found myself glaring at an alarm clock. 7:16pm. I suspected I'd been knocked out for quite a few hours. I scanned my eyes to the left, and saw the suitcase I'd taken up to the coast with me. It had been opened, and my belongings were spilling out over the floor. I then scanned my eyes to the right, and saw a window. Outside the window, I saw the Sydney Harbour Bridge and the city skyline.

The back of my head seemed to throb with every thought, but somehow I pushed myself up from the bed and went to investigate my new surroundings.

After stumbling outside the bedroom, I found myself standing at the top of a staircase, looking down at a swanky open-planned apartment. This was supposed to be my accommodation while I completed the project? Flashy. This apartment had been intended for Bruno Samuel, but now I was here to fill his shoes.

I clambered down the stairs and to the bottom floor. Immediately, I was drawn towards the kitchenette, desperate to satisfy my thirst. I opened up a cupboard above the fridge, found a glass, and filled it with water from the tap. I drank it down, gratefully.

When I had finished, I placed the glass on top of the kitchenette bench. It was then I noticed the manila folder and the apartment keys resting beside the sink. Realisation hit me like a punch to the gut. Those sons of bitches had my girlfriend. They were keeping her hostage, and they wouldn't let her go until I completed my mission.

Anger pulsed through my veins. Rochelle shouldn't have been brought into this. I wanted to blame my new adversaries, but instead I blamed myself. I should have protected her. I should have done something. Worst of all, I didn't know where she was being held captive. I'd been unconscious during my trip to and from the house, so locating her would be impossible. She was alone, defenceless.

My mind was failing me. I couldn't concentrate. All my thoughts were of Rochelle, and the sound of her weakened voice. I wanted to break down, but for once, I kept myself together. I needed to be strong. I needed to think this through rationally. I guess my only option was to finish the task that had been assigned to me.

I opened the manila folder to begin reading, when I found a note from Mal Lawson lying on top of the files. I read it. The message was brief, but clear,

*Mr. Kennedy,*

*One more thing I forgot to mention; this project you've signed on to do is confidential, so don't speak a word of it to anyone, or you'll be a dead man.*

*- Mal*

I had assumed so from the start. This wasn't the first time I'd dealt with criminals.

I picked up the rest of the folder, and began to flick through it. There were dozens of documents. All about Nathan Burwell. As I read through the folder, I caught an insight into Nathan's life, and although I'd never met him, the information was proving to be useful.

I continued to read, before sitting down at a spacious, glass dining table. I was focused. I knew what I had to do, and although I didn't like my situation, I had come to terms with it. In order to rescue Rochelle, I had no choice but to work with the enemy.

# 11

*July 26th*

I dragged myself to work on Monday.

I'd spent the rest of my weekend recovering from my injuries, and drugging myself with painkillers to the point where I almost felt numb. The gash at the back of my head had begun to heal, but since I kept my hair quite short, the wound was very noticeable. Before I left for work that morning, I found a cap in my suitcase and put it on. I felt like a bit of an idiot, mainly because I was wearing a cap indoors while it was raining outside, but I didn't want anybody to see my injury. I was in no mood to answer questions.

I left the apartment just before eight o'clock. I figured I'd need to catch a bus, but Mal Lawson had kindly arranged for my own mode of transport—a Black BMW. A very flash car indeed. Then of course, memories surfaced. I remembered back to last year. This car had originally belonged to Bruno Samuel.

For a moment, I hesitated. Bruno had committed crimes using this car. It seemed wrong to use a vehicle that had been linked to so much evil, but then I disregarded my stupid superstitions, and slid behind the wheel.

\*\*\*

I was late.

It was just after nine-thirty as I stumbled through the front door of Jeff's Music. Sydney traffic was never pleasant, and when it was raining during peak hour, it was even worse. Nevertheless, Cosmo didn't question my tardiness, but maybe it was because he was busy making a sales pitch to a doting father, trying to buy his ten-year-old son his first guitar.

I slipped behind the counter and started entering amp orders into the system, pretending like everything was as it should be. I tried to forget about Mal Lawson, Bruno Samuel and Nathan Burwell—but I was struggling, because Rochelle's voice was plaguing my every thought.

After Cosmo successfully scored the sale, he processed the payment, and wished the customer a pleasant day. He was a total suck up. But of course, I knew him for who he really was, and when the store was empty—Cosmo let his true personality emerge.

"So how was your weekend away?" he said, smiling as he approached the counter. "Did you get laid?"

"Bugger off," I snapped.

"Hmm, so I'll take that as a no?"

I ignored him. I wasn't in the mood for Cosmo's bullshit games. Eventually, he slinked away to the back of the store and began replacing the strings on vintage guitars. Good. I wanted him to keep his distance. I just wanted to be alone.

As my head continued to throb, I tried to concentrate on my work. There were hundreds of orders to process. My fingers clacked across the computer keys, as I entered dozens of digits. Strangely enough, I was finding work somewhat therapeutic, probably because it was enabling my mind to focus on something else. However, Cosmo was doing all he could to break my concentration.

"Hey Kennedy," he called from across the room. "Wanna come to Kings Cross tonight?"

"No," I replied, not looking up from the computer screen.

"Come on. I'm sure your girlfriend won't mind if it's a one off."

"I said no."

He watched me uneasily, sensing something was playing upon my mind.

"By the way, what's with the cap?" asked Cosmo. "You look like a douchebag."

"Shut the hell up!" I shouted, unable to suppress my anger.

He scowled at me, stopped what he was doing, and approached the counter.

"Hey, what the fuck is wrong with you today?"

"Cosmo, please, just leave me alone!"

"You got issues, man. Just tell me what's going on?"

I grunted and jerked my head away from him. Cosmo lost patience with me—he hated being ignored—so he lunged out his hand and snatched the cap off my head.

"Fuckin' look at me when I'm talking to you!" he shouted.

I kept my head low, and turned away, forgetting that the gash on the back of my head was clearly exposed. Cosmo noticed it too.

"Jesus!" he said, eyeing the wound. "What the hell happened to your head?"

"It's nothing. Give me my cap back."

"Did Rochelle do that to you?"

"Of course not!"

"Then who the fuck did?"

Fighting my own apprehension, I turned away once more. Maybe I was embarrassed, or maybe I was ashamed—I wasn't sure—but I knew I couldn't deal with this situation alone. I was weak. I was afraid. I needed somebody to help me. Mal Lawson had threatened my life if I dared to reveal the details of my own personal hell, but for a moment, I ignored the risk. There was no way I'd survive without the trust of a true friend, so I turned to Cosmo, and I spilled my secrets.

I told him everything. A burden was lifted from my shoulders. Cosmo stood, a vacant expression on his face, as he took it all in. I went into every detail, leaving nothing out. I liked to think I was honest with people, but as I unleashed one fact after the other, I could see just how secretive I was.

As I continued to explain what had happened, a feeling of guilt rose from within. What was I doing? It was not fair to dump my problems on Cosmo. Yet as I spoke, he seemed to understand. I could only hope that he would help me.

When I had finished, there was a silence. He stared at me, blankly, while I fought to keep myself together.

"Seriously?" he asked, eyes wide. "No bullshit?"

"It's all true, Cosmo. These people have taken Rochelle away from me."

He opened his mouth to say something, but then closed it. For the first time, Cosmo was speechless. I'd always kept my past a secret. To me, only the future mattered.

It was then I tried to explain the task I'd been assigned. I mentioned Nathan Burwell, and Cosmo seemed to recognise the name, but he had already made up his mind. He offered to help, and assured me he would do all he could.

Before I could thank him, Cosmo rested a hard hand on my shoulder.

"We'll find Rochelle," he said. "Whatever it takes, man."

***

The store had been closed for a few hours, but Cosmo Rowland hadn't left work yet.

He liked to stay behind, playing a guitar, dreading the thought of returning to his trashed studio apartment, cold and isolated. And although taking a trip to Kings Cross always brightened his mood, money was tight. He'd have to wait until pay day.

His fingers slid across the frets, which was the most natural feeling in the world. Cosmo sat on a stool, behind the counter, with a guitar in his hands. When he played, the rest of the world faded away, and the music was all that mattered. Cosmo closed his eyes, still playing. He enjoyed losing himself in the moment, just listening to the sound of the amps gently humming with each strum.

Unfortunately, the sound of a car screeching outside the store broke his concentration. Cosmo jerked his head around, squinting at two headlights beaming from the car park. Two figures suddenly emerged from the car and headed towards the store. They were men. They were wearing suits. The shorter man stepped in front of the entrance doors, tugging on the handles as he tried to gain access.

"We're closed!" called Cosmo. "Come back tomorrow!"

Without warning, the doors were kicked in and the glass frames shattered to the ground. Cosmo stared, barely believing it. A hand snaked through the broken frames and unlocked the front doors from the outside. The two men stepped inside the store and headed straight towards Cosmo.

"Hey!" he shouted, rising from the stool. "What the fuck do you think——?"

A gun barrel was shoved under Cosmo's chin, hushing him mid sentence. Before he could come to terms with his newfound situation, Cosmo was pushed up against the back of the wall, the gun digging into his flesh. He tried to shove the intruder away, but the second man grabbed Cosmo by the wrists, and dug his shoulder into his rib cage. Cosmo was pinned. He was going to die.

"What the hell is this?" hissed Cosmo.

"Please, Mr. Rowland, keep quiet," said the shorter man, resting his finger on the trigger.

"H-how do you—?" began Cosmo, failing to comply with the stranger's demand. "How do you know my name?"

"I know a lot more than that, Mr. Rowland. I know you very well."

"So what are you going to do? Shoot me?"

"No, I'm not here to kill you," he continued, retracing the gun away. "I'm here to propose a deal which I think you may like."

Before he could ask questions, the taller man relinquished his grip around Cosmo's wrists, and let him off the wall. By natural instinct, Cosmo raised both fists, preparing to defend himself in case of another attack.

"Please, take a seat. Relax, Mr. Rowland."

"Who the fuck are you guys?" he snapped. "And what do you want?"

"My name is Mal Lawson," said the shorter man, "and this is my assistant, Isaac."

The taller man made a crooked smile and nodded his head.

"But—? What the hell are you both doing here?" hissed Cosmo, losing patience.

Mal instructed Cosmo to take a seat, but he remained standing, with both fists still raised.

"We need your help," began Mal, "because earlier today Jordan Kennedy revealed a secret to you he was not meant to tell, and because of that, you are now involved."

Cosmo dropped his fists.

"How do you know what Kennedy told me?"

"Two days ago we installed a listening device into Jordan's wristwatch. He is unaware of it, and it must remain that way," said

54

Mal, placing both palms on the counter top. "Every word he says, we hear. Every time he thinks he's in a private conversation, we will be listening in. Jordan Kennedy is being closely monitored until he completes the task assigned to him."

The pieces quickly came together. These strangers were the people keeping Rochelle captive. Cosmo was almost certain of it.

"So what is it that you want from me?" hissed Cosmo.

"Two things," said Isaac, speaking for the first time. "We want you to ensure Mr. Kennedy doesn't fail, and we want you to oversee his actions too."

"How do you mean?"

"We want you to supervise him," explained Mal, "Mr. Kennedy can be unpredictable at times. I don't understand how his mind works, so I want you to observe him closely. If Mr. Kennedy begins planning something irrational, you are to report it to us."

"Fuck that. I'm not going to betray a friend."

Mal smiled, leaned closer and said,

"Not even if it benefits you?"

Cosmo stood his ground. He had been gifted with the ability to decipher the hidden motives of others, and he knew these men could not be trusted. However, Cosmo had his weaknesses too, and his curiosity dominated over rationality.

"How would it benefit me?" asked Cosmo, crossing his arms.

"I know you well, Mr. Rowland," replied Mal.

"Oh yeah? Then humour me, fuckwit."

Mal smiled, just before he unleashed the past Cosmo had tried to forget,

"You were a high school dropout, and spent the majority of your time drinking, partying and chasing women. You are a self-proclaimed rebel, with a poor track record when it comes to responsibility—yes, I know all about your annual trips to Thailand. Desperately trying to get your life back on track, you aspire to become a tattoo artist. Eventually you gave up that dream and turned to crime. At the age of twenty-two you were involved in an armed tattoo parlour robbery, driving the getaway car and carrying an unlicensed pistol. You were sentenced to twenty-four months and served out your time at the Chelsea Hill Correctional Centre. After prison, you turned to gambling. Blackjack became your life, you wanted to play it professionally and make a career out of it. However, one bad hand robbed you of all your earnings, and to this very day you struggle to get by. Two years ago, you turned to music and drugs, and they've acted as your salvation ever since."

Silence. The memories had resurfaced, but Cosmo tried to push them from his mind. Instead, he tried to focus on the central issue—how the hell did this stranger know about his darkest secrets and deepest regrets? Cosmo had never told anyone his history. He had tried to start a new life, abandoning his friends and family, in order to get a clean slate. Cosmo tried not to seem astounded—he just let his aggression take control.

"How the fuck do you know all this?" barked Cosmo, his voice steady.

"Your name is Cosmo Rowland. That's all the information I need to dig up your past and discover all your personal demons."

"Nobody knows about my past, and I plan to keep it that way."

"And you can," said Isaac. "If you help us."

"That's fuckin' blackmail."

Isaac and Mal exchanged glances, both smiling. Cosmo waited, and before long Mal took a stride closer to him, and simply said,

"Then how about I sweeten the deal? How does five hundred thousand sound?"

At first, Cosmo was sure it was a bluff, but the tone in Mal's voice had seemed genuine.

"You serious?" he eventually asked. "Five hundred thousand bucks?"

"I'm quite serious, Mr. Rowland. You will be paid in cash and we will help you launder the money. Just as long as you assist us, you'll be rewarded."

Cosmo liked to think he was a loyal friend, and the majority of the time, he was. However, money divided people. Everybody needed money. Cosmo was no exception. And now that he was hovering just above the poverty line, temptation overpowered loyalty.

"Then I want to be paid in advance," said Cosmo, "right now."

Mal seemed surprised by his sudden change of heart, but Cosmo refused to feel the guilt. He was struggling, and he needed money to survive.

"I'll pay you half now, and half when the task is complete."

Cosmo thought about arguing, but he didn't want to risk losing the deal. Instead, he stuck out his hand. Mal shook it. The agreement had been made.

"And I want the first payment by tomorrow," said Cosmo.

"Done," replied Mal, "and starting tomorrow you will begin monitoring Jordan Kennedy."

Cosmo nodded. The duty seemed simple enough.

"And one more thing; I told Mr. Kennedy he would be killed the moment he told anybody of the situation, but since I'm feeling charitable today, I've allowed him to keep on living. And better yet, now he has your assistance..."

"Yeah, he's a lucky bastard."

"—But rest assured, if you tell a soul about what's going on, then I *will* kill you. Is that perfectly clear, Mr. Rowland?"

"Is this the part where I shit my pants?"

"I will not tolerate sarcasm."

"Then what the fuck are you going to do about it?"

There was no reply, but there was a reaction. Mal's fist came into contact with Cosmo's right cheekbone. The blow was powerful. Before Cosmo had the chance to retaliate, Mal jabbed an elbow into his throat. Cosmo collapsed, defeated, and gasping for air. The entire attack had happened in less than four seconds.

"Do not question my ability," said Mal, staring down at Cosmo. "I could crush your windpipe if I wanted to, and you'd be dead within minutes."

"F-fuc-k...y-you," he coughed.

"You need to learn how to behave, Mr. Rowland. You don't want me as an enemy."

Summoning the strength, Cosmo pulled himself off the floor, and considered making a reprisal. However, Mal and Isaac had already left the store, and had headed back towards their car. Cosmo dashed outside, still wheezing, as the car faded into the distance.

# 12

When I arrived at work that morning, I found Cosmo on his hands and knees, sweeping up shards of glass from the middle of the doorway.

"What happened?" I called from across the car park.

"A break in," replied Cosmo, without even looking up from the ground.

"Shit. Was anything stolen?"

"I don't think so. I think somebody kicked the doors in and then ran off."

I looked inside the store. Nothing seemed to be missing.

I tried to help Cosmo clean up, but he insisted he didn't need a hand. Something about his behaviour was a little off. He was quiet and evasive. I watched as Cosmo finished sweeping up, dumping the glass shards into a dustbin inside the store. I followed him inside, and stepped behind the counter. It was then that I noticed a bruise on his right cheekbone.

"What happened to you?" I asked.

He was silent for some time.

"Bouncer at a strip club roughed me up," he said, eventually. "We got into an argument, I called him a douchebag, and then he took a swing at me."

Typical. Cosmo's temper never failed to land him in hot water.

"By the way, we both have the afternoon off," he explained. "I called Jeff this morning and he's going to cover both of our shifts. That way, you and I can go into the city and talk to this Nathan Burwell dude."

I was surprised by his initiative, but didn't question it.

"Thank you, Cosmo."

He said nothing, and began flicking through a phone book, trying to find a service that could do a quick glass replacement. I kept wondering to myself why somebody would take the effort to break into a music shop, but not steal anything. Some of our equipment was worth thousands of dollars. Why was nothing taken? Then again, it was a blessing. A big break in had the potential to destroy our business, so I let it go and moved on with my work.

The morning went quickly. For a Tuesday morning, we certainly had a lot of customers. We sold six guitars, two bass cabinets and a drum kit within two hours. It was probably one of the busiest mornings we'd had in a while.

Just after twelve thirty, Jeff arrived at the store and gave Cosmo and I permission to leave. I felt guilty leaving my boss to cover both of our shifts, but he didn't seem to mind.

Cosmo and I left the store, and headed towards my car—or perhaps more accurately, the car Mal Lawson and Isaac Fuller had lent to me. I wasn't used to driving such a flashy car.

Clearly, I had forgotten to tell Cosmo about my temporary vehicle because he stopped and stared, eyes wide in disbelief, as I began unlocking the driver's side door.

"Shit," said Cosmo, eyeing the black BMW. "Is this yours? How did you afford it?"

"It's not mine. It belongs to *them*."

Cosmo just nodded. He needed no further explanation.

\*\*\*

I had spent the previous evening researching Nathan Burwell, and I had learned a lot.

He was forty-two, resided in Sydney and lived with his wife and four children. Nathan had worked for Channel 5 over the last two decades, and had been the owner and CEO ever since. He had many interests, the main ones being golf, politics, the environment and—perhaps the most important to him—art. Nathan had completed an advanced Bachelor of Arts at university, and had several of his paintings on display in galleries around Australia.

Learning about his interests enabled me to hatch a plan. I was going to pretend that I was a writer, with a desire to interview Australian artists in order to complete my book. I was going to ask to interview Nathan Burwell, for his views on contemporary Australian art and play up to his interests. I would arrange the interview inside his office, and when I was alone, I would bug his office with listening devices and surveillance cameras.

However, there was a flaw in my plan. Nathan Burwell would never leave his office during an interview, unless he was called upon to deal with an urgent situation. The plan? I needed Cosmo to create a diversion. Hopefully, it would allow for some time alone inside Nathan's office.

"When we get there," I began, "I'm going to try and arrange a quick meeting with Nathan. I'll suggest we have an interview in his office. Once I've been inside for roughly ten minutes, I need you to distract Nathan and call him away from his desk. I need to be left alone inside his office for at least three minutes."

"And how am I supposed to do that?" asked Cosmo.

"I don't know. Be creative."

He grunted at me, and we fell back into silence.

As we drove along, I tried to recall details about the contemporary practices of current Australian artists. I had researched a few last night to arm myself with knowledge. After all, I didn't want Nathan Burwell to discover my true intentions.

After much thought and consideration, I had decided spying on Nathan would be the only way to unearth his secrets. I'd also figured his office would make the best point of attack. I felt guilty about it, but it had to be done. I just wanted Rochelle back, safe and secure in my arms. I'd do anything for her—even if it meant criminal activity.

Finding Nathan Burwell's network building was simple enough. A gigantic number '5' had been inscribed down the side of the building, and was visible from the far distance. I found my way into an underground car park and killed the engine.

By luck, I had already loaded up the boot of the car with useful equipment to aid my assignment—including spy gadgets.

The apartment Mal Lawson had loaned to me had a cupboard full of firearms and high-tech gizmos. I had no need for the guns, but I wanted the gizmos. The technology was quite surreal to me—computer trackers, listening devices and hidden surveillance cameras. Although it seemed like they would be difficult to use, I had been mistaken. I'd spent the previous evening learning how to use the technology, and nothing could be simpler.

In fact, the hardest part of my task would be meeting Nathan Burwell.

I stepped out of the car and opened up the boot. Cosmo followed.

"What are you doing?" he asked.

I pulled out a suitcase I had packed earlier, filled with the necessary equipment. I flicked the buttons down and watched as the case popped open.

"What's all that stuff?" asked Cosmo, peering inside.

"Spyware devices," I replied.

Without asking permission, Cosmo began picking up the devices, and inspected them. Judging by the look on his face, he had no idea how the gadgets functioned—but I did. I found myself amused as Cosmo queried each piece of equipment.

"What's this thing?" asked Cosmo, holding up a tiny wireless box.

"It's a video camera," I replied.

"Then why is there a pen attached to it?"

"No," I said, "that's a voice recorder."

He blinked twice, but a smile quickly followed.

"This shit is awesome," said Cosmo, as he continued to rifle through the suitcase. "I feel like *Inspector Gadget*, man."

I rolled my eyes, snatched the equipment off him, and closed the suitcase. I decided I would bring everything with me, as I was unsure what to expect.

With a confident stride, I crossed the car park and headed towards the elevator. Cosmo followed. We took the elevator to the first floor, and stepped out to find ourselves in the main foyer. Dozens of men in suits swarmed across the floor, each with a mobile phone glued to their ear. I suddenly felt out of my comfort zone, and completely underdressed. I wore a maroon hoodie matched with dark grey cargo pants, while Cosmo wore a ripped pair of jeans and a band t-shirt featuring a winged skeleton clutching a machete. We stood out for all the wrong reasons.

Disregarding my insecurities, I cut through the crowds, and approached the administration desk at the very back of the foyer. I was preparing to go and talk to the woman sitting behind the desk, but Cosmo grabbed me by the arm and pulled me back.

"What are you doing?" he demanded.

"I'm going to talk to the lady—"

"—And say what?"

I arched an eyebrow, puzzled by his sudden curiosity.

"I'll say that my name is Jordan Kennedy and I want to see Nathan Burwell."

"Are you insane?" he cried. "You *can't* use your real name. You need to make one up."

"Like what?

"Anything!"

I thought for a moment, and came up with the first name that sprang to mind,

"Jack Smith."

"No, that's too common," he replied. "It needs to be unique."

I sighed.

"Then you make one up for me."

"How about Milo Zimmer?"

"No way." I protested. "That sounds like the name of a porn star."

He smiled, amused, and let go of his grip around my arm. I turned my back on Cosmo and headed towards the front counter once again. The woman behind the desk was now talking on the phone. I crossed my arms and waited. I waited almost ten minutes for her to get off the call. At last, she acknowledged me.

"Hi, how can I help you?" said the woman, as she placed the phone in its cradle.

"I'd like to talk to Mr. Burwell, please."

"And what is your name?"

I paused, and hesitated as I said,

"Milo Zimmer."

"And do you have an appointment, Mr. Zimmer?"

"Do I need one?"

"Yes," replied the woman, matter-of-factly. "Mr. Burwell sees no one without an appointment."

"Then when can I make an appointment?"

"Are you a client of his?"

"No," I replied, growing impatient.

"Then I doubt you'll be able to make an appointment. Mr. Burwell only sees clients."

I was beginning to assume Nathan Burwell was harder to meet than the Queen of England. I rested both palms on top of the counter.

"Please," I said, using the most placid tone I could manage. "Could you please call Nathan and tell him Milo Zimmer would like to interview him about his art."

"Sorry," she said. "I can't do that."

"Not even if I pay you a hundred bucks?"

Her eyes lit up. Money. Everybody likes money.

"I would," she began, "but Mr. Burwell is out to lunch. Perhaps I could leave a message?"

"Thanks," I said, placing two fifty dollar notes on the counter. "I'd appreciate it."

The woman snatched the money, tucked it into her bra, then turned to her computer and began clacking away on her keyboard. I could only assume she was emailing Nathan, but even if she didn't follow through with the arrangement, I wouldn't lose hope. I would contact Nathan Burwell by any means necessary.

I walked back over to where Cosmo was standing. He was leaning up against the marble wall, arms crossed, and receiving dirty looks from every person that dared to pass by him. Cosmo had taken notice too, and he was enjoying it.

"I don't think these businessmen like me," said Cosmo, amused. "What is it, the tattoos? The piercings? What is it that's too much for them, man?"

"I'd say it's a combination of both," I replied. "And maybe the clothes too."

"Huh? What's wrong with my threads?"

"Nothing, but these businessmen are too clean cut to appreciate them."

Cosmo shook his head, still smiling and said,

"What a bunch of boring fucks."

I was quick to move the conversation onto more serious matters. I told Cosmo what the woman behind the desk had told me. I tried to go into details, but he was no longer listening to me. Cosmo was staring over my shoulder.

I turned around and noticed what Cosmo had detected—a black Mazda with dark tinted glass had pulled up outside the front of the building, and four or five security guards stood around the car, observing everyone who walked by.

"Correct me if I'm wrong," said Cosmo, pointing towards the flashy car, "but I suspect Nathan Burwell is the man in the backseat."

And Cosmo was right. One of the security guards opened the back door, and I recognised the man stepping out of the car— Nathan Burwell. His photographs were constantly plastered over newspapers, magazines and current affairs.

Nathan looked younger than his age. Despite being forty-two, he could easily pass for somebody in their mid-thirties. Nathan had sandy blonde hair, neatly parted on the side. He was also tall and lanky, which made me think he would make a better professional basketball player than the CEO of the highest rating television network in Australia. That said, I knew I was blatantly stereotyping the poor bastard.

Nathan's paranoia was clear to me too. As I gazed around the foyer, dozens of security cameras lined the walls, and from the moment he stepped out of the car, muscular giants had surrounded him.

Nathan Burwell would not be an easy man to expose.

Nevertheless, I pushed away my doubts and watched as Nathan entered the building. Businessmen stepped out of the way to make room for Nathan and his guards, and no one that passed by would even risk a glance in his direction. I knew this was my only chance to make a move. I had to speak to Nathan, and Cosmo had the same idea too.

Cosmo stepped forward, but I stopped him in his tracks.

"No, you wait here," I said, holding him back. "I'll talk to Nathan."

"What? Who made you boss?"

"I did. This is my mission."

Cosmo rolled his eyes and laughed.

"Mission?" he replied. "Sure, whatever you say, sergeant."

I ignored Cosmo and crossed the room. As I headed towards Nathan Burwell, the nervousness kicked in. This first introduction would be vital—it would either lead to my success or my failure. I prayed that I wouldn't mess it up. Rochelle's life was on the line.

Just metres away, Nathan began talking to one of his security guards. I panicked at the very thought of having to intervene, but I had no other options.

"I'm sorry to interrupt," I said to Nathan Burwell, as I stood directly in front of him, "but I was wondering if I could have a word with you, Mr. Burwell?"

"No," said one of the security guards, answering on behalf of Nathan. "So, bugger off."

"There's no need for that, Dustin," said Nathan, scolding his guard. He then turned to face me, offered a warm smile and said, "What is it that I can do for you Mr...?"

"Zimmer," I said, sticking out my hand. "Milo Zimmer."

Nathan shook my hand and waited for me to speak.

"I'm a writer, and my debut book is a collection of interviews with Australian artists—"

Nathan's eyes lit up. I continued.

"—So I was wondering, Mr. Burwell, if it's not too much trouble, could I conduct a short interview with you today and ask for your views on contemporary Australian art?"

He maintained his smile and replied,

"Well, it certainty is an intriguing offer..."

"I won't take much of your time. I promise you."

He seemed a little reluctant, but curious. I waited patiently as Nathan considered it. As I held my breath, desperate for Nathan's approval, I noticed he was holding onto a briefcase, which had been handcuffed around his wrist.

It was only natural to ponder what was inside the briefcase.

"Perhaps in ten minutes I could fit you in?" said Nathan, grabbing my attention.

"Really? So you'll do the interview?"

"Sure."

"In your office?" I asked, hopefully.

"Of course," replied Nathan. "Take the elevator to level fifteen. I'll see you shortly."

Without more to say, he continued to walk on, and his guards glared at me as I walked by. I tried not to feel intimidated, but I think I failed. Once they had gone, I rushed back towards Cosmo. He was still leaning up against the goddamn wall.

"I've got the interview with Nathan," I began. "In just ten minutes time."

"Stand tall, Kennedy. You executed the mission perfectly," he replied.

For the second time that day, I ignored his childish behaviour.

"So during my interview, I need you to call Nathan away from his desk so I can be alone in his office. He needs to be gone for roughly three minutes so that I can install the technology. Can you do that for me, Cosmo?"

He nodded vigorously.

"So you'll make the diversion?" I asked.

"Affirmative," said Cosmo as he gave a salute. "At exactly fifteen hundred."

I looked him up and down.

"Do me a favour," I said, moments before I headed towards the elevator. "Stop being a douchebag."

# 13

Just as I was instructed, I took the elevator to the fifteenth floor.

I hadn't been nervous at all, but as the doors opened up, and I came face to face with a familiar buffed-up giant—I instantly felt nervous. He was one of Nathan Burwell's security guards. I'd met him in the foyer just minutes ago.

"My name is Dustin Pinfold," said the guard, running through his typical protocol. "I am Nathan Burwell's bodyguard and loyal employee. Before you meet with Mr. Burwell, you will need to go through some security checkpoints."

Security checkpoints? Shit. I should have expected that. By instinct I took a step back towards the elevator, but Dustin advanced towards me. Suddenly, he dropped his professional demeanour and I saw a brief glimpse of his true personality.

"I have to admit—you've got some balls," he said, his voice booming. "Not many people would have the guts to request an interview with Mr. Burwell."

"And why is that?" I asked, anxiously.

He evaded the question. Instead he made a smirk and simply said,

"Nathan will see you in a moment. Follow me."

I complied, not daring to speak unless I was spoken to.

He led me down a long corridor. I couldn't help but notice the dozens of paintings lining each side of the wall. Most of the art works were colourful and abstract. Nathan's taste in art surprised me, because I certainly couldn't see the beauty in messy painted canvases that a young child could have created. But maybe that's why I'm not an artist?

We turned left at the end of the corridor, and in front of us, was a wooden oak door with a golden plaque bearing Nathan Burwell's name placed in the centre. I waited to be led inside, but Dustin pulled a paddle out of his coat and said,

"Spread your legs and stick out your arms."

"Pardon me?" I asked.

"The security checkpoints, remember? We have these strict procedures in place and they are mandatory for anyone who wishes to see Mr. Burwell. I'll need to scan your body to ensure you are not carrying any prohibited items. So please, spread your legs and stick out your arms."

I hadn't been aware there were security procedures, but I had been naïve to think meeting Nathan would be so easy. However, I obeyed Dustin's demands, regardless of how ridiculous and awkward I felt.

Without delay, Dustin waved the paddle over both sides of my rib cage, and then hovered it under my arms. After scanning my back, he placed the paddle between my legs before waving it across my sternum. Finally, after what seemed to be an eternity, he finished.

"All clear," said Dustin, "but you'll need to leave your suitcase in a safety vault."

"What?"

"You can't take that in," he said firmly, gesturing to my suitcase. "You'll need to leave it in the safety vault, and then you can pick it up after the meeting."

I panicked. I needed my suitcase. All of the devices were inside, and without them, the plan would fail. Thinking quickly, I tried to bargain with Dustin.

"Can I take my valuables out?" I asked, hopefully.

"They'll be perfectly safe inside the vault, Mr. Zimmer."

"Just my USB and a pen—it's for the interview. Please."

At first, he scowled at me, but eventually, agreed. I thanked him and opened up my suitcase. As I took out the items, Dustin peered over my shoulder and gazed upon the gadgets I kept inside. I'm sure he was probably wondering what they were, but he didn't question it. I was thankful.

I tried to put the USB and pen into my pocket, but Dustin stopped me. He wanted to inspect the items first.

"Give them here for a sec," he said, holding out his hand.

I reluctantly handed them over, and he immediately began studying them. My heart was beating so rapidly inside my chest that I feared it might stop.

Dustin's face was fixed to suspicious as he clicked open my USB. I prayed he wouldn't discover its secrets. Although it looked like a regular USB, it had the ability to track and expose the most private and secure files on anyone's computer. As for the pen, removing the spring from the inside would trigger a listening device to activate, but I hoped he wouldn't figure that out. Dustin clicked the pen several times, drew a line on his wrist to be sure it was real, and then handed the items back to me. I thanked him, overwhelmed with relief, and tucked them into my pocket. Dustin then placed my suitcase into the vault in the wall and locked it.

"Mr. Burwell will see you now," said Dustin, and without further delay, his office door was opened and I was let inside.

I was led into a spacious office, overlooking the city skyline. There was also a gigantic canvas plastered on the back wall. The painting was of a tiger hiding amongst African shrubs. And while it wasn't to my taste, it truly was spectacular.

I looked to my left, to see Nathan Burwell sitting at his desk, working on his computer. As I entered his office, he stood, smiled, and told me to take a seat. I didn't waste time and quickly sat opposite Nathan, eager to get it all over and done with.

However, before I could get started, I noticed that Dustin had followed me inside. He also closed the door behind him, crossed his arms, and watched me like a hawk. Nathan quickly noticed my anxiousness.

"I hope you don't mind," said Nathan, "but Dustin sits in for all my meetings."

I nodded and smiled, pretending I didn't mind at all, but truthfully? It was like a punch to the gut. I had underestimated Nathan's paranoia. He truly was a man on the edge. I had never assumed a security guard would watch the meeting and it posed a problem. I needed Dustin to leave. I tried to think of what to do, but Nathan was waiting for me to begin the interview. I'd have to work it out later. For now, I had to put on my façade.

"So," I began, struggling to put words together. "I- uh, wanted to thank you very much for agreeing to this interview. I truly appreciate it."

"You're most welcome," he replied.

"So uh, I was just wondering, what views you have on contemporary Australian art?"

I thought I'd need to bullshit my way through the interview, but Nathan hardly needed my input. He was deeply passionate about art, because he spoke non-stop about it. I'd only asked him one goddamn question too. I nodded occasionally, pretending I was intrigued—although truthfully, I didn't have the slightest clue what he was talking about.

The first nine minutes flew by. While Nathan was busily telling me about his predictions for Artist of the Year nominees, I tuned out and wondered what Cosmo was doing to create the diversion. I thought calling Nathan away from his desk would be easy, but now with Dustin in the picture, I was unsure what would happen. Would Nathan take his security guard with him? Or would he remain? Would Nathan go at all? Or would I be the one asked to leave? The questions circled my mind like a spinning top losing control.

"Are you a painter yourself, Mr. Zimmer?" Nathan asked me, breaking my train of thought.

"Sure," I replied, forcing a smile.

"Excellent," beamed Nathan. "So what do you use as your medium?"

I fell silent.

"Pardon?"

"Well, do you use oils, acrylics, watercolours?"

I paused for a while, trying to work out the best way to answer the question without looking like an idiot. Maybe I would have to bullshit my way through the interview after all.

"All of them," I eventually replied.

"Really?" asked Nathan, raising an eyebrow. "You must be quite a diverse artist."

"Yeah, well, I try not to limit myself creatively."

I thought I heard Dustin snigger at my response, but when I looked over my shoulder, he had a straight face. Nathan seemed to buy into my answer though, but his questions kept coming.

"I must ask, just out of curiosity, do you have a favourite artist?"

"Yeah," I replied, a little hesitantly.

"And who would that be?"

I paused again. I was tempted to reply and simply say 'you', but surely Nathan Burwell would see right through my false act. Thinking quickly, I said the name of the only other artist I knew about,

"Picasso."

Silence.

"Oh," he finally said, sounding a tad disappointed.

Before Nathan had the chance to fire more questions at me, the intercom on his desk buzzed. I watched and waited anxiously.

"Mr. Burwell," said a woman's voice, that I instantly knew belonged to the woman at the administration desk. "I'm sorry to interrupt, but I need you to come down to the main foyer for a moment."

Cosmo was an absolute legend. I didn't know how he managed to pull it off, but I knew he wouldn't let me down.

"What's wrong, Susan?" asked Nathan, talking into the intercom.

"It's urgent, Mr. Burwell. You need to get down here immediately."

Nathan sighed, but eventually rose from his desk.

"I'm very sorry, Mr. Zimmer. But I will have to step out for a moment. I'll be back shortly."

"No problem," I said, trying to suppress a smile.

Nathan left promptly, making no delays. However, I still had a problem to overcome. Dustin had remained behind, and I couldn't install the equipment while he was watching. What the hell was I supposed to do? I tried not to panic, but I could feel my hands shaking as I rested them upon my knees. I needed to distract him. But how? Dustin's job was to watch my every move, so making a diversion would be damn near impossible. I scanned my eyes around the room, trying to figure out what to do. I needed three minutes to myself, but I was running out of time. Activating the devices would be simple enough, but where to put them? And how could I do it without being caught? I tried to disregard my anxiousness, but I didn't want to fail today. I had to succeed; otherwise I might never see Rochelle again.

The very thought was enough to ignite a panic attack.

This was not the time to break down. I had to stay calm, but my body was betraying me. My breathing became heavier. I could see my chest rising and falling through my shirt. As the room started to rotate around me, the world began to fade.

"You OK?" asked Dustin, his voice seemed distant.

"Not really," I wheezed.

"You're not going to faint on me, are you?"

Before I could answer, something clicked inside my head. I was not powerless in this situation. My actions would be enough to get Dustin to leave the room, so I began playing up to my anxiety attack.

"I think I'm going to pass out," I said, swaying in my chair— just for effect.

"Just breathe, mate. Calm down," replied Dustin, sounding as anxious as me.

It was working. For once, my panic disorder was benefitting me. I pretended to breathe harder, and forced myself to shake. Although I was feeling quite fine now, I knew I had to continue the façade. It was the only way I could succeed.

At last, I rolled off my chair and collapsed to the floor. I kept my eyes shut and remained perfectly still. While I'd never practiced fainting before, I had a feeling I'd done a fairly convincing job.

I heard Dustin's feet dash towards me, but I kept my eyes shut.

"Oh shit," I heard him say, as he nudged my body. "Oi, mate, wake up."

I remained perfectly still, and made a silent prayer that he wouldn't do anything rash like attempt CPR. Dustin placed a firm hand over my back and shook me. I refused to react. I wanted Dustin to think that I was out cold.

And it worked too, because seconds later I heard Dustin's footprints fade off into the distance, muttering more profanities as he exited the office.

He closed the door behind him. I was alone.

I wasn't sure how long Dustin would be gone for, but I couldn't waste a second of it. He could return at any moment, and Nathan probably wouldn't be gone for too much longer either. I opened my eyes, rolled over and pushed myself to my feet. Dunking my hand into my jacket pocket, I pulled out my pen and USB. First, I installed the USB by shoving it into the port at the back of the computer. A window popped up on the screen, so I scrolled down and clicked 'Open to view files.' Instantly, the spyware automatically installed itself on the computer. The process took two minutes, so while it was loading; I turned my attention to the listening device, disguised as a pen.

I unscrewed the pen top, removed the spring from the inside and then connected it back together. The listening device had been activated. As long as the pen remained in the room, I would be able to hear every word spoken within the walls. I had to hide it. But where? I figured Nathan would spend most of his time at his desk, so I decided to conceal the pen underneath it. I dropped to my knees and glanced under the table. I needed something to hold the pen in place. Acting quickly, I located a reel of sticky tape on Nathan's desk. I sliced off a few pieces and stuck the pen under the rim of the desk.

Once again I looked up at the computer screen. The spyware had been installed. From now on, I would see every email Nathan sent. Every key he touched, I would know about it. This was perhaps the most vital piece of equipment I had, because now his private life would be exposed to me.

I heard footsteps. They were gaining. Somebody was heading directly towards the office. I quickly yanked the USB from the port, and resumed my unconscious position on the floor. Just as I closed my eyes, I heard the office door burst open. At that moment, I pretended to wake. I slowly opened my eyes, held my head in my hand and groaned. Dustin stood a metre away from me, clutching a cup in his hand.

"You OK now?" he asked, without a note of sincerity to be detected.

"Y-yea-h," I stuttered. "S-sorry I was n-nervous."

He crouched down a few inches and held the cup towards me.

"Here," he said. "I brought you some water."

I forced my arm to shake as I reached out towards the cup. I took it from him, and purposely spilt a bit as I tried to bring it to my lips. Dustin said nothing. He remained standing, as a vexed expression crossed his eyes. I continued to sip the water, as I sat there thinking.

There was so much more Dustin could have done to assist me during my fainting episode, but he clearly didn't know what to do in that situation. Then again, it had worked in my favour, because now the devices were activated and in place.

Once I had finished my water, I pulled myself to my feet and I sat down at the table, pretending nothing had ever happened. I wondered if Dustin would mention to Nathan that I had fainted in his office, but when Nathan returned two minutes later, he stayed silent.

"Sorry about the delay, Mr. Zimmer," said Nathan, as he crossed the room and sat down at his desk. "We had a disturbance in the foyer that I had to take care of."

I tried not to smile. I still didn't know what Cosmo had done to create a diversion, but whatever it was, it had been bloody brilliant.

"No problem," I said, tenting my fingers.

"Now where were we?" asked Nathan.

"How about we wrap up the interview with one last question; if you could collaborate with one Australian artist on a painting, which artist would you pick?"

I wanted to end the interview quickly, but Nathan picked at least seven different Australian artists I'd never heard of, and explained each answer thoroughly. Half an hour dragged by, and at last, we were done.

"Thank you for being so generous with your time," I said, rising from my seat.

"My pleasure," replied Nathan. "I look forward to reading your book."

We made our goodbyes, shook hands, and not a moment later Dustin escorted me from the office. The door was closed behind me, and I was led to the safety vault. Dustin never said a word as he returned my suitcase to me, nor did he say goodbye. He merely pointed to the exit, then turned around and left. I quickly headed towards the elevator. I didn't want to overstay my welcome.

***

When I stepped out into the main foyer, I expected to find Cosmo waiting for me, but he was nowhere to be seen.

Where the hell did he go? I started feeling a little concerned, so I pulled out my mobile and tried to call him. The reception was poor. I couldn't reach him. I marched across the foyer, through the swarm of businessmen, and outside into the cool Sydney air.

I tried to call Cosmo from outside, but there was no need. He was standing across the road, arms crossed, staring at me. I made a *'what gives'* shrug. Cosmo saw me and beckoned me over. When the cars cleared, I crossed the road.

"What are you doing out here?" I called, just metres away from him.

"I was about four seconds away from having someone call the cops on me," explained Cosmo, "so I had to do a runner, or risk a night in a cell."

"What happened?" I asked, intrigued.

"I made a diversion. Just like you asked me to do."

"But how? What did you do?"

"I threw my body on top of the administration desk and refused to move until I spoke to Nathan Burwell."

"Right…"

"And some of those security guards we saw earlier tried to pull me away, but I didn't budge. Eventually, they gave in and called Nathan down to the foyer."

"And what did you do when Nathan came down?"

"Said hello to him and then ran like hell."

I smiled, shook my head and said,

"I'm sort of disappointed, Cosmo. I was expecting something more from you."

"Well, I did consider stripping naked and chaining myself to the main doors, but I figured I'd go with the safer option."

I chuckled, and then explained what had happened during the interview. I told Cosmo about the high security level, and my fainting performance. I also mentioned I didn't have an opportunity to install a surveillance camera, but the listening device and computer tracker were of more use to me anyway.

Cosmo and I headed back towards the car in the underground car park, taking the long way around rather than having to enter the Channel 5 building again. We located the black BMW, and I slid behind the wheel.

"Do you reckon this Nathan guy has skeletons in his closet? Or do you think he's too squeaky clean for that shit?" asked Cosmo, climbing into the passenger's seat.

"Don't know," I replied, fastening my seatbelt. "Only time will tell."

# 14

Unearthing Nathan Burwell's secrets had been far harder than I had first anticipated.

I had believed that everyone had a past they'd rather forget, or a secret so deep that they'd blocked the memory from their mind. But if Nathan was hiding anything, it was well hidden, because spying on him from his office had proved to be a waste of time. He was clean.

Cosmo and I had spent every evening in the Sydney apartment, monitoring Nathan's actions, but uncovered nothing. Nor had we found anything suspicious. The listening device I'd installed under his desk had recorded nothing of interest, just dull meetings with clients that seemed to drag on for an eternity. The computer tracker had been unsuccessful too. Nathan only used his computer to email clients about the network, or occasionally to write a pleasant email to his wife. There was nothing else. When he used the Internet, it was purely for work. He didn't use social networking sites such as Facebook, or watch YouTube videos, and much to Cosmo's surprise, Nathan didn't even visit porno sites.

It was half past midnight, but Cosmo and I were still up, trying to figure out a new plan of action. Even though we had only tried one thing, we were already fresh out of ideas.

"Maybe we ought to try and bug his house?" suggested Cosmo, as he sat down in the armchair opposite me. "We're bound to find something."

"No," I said, grimly. "Nathan Burwell only invites friends to his mansion. No clients."

"Then try and befriend him. Gain Nathan's trust."

"That could take months, Cosmo. And time isn't on our side."

He thought about it, and eventually nodded. Our brainstorming session was getting us nowhere. Besides, our options were running short, and I didn't know how long I could continue without Rochelle. I hadn't seen her in over a week, and each day was getting harder. Was she being looked after? Or treated like an animal? Was she coping? Or was she on the verge of giving up? Rochelle had been thrown into a situation beyond her control, and I didn't want her to be a part of it anymore.

If Mal Lawson needed my assistance, I would help him in order to restore a bit of normality, but it was not fair on Rochelle. She deserved better than this, and I knew what I had to do.

"I guess we've only got one option left," I said, after some time.

"And what's that?" asked Cosmo.

"I'm going to have to involve the police."

"No!" shouted Cosmo, catching me off guard. "Are you fuckin' crazy, Kennedy?"

"These men have Rochelle for Christ's sake! I have to do something."

"But they'll kill her! If you involve the police, I can guarantee those bastards will put a gun to her head. You can't risk it, man."

As much as I didn't want to admit it, Cosmo was right. I couldn't jeopardise Rochelle's safety. I needed a new approach to my current situation, but calling the coppers was not the way to go. Besides, I didn't even know where Rochelle was. Her location was unknown to me, so what the hell could the police do anyway?

"Then we need to come up with a new idea," I said, sitting back in my chair. "And we need to think of it quickly, because I don't want to deal with this anymore."

"We'll think of something, but we have to be rational about it."

I sunk a little lower in my chair, and tried to stay strong. I was far from any kind of hero, but I'd have to try if I had any chance of seeing Rochelle again. I wanted to hold her. Being so far away from the ones you love can be brutal, but knowing the ones you love are in danger? It's excruciating.

I wasn't sure how much more I could take.

Suddenly, I watched as Cosmo dunked his hand into his top pocket, and pulled out a lighter along with two pieces of rolled up paper. He put one of the cancer-sticks between his lips, ignited the end and sucked in the poison. He then tried to offer me one.

"Take one," he said. "You need to relax."

"Cosmo, you know I don't smoke."

"Yeah, but these aren't regular cigarettes..."

I looked at him sternly and replied,

"If you're going to smoke that, take it outside—away from me."

"Fuck, you're a goody-two-shoes. Can't you learn to live a bit?"

"Take it outside, Cosmo."

He rolled his eyes at me, muttered an insult under his breath, and went outside to the balcony to smoke his joint. I made sure he closed the sliding door behind him.

Once again, I was alone, and loathing every minute of it. I considered going to bed, but I knew all too well that sleep would not come. Despite the fact I had work first thing tomorrow morning, I picked up my car keys and headed to the front door. I didn't say goodbye to Cosmo or bother with an explanation, because I knew he'd try to stop me. But I needed to leave. I wanted to go to my tiny rented home amongst the towering trees. Without reconsidering, I made my departure.

# 15

Shortly after two in the morning, I pulled up outside the only other place I had ever called home in this country.

I was back in Middle Dural. I had not been home since Rochelle and I left for our getaway almost two weeks ago. That day actively kept replaying in my mind, and I continuously wondered what would have happened if I'd just stayed at home. Maybe I should have. Maybe they wouldn't have involved Rochelle at all.

Shaking the thoughts from my head, I stepped out of the car and walked up to the front door. It took me a moment to find my keys, but I was glad to be back home. It was nice to have some familiarity back in my life.

Roaming through the main room, I found myself feeling more at ease. Sure, the house was a mess—just like it always was—but it was somewhat therapeutic for me. I noticed the newspaper sprawled across the coffee table, the unwashed glasses carelessly dumped in the kitchen sink, and the half eaten apple on the kitchen bench that had rotted into a brown pulp. However, I decided to leave the house exactly the way it was. When Rochelle returned, I wanted her to know that nothing had changed. And hopefully, nothing would ever change.

Suddenly, a blinking red light caught my attention in the distance. It was the answering machine, and to my surprise, thirty-four messages had been left for us. Instantly, I began to playback the messages. A few were from Rochelle's work, stating that her position had been terminated due to her absence. I felt enraged. The bastards had sacked Rochelle even though they did not have the power to do so. Besides, why hadn't they investigated her absence? Why had they assumed she wasn't coming back? I felt like calling them back and abusing them, but what could I say? Besides, my attention was quickly redirected to the remainder of the messages, as most of them were from my sister, Amy. The messages seemed quite frantic, demanding me to return her calls.

I picked up the phone and instantly complied. After dialling in a billion numbers, Amy picked up after only a few rings.

"Hey, Amy. It's me," I said.

"Where the *hell* have you been?" she snapped at me. "I haven't heard from you in weeks!"

"So? I've been busy."

"But you *always* call, Jordan. You had me worried!"

Even though I was the older sibling, Amy had a habit of treating me like the younger child.

"What's been going on? Are you alright?"

"I'm fine," I replied, but I struggled to make it sound convincing.

"What about Rochelle? Is she OK?"

"Yeah."

Silence. I wasn't sure if Amy believed me or not, but I wasn't prepared to tell her the truth. My sister had already been through so much in her short life, and it was my duty to protect her. Besides, there was nothing Amy could do to help me anyway.

However, a question lingered on my mind. And while I wasn't comfortable bringing up the topic in a conversation, I knew I had to. My question would not benefit my current situation in any way, but I was curious, and I had to know the answer.

"Can I ask you something, Amy?"

"Yeah, what is it?" she asked, but I could already hear the suspiciousness in her voice.

"Do you ever think about Eamon?"

Once again, she fell silent. I knew I'd crossed the line.

"Jordan," she said after some time, her voice solid and firm. "I thought we promised we would never mention *him* again."

"I know, and I'm sorry," I began, "but I just wanted to know."

Truthfully, I believed the world was a better place without people like Eamon Bronson, but still, he had changed the course of my sister's life. What would she think if she knew he was dead? Then again, it was not my place to tell her. After all, what was I supposed to say? How could I tell Amy her ex-husband had been brutally murdered? It was impossible.

However, Amy sensed there was something amiss.

"What's going on, Jordan?" she asked, breaking the silence.

"Nothing."

"Bollocks. Don't lie to me."

"I'm not, Amy."

"Has Eamon contacted you? I thought he was in jail."

"Well, yeah, he was."

"What do you mean by *was*? Why isn't he still there?"

I'd already said too much.

"Look, it's really late over here," I said, abruptly. "I'd better go."

"No. Not until you tell me what's going on."

"I'm sorry, Amy."

Click. I hung up on her without more to say. She tried calling me back—several times—but I wouldn't pick up. It had not been my intention to involve Amy in my predicament, so now I'd have no choice but to ignore her.

I stepped away from the phone, and wandered into the bedroom. Everything was just as I'd left it. Our clothes were carelessly scattered around the floor, and the bed was still unmade. I crossed the room and sat down on my usual side of the bed. I closed my eyes. Even with all the thoughts running through my head, I knew I needed sleep. Feeling a little dreary, I crashed down onto the mattress. I found the darkness somewhat comforting and tried to fall asleep. However, I simply couldn't switch off my brain.

I rolled over, feeling the empty space beside me. I opened my eyes again. Suddenly, being here alone was painful. Rochelle always slept beside me, but she was not with me tonight. God knows where she was. I knew I was on the verge of a breakdown, but I had to be strong—not only for Rochelle's sake, but for my own too. I reached my hand across the cold bed sheets, and tried to visualise her lying next to me. As the minutes passed, I faded into sleep, dreaming about holding her, safe and secure in my arms.

***

*August 4th*

He was anxious.

Mal Lawson had put his faith in Jordan Kennedy, but why? Why had he trusted a stranger's recommendation? Jordan did not seem capable of completing his task, and no progress had been made whatsoever.

Nathan Burwell was still untouchable.

Time was slipping away, and Mal hadn't earned a cent. People had started losing patience with him too, because they'd invested millions of dollars into the Nathan project, but that had been well over a year ago. Mal's associates wanted a profit of at least five million each, and at the moment, that seemed unlikely.

But maybe Mal was being too pessimistic. He'd heard Jordan Kennedy was capable of doing the impossible, so maybe he was worrying for nothing.

Enough. Mal had been thinking too much today. Immediately, he poured himself a large glass of brandy and tried to numb his mind. Sure, it was cliché, but goddamn it, the alcohol worked. Mal took a seat at the dining table—bringing the bottle with him—and tried to relax. However, he was disturbed by a knock on the door.

"Come in," Mal called, not bothering to leave his seat.

Isaac opened the door and stepped inside, clutching a few sheets of paper in his hand.

"What is it?" asked Mal.

"I figured you'd like an update on Kennedy."

"Unless he's made progress I don't want to hear about it."

"Fair enough," replied Isaac, as he dumped the papers on the dining table.

Mal turned and looked out the window, trying to find a way to rectify his situation. How much longer was he prepared to wait for Kennedy to make his move? Or would Mal simply have to hire somebody else and remove Jordan Kennedy from the picture?

Perhaps he should have done that from the start.

Mal decided he'd sleep on it for another week, before stepping in and taking action.

Failure, of course, was not an option.

# 16

*August 5th*

The call came through a little after one in the morning.

I had been maybe only seconds away from falling into a deep sleep, when my mobile sounded, startling me half to death. I flicked on the bedside light and sat up, both a little dazed and disorientated. I picked up my mobile, which was flashing and vibrating uncontrollably across the wooden dresser. I pressed the green button and answered the call.

"Hello?" I asked, holding my forehead in my palm.

"Kennedy," said the voice that could only belong to Cosmo Rowland, "I have the best-fuckin'-idea...ever!"

"What? Do you have any idea what time it is?"

"Are you sitting down?"

"What—no?"

"You'd better sit down."

Barely conscious, I stumbled back towards the bed and sat down. I held the phone to my ear and waited for Cosmo to continue.

"Are you sitting down now?" he asked.

"Yes," I replied, irritably.

"Good, because my idea is so fuckin' awesome, that I didn't want you to faint on me."

"Are you drunk, Cosmo?"

"Of course not!"

"Stoned?"

"Hmm...a little bit."

I was tempted to hang up the phone. I didn't want to talk to Cosmo when he was in an incoherent state of mind, struggling to string two words together. However, I was curious to know what his idea was. Then after, I would hang up the phone.

"So what is it, Cosmo?" I asked, cutting straight to the point.

"Well, I figured it's going to be fuckin' impossible to reveal Nathan Burwell's secrets and shit, but why do we want to know his secrets? All we want is money, right?"

"Right..." I said, unsure what he was getting at.

"Well, fuck the secrets. We can blackmail him in other ways, yeah?"

"But how? Nathan's clean."

"Ah, but suppose Nathan is cheating on his wife? What if we had the evidence to prove it? He'd be easy to blackmail!"

"But we don't have anything on him. As far as we know, Nathan is faithful to his wife."

"Maybe he is, but that doesn't mean we can't set him up."

I'd heard it, yet still, my mind failed to comprehend it.

"What?" I asked, not knowing what else to say.

Cosmo giggled to himself and tried to explain his plan. Before he'd even said a word, I could sense Cosmo was struggling to contain his excitement.

"One night, you can take Nathan out somewhere, like a restaurant. You following me so far? Good. Next, you can drop a roofie into his drink, and then set him up getting hot and heavy with some chick. Then finally, we take pictures for evidence! You get me?"

"Not exactly. What's a roofie?"

"Rohypnol."

I was silent.

"It's a date rape drug, Kennedy!" cried Cosmo. "Jesus, you've lived a sheltered life."

I could barely register it. I was stuck somewhere between outrage and astonishment. While I wanted to succeed in my task, there were limits. I would lie without hesitation, but there was no way I would drug an innocent man, and possibly destroy his marriage, not to mention his career and image.

"I can't even believe you would suggest such a thing," I said, unable to disguise my repulsion.

"Don't get all fuckin' weird on me now, man. I've never used a roofie on anyone, but I know what they're capable of, and I know where to get them from."

"No," I said firmly. "We're not drugging anyone."

"Why not? It's the solution to everything."

"No! It's immoral and wrong."

"You need to harden the fuck up, man."

I'd had enough. Without bothering to say goodbye, I hung up on Cosmo. I switched off my mobile too so he couldn't call me back. Feeling wearier by the minute, I lay down and switched off the bedside lamp. Darkness filled the room once more, but my mind was still racing. I couldn't switch it off. And even though Rochelle's safety was my main priority, how far was I prepared to go? Eventually, my body began shutting down for the night. I needed my sleep. I pulled the sheets up to my neck, as my mind floated off into nothingness.

# 17

I arrived at work before Cosmo.

It was a rare occurrence, but I liked it. I enjoyed being in the store alone, because it was always so peaceful, and it gave me the opportunity to play the piano. For the best part of half an hour, my fingertips danced across the keys. It'd been a while since I'd played, and I truly had missed it. Just before nine o'clock, Cosmo rocked up.

"You're a prick," he said, seconds after entering the store.

"What for?" I asked, innocently.

"You hung up on me last night, man! You should've heard me out."

I turned and faced him. Since Cosmo had been high as a kite when he'd made the call, I was hoping he would have forgotten. But I had been mistaken. I rose from the piano stool and closed the fallboard over the keys.

"I knew exactly what you were suggesting," I began, "and I clearly said no."

"But this is our best fuckin' option, dude."

I wanted to tell him it wasn't, but I didn't know what else to say. I was out of ideas and each day my desperation increased. I just wanted Rochelle back, and I knew I wouldn't see her again until I finished my end of the deal. I'd have to bring Nathan Burwell down, and perhaps setting him up was the only way to achieve my goal? But surely there was another way to frame him? A few suggestions came to mind, but they were minor, and it wouldn't be enough to black-mail Nathan. It needed to be big, and although I still detested the idea, perhaps Cosmo's plan truly was the only choice I had left?

I rubbed my thumb and index finger across my forehead, feeling a headache surfacing, and faced Cosmo once more.

"Alright," I said, "go through your plan again."

Cosmo grinned and pulled out a scrap bit of paper from his jeans pocket. Christ, he'd even written it out. He held out the paper in front of him and started to read out the steps. I tried to read his plan for myself, but I couldn't make sense of his handwriting.

"Basically all you've got to do is call up Nathan Burwell and ask to meet with him again," began Cosmo, "and it's very important you meet in a public place—namely, a restaurant."

"What kind of restaurant?"

"One with a back entrance or a fire exit. In fact, there's a seafood restaurant in the city called *Hardyheads* and I know for a fact that in the men's bathroom there's a fire exit leading to a back street. And that's important, because we would need to get Nathan out of the building without anybody seeing us."

"That's going to be impossible, Cosmo. His guards will follow him everywhere."

"Even into the toilets? I don't think so. He can't be that fuckin' paranoid can he?"

"You'd be surprised."

Cosmo waved it off and continued to explain his idea.

"Anyway, if we bribe the right person at the restaurant, I'm sure we can get someone to keep that fire exit unlocked for us."

"But how the hell do we get Nathan into the bathroom anyway?"

"With the roofies, man."

Instantly, I cringed and felt uneasy. And Cosmo only fuelled my anxiety as he pulled a small plastic sachet from the back pocket in his jeans. He held the sachet out to me, to reveal at least half a dozen tiny white pills. I was not impressed.

"I picked them up from a mate's house this morning," said Cosmo, "and we're going to need these if we have any chance of pulling this shit off."

"Why can't we just bribe someone to spike Nathan's drink? We can get him drunk instead. I'd be more comfortable with that. I don't want to drug anybody."

"Getting someone drunk isn't going to do shit! Roofies are fuckin' powerful, man. Do you have any idea what they're capable of?"

"Clearly not."

Cosmo rolled his eyes at me and tucked the pills back into his jeans.

"If you drop a roofie into Nathan's drink, you can fuckin' own him. They have the ability to erase your memory, and the pills can affect people very quickly—within twenty minutes, man. The person you use it on will usually start to feel disorientated, dizzy and maybe even nauseous. Now if Nathan feels these symptoms, I reckon he'll go to the bathroom, which is where I come in. I can keep a car behind the restaurant, and when Nathan is alone, I'll grab him, take him out the fire exit, and put him in my car. And since roofies are so powerful, and Nathan's only a small guy, I reckon it'll completely knock him out."

"But are they dangerous?"

He was silent for a long time. It worried me.

"Not really," he replied, but I could tell he was lying.

I shook my head. Every part of me was against Cosmo's plan. How far was I willing to push the boundary? I exhaled and pressed for more answers.

"So what will you do once Nathan's in your car?" I asked.

"Well, firstly I'll drive off and get the hell out of there. I'll take Nathan back to a motel or something, and waiting inside the motel room will be a beautiful woman. Hopefully by then Nathan will either be out cold or so out of his fuckin' head that he won't have a clue what's going on. And then, the gorgeous girl will fool around with Nathan and shit, and I'll take photographs. Next, I'll get the photos printed as soon as I can, and then we're going to blackmail that son of a bitch. And if he fails to obey our demands, we'll leak a photograph to his wife, and if he still doesn't pay up, we'll leak the rest of the photographs to the whole fuckin' media! Imagine it—the other networks would pay top dollar to name and shame their biggest competitor. And Nathan loves his squeaky clean reputation, so he won't allow the photographs to go public. He'll pay us any sum to keep us quiet. I guarantee it."

90

I was disgusted—not only with Cosmo, but also with myself. My desperation to have Rochelle back was too much to ignore. I had no choice but to play dirty, and potentially ruin the life of an innocent man. I forced down my apprehension, and accepted Cosmo's idea.

"Right," I said, gruffly. "And where do you suppose we'll find a beautiful woman willing to be in on this?"

"Man, I'm way ahead of you. I've already got the perfect woman to help us pull it off. She's my new girl. Her name is Daphne and she's willing to help us out."

"New girl? But whatever happened to your last girlfriend?"

"Who? Christine? Man, I dumped her like a week ago. She was a lousy root."

"Root?"

"Fuck, Kennedy. It means she was rubbish in bed."

"Oh," I said, feeling slightly awkward. "I hope you didn't tell her that."

"Yeah, of course I did. In fact, I told her several times."

"Charming."

He ignored me. Either he didn't care what I thought, or didn't want to get into a petty argument with me. It was probably a combination of both.

"So, we're gonna go through with it?" asked Cosmo, testing my morality.

"Yeah," I said. "I guess so."

Cosmo grinned and shredded the scrap piece of paper he'd written the details on. Good. I didn't want any record of what we were planning to do. Apart from Cosmo and myself, no one else could learn of our despicable ideas. As a matter of fact, I wasn't even sure how I was going to live with myself.

"Well," said Cosmo, drawing me away from my apprehension. "You know what you've got to do now, don't you, Kennedy?"

"Find a confession box and declare my sins?"

He sniggered.

"Nope. You need to pick up the phone, man. It's time to make the call."

Cosmo didn't need to elaborate. I knew what he meant. The first step of our scheme needed to be put into action—call Nathan Burwell and arrange a meeting. I recalled the name of the restaurant Cosmo had suggested and pulled out my mobile from my top pocket of my jacket. I'd saved the network headquarters number into my mobile. However, before I could even talk to Nathan, I knew I needed to get past the administration desk first. I was about to make the call when I realised I couldn't use my real name. I'd used a fake one, but I couldn't remember it. I turned to Cosmo.

"Hey, what's my name again?"

"Huh?" asked Cosmo, tilting his head like a dumb puppy.

"My name! The false identity you thought up for me. What was it again?"

"Jesus, man. You have the memory span of a fuckin' goldfish. It's Milo Zimmer. Remember?"

I nodded and turned my attention back to my phone. I began scrolling through my contact list, and when I'd found the number I wanted, I pushed the green button, pulled the phone to my ear and waited. The ringing seemed to last an eternity, but I was thankful for it. It gave me a moment to collect my thoughts. After all, I'd sunken to a new low. How would Rochelle feel if she knew what I was planning to do? Disgusted or grateful? But then again, it didn't matter. Rochelle would never know of the shameful acts I had committed to ensure her safety, because I'd already decided that I would never tell her.

It was for the best.

# 18

*August 6ᵗʰ*

As Cosmo and I pulled up outside the restaurant, I reminisced about all the bad things I had done over the duration of my life.

I had certainly made a fair few mistakes in my short time, and I was far from perfect, but I was about to commit an appalling crime. Nathan Burwell was a good man. More importantly, he was innocent. I was about to turn his world upside down, and for what? A stranger's benefit. I guess it's true what they say—it's a dog eat dog world.

I had succeeded in arranging a dinner meeting with Nathan Burwell, but the only time he could fit me in was tonight, so we would have to pull off everything perfectly. We could not afford mistakes.

I had gone over the plan a million times in my head, and I knew exactly what I had to do, but I was still nervous. I was going to drug the multimillionaire CEO of Channel 5. The very thought sent chills through my body.

I checked the time. It was a quarter to seven. Nathan would be arriving soon.

"You got the roofies?" asked Cosmo, breaking my train of thought.

"Yeah," I said, as I checked my trouser pocket. "I've got them."

"And remember, put the pill in his second drink. The more alcohol in his system the better."

I nodded, feeling the pressure build under my chest with every second.

"You OK, man?" asked Cosmo, noticing my anxiousness.

I didn't answer him, because I knew I'd only lie. I checked my watch again. Time was slipping by and I was only making myself more nervous.

"So is the back door in the men's bathroom open?" I asked.

"Yep. I've already paid one of the waiters a hundred bucks to open the fire exit for us, and then paid him another hundred to keep his mouth shut about it."

"OK. Well, I suppose I ought to go in. You'd better park around the back."

"Yep, and send me a text if anything goes wrong."

"Will do," I replied, but I was secretly hoping it would all go to plan.

Without more to say, I opened the passenger's side door and stepped out into the bitterly cold air. I closed the car door behind me, and watched as Cosmo drove off. I was alone now. Alone and close to breaking point. Stepping towards the seafood restaurant, *Hardyheads*, I could feel my hands shaking by my sides.

I entered through the main doors and approached the front counter. A young waitress caught my eye, offered a warm smile and said,

"Good evening, sir."

"Hi," I said, forcing a smile. "I made a reservation under Zimmer."

"Yes. Right this way, Mr. Zimmer."

She led me through a swarm of tables—each one already crowded with people—and directed me to a small table at the very back of the room.

When I'd called Nathan to make the booking, he had requested a table for three. I assumed the third one was for his bodyguard, Dustin, and he posed as my biggest problem. Bodyguards were trained professionals, so how was I supposed to slip a pill into Nathan's drink without Dustin knowing? Cosmo had taught me a technique he thought was bulletproof, but I still had my doubts.

Twenty or so minutes passed. I waited eagerly. The waiter brought three glasses and a jug of water over to the table, so I poured myself a drink and gulped it down. Another two minutes passed and Nathan Burwell arrived.

Without delay, I stood from my seat and watched as they approached. Nathan's bodyguard, Dustin, walked beside him. It didn't surprise me. I knew he'd be here. However, a much younger man was trailing behind Nathan. I had never seen him before, and instantly, my fears took hold.

This was not right. Who the hell was he? Why hadn't Nathan told me he was bringing someone else? I'd only booked a table for three, and surely he knew that? They were approaching quickly, heading towards me. I straightened my jacket and exhaled deeply. I wasn't sure what I'd gotten myself into, but it was too late to back out now.

"Good evening, Mr. Zimmer," said Nathan, offering a smile. "How are you?"

"Good," I heard myself say, but all my attention was focused on the stranger.

Nathan noticed it too.

"This is my step-son, Brad," said Nathan as he introduced the young man. "I hope you don't mind him joining us tonight. He's my apprentice in training."

Surprisingly, the news brought me relief. He was just an apprentice. No threat. Perhaps it would be harder to sneak Nathan a pill with another pair of watching eyes, but I had to stay positive. Otherwise my fears would lead to failure.

"So," I began, looking at Nathan. "I suppose I ought to get a waiter to bring us another chair?"

"No, that won't be necessary. Only three of us will be dining, and Dustin will wait at the door until we've finished."

It felt like somebody had cut the noose from around my neck and I could finally breathe again. It brought me some comfort knowing that Dustin would not be dining with us. Perhaps I could pull off the stunt after all? I'd still have to be cautious, but my concerns lessened in an instant.

"Oh," I said, disguising a smile, "in that case let's all take our seat."

I sat down, and Brad did too, but Nathan appeared to be tinkering with his briefcase. It was then I realised the briefcase was attached to his wrist by a pair of handcuffs. I'd seen it before. When I'd met Nathan Burwell for the first time, he'd been carrying it. It must've had something valuable inside, but what? And why had he brought it with him when tonight's meeting was casual, with no relevance to his network? No answer came to mind.

I watched uneasily as Nathan unlocked his end of the handcuff, seconds before Dustin took the briefcase and attached the handcuff onto his hand. Nathan thanked his bodyguard and asked him to wait by the door.

"Are you sure you don't want me to stay, Mr. Burwell?" asked Dustin, eyeing me as he spoke.

"Of course not, Dustin," he said. "I have no enemies here."

Dustin nodded and walked away, clutching the briefcase as he stepped. He waited by the door just as he was ordered to do, but watched us carefully from afar. I knew Dustin was monitoring me closely, but I paid no attention.

Finally, Nathan took his seat. In perfect sync, we picked up our menus and began reading. I didn't particularly like seafood—in fact, I downright despised it—but I figured I'd be safe ordering fish. The difficult task would be trying to work out what kind of fish to order. I wasn't very familiar with any of them.

The food wasn't important though; it was the drinks that I cared about. Cosmo had told me to ensure Nathan ordered a dark coloured drink, preferably red wine. It would be too obvious to drop a pill in a drink you could see right through, but luckily red wine happened to be Nathan's drink of choice.

"I'd quite like to order a bottle of red wine," he said, grabbing my attention. "Do you have any preferences, Mr. Zimmer?"

"Can I recommend the Smithson Hills 1998 Merlot? My treat of course."

"Well, that's certainly an offer I can't refuse."

I forced myself to chuckle and resumed reading my menu.

"What about you, Brad?" said Nathan, looking towards his step-son. "Are you going to order a soft drink or would you like some of the red wine too?"

Brad nodded, barely making eye contact.

I'd researched Nathan Burwell's background quite profusely, and I knew he had four children. I could even remember their ages—four, eight, fourteen and twenty-three. I also knew that three of the children were biologically his, and the eldest one was a step-son. Nathan's current wife had previously had another child through a failed marriage. It was clear that Brad and Nathan were not related. However, they did share the same surname. I knew that over a decade ago Nathan had legally changed Brad's surname to Burwell. Initially, Brad's birth father had not agreed to the change, but eventually he signed the documents. If you ask me, I didn't understand why it was so important, but clearly Nathan's surname was an important part of his reputation.

As I flipped through the menu, I compared the differences and similarities between Nathan and Brad. Although they were both the same build with an identical haircut, their facial structures were completely different. Nathan had a well-rounded face, while Brad's was gaunt, with perfectly chiselled cheekbones. And clearly, their personalities were at the opposite ends of the spectrum too, as Brad hadn't said a damn word yet.

Time passed, and we each made our decisions. A waitress approached our table and took our orders, and the bottle of red wine was brought to us within three minutes. The waitress poured our drinks and conveniently left the bottle in the middle of the table, well within my arm's reach. Good. I wanted it that way.

Nathan was the first to take a sip. I watched him carefully, wondering how long it would be before I could try slipping him the pill. However, my focus was diverted, as art was all Nathan wanted to talk about. Once again, I'd have to bullshit my way through another conversation. He began discussing the concepts behind his work, and I tried to pay attention. Nathan was clearly a creative individual—and

I was too—but his passion for art was something I truly didn't understand.

Luckily for me, our entrées were brought out quite quickly. Top-notch service. I'd definitely have to leave them a tip tonight.

Nathan dug into his Oysters Kilpatrick, while Brad and I took the safe bet and had garden salads. We ate quietly, but the sound of moderately drunk patrons talking far too loudly filled in the awkward silence. Besides, I had nothing much to say. I kept monitoring Nathan's wine glass. To my luck, Nathan finished his first drink with his entrée.

This was my opportunity.

I carefully slid my hand into my trouser pocket, and pulled out the sachet of pills. My movement was so minor, that Nathan and Brad were none the wiser. Underneath the table, I used one hand to open the sachet and pulled out a pill. That was the easy part. It was increasingly more difficult to reseal the sachet and put it back into my pocket, but somehow I managed to do it without anybody noticing.

I risked a glance over my shoulder, scanning my eyes towards the front entrance. Dustin was still standing there, but he was looking at his mobile phone. Perfect. I needed to act now or I'd let the chance slip by.

I wedged the pill between my index and middle finger, and held it in place.

"Mr. Burwell," I said, trying to keep my voice calm. "Can I top you up?"

Nathan looked at me, and then looked at his empty wine glass.

"Yes, please," he said, grinning.

I picked up his glass with my free hand, and placed it in front of me. I raised my other hand and picked up the bottle from the centre of the table—keeping the pill wedged in place—and poured Nathan's drink. My hand was slightly shaky as I poured, but Nathan was still too busy picking at his oysters' shells to pay any attention to me.

98

I looked at my right hand. I could see the tiny white pill poking through from between my fingers. I had to drop it into his drink before somebody noticed. It was then, that I began to fear that maybe I would fail. What if the pill didn't sink? What if it floated on the surface? Or, what if the pill didn't dissolve like it should? What if it stayed at the bottom of the glass after Nathan had finished drinking from it? Panic rose from within, but I had to do it. This was the only option I had left, and if I didn't succeed then I may never see Rochelle again.

Her name was all the motivation I needed.

When Nathan's glass was full, I placed my hand over the top of his drink, and wedged my fingers apart. The pill dropped in and sank like a stone. I placed the drink back in front of Nathan, and quickly began pouring my own.

"Thank you," said Nathan as he picked up his glass and began to drink.

I'd done it. Nathan hadn't noticed, and I don't think Brad had either. I looked over my shoulder to see what Dustin was up to, and he was talking to a young waitress. Instantly, I scanned my eyes around the room and stared at the other patrons. Nobody had noticed.

I felt like I wanted to unwind, but I couldn't. The first step to the plan had only just been taken into action and there was a long night ahead of me. I began drinking down my own glass of wine— perhaps more quickly than I usually would—and tried to maintain my focus.

Within five or so minutes, our plates were cleared, and the table was set for our mains. As Nathan sipped on his wine, he resumed telling me about his art. I barely had to say anything—Nathan did all the talking.

Another fifteen minutes passed, and Nathan had finished his drink. The glass was empty and the pill was gone. From what Cosmo had told me, within half an hour or so, the effects would begin to take hold, but the pill worked faster than anticipated. Only ten minutes passed and Nathan complained about feeling sick.

"I feel a little nauseous," he said, his words slightly slurred.

"Oh," I said, still playing my part. "Perhaps you should have some water?"

Nathan listened to me, and picked up his glass of water. He took small sips, but as the minutes passed, he began swaying in his seat. I looked over at Brad. He didn't look concerned at all. Good. Clearly Brad didn't suspect a thing.

"I'm sorry," said Nathan, resting his forehead in his palm. "I'm not too well. I'm just going to go to the rest room for a moment."

Instantly, Nathan stood, moving awkwardly towards the bathrooms. Unfortunately, Dustin noticed and began stepping towards Nathan. My heart began pounding uncontrollably, and a moment of anxiety constricted my breathing. However, Nathan saw Dustin coming, and waved him off. Dustin listened to his boss and stopped in his tracks.

I think I may have sighed out loud in relief.

I watched as Nathan disappeared into the men's bathroom. He was gone, and nobody suspected a thing. Maybe I would get away with this after all. In fact, I was feeling so positive about tonight that I finished off the bottle of wine. Even though my actions would be forever regarded as despicable, I'd achieved the damn near impossible.

"I knew it," said Brad, speaking for the first time.

His words stunned me, feeling like a blow to the chest.

"Pardon?" I said, jerking my head in his direction.

"I knew Nathan shouldn't have had the oysters as an entrée," he explained, "because they always seem to make him sick."

"Oh. I see."

I didn't know what else to say. I hadn't expected Brad to speak to me, and now that we were sitting alone at the table together, I felt obliged to start a conversation, but I wouldn't know where to begin.

I had more important things to concentrate on anyway. After all, Nathan Burwell was about to be kidnapped. I sat back in my chair and tried to play it casually. But I couldn't relax. Not just yet.

100

***

Stumbling through the men's bathroom door, Nathan Burwell clambered towards the basins.

He grabbed hold of the tap and turned it, releasing a stream of cool water. Nathan furiously splashed water onto his face, but it proved to be useless. His nausea would not be cured so easily, so the only option left would be to ride it out.

But how the hell had this happened? Why was his body betraying him? Nathan raised his head and tried to catch his reflection in the mirror. His vision was somewhat blurred, but he still noticed the man standing over his shoulder.

A sweaty palm was wrapped around Nathan's face, covering his mouth. He panicked as breathing became more difficult. A second hand was wrapped around his chest, practically crushing his lungs. Without warning, Nathan was pulled back. He stared up at the bathroom lights as they moved past him. No, the lights weren't moving. Nathan was. Somebody was dragging him away, and before Nathan had the chance to struggle free, he found himself outside, staring up at the night sky.

For a brief moment, the cold air felt good against Nathan's skin. But it didn't last long, because his body came in contact with the muddy earth below. His hands were bound. His feet were bound. It had happened so quickly, that Nathan never had an opportunity to let the situation sink in. At last, he was yanked up from the ground and placed inside the backseat of an unfamiliar car. Although Nathan's surroundings were dark, everything seemed to become darker by the second.

"D-Don't," croaked Nathan, his voice sounding strangely distant.

The man looked down on him from above, but Nathan's vision was too blurry to make out any features. A hand patted Nathan on the cheek a few times, and then he heard the man's muffled voice,

"Just try and relax, dude. I've set you up for a fun night."

# 19

I checked my watch.

Nathan had been gone for some time now—almost twenty minutes. Our main meals had already been brought to the table, but neither Brad nor I had touched them. We'd said we'd wait until Nathan returned, but I knew he wouldn't.

Cosmo had followed through with his side of the plan. I was sure of it.

I noticed that Brad had begun picking at his dinner, nibbling on a beer battered chip.

"My chips are getting cold," explained Brad, defending his lack of patience.

"You can eat," I said. "I'll just wait until Nathan returns."

"He's probably having a chunder. He might be ages."

"Pardon? What's chunder?"

"Vomit."

"Oh."

"But I can go and check on him if you like," replied Brad, standing up from his seat.

"Sure. That sounds like a good idea."

Brad nodded and ambled towards the bathroom. I looked over my shoulder. Dustin was watching again. I turned back to my meal and tried to keep calm. I was so close to the finishing line that I didn't want to stuff it up now. I poured myself a glass of water, and waited. Brad was gone for no longer than a minute. When he finally emerged from the men's bathroom he walked straight past the table, and headed towards Dustin.

Adrenaline pounded in my veins and my heart trembled inside my chest. I knocked back the rest of my water just as I saw Dustin race towards the men's bathroom. He darted inside, and then reappeared only moments later. The sheer look of panic in Dustin's eyes confirmed what I already knew—Nathan Burwell was gone. Immediately, Dustin marched towards me, and Brad trailed behind him. I placed down my empty glass, turned around, faced them, and made my best attempt at a guilt-free smile.

"So?" I said. "How is Nathan?"

"He's gone," snarled Dustin.

"I'm sorry?"

"He's not here anymore. So where the hell did he go?"

"Nathan went into the bathroom."

"Jesus Christ, aren't you listening? He's gone!" shouted Dustin, attracting the attention of several curious onlookers. "And Mr. Burwell *never* leaves without me!"

"Maybe he went home," said Brad, offering a suggestion. "Nathan said he was feeling crook, so maybe he felt embarrassed and snuck out?"

"Oh, I hope he's alright," I said, still playing my part.

Dustin gazed at me with uneasy eyes. I knew he wanted to make accusations, but without the proof, he'd only make a fool of himself.

"We're leaving," said Dustin, as he turned his back on me. "Come, Brad."

Brad obeyed, and followed with no more to say. They walked directly out the front door, without looking back once. Finally, I was alone, and I'd accomplished the impossible. If I hadn't felt so disgusted with myself, I think I may have felt proud.

Acting casually, I pushed back my chair and stood from my seat. I strolled towards the front desk and paid the bill. Since none of us had even eaten our main course, I tried to get a discount, but no such luck. I had to pay in full.

After coughing up almost three hundred dollars, I stepped out into the chilly winter's night. I scanned my eyes around the street. By luck, I spotted an available taxi, so I slipped into the backseat and gave it a destination.

# 20

*August 7th*

Sunlight spilled through the open window, but I refused to open my eyes.

I was caught in the state of semi-consciousness. I was aware of my surroundings, but I remained inside the dream I'd been having all night. However, I still couldn't decipher whether I had dreamt it, or if it had truly happened. In the vision, I'd been holding Rochelle in my arms, safe and very much alive. I could even recall how soft her blonde hair had felt under my fingertips, and the warmth of her body next to mine.

However, when I finally opened my eyes, I was brought back to a disappointing reality.

I was alone, and Rochelle was still in danger. But before I could get too bogged down in my own self-pity, my mobile sounded a musical chime. I rolled over, pulled back the duvet and picked up my mobile from the top dresser. I checked the caller ID—Cosmo Rowland. I pushed the answer button and put the phone to my ear.

"Hi," I said.

"We did it, man. We fuckin' did it."

"What?"

"The motel pictures! I've got them!"

The words didn't register at first, but then last night's memories resurfaced—I'd drugged Nathan Burwell with a roofie, and then Cosmo had kidnapped him. Nathan had then been taken to a motel room and set up with another woman.

However, blackmailing the target would be impossible without the evidence to prove the scandal, so Cosmo had taken photographs of the staged betrayal.

Still a little disorientated, several thoughts and questions entered my mind but I struggled to say anything at all.

"Hello? Are you still there, man?" asked Cosmo.

"Yes—are you telling me you've got the photos already?"

"Yeah. Snapped them, and printed them. I've got them right here in my hands."

"Jesus Christ."

"I'll be over in ten minutes. So have a cold one ready for me when I get there."

"Cosmo, it's only eight thirty in the morning."

"Yeah, but I haven't slept."

End call. Without wasting a minute, I dressed for the day and grabbed something to eat. I was in the middle of finishing my toast when Cosmo knocked at the front door. I let him inside the Sydney apartment, but we didn't greet each other. Instead, Cosmo took a seat at the dining table and pulled out a stack of photos from his leather jacket. He sprawled the photographs across the table. I leaned over and picked up an image.

Cosmo had captured the scene just like he said he would. The setting was perfect. Cosmo had selected a rundown, gritty motel room, just adding to the sleaze factor. Two half-dressed bodies were in the centre of the photograph, lying on a bed. The woman in the photo had Nathan's arms wrapped around her waist, her lips firmly pressed against his.

These photographs were filthy, despicable, and best of all—convincing. Anyone who saw the shots would be convinced Nathan Burwell had committed adultery.

"How did you manage to make them look so realistic?"

"Nathan was out cold the entire time, and Daphne knows how to make it look like the real thing," said Cosmo, before adding, "and of course, I'm a fuckin' awesome photographer."

"Hang on, how long was Nathan out cold for?" I asked.

"Dunno," replied Cosmo, matter-of-factly. "He was still un-conscious when I dumped him outside the Botanical Gardens."

I looked up from the photographs and met his gaze. Although I was sure of what I'd heard him say, I still found myself asking,

"What?"

Cosmo continued to stare, and then confirmed what I had feared.

"I dumped Nathan outside the Botanical Gardens. What else was I meant to do?"

A million different questions entered my head all at once.

"How could—? Why did you—? Where is he now?"

"Man, you don't watch the news much do you?"

"I've only just gotten up for Christ's sake!"

Cosmo shook his head at me and stood from his seat. He found the television remote sitting on the arm of the chair, and flicked it on. I stared at the moving pictures on the screen, as the Channel 3 news anchor recapped the headlines. I heard her mention Nathan Burwell's name, and then she mentioned something about alcoholism.

"What's going on?" I asked, dumbfounded by the reports.

"Nathan Burwell was found asleep under a tree in the Botanical Gardens by an early morning jogger," explained Cosmo. "He was taken away by an ambulance to a local hospital, but was quickly discharged. However, since the Channel 5 network have refused to comment on the incident, other media stations are suggesting he was under the influence of alcohol after a night of binge drinking. But you and I know, it's a story they've pulled out of their arses."

"Shit," I heard myself say, "but Nathan's going to report us, isn't he?"

"Of course not. Nathan has no recollection at all, which is why his network has refused to make a comment. The roofies are good like that, because they can wipe out the memories completely. I doubt he'll ever remember a thing."

"So, you think we've gotten away with it?"

"Yeah. Without question, man."

At last, I felt like I could breathe. Cosmo and I had achieved the impossible by lining up the perfect blackmailing opportunity. I'd accomplished what I'd set out to do, and the end of this nightmare was in sight.

Cosmo wandered over into the kitchen, and returned with two beers. He offered me one, but I declined. Although I felt like I ought to be celebrating, it was still too early for me. Instead, I returned to the dining table and focused my attention towards the photos. The images were destructive, but they were also my ticket to ensuring Rochelle's safety.

"So, what happens next?" asked Cosmo, unscrewing the cap from his bottle.

"We've done our part," I explained, gathering the photographs in a bundle. "So now it's up to Mal Lawson to hold up his end of the deal."

***

After rummaging through a manila folder filled with nearly a hundred loose sheets of paper, I found Mal Lawson's contact number.

I was nervous about calling him, but I knew it had to be done. Cosmo watched me anxiously from the kitchen as I picked up the phone. I began dialling numbers, but I stopped, and hung up the receiver into its cradle.

"What am I supposed to say?" I asked helplessly.

"Don't be a pussy," he snapped back at me. "Call him and tell the douchebag you've got enough evidence to blackmail Nathan."

I nodded my head and mentally prepared myself once again.

I hadn't seen or spoken to Mal since the first day we'd met, which I found bizarre, because I thought he would've wanted to know how I'd been progressing. Or maybe he had more faith in me than what I had realised? I couldn't be sure. Shaking the thoughts from my head, I picked up the phone and began dialling. Somebody picked up after the second ring.

"I've been waiting to hear from you, Mr. Kennedy," said Mal.

His voice startled me at first, but I recovered.

"And how did you know it was me?"

"Nobody else can call me on this number. It's your own private line," he explained, before adding, "I bet that makes you feel special, huh?"

I evaded the question and went straight to the point of my call.

"I've got what you wanted—"

"I'm very pleased to hear that, Mr. Kennedy."

"—So I demand we make an exchange later today."

Mal was silent for some time, but eventually said,

"What exchange?"

"You know what. I have the evidence you need so that you can blackmail Nathan, and now you must return Rochelle safe and unharmed. That was the deal, Mal."

He fell silent again. I panicked. Had he forgotten our initial agreement, or was he disregarding it completely? I'd tried so hard and worked myself to the bone—surely I had reached the end of my hell? Unfortunately, matters would not swing in my favour. Mal decided to screw me over, yet again.

"Well, I changed my mind," he eventually said. "You blackmail Nathan yourself, and then you'll bring us the money. Once we have it, you'll have your girlfriend back."

"No," my voice was unnaturally steady. "I've done what you asked me."

"Mr. Kennedy, you're not in a position to disagree with me."

"Well I am, goddamn it!"

Mal sniggered at the other end of the phone. My attempts to intimidate him had failed, and he was finding my anger amusing.

"Fine, suit yourself," he replied. "I'll hold onto Rochelle for a while longer, after all, I'm starting to like the company. Your girlfriend certainly has quite the fight in her."

"What's that supposed to mean?"

"Just get me the money, Mr. Kennedy. That's all you have to do."

"You'd better be taking care of Rochelle because if you—"

"—She is alive, but I can't guarantee what condition she'll be in when I return her to you."

I erupted. I hadn't even predicted it, but I couldn't contain myself from shouting abuse down my end of the phone, using every profanity I knew, as I made violent death threats. When I'd finished, I was left drained and surprised by my sudden outburst. I didn't know I was capable of saying such disgusting, vile things. Even Cosmo seemed quite stunned as he gazed at me from behind the kitchen bench. I exhaled deeply, and waited for Mal's reply.

"Are you done, Mr. Kennedy? Do you feel better now?"

At first, I didn't answer him. Truthfully, I did feel better, but I knew my words meant nothing to him. Once again I had been left with no choice. There was nothing I could do than obey my enemy's demands. The realisation that I'd have to finish his dirty work sank in quicker than I had anticipated, so I took a deep breath, and continued the conversation.

"Fine. How much money am I supposed to get off Nathan anyway?"

He sniggered, pleased that I had come to terms with my situation.

"You will demand fifty mil in cash," he eventually replied. "Cheques or electronic transmissions are not acceptable."

"I'm sorry, fifty million dollars?"

"Yes. You heard correctly, Mr. Kennedy."

It was a sum I could barely comprehend, but if Mal wanted it, I'd have to get it. He began talking me though possible complications, but I wasn't listening. I could feel the disappointment well up inside me, before exploding into tiny fragments. I truly thought this was the end of my ordeal, but I'd been let down. Living without Rochelle was almost impossible, and I wondered how long it would be before I cracked.

"—And you'll need to arm yourself," said Mal as I snapped back into the conversation.

"Arm myself? With what, a gun?"

"Of course. Blackmailing Nathan isn't going to be easy."

I didn't doubt it. Not for a second.

As our conversation came to an end, I had one final remark to make. I knew it wouldn't do any good, but I wanted to shake him up a bit.

"And for the record, Mal," I began. "You're a coward."

"Pardon?"

"If you were any kind of man you would come out of hiding and face this yourself. You're scared, which is why you're getting innocent people to do your dirty work."

"I am not scared."

"Then prove me wrong."

Mal fell silent for some time.

"66 Gilmore Road, Arcadia," said Mal. "Now you know exactly where I am. I am not a coward, and I do not hide."

I could sense the aggression in his voice. Good. I'd hit a nerve. That's exactly how I wanted it. However, I had not expected him to tell me where he was. Did that mean Rochelle was there too? Or was the address a fake? But without more to say, I hung up the phone. I then gazed up at Cosmo. He stared at me, so I stared back.

"So uh, judging by the pissed off look on your face, I take it the conversation with Mal didn't go so well?" asked Cosmo, sounding a tad uneasy.

I didn't answer him; instead I accepted the beer I'd originally rejected. It was still only a quarter past nine in the morning, and I'd never used alcohol to drown my sorrows before, but right now I needed it. I untwisted the cap and began to drink. I finished it within a few minutes, and then I grabbed a second one from the fridge. Cosmo watched me, surprised by my actions, but he did not condemn my behaviour, instead, he had a better idea.

"Want a joint?" he asked, not knowing what else to say to console me.

"Do you really think that's what I need right now?"

It was a rhetorical question, but Cosmo answered anyway.

"Hell yeah, man. You need it—it'll chill you out and take the edge off."

I despised Cosmo's cannabis use, but right now I disregarded my morals and accepted his offer. I'd only ever smoked a handful of cigarettes in my life, but I had never tried weed. However, I was up for anything right now. All I wanted was to feel numb.

"Alright. I'll try it."

Like an excited puppy, Cosmo pulled out his stash, chopped up, then rolled out two joints. He ignited the ends of both, and handed me one. I put the joint between my lips and inhaled the poison. It was revolting, and I felt disgusted with myself. I didn't pretend to like it, but I knew what the drug was capable of, and I wanted it to drown out my problems.

"You might wanna sit down, man," said Cosmo, taking a deep drag from his own, "because this is a new sensation for you, and you're going to love it. So relax and enjoy it."

We moved from the kitchen into the lounge room. I kept smoking. Crossing the room, I took my seat on the sofa, while Cosmo flopped down into an armchair opposite me. After a few minutes, I began feeling the effects. I closed my eyes, as my worries and concerns faded from my mind, leaving me with a satisfying emptiness.

# 21

*August 9th*

From the moment I opened my eyes, I was overcome by a sense of regret.

I found myself lying on the bare ground, still wearing the same clothes I'd been in two days ago. My head was spinning. My mouth was dry. If I hadn't known better, I would have thought I was dead. Using what was left of my energy, I pulled myself from the ground and sat upright. As my eyes adjusted to the scene, I surveyed what was left of my apartment.

The place was a mess. Dozens of beer bottles were lined up across the coffee table, and empty chip packets were scattered across the floor. The room was intoxicating. Each breath made me inhale second-hand smoke, and sometimes I felt like I was choking on the air. I coughed a few times, and placed my palm across my sweat-drenched shirt. I could feel my heart beating rapidly beneath my chest like a bomb ready to explode.

The windows and blinds were all closed, making the apartment pitch black. Hell, I couldn't even tell what time of the day it was.

Staggering to my feet, I took a moment to compose myself. I couldn't remember a time when I'd felt so ill, because every movement I made took effort. I was hungover and stoned. Not a good combination. I forced myself to cross the room, and opened up the blinds.

Daylight spilled through the window, temporarily blinding me.

The sun was only just peeping up from behind the city skyline—it was morning. I would not waste another day dwelling on my sorrows. Today, I would take action. I was without a plan and perhaps out of my mind, but I would blackmail Nathan Burwell, and I would succeed. I figured being pessimistic had gotten me nowhere, so I'd decided to turn over a new leaf.

Once again, I turned my attention to the state of the apartment. It would need to be cleaned up later—I had more important matters to worry about. It was then that I noticed Cosmo. He was asleep on the sofa, wearing nothing but briefs. Yes, not boxers, but briefs. I cringed and turned away. It was more of Cosmo than I ever wanted to see.

But he had to be woken up. Daylight was burning and I was determined to make the most of it. I approached Cosmo and gave him a poke in the shoulder. He didn't move. Losing patience, I poked him again. Harder. When that didn't work, I delivered a powerful slap across the face. He woke up immediately, shot upright, fists at the ready. I wasn't sure what he had been expecting, but as he adjusted to his surroundings and saw me, his fists dropped. But he was furious. No question about it.

"What the fuck was that for?" he snarled.

"Get up," I replied. "We've got plans today."

"Like what?"

"We're going to blackmail Nathan Burwell for fifty million."

"What?" he scoffed. "Right now?"

I didn't answer him. I would complete the task with or without his help—although having his help was much preferred, of course. I swiftly left the room and prepared to make my departure. I grabbed the stack of photos from the kitchen bench and slipped into my jacket. Just as I was about to step out the door, I heard Cosmo call my name. I turned around to see him rushing towards me, still wearing nothing but the briefs. Extremely *tight* briefs. I cringed once again and turned my head.

"Hold up, Kennedy. You can't go yet," said Cosmo.

"I have to. I can't just wait around—"

"—Yeah, I get that. But you're in no state to meet a fuckin' CEO right now. Like, I don't mean any disrespect, but you desperately need a shower, man. Seriously, you smell like you've spent the night lying in horse shit."

I tried not to take offence.

"That bad?" I asked after some time.

"Oh yeah. It's fuckin' vulgar."

I checked my watch. 7:13am. Nathan Burwell probably hadn't even arrived at his office yet. He'd probably be sitting down to breakfast with his children, or suiting up in his flash business attire. I could afford to spend some time preparing for the day.

"Alright, I'll go fix myself up," I said, as I headed towards the bathroom. "And while I'm gone, please, do me a favour and put some goddamn trousers on."

# 22

I had spent the morning resurrecting what was left of my dignity.

I'd showered and shaved—and the process truly had been therapeutic. I also felt more focused, because the time I'd spent getting ready had allowed me to come up with a plan of action. I would meet with Nathan Burwell, request that the meeting be private, show him the pictures, and bribe that poor bastard for all he was worth. A little after ten thirty, Cosmo and I planned to make our departure.

I found him sitting at the breakfast bar, pulling the zipper across a large black backpack. When he saw me approach, he seemed a little on edge, and I think I knew why. I eyed the backpack, and pointed towards it. Cosmo picked it up and slung it over his shoulder, not daring to give an explanation. Since I had known Cosmo for quite a while now, I knew his mannerisms, and I could tell when he was feeling guilty.

"What's in the backpack?" I asked, although I was almost positive of the answer.

"Tools of a useful nature," replied Cosmo.

"Such as?"

"That's my little secret, Kennedy."

I had a strong suspicion that Cosmo had been rifling through the weaponry cupboard while I had been dressing, and I was sure he had armed himself. I really detested the idea of Cosmo with a gun. Did he even know how to use one? However, I let it slide. Regardless of my concerns, I'd rather Cosmo be armed than myself. Despite all those times I'd held a gun in my hand, I still felt uncomfortable with it. A gun was designed for only one purpose—to kill, or at least seriously injure—and that never settled well with me.

Checking the time once more, we decided it was time to leave. For once, I did not feel nervous. Perhaps I was over-confident, but I couldn't see the harm in it. I had the upper hand, and I had the power to lead Nathan Burwell to his peril.

We pulled into the Channel 5 underground car park a little after eleven o'clock.

For once, I felt prepared. I knew exactly what I had to do, and now it was only a matter of executing it. Today, I would face Nathan alone. Cosmo was purely with me for moral support, although truthfully, I saw him as a safety net too. Just in case matters turned sour, I was relieved to know that Cosmo would not be too far away. He had nerves of steel—which was something I deeply envied.

For the millionth time today, I flicked through the photographs. I wondered how Nathan Burwell would react when he first laid eyes on the images. Would he play it cool? Or fall to pieces? I figured it was time to find out, so I unbuckled my seatbelt and stepped out of the car.

"Keep your mobile with you," said Cosmo, "and call if you need assistance."

"Will do," I said, but I doubted I'd ever have the chance to contact him, even if I needed to.

Without more to say, I turned and left Cosmo standing by the car. I dug my hands into the pockets in my jacket, and made my way towards the elevator. I rode it to the first floor, and stepped out into the main foyer. It was just as busy as the last time I'd been here, and I figured I'd have to go through a similar procedure in order to see Nathan Burwell—but I was mistaken. Only seconds after stepping out of the elevator, Nathan's main bodyguard, Dustin, was standing directly outside. He had been waiting for me.

"Mr. Zimmer," said Dustin, beckoning to me.

"Hi," I said with a causal smile, feeling unnaturally at ease. "How are you?"

Dustin evaded the question, and simply replied,

"If you have a moment, Mr. Burwell would like to see you."

"Brilliant, because I'd like to see him too."

Without another word to say, Dustin escorted me back into the elevator, and to the fifteenth floor. He led me down the same long corridor, and I went through the same security procedures. Dustin scanned my body, and then locked my belongings in the safety vault. I asked to keep my mobile phone on me, but he denied my request, and I had to hand it over. When all my possessions were securely locked away, he led me to the wooden oak door with a golden plaque at the end of the corridor. He opened the door for me, and I stepped inside.

But Dustin did not follow. Once I was inside Nathan Burwell's office, he closed the door behind me. I was taken by surprise, but I remained calm. I scanned my eyes around the office, and found Nathan standing behind his desk, looking out the window. He had his back turned to me. Nathan knew I had betrayed him.

"I was wondering when you'd show up," he said, his voice low and bitter.

"I've been very busy," I said, lying through my teeth.

"That night when you invited me out to dinner—you set me up."

There was no point in denying it.

"Yeah," I agreed. "I did."

I heard him exhale deeply. A silence lingered in the air, but I remained standing by the door. I was not sure of what thoughts were running through Nathan's head, so I kept myself focused. I still didn't know what he was capable of.

"Your name," said Nathan, making eye contact with me at last. "It's not Milo Zimmer, is it?"

I was honest with him.

"That's right. It's not."

"And now that I know, are you going to tell me your real name?"

"Of course not, Mr. Burwell," I said, offering a polite smile.

He moved away from the window, and sat down at his desk. He told me to take a seat, but I remained standing. I was on high alert, and I wouldn't let my guard down just yet.

"I don't deserve this," said Nathan, his voice cracking slightly.

He was using his emotions to weaken me, but for once I refused to feel the guilt.

"The last thing I remember was having dinner with you, and feeling sick," began Nathan, as he started to reminisce. "I think I blacked out, and then when I woke up, I found myself in the Botanical Gardens, with no recollection of how I got there. I was then rushed to the hospital and they took some tests," said Nathan, but then he paused and looked directly at me. His gaze was so cold I could almost feel it. "The doctors found Rohypnol in my system. You drugged me."

Nathan had worked it out, so without a word to say, I stepped closer, plucked the photographs from my jacket and spilled them across the desk.

I'd never seen the colour drain from a man's face so quickly.

He picked up a single photograph and stared at it for the longest time. I could tell Nathan wanted to be furious with me, but he was more furious with himself. Despite how cautious he'd been, I'd managed to get one over him.

I gave Nathan some time to compose himself before getting down to business.

"I will leak these pictures to your wife, your children and the entire country unless you cooperate with me. Do you understand?" I said, using a much firmer tone than I was used to.

"And how much do you want?" asked Nathan, cutting to the chase.

"Fifty million. In cash."

"You bastard."

I shuffled the photographs from the desk and collected them, and then snatched the final photograph from Nathan's hand. I tucked them back into my jacket pocket and crossed my arms. I needed to show him that I was not bluffing.

I could see the sheer panic in Nathan's eyes. Good. I wanted it that way. He rested his hands in front of him and tried to calm himself. No such luck. I could see his knee jack hammering the floor below. He was nervous, and he knew there was no choice but to bow down to my demands.

"You know," Nathan began, finding his voice, "I have my office swept every week for bugs."

"Bugs?" I queried.

"Yes—spyware bugs to be more specific, and recently a listening device and a computer tracker were found. So tell me, was that your handy work?"

"Maybe, maybe not."

"I'd like a straight answer, because I need to know, how the hell did you do it?"

I think I smiled. I didn't mean to, but it was satisfying to know I'd outsmarted the man behind a multi-million dollar network, and his over-the-top security measures had failed him.

"Just out of interest, how ignorant do you think I am?" asked Nathan, his eyes fixed on me.

"Oh, you're not ignorant, but that doesn't mean I can't play you as a fool."

"Good," replied Nathan, "because as we speak I am well aware you have an accomplice waiting for you by a black BMW in the downstairs car park."

"Impressive. How did you work that out?"

"Because my building has security cameras at every corner and I saw you arrive with him."

It explained why Dustin had been waiting for me at the elevator. Obviously, they had been watching out for me for days now. They knew all too well that I was the one responsible for Nathan's disappearance at the restaurant.

"Those photographs," said Nathan, "how did you print them? Did you go to a shop or...?"

"We hooked up the camera to a printer, and printed them off that way."

"Then if I pay you this money, I demand to have any extra copies you've printed off, and I also want the camera used too. I want all records of these photographs to be destroyed, as if it never happened. Do we have an agreement?"

After so many tumultuous weeks, I could see the light at the end of the tunnel. I had accomplished the task that I'd been assigned to do. The very thought made me smile.

"We've got a deal," I said, pulling the photographs from my jacket once more and handing them over to him. "So get me the money and I'll be on my way."

Nathan closed his eyes for a moment, and sat perfectly still. He kept the photographs clutched tightly in both hands. Finally, acknowledging his defeat, he tucked the photographs away, opened a desk draw to his left and pulled out a chequebook. He opened the book and began to scrawl across the first cheque.

"No, I don't want a cheque," I said, raising a palm. "Cash only."

"I know," said Nathan, continuing to write. "This cheque is not for you."

I sat back in my chair and watched him. Surely this was not the time to lapse back into his own business? My demands needed to be met first. Soon enough, he ripped the cheque out of the book, and then pressed a button on his intercom.

"Dustin, you can come in now," said Nathan.

Without delay, Dustin Pinfold opened the office door and stepped inside. He stared directly at me, eyes like a wild animal. I refused to feel intimidated. It was at that moment I noticed that Nathan had folded the cheque in half, and had slipped it into Dustin's pocket. Strange.

"Dustin, please take Mr. Zimmer and his friend waiting in the car park to the vault room. They request cash, so pay these men their sum, and let them leave."

"Of course," replied Dustin, still staring.

I was fairly sure Dustin knew what was going on, but I was also sure he wouldn't do anything without Nathan's permission. I saw Dustin as his pet on a leash, and he had no choice but to obey his master's commands.

120

"Goodbye, Mr. Zimmer," said Nathan—I could sense he felt uncomfortable using a name he knew was fake. "Good luck with your future endeavours."

I thanked Nathan, and left with Dustin. The office door was closed behind me, and my possessions were returned. However, just before Dustin returned my mobile, he took the liberty to switch it on and said,

"Call your friend in the car park. Tell him to meet us on the fifth floor."

I took my mobile and complied. I dialled in his number, and Cosmo picked up without delay.

"Kennedy, you alright? What's happening?"

"Everything is fine," I replied. "We're getting our payment and then we can go. So meet me at the fifth floor right now. OK?"

"Got ya," he said, and he hung up.

Seconds after slipping the mobile back into my pocket, Dustin instructed for me to follow. I obeyed. We took the elevator to the fifth floor and waited.

I was just moments away from being freed from my assignment, and then I could claim what was rightfully mine—Rochelle. There was no greater feeling than knowing that after all I had endured, she and I could finally go back to living life as normal.

# 23

Fifty million dollars—it was more than I could comprehend.

I was already thinking ahead, and trying to work out the best way to deliver the money to Mal and Isaac. Or perhaps I could be the one to call the shots now? I'd have what they wanted, so I'd demand that Rochelle be released before I showed them a cent of the money. The last few weeks had built up my confidence, and I liked it. I wasn't weak and powerless after all.

A few minutes passed, and finally Cosmo arrived outside the elevator, on the fifth floor. He approached Dustin and I, bringing along his cocky smile. It was then I noticed Cosmo had his backpack slung over his shoulder. Dustin saw it too and grew suspicious.

"What's in the backpack?" asked Dustin, giving Cosmo his filthiest stare.

"None of your fuckin' business, mate," he replied.

Dustin shot his hand out and snatched the backpack from Cosmo's shoulder before he had the chance to blink. Cosmo looked as if he wanted to retaliate, but knowing better, he kept still. But I was panicking. I was sure Cosmo had packed a weapon—namely, a powerful handgun. It could ruin the deal, and I felt close to breaking point. Cosmo, on the other hand, was completely calm.

I watched uneasily as Dustin unzipped the backpack and rifled through the inside.

"There's a laptop, a camera and half an eaten protein bar in there," said Cosmo. "I don't know what you're looking for, but that's all you're going to find inside that backpack."

I exhaled with relief. I'd been expecting the worst, but clearly I didn't know Cosmo was well as I thought I did. At last, Dustin finished inspecting the bag, and then returned it to Cosmo.

"By the way, what's with the sour face?" Cosmo asked Dustin, as he slung the backpack over his shoulder again. "Would it kill you to smile?"

Dustin grunted, and then turned around and began walking down a corridor. Cosmo and I followed behind. We came to a room with a plain white door. Dustin opened up the door, and instructed us to go inside. We complied. Cosmo and I found ourselves in a dull grey room filled with boxes stacked up against a wall. Where the hell was the vault? I scanned my eyes around the room and spotted another door across from us. I stepped towards it, but without warning, it opened up and four men stepped out. I spun my head around to see that Dustin had entered the room with us, closing the door behind him.

There was no vault. They had played us, just as we had played them.

Cosmo had worked it out too, and within a split second, he pulled out a gun he'd been hiding—tucked in the back of his jeans—and aimed it at Dustin. He had his finger on the trigger, ready to fire, when a second man grabbed Cosmo from behind. The gun was forced from Cosmo's hand. It dropped to the floor. I dived to the ground in the hopes of reaching it, but Dustin kicked it away. I sprung back to my feet, ready to defend myself, when I too, was grabbed from behind. The man was trying to force me to the floor again, but I knew all too well that if I allowed it, no doubt it would be the end of me. I tried to maintain balance, but my knees gave way and I fell to the concrete floor below. The man holding me then put his body weight on my spine and applied pressure. I screamed. I felt the man's hot breath on the back of my neck, his cold sweat dripping onto me. A second set of hands snaked around my neck and forced my face to the floor. I panicked and tried to break free.

Suddenly, a foot came into contact with my jaw, followed by a jab to the rib cage. I tasted blood in my mouth. I took beatings from each direction, and I closed my eyes and waited for the end to come. But it didn't. The flogging continued.

I was yanked up from the floor, and forced to my feet. Somebody kneed me in the groin, and I buckled to the ground once again.

"Get up, motherfucker!" somebody yelled into my ear. "On your feet!"

Before I could summon the strength, I was pulled up again, almost forcing my shoulder out of its socket. My arms were held behind my back. I tried to squirm free, but they were twisted, and in the firm grip of somebody else's hands. I was stuck.

I raised my head and focused my eyes. I saw Cosmo across the room, being held to his knees by three men. He too, was unable to move, but that didn't stop him from trying.

I heard a laugh. I turned my head to see Dustin standing to my right, lighting a cigarette. He then bent down and picked Cosmo's gun up from the floor, his finger resting on the trigger.

"Right from the start, I knew you couldn't be trusted," said Dustin, staring directly at me. "And I told Nathan my concerns, but he disregarded it. But of course, I was right. Hell, I should be the one running this company. I always get it right."

I said nothing, but Cosmo barked a string of insults from across the room. The men continued to beat him, but it wasn't enough to diminish his anger.

Dustin put the cigarette to his lips and inhaled deeply. He then breathed out, and blew the smoke in my face. I tried not to show my fear, but I had surely failed.

"Do you know how many men try to blackmail Mr. Burwell every year?" said Dustin, his face just inches from mine. "Dozens. You're not the first wankers that have tried to pull a stunt like this. Now I'll admit you came the furthest out of all of them, but you failed, just like the rest."

I had been naïve to think I would succeed. I wished somebody had talked some sense into me before undertaking the task assigned to me. I should have spent my time trying to rescue Rochelle, instead of wasting my time on the impossible.

"Now let me show you something," said Dustin, and he pulled out the cheque that Nathan had placed in his pocket just moments ago. Dustin unfolded the cheque, and placed it in front of my face so I could read it. In black, bold letters it read,

*SEND THESE MEN TO HELL.*

I read the words. Then I read them again, before closing my eyes and hanging my head.

"You're going to kill us," I said, as if I'd already accepted my fate.

"Personally, I'd like to, but that's too much mess," replied Dustin, "but rest assured, you'll be going through hell. After today, you'll probably wish we killed you..."

"Bring it on, fuckwit!" yelled Cosmo, fighting for his freedom.

One of the men delivered a punch directly into his sternum, and then kneed him under the chin. I turned away, unable to watch anymore. I listened as they pounded their fists into Cosmo's body. How could one man take such brutal punishment?

When the beating stopped, I looked back at Cosmo. His face was swelling with bruises ready to surface, and blood trickled from his scalp down the side of his face.

"You probably know," said Dustin, grabbing my attention once more, "but I overheard your conversation with Mr. Burwell today. I'm aware that you drugged him with a roofie, and I know about the photographs."

"I already gave the photos to Nathan," I said. "He has them now."

Dustin pulled the cigarette from between his lips, and pressed the butt onto my neck. My skin burned, as if there was a searing hot bullet slowly penetrating through my flesh. I yelped in pain. I tried to struggle free. Dustin held the cigarette in place, and when I could take no more, he dropped it onto the cement and stomped on it.

"But the photos must still be on the camera, correct?" asked Dustin.

"It's in my backpack," said Cosmo, as blood filled the lines in between his teeth. "Take the camera, and then let us go."

I spotted Cosmo's backpack lying beside one of the doors. Dustin picked it up and unzipped the bag, and pulled out the laptop and camera. Dustin carefully put the laptop aside on one of the boxes behind him. He then seized the memory card from the digital camera and snapped it in half. He then threw the camera to the floor, and stomped on it until it smashed into tiny fragments. All that was left was a shattered mess.

Finally, Dustin gained eye contact with me once more.

"But you must have backup photographs kept somewhere else, don't you?" he asked.

"No," I replied. "That's it. You have everything now."

"I don't believe you."

"But it's the truth..."

"The truth means fuck all coming from your mouth."

I fell silent. I had nothing more to offer him. After all my hard work, they had the photographs, and they had destroyed the evidence. Why wouldn't he believe me? Then again, maybe he just didn't want to.

"His wrist," said Dustin, pointing at Cosmo. "We'll start off easy on him."

One of the men sniggered, and held a firm grip around Cosmo's left wrist. Cosmo tried to break free, but he was being held too tightly. For the first time, I think I saw fear in Cosmo's eyes. We both knew today would not end well.

"Tell me," said Dustin, igniting a fresh cigarette. "Where do you keep your back up photographs? Are they saved on a hard drive, or did you print more copies?"

"You have everything. I promise."

"Don't lie to me, or we'll start breaking bones."

"I'm not lying!"

Dustin turned his head, nodded towards the man holding onto Cosmo's wrist. The man grinned wickedly, and began to apply force. Cosmo gritted his teeth, trying to hold back the pain. I couldn't take it. This was not Cosmo's battle.

"Please! Don't!" I shouted.

My pleas proved to be useless, and it wasn't long before I heard a chilling snap. Cosmo's eyes seem to bulge out of their sockets. He tried to hold back every urge to scream. I stared helpless-

126

ly, as Cosmo's wrist hung loosely from his arm, with his fingers dangling motionlessly. The bone was broken. I was sure of it.

Dustin laughed at my reaction, enjoying every second of it. He then crouched down beside me, directly at eye level. He blew smoke in my face once again.

"Don't feel as though you're being left out," he said. "It'll be your turn next."

I closed my eyes and tried not to think about it. Dustin laughed again. If it weren't for the fact I was being held, I would have struck him. Fear was fading, and anger was resurfacing.

"Now let's take this up a notch," said Dustin, grinning ear to ear. "The femur is one of the strongest bones in the body. But guess what? My boys can break it."

My feet went numb as I spotted a mallet resting in the corner of the room. Without warning, Dustin stood up, and picked up the mallet. He gave it to one of his men, pointed at Cosmo and instructed him to take the hit. I begged for mercy.

"So are you going to tell me where you keep the extra photos?" he asked me.

"Yes," I said, hoping a lie would save Cosmo from enduring another broken bone. "They're saved on the laptop you've got. I promise!"

Dustin smirked, and whispered icily,

"You're full of shit." Redirecting his attention, he stared at the man with the mallet, nodded and said, "Break it."

The man held the mallet over his head.

"No!" I screamed. "Please! Don't!"

The mallet was brought down over Cosmo's leg. He yelled out in pain, unable to disguise his distress. However, he continued to jolt his body, trying to escape. The man then touched the back of Cosmo's leg. He seemed a little confused, before turning to face Dustin.

"It's not broken," said the man, dumbfounded.

"Then try again," replied Dustin.

The man shrugged, and lifted the mallet up once again.

"For Christ's sake!" I shouted. "Stop it! Take anything you want, but please, let us go!"

"Wait," said Dustin, raising a hand. "Hold on for a second there."

I don't know if what I'd said had worked, but Dustin had seemingly had a change of heart. But I wasn't the only one surprised, the rest of the men were too.

Dustin stepped towards me. All that could be heard was his footsteps thumping across the cold cement below. Once again, he crouched down beside me.

"Correct me if I'm wrong," began Dustin, "but you have a BMW downstairs, don't you?"

At first, the question came as a surprise, but then I realised this might be my one chance to leave without further punishment.

"Yeah," I said. "If you want it, it's yours—as long as you let us go. Right this second."

"Where are the keys?" asked Dustin, lowering his voice.

"Cosmo has them. Check his pocket."

Dustin nodded towards one of his men, and demanded they empty Cosmo's pockets. They pulled out the keys and tossed them towards Dustin. He clutched the keys in his hand, studied them, before tucking them away.

"Let the pricks go," said Dustin.

Immediately, the grip around my arms loosened, and I crashed to the ground. The men let Cosmo go too. I half expected him to fight back, but he had already taken too much. I scrambled off the floor and back to my feet. I tried to help Cosmo up, but he refused my assitance.

Without delay, the four men left through the door they had entered in, and once again Cosmo and I were alone with Dustin. But he hadn't finished taunting us—not just yet.

"When you gentlemen leave this building, take one thought with you," hissed Dustin. "You are both not welcome here, and if I see you, I will not hesitate to shoot you dead."

128

He aimed the gun towards us, held it steady for a few moments, before lowering his aim.

"You won't see us again," I promised.

"Good. Then get the fuck out of here."

Cosmo and I didn't need to be told twice. We immediately left the room, staggered down the corridor and took the elevator to the ground floor. We darted across the car park and made our way back to the streets. Cosmo and I never looked back. Not once.

# 24

I'd been a foolish, ignorant idiot.

Trembling with each step, aching each time I blinked, I came to the realisation I should have seen earlier—I'd been assigned to do the impossible. Mal Lawson had set me up to fail.

The thought made my insides drop like an anvil, or maybe that was because of the pain? The beating had drained me of almost all my energy, and I could hardly believe I was still standing. Then again, Cosmo had copped it far worse than I. After all he had just endured, I really couldn't be the one to complain.

We staggered down the streets of Sydney, in full daylight, looking like we'd spent the night in a lion's cage. People eyeballed us as we shuffled past, but I refused to let them get to me. Cosmo didn't seem to care either, because he kept it no secret that he was in agony. He walked on muttering every profanity he knew under his breath, and occasionally allowed himself to growl in pain. As the minutes passed, he grew more agitated. I had no choice but to listen to his rants.

"My fuckin' wrist!" shouted Cosmo, nursing the broken bone. "It fuckin' hurts!"

"We'll go to a hospital," I said for the umpteenth time.

"And say what? I fell? Come on, look at me. I'm a fuckin' mess."

I shrugged, not knowing what else to say.

"Man, it's already swelling," said Cosmo, studying his wrist. "It's like there's a fuckin' golf ball stuck under my skin."

"And how's your leg?"

"In fuckin' pain," he hissed, "but at least they didn't crush it."

I nodded, although I think I was only half listening. I was too preoccupied with my own thoughts. How was I meant to rescue Rochelle now? It'd been weeks since we'd last seen each other, and the longer we were apart, the more I'd fear that I'd never see her again. Was she OK? Was she being treated right? I needed to know. I couldn't go on without knowing her fate. Rochelle was my priority. I didn't give a shit about getting the money or finishing the assignment—I just wanted my girlfriend back.

I needed to change my approach. I'd failed twice, and I refused to fail again. Rather than obeying Mal Lawson, I would take matters into my own hands. Besides, the address he had told me seemed legit, so I would investigate. If Rochelle was indeed there, being held captive against her will, I would break her out and beat those bastards at their own game.

The thought of outsmarting those sons of bitches was all the motivation I needed.

I picked up the pace, leaving Cosmo trailing behind. He tried to catch up, but his injured leg prevented him from moving any faster. Fairly soon, I was far ahead of him.

"Where are you going?" Cosmo called out to me.

"Home," I said, without looking back.

"You should probably get checked out too. You took some big hits."

I ignored him and continued walking.

"Fine then," he shouted. "I'll see you back at the apartment."

But he wouldn't see me there. I wasn't going to the apartment. I was going home—the only place where I truly belonged.

\*\*\*

They had failed him, and failure deserved punishment.

Mal Lawson sat, staring vacantly into a computer screen. He had heard the audio from the listening device inside Jordan Kennedy's watch, and what had just transpired did not please him. Once again, he had failed to blackmail Nathan Burwell successfully, and the money was out of reach.

Mal's clients were losing patience with each day that passed by. Death threats had been made. It probably wouldn't be too long before somebody took a shot. Mal needed the fifty million, and he needed it soon—but staring into the computer screen wasn't doing any good.

There was a knock on the door, and after being granted permission, Isaac stepped inside the room. He had come to break the bad news to Mal.

"We should have hired a professional," mumbled Mal, still staring at the screen.

"But nobody wanted to take the job."

"But we should have kept searching...because this is pointless, Isaac. Kennedy is wasting our time. He doesn't have the skills to pull this off."

"So what now? Do we kill him?"

"Not yet," replied Mal, "but his failure cannot be dismissed."

# 25

It took two buses and an overpriced taxi ride to get back home to Middle Dural, but it was worth every cent to me.

The taxi drove down the narrow dirt road and dropped me off directly in front of the house. The grass—and there wasn't much of it—had grown wildly, and our letterbox was almost overflowing. I paid the taxi driver his fare and slipped out of the car. He drove off without delay, kicking up a storm of dirt as he departed. Once again I was alone. Cold and isolated.

I emptied the letterbox first and flipped through the stack of bills that urgently needed paying. I doubted I'd be able to afford it.

Cosmo and I had skipped more days of work than I cared to keep track of. Jeff had called us a couple of times, demanding that we return to work immediately. Our excuses were wearing thin, and Jeff had threatened to hire new staff in our absence. We were on the verge of losing our jobs.

Rochelle's Ute was still parked a few meters away from our granny flat. Although I now needed a new set of wheels, I would be unable to drive Rochelle's car because she drove a manual—and I didn't have a damn clue how to drive one.

Strolling towards the front door, I checked my pockets for my keys. I'd left them back at the apartment. Luckily, we had hidden a spare key behind a false brick in the wall—and only Rochelle and I knew about it. I crouched down, and carefully pulled out the brick. After grabbing the key, I shoved it into the front door and opened it up.

Stepping inside, I was overcome by a sense of loss. I'd come home thinking that I'd find comfort in the familiarity—but this time, I didn't. It only reminded me of what I was missing.

Now that I knew what I was without, I could appreciate just how fortunate I had been. Hell, I'd had it good. Earlier this year I thought living the mundane wasn't enough, but I was dead wrong. I'd give anything to have my life back again. But I had been growing more desperate each day, and I'd reached the point where I'd gladly exchange my life to ensure Rochelle's safety and wellbeing. I wasn't sure how much longer I could carry on knowing she was in danger, probably scared and thinking death was inevitable.

Growing weaker by the minute, I sat down on the second-hand leather sofa in the centre of the room. Memories flooded back. I could recall the evenings I'd spent with Rochelle on the sofa, sitting in front of a toasty fire, with her head gently resting on my chest. Sometimes, we even made love on the sofa—usually while the TV was on, during episodes of *Deal or No Deal*. For a brief moment I smiled, but the happiness quickly faded as reality set back in.

God, I was losing my mind without her.

I scanned my eyes around and eyed the phone. In a moment of weakness, I wanted to call my sister Amy. I wanted to tell her everything—but I knew I couldn't. Nobody else could learn of the mess I was in. Besides, how could I tell her about Eamon Bronson's death? She'd been married to him. She had loved him. I simply didn't have the strength to tell her the truth. Amy could never know what I knew. She'd finally gotten her life back on track, and I didn't want to be the one to ruin it.

The injuries I'd sustained just a few hours ago were beginning to take their toll. My body ached, my head was pounding and I was in no state to think rationally. I crashed down on the sofa, and folded my hands across my chest. Thoughts weighed heavily on my mind, but I was delirious. I closed my eyes and faded into a pleasant state of unconsciousness.

# 26

*August 10th*

I awoke in a cold sweat.

As my eyes adjusted to my surroundings, I was surprised to see I was still resting on the sofa, inside my tiny rented house in Middle Dural. I'd been in so much agony, it seemed the pain had been enough to knock me out cold. I checked my watch. 6:53 AM. The start of a new day.

Perhaps I should have closed my eyes again, and tried to sleep some more in order to fully recuperate—but there was too much to do. I sat upright. I was overwhelmed by dizziness. The walls were rotating around me, and the floor was spinning beneath my feet. Maybe this was a sign from a higher power telling me to lie down and rest? But my newfound determination made me rise to my feet, and walk out the front door.

I staggered my way to the bus stop, which was a good thirty-five minute walk from my house. Somehow, I survived the journey and I caught the first bus into the city. When I arrived, I wasn't sure where I was. The city was still a somewhat unfamiliar place to me. Luckily, I managed to ask a bunch of tourists with a map how to get to Millers Point, and they were more than helpful. I took a train ride to the other side of the city, and then walked the rest of the way. Finally, I found the apartment block.

I took the elevator to the top floor, and stepped out into the corridor. I'd started feeling better too, but I knew it might take days to fully recover. Walking down the corridor, I found Cosmo sitting down in front of the door. His arm was in a cast, and his face was black and blue with bruises. Cosmo raised his head and made eye contact with me. Dark circles surrounded his eyes, which made me wonder how long he'd been sitting outside for.

"Where the hell have you been?" asked Cosmo, his voice rougher than usual.

"Sorry," I replied, although I truly wasn't. "I went home for a little while."

Cosmo stared, and I could tell he was tempted to question me about it, but knowing better he kept his mouth shut and let it go. I was thankful. I wasn't in the mood for an argument.

He pulled himself off the floor—which was a great effort—and waited for me to open the door. We stepped inside the apartment to find the place was still trashed. Although I was sure Cosmo was responsible for the majority of the mess, I let it slide. I would harass him to clean up another time. Besides, he barely had the energy to stand. I watched as he limped his way towards the sofa, and crashed onto it.

"How's your leg?" I asked.

"Pretty screwed up. I've got a bruise on the back of my thigh the size of a fuckin' football."

He was lucky there was no fracture. I doubted many people would walk away from a mallet to the femur with minimal damage. I know if I'd been in his position, my bone would've snapped cleanly.

"And what about your wrist?" I asked, eyeing the cast.

"The fucker that broke it snapped it in the worst place possible," he mumbled, kicking off his shoes. "It'll be in a cast for a while."

I nodded, and thought about offering my sympathy, but I knew Cosmo would only reject it. I was still standing in the doorway, and although I hadn't moved, I knew what I wanted to do. There was only one reason why I had returned here, and I would be leaving soon without delay. The only obstacle in my way was Cosmo. I hadn't expected him to be here, and I knew he would never approve of what I was planning on doing.

"So where to from here?" asked Cosmo, as if he was reading my mind. "I guess we're pretty much back at square one. How do you suppose we get the money?"

I thought about lying, but I was lousy at hiding the truth.

"We don't," I said, without bothering to elaborate.

Cosmo stared. I maintained a vacant face.

"Don't talk stupid, Kennedy," he said after some time. "There's no way in hell we're giving up now. We've been through too much shit to suddenly drop everything."

"I don't intend to give up, but after yesterday, my priorities have changed."

"Huh? What the hell are you getting at?"

I couldn't be blunt with him, even thought I wanted to.

"I don't give a damn about getting the money, Cosmo. All I care about is Rochelle," I said, my voice becoming firmer with every second. "And I know where she is, so I'm getting her back. To-night."

Cosmo stared, dumbfounded. However, it wasn't long before he started to abuse me, calling my idea pure idiocy. I didn't care what he thought. I would go through with my plans. Even though calling the police was tempting, I didn't want to risk losing Rochelle. If I wanted her back, I knew I would have to do it alone.

Without wasting any more time, I turned and walked over towards the weaponry cupboard. I opened up, and selected my weapon of choice—a semi-automatic handgun.

It had been a while since I'd held a gun, but strangely enough, it felt natural.

Although the day was young, I wouldn't make my move until tonight. I wanted to leave and investigate the area where I believed Rochelle was being held captive. Being one-step ahead was my key to success. I tucked the gun in the back of my jeans and hid it behind my jacket. I headed towards the door.

"Wait," called Cosmo. "What are you planning on doing? Where are you going?"

"66 Gilmore Road, Arcadia. That's the address Mal gave me."

"Don't risk it! He'll kill you and Rochelle on the spot."

"Everything else has failed," I hissed, "and this is my only option left."

Cosmo fell silent. I stared. Why was he being so uncooperative? Couldn't he understand what it was like for me being away from the one person I cared for most of all? I had wanted Cosmo's support in my decision, but I could see I wasn't going to get it.

"Don't do it," said Cosmo, his voice sounding more like a plea than a demand.

"I'm sorry," I said, turning my back and walking out the front door, "but I have to."

***

He was a traitor, a deceiver.

Cosmo Rowland had been keeping a secret for a long time, and although it was constantly on his mind, he refused to mention it to anybody. He had been paid off by Mal Lawson to monitor Jordan, and up until now, he'd had nothing to report. It all changed today. Cosmo knew he would have to make the call.

Rifling through the files inside the manila folder on the kitchen bench, Cosmo found Mal Lawson's contact details inside. He took a seat at the breakfast bar, and began dialling. Somebody picked up after just a few rings.

"Jordan's coming for Rochelle," said Cosmo, without bothering to stall time, "and he's armed with a gun too."

"So I've heard," said a voice belonging to Mal Lawson. "Isaac gave me an update just moments ago, but thank you for calling. You have shown your loyalty to me."

"I didn't do it for you, douchebag. I'm calling for Kennedy's sake."

"What do you mean?"

"Don't kill him," replied Cosmo. "He's put his arse on the line for you."

Mal chuckled, but the laughter was not kind.

"Is that so?" hissed Mal. "Because from what I've heard, you've been taking the beatings for Kennedy's errors. So tell me, how is that fair?"

Cosmo didn't reply, because he had no answer to the question.

"I've grown a fondness for you, Mr. Rowland," began Mal, "I've been listening in to you and Kennedy very closely lately, and I admire your spirit and perseverance. In fact, I should have given this task to you. I'm sure you would have succeeded."

"Then why the fuck didn't you? Man, you should have kept Kennedy and his chick out of this."

"Well, it's too late for what should have been. Besides, I'm sure he'll be here soon. I need to make the necessary arrangements for his arrival."

The phone call had been pointless. Mal wasn't backing down.

"Just remember you need to keep Kennedy alive to fulfill this assignment," said Cosmo, in a final effort to save his friend's life. "I'll think up a new plan and get you the money from Nathan Burwell, but I need Jordan's help. I promise we'll get the task done."

The phone went dead. Mal had already hung up the phone. Had he listened to Cosmo? Or had Mal already made up his mind? Cosmo remained seated at the breakfast bar, wondering what else he could do. However, he had already tried to reason with the enemy, and this was not Cosmo's fight.

# 27

Night had fallen, and the winter chill had set in.

Each time I inhaled, the icy air seeped deep inside my lungs, making each breath difficult. From the distance, I could see a house hidden amongst the towering gumtrees. The lights were on. They were home. It didn't faze me though—I would attack tonight regardless of the dangers.

The night was still young, and I was prepared to wait in the bitter cold until the early hours of the morning. I wasn't exactly sure how to break into a house, or even more so, what to expect once I'd achieved that—but I didn't care. I had my weapon. It was all the security I needed.

Without warning, a light switched off, followed by another one. I watched and waited until every single light in the house had been switched off. Were my adversaries already calling it a night? At 8:15pm? The unmistakable sound of gears rotating interrupted my thoughts. The garage door had just opened up, and the headlights of a car beamed through the darkness. Slowly, the vehicle began to move down the driveway. They were leaving. I'd picked the best possible night to strike.

The garage door closed again, and the car drove off. Had Mal and Isaac been in the same car? I could only hope so. But I prayed they hadn't taken Rochelle with them, otherwise tonight would be all for nothing.

Breathing in my hands in an attempt to escape the chill, I began walking closer to the house. I was cautious with each step, monitoring my surroundings from every angle. Part of me thought about trying the front door, but I knew it would be locked. I'd have to break in through a window on the lower floor. The only problem was that I wasn't sure if the house was alarmed, and the slightest noise could potentially be the death of me.

I approached the window from the side, and I couldn't see any signs of an alarm. Good. Luck was on my side tonight. Pressing my hands upon the icy glass, I tried to figure out the best way to break through. I pulled out my weapon for the first time that night, and gripped the end of the muzzle. I tapped the glass with the handle, and waited. Silence. Gripping the gun a little tighter, I brought my arm back, and then cracked it through the glass. Tiny fragments shattered around me, and my force had been so strong that my arm had gone through the window too.

I brought my weapon back and took aim. I waited. Nothing happened. No alarms sounded and no one came running. Carefully, I chipped more glass away, making a bigger hole in the window. I then peeled off my jacket, and laid it down across the bottom of the windowsill. Planting my palms firmly onto the frame, I hoisted myself up and climbed through. I slipped down to the floor, tucked my knees in, and rolled onto the broken glass fragments. I cut my elbow on a piece of glass on entry, but I would tend to the wound later. For now I needed to stay alert.

I wasn't sure which part of the house I was in, but it was pitch black. I waited for my eyes to adjust to the darkness, and finally, I could faintly see a door across from me. I stepped across and ran a hand down the wall, beside the doorframe. I found a switch, and flicked it on. Light had barely filled the room when I put my back to the wall, taking aim.

I waited again. I was standing in a corridor, stretching a long distance across the house. Half a dozen doors lined the walls, including one door at the very end of the corridor.

Memories flooded back. The thoughts confirmed what I already had suspected—I had been here before. This was the same house they'd brought me to when Rochelle and I were abducted. I could remember being dragged down a staircase, arms bound behind my back, and hearing Rochelle's weakened voice from the room at the end of the corridor.

My blood chilled at the very thought, but I had already begun walking towards the door. I kept my gun steady and I moved as swiftly and as quietly as I could. I approached the door and noticed a latch. The door had been locked from the outside, so I carefully pulled back the latch and placed my hand on the door handle. Before turning, I put my ear to the door. Silence.

"Rochelle," I whispered from the outside, but there was no response.

Without waiting a second longer I pushed open the door and stepped inside. At first, I saw nothing but darkness, so I searched for a switch, and turned on the lights. One dim bulb flashed on, dangling limply from the ceiling. The room was tiny and unkempt. There was a mouldy mattress underneath a single window, but the window had been boarded up with wooden planks, nailed into the walls. Broken beer bottles littered the floor, as well as hundreds of half smoked cigarettes.

Devastation consumed me as I accepted the reality—she wasn't here.

Maybe I was too late. Had my failure cost me the woman I loved? Desolation filled my heart, and I was on the verge of a breakdown. But before I could drown in my own self-pity, a firm hand was clasped around my rib cage, as a cold blade was pressed gently onto my neck.

"Drop your gun," a husky voice whispered in my ear.

I'd heard it, but my body had frozen, and although I wanted to move, I was paralysed by fear. The grip around my rib cage tightened, and the blade on my neck was pressing deeper into my flesh—at any moment my throat would be slit.

I went limp, and finally I allowed my gun to slip from my fingertips. But without warning, the grip around me loosened and the knife retracted away. Before I could believe my luck, I received a powerful blow in the back of the head, and darkness surrounded me.

I think I may have been knocked unconscious on my feet—if that's even possible—but it seemed like I had been out for a couple of minutes when I first opened my eyes, gazing up to find Mal Lawson staring down at me. Immediately, I tried to curl up in the foetal position as an attempt to protect myself, but Mal began kicking me directly in the sternum. I wheezed for air and rolled over. Unfortunately for me, Mal took advantage of my careless move, and stomped on my back. I howled in pain.

Just a metre away, I spotted my gun lying on the floor beside me. I shot my hand out and tried to reach for it, but Mal beat me to it. He then crouched down beside me and forced the barrel of the gun into my mouth. He pulled down the hammer and rested his finger on the trigger. I began to gag and choke as he tried to force the gun deeper into my throat. He hushed me, told me to relax and listen—but I was finding it somewhat difficult under the circumstances.

"I have been more than fair to you, Mr. Kennedy," began Mal, his eyes staring into mine. "And for all I've done, you still decide to betray me."

My hands were trembling as they lay limply on the floorboards. If he was going to kill me, I wanted him to take the shot right now and spare me the mental torture.

"You knew what was at stake. I made it perfectly clear. So why do you continue to fail me? I was told you were the man for the job. I guess somebody lied."

I gagged again, but Mal kept the gun steady.

"I want to burst your brains all over these floorboards, just so I know you'll never disappoint me again," hissed Mal, but after a few seconds, he pulled the gun from my mouth, "but not tonight. I've had a change of heart."

I could barely believe my ears—or my luck—once again my life had been spared. However, my safety wasn't important right now—the wellbeing of my girlfriend was the only thing that I cared about.

"Where's Rochelle?" I asked.

"She's alive," replied Mal, "at least for now."

I wanted to abuse him, scream words of hate and vent my frustration—but instead I kept silent. Mal wanted to see me break, but obviously he didn't realise I had already shattered into a thousand pieces.

"Isaac has moved Rochelle to a new location," continued Mal, "but rest assured I'm giving you one last chance to give me what I want, or she will be dead within a week."

I'd heard it, and in some bizarre way, I could see a comfort in the deadline. I promised myself this entire ordeal would be finished in a week, and I would have Rochelle back with me, safe and protected. I had no idea how I was going to achieve the desired outcome, but I would make it happen.

"Now get up," said Mal, "and show yourself out."

I didn't need to be told a second time. I forced myself onto my feet—using what was left of my strength (and there wasn't much of it)—I staggered out of the room, down the corridor and through the broken window. Then I started to run, and I didn't stop. Not even for a second.

# 28

I'd spent the night curled up on a bus stop bench, trying anything to keep warm.

I wasn't sure if I'd slept at all, but if I had, I couldn't remember it. After my encounter with Mal last night, I'd been so mentally and physically exhausted that I'd given up and had taken refuge at a bus stop. The night had been long and torturous, but at last daylight was on arrival.

I sat up—which took the greatest effort—and tried to focus. Several other patrons waiting for the bus were staring at me, delivering their most disgusted looks. Maybe they thought I was homeless, or maybe a drug addict, but I didn't care. I stood up from the bench, and began my journey home.

As I walked, I pulled out my mobile phone and called for a taxi. My credit card was basically maxed out, but I was hoping I'd still have enough to get me home. I waited outside a little bakery at Galston, and twenty minutes passed before my taxi arrived. I slid into the backseat and told the driver my destination. At last, I allowed myself to get some shuteye.

I woke up forty minutes into the journey, but already I could see the city skyline. I glanced at my watch. 8:15am. And as I stared into the Rolex, watching the second hand tick by, something that hadn't originally occurred to me, had finally surfaced—this watch had been given to me by my enemies, so surely there had been a hidden agenda. Why else would they give me what seemed to be a genuine Rolex? It was bugged. I was sure of it. How else did Mal Lawson know that I'd planned last night's break in? And how else would he have known to move Rochelle to a new location? I'd been naïve to think they hadn't been watching me. After all, the fate of their business was in my hands.

I arrived at my destination. I handed the driver my credit card, I was charged, and without giving it a second thought, I gave the Rolex to the driver. His eyes lit up, and he accepted the gift with no questions asked. The taxi drove off, along with the tracking device.

But I was still convinced there were more bugs and tracking devices. I knew I'd have to discard my electronics, because I couldn't trust that they hadn't been tampered with. I then dumped my mobile phone in a rubbish bin as I headed towards the apartment block. I took the elevator to my floor, walked down the corridor and opened up.

I found Cosmo slumped over at the dining table, reading up on documents from Nathan Burwell's file. He jumped up from his seat from the moment he saw me, with both palms up turned, waiting for an explanation.

"Well?" he asked. "What the hell happened last night?"

I avoided the question, and cut straight to the chase.

"We have to leave," I began, "this apartment is probably bugged with listening devices and surveillance cameras. Mal Lawson has been watching us, so we need to get rid of any electronics and find a new place to stay."

I moved quickly. I needed to start packing my belongings. Cosmo was watching me, waiting for an answer, but I ignored him as if I was unaware. Besides, I didn't need to answer to anyone.

"What?" he finally said, pushing back his chair. "Where's all this come from?"

"Mal knew what I was planning last night, Cosmo. He was there. Waiting for me."

"Nah, you're talking shit," scoffed Cosmo.

I didn't care what he thought, because I knew the truth. How had I been stupid enough to think that high-profile criminals would trust me with a task this important? I should have known they'd be keeping an eye on me somehow. However, there was still something I didn't understand. Mal had told me several times that I'd been recommended by another person to do the job—but who the hell had recommended me? I tried to think of an answer, but nothing came to mind.

I climbed the staircase and entered my bedroom. Cosmo followed.

"So where are you going to go?" he asked, in a tone firmer than what I was used to.

"I can't tell you that," I replied. "Mal and Isaac are probably still listening."

"Do you realise how fuckin' paranoid you sound right now?"

I began piling my clothes back into my suitcase. I wasn't even sure myself where I was going, but I knew I couldn't stay here. I entertained the idea of going back home to Middle Dural, but that's the first place Mal would expect me to go. I'd probably have to lay low at a motel for a while, using nothing but cash so I couldn't be traced.

Within a few minutes, I was packed and ready to go. I exited the bedroom, walked back down the stairs and headed towards the front door. I was just about to leave, when I made a conscious decision to take one final item with me. I placed my suitcase on the floor for a moment and stepped towards the weaponry cupboard. I selected a new gun, and enough rounds of ammo to get me through the next week. Just as I finished tucking the weapon into my suitcase, Cosmo appeared from the bedroom, and stood at the top of the stairs.

"This is fuckin' stupid, Kennedy," he said, walking down one step at a time. "Besides, it doesn't matter where we go. They will find us."

I ignored him. Once again I walked back over to the front door and picked up my suitcase. I turned the door handle and stepped out into the corridor. I was about to close the door, when I looked at Cosmo one last time.

"I'm sorry that I've dragged you through all this," I began. "This is my problem, and I shouldn't have involved you. I appreciate all you've done for me, and I understand if this is where you leave. Thank you, and I'll see you when this is all over."

Without another word to say, I closed the door behind me and began to walk away.

It was maybe only four seconds later when I heard the door open behind me, and a pair of footsteps followed me to the elevator. I smiled. After all we'd been through, I knew Cosmo wasn't ready to abandon me yet.

# 29

I had to get away from the city.

Mal Lawson would be searching for me, and knowing my luck, he'd probably find me without any difficulty. When Cosmo and I stepped out of the apartment block, we discarded all of our electronics. Mal had found me twice in the past, so this time around I would be more vigilant.

I needed to keep a low profile. I figured booking into a hotel would be the best option, but Cosmo had a better idea. He told me about a rehearsal warehouse in Alexandria. He said he and his band rehearsed there a lot, and the owner of the warehouse was a good friend of his, and would probably let us stay there. Cosmo also explained the place was hard to get to, with top-notch security. I liked the idea, so we called for a taxi to take us to the warehouse.

Cosmo wasn't kidding—the place was not easy to find. It was tucked away behind a one-way street, opposite a seedy looking petrol station. The taxi driver wasn't sure where exactly to take us, so we were dropped off by the side of the road. Cosmo led me down another dodgy looking street, and we came to a rolling door.

"Are they closed?" I asked.

"Nah," he replied, "but they won't let in any old douchebag off the street."

I wasn't entirely sure what he meant, but Cosmo walked up to the rolling door and pressed an intercom button. We waited a while, but eventually somebody answered.

"Hello? Is that you, Cosmo?"

"Yeah, man. How's it going?"

"Shit. Haven't seen you in ages! Where are the boys?"

"Just me today. Can you open up? I got a proposition for you."

Not a second later, the rolling door was activated and it opened up. Cosmo walked inside. I followed. We walked through a dark car park, and came to an elevator. He pushed the button and we stepped inside, taking the elevator to the next floor. When the elevator doors opened up, we stepped inside an enormous room, littered with instruments and amps everywhere. There was noise pollution like you wouldn't believe—screeching guitars, booming bass and pounding drums. I could even hear some vocalists singing—or screaming if you like—and already my ears were ringing.

In the centre of the room, there was an ancient TV set with terrible reception—seriously, the pictures on the screen were barely visible. To my left, lined up against the wall were half a dozen pinball machines, along with old school arcade games like *Frogger* and *Space Invaders*. I'm sure this place had seen better days, but nevertheless, it had a nice feel about it.

Suddenly, a balding man in his late forties approached Cosmo and I. He greeted Cosmo with a firm handshake, and offered me a polite smile.

"This is my mate, Jordan Kennedy," said Cosmo as he introduced me to the stranger.

"I'm Alex," said the man as he shook my hand. "And any mate of Cosmo's is a mate of mine."

"I'm glad to hear that," began Cosmo, "because I was wondering if we could ask you a favour."

"I'm all ears," replied Alex.

"Any chance we could stay here for a while? Kennedy and I need to lay low and figure some things out, and I know we'd be safe here."

"Ah shit, Cosmo. All my rehearsal spaces are booked out today."

"I'll pay you a hundred bucks a day."

"Done," said Alex without a second thought. "You can take Room B."

Cosmo thanked him and began to walk away. I followed again. We walked down a narrow corridor with band posters cluttering up almost every inch of the walls. After being led down what seemed to be a maze of corridors, we came to a door clearly labelled 'B.' Cosmo pulled open the door to reveal a second door, and after pushing that one open we stepped inside. The moment I closed both doors behind me, there was an immediate and complete silence. I could no longer hear the bands playing. Blimey, I was truly impressed at how these rooms had been made so sound proof.

Scanning my eyes around the room, there were no windows, just four dark walls layered with thick materials. There was also a PA system, a couple of microphone stands and empty milk crates scattered everywhere. Our accommodation was a bit of an eyesore, but it was safe, and we wouldn't be tracked.

"Look, I'm going to go. I bet you're feeling pretty tired, so I'll give you some time to yourself to rest," said Cosmo, and he backed away to the door.

"There's no time to rest, Cosmo. We've only got a week."

"A week? What?"

"Yeah, I didn't mention it before," I said, placing my suitcase onto the ground. "But Mal's serious about getting the task done, so now we've got a deadline. We need to get him the cash by the end of the week."

"Or else what?"

I stared at him, barely believing his naivety.

"Do you really need me to clarify it for you?"

Cosmo said nothing. We both knew what failure would lead to.

***

He sat across from his adversary, hands folded together, feeling completely out of his comfort zone.

"Mr. Rowland," began Mal Lawson, clasping a bottle of beer around the neck, "when we first met I sensed that you could not be trusted, but once again you have proven me wrong."

"Then you're a fuckin' idiot," hissed Cosmo, "because I'm not to be trusted. Ever."

"And yet here you are," he sneered, taking a sip from his bottle.

While Jordan Kennedy had been busy making arrangements for the new plan of attack against Nathan Burwell, Cosmo had secretly snuck away in order to tell Mal of their new accommodation. Finding Mal had been easy; it was just a simple matter of giving him a call on the payphone outside the rehearsal warehouse, and demanding an immediate meet up. Mal had told Cosmo of their latest hideout—still in Arcadia, just a different street—and he had caught the first available taxi to the new location.

Cosmo had arrived outside a two-storey house in the middle of nowhere—perfect for keeping hidden. And he had told Mal everything— Jordan had figured out they were being watched, and now they were keeping a low profile in a rehearsal warehouse. Cosmo never wanted to tell Mal Lawson a single thing, but he knew if he didn't, then the rest of his money would be in jeopardy. Mal still owed Cosmo two hundred and fifty thousand, and he wasn't prepared to lose it. After all, there wasn't much money left from the first payment.

"From now on you're going to have to wear this," said Mal, pushing a Rolex across the table. "It has a listening device hidden inside, so we'll be able to monitor Jordan again."

Cosmo stared, before pushing the watch away from him.

"Fuck that. I'm not wearing it," hissed Cosmo. "Firstly, Kennedy figured out his own watch was bugged, so if I rock up with a new Rolex, he'll fuckin' know I'm in on this. Secondly, I'm already keeping an eye on him, so I'll let you know if anything changes."

Mal sat back in his chair and smiled.

"A fair point, Mr. Rowland."

"Look, I came here to give you an update, and now I'm leaving," replied Cosmo, standing up and pushing back his chair.

"Can I offer you a beer?"

Cosmo ignored him, and began walking towards the door.

"You know, I'm surprised you haven't asked about Rochelle. Don't you care about her welfare?"

Cosmo stopped, turned around, eyes fixed on Mal's. Was this one of his sick mind games? Or was the question genuine? Curiosity always got the better of him.

"Where is she?" asked Cosmo.

"Second door on your right as you walk out," replied Mal. "She's locked in there, so you won't be able to see her, but maybe she'll speak to you. Depends on what mood she's in."

Cosmo nodded, and without more to say, he opened up the door and walked out. Isaac was waiting directly outside, smirking as he brushed past Cosmo.

Second door on the right. He saw it. Regardless of what Mal had just told him, Cosmo tried to open up the door. Pointless. It was locked. So instead he put his ear close to the door and gave a quick tap on the wood. Silence.

"Rochelle?" he said, pressing his ear to the door.

Cosmo thought he heard a weakened voice, but then again, maybe he heard nothing at all.

# 30

How had I not seen it before?

Mal Lawson had given me a manila folder filled with information about Nathan Burwell, so why didn't I read through every single document? Why had I simply skimmed over a few pages and assumed I knew what I was doing? I was stupid. I was ignorant, but I would chalk it up to experience and learn from my mistakes.

During the afternoon, I had read through every single page and every single document—twice. There had been details I had missed, and while some were not important, others were the key to success. Just hours ago I was a broken man, but at last I had regained my footing.

Suddenly the rehearsal room opened up, and Cosmo stepped inside.

"Where have you been?" I asked, looking up at him from the folder.

"For a drink," he replied. "There's a pub just over the road."

"And it took four hours?"

"Then I'll admit it," he said. "I had a few drinks."

Typical. But I dropped it and beckoned Cosmo over to have a look at the documents I'd found.

"Take a look at this," I said.

He pulled up a milk crate and sat down opposite me. I handed Cosmo the very document that had captured my interest.

"And what is this?" he asked, gruffly.

"I found a booklet containing Nathan Burwell's typical weekly regime. I hadn't taken any notice of it before, but every Friday lunchtime Nathan visits an Italian restaurant in the city."

"And why is that significant?"

"Because according to this," I said as I handed Cosmo a second document, "it's the only occasion where Nathan is without his security guards."

As I predicted, Cosmo's eyes lit up.

"No shit?" he asked. "Man, why hadn't we seen this before?"

"Guess it pays to do our homework."

Throughout the entire ordeal, Cosmo had been strong, because Lord knows that I'm not. Earlier today I was convinced Cosmo was ready to throw in the towel, but once again he proved me wrong. He truly was in it for the long haul.

"Alright, so what do you reckon we should do?" asked Cosmo.

Luckily, I had already worked it all out.

"The moment Nathan Burwell is alone without any security, I'm going to pull a gun to his head, force him to come with us, and demand immediate payment."

Cosmo raised an eyebrow.

"Fuck, Kennedy. You're not playing around this time, are you?"

"We've got a deadline, and I can't jeopardise Rochelle's safety any longer."

Cosmo was silent at first, but then offered a nod of approval. In the beginning, I'd been focusing on digging into Nathan's history and blackmailing him, but all I needed was the money. Why blackmail when I can make threats? After all, I'm sure Nathan wouldn't need too much persuasion when his life was on the line.

"But you and I know Nathan isn't an easy bloke to get alone," I began, grabbing Cosmo's attention once more, "so we may only have a few minutes to strike. This afternoon I researched the restaurant and it's on the top floor of a hotel—The Harrison Inn. I even found uploads of the hotel's infrastructure, and judging by the layout, I figure we're better off making our move while he's taking the lift up to the restaurant."

"But how's that going to work? There's no guarantee he'll get in the elevator alone, and secondly, there's no way in hell Nathan will get inside if you're there waiting for him."

"Look, I know there is a chance others will be in the lift with him, but hopefully he'll be alone. But if he isn't, then we'll have to scrap the plan. I don't want any innocent bystanders involved. And I'm not going to wait for Nathan inside the lift either, I'm going to stop the lift just before the fifth floor, gain access while it's stopped, and then I'll raise my weapon."

Cosmo shook his head. His scepticism was seeping through.

"And how do you suppose you'll pull that off?" he asked.

"The hotel was built decades ago and is operated on an old pulley elevator system. There is a control room located on the top floor of the building, same as the restaurant, so it's just a matter of gaining access to the control room and flicking a switch. That'll be your job."

"Do we really have to stop the elevator? Can't you just surprise Nathan by riding the elevator with him a few floors up from where he takes it from?"

"No, Nathan needs to be trapped. I can't risk more people boarding the elevator at different levels, and besides, the negotiation might take longer than a few stops between floors."

Cosmo nodded, taking it in.

"And as for me getting inside the lift," I continued, "the moment the elevator is stopped I can gain access by jimmying open the elevator doors on the fifth floor, and then I can climb into the shaft and on top of the elevator, and get inside through the ceiling hatch."

"You make it sound so easy."

"It won't be, Cosmo. But I'm sure we can pull this off."

"Alright, but how are we meant to get Burwell from the elevator to the bank? I've got a feeling he's not going to come quietly," said Cosmo.

"You and I both know just how paranoid Nathan truly is, and when that gun is in his face I'm positive he'll buckle down to our demands without a second thought. So we'll hire out a car and get Nathan to come with us. Once he's paid up, we'll let him go. By the time his security finds out, we'll be meeting with Mal, handing over the money and getting Rochelle back."

Cosmo handed the documents back to me and crossed his arms.

"I reckon we can do this, but damn, we're going to need to be at the top of our game."

"And we've only got a couple of days to prepare. Friday is only around the corner, so we'll hire the car first thing tomorrow morning, and visit the hotel so we know exactly what we need to do."

"And there's one more thing," said Cosmo. "The gun. You need to get one."

I pulled my suitcase to my side, opened up, and pulled out the weapon I'd chosen to take moments before leaving the apartment.

"No need," I said, replacing the magazine. "I've already got one."

# 31

*August 12th*

I'd barely slept throughout the night.

For hours I'd been mentally going through each step of the plan. I was positive this would be my last chance, so I needed to get it right. Naturally, I was nervous as hell, but I'd have to find a way to suppress it. I could not afford to let my fear seep through.

Today was Thursday, which meant that Cosmo and I would only have one day to prepare. Knowing that each minute was crucial, we left the warehouse early that morning and set out to hire a car.

Luckily, we had the car organised within an hour. We'd selected a silver Holden Commodore—a common car, meaning it would be easier to stay under the radar, because riding around in a black BMW had never been wise. We had always drawn attention to ourselves.

Once we had the car, we wasted no time and drove directly to the Harrison Inn—the hotel where we would make our attack. On arrival, I had expected valet parking and bellboys waiting outside the front to wish us a pleasant stay, but the hotel's car park was already full. Cosmo and I ended up parking almost four blocks away.

We walked back to the hotel, straight through the front doors and made our way towards the elevator. I had expected somebody at reception to welcome us or at the very least give us some kind of acknowledgement, but we were outright ignored.

Cosmo pushed the up button, and the elevator doors opened up straight away. We stepped inside and Cosmo tried to push the button for the top floor, but I stopped him.

"What?" he queried, "aren't we going to the restaurant?"

"Nope. Fifth floor," I replied, pushing the button.

I was adamant about practising my point of entry into the elevator.

The elevator slowly dragged itself up to the fifth floor, and by God, it was the noisiest elevator I think I'd ever been in. The sheave roared as it rotated furiously, and call me paranoid, but I was terrified about the cable breaking. Yeah, this elevator truly didn't sound too healthy.

At last it came to a sudden stop, and a slight drop, followed by the elevator doors opening. Cosmo and I stepped out, turned left and began to inspect our surroundings. Numbered doors lined the corridor. I was quite surprised at the number of doors with 'Do Not Disturb' signs hanging out the front. They seemed to be on almost every single door. In fact, one opened up just a few metres in front of us. A man stumbled out, fixing his tie. He spotted us and seemed a little startled, so he dropped his hands to his sides and quickly passed us.

Could he make it any more obvious?

I guess when Sydney men wanted to hide an affair, they didn't go to dodgy motels in the middle of nowhere—they came here, still wanting a little taste of luxury.

I couldn't help but wonder—had Nathan Burwell ever come here with another woman? Or did he come here purely to dine at the restaurant? No, his history was clean. Besides, Nathan was proud of his reputation and would never chance a quick fling.

"So what exactly are we looking for?" asked Cosmo, fidgeting with his lip piercing.

"We're just scoping the floor," I explained. "I'm checking for surveillance cameras, but there doesn't appear to be any on this level. Perhaps they're only active in the main foyer."

"Does it matter?"

"Well, yeah, I don't particularly want to be spotted breaking into an elevator shaft."

Once Cosmo and I had walked the entire loop of level five, we returned to the elevator. I stood in front of the metallic doors, surveying the area when I found the access hole in the top right hand corner. The hole was tiny. Probably half the size of a five-cent coin.

"So how the fuck do you get inside?" asked Cosmo. "Don't you need some kind of key?"

"A drop key, yes, but apparently a flexible piece of metal can do the trick," I explained. "I've read that some people are able to hack into elevator shafts by using a bike spoke."

"A bike spoke? Sounds like bullshit to me."

"Then how about we test the theory?" I quipped, seconds before fishing out the spoke from the inside of my jacket. "While you were out yesterday I went and picked a bunch up from a bike shop—so here's hoping it works."

"Alright, give it a try and I'll keep a look out. Just be quick."

Without delay I gently bent sections of the bike spoke and slotted it through the tiny access hole in the elevator door. I manoeuvred the piece of metal in all directions, hoping to disengage the lock. However, it was proving to be harder than I had first thought.

I poked and prodded the spoke around the hole and tried to pull the doors apart. No such luck.

"This is a waste of time," groaned Cosmo. "This is never going to work, man."

Suddenly, I felt the bike spoke catch onto something, and I quickly turned it clockwise. I heard a faint click sound, signalling that the locking mechanism behind the door had been disengaged. I pulled the bike spoke out from the access hole and pried open the elevator doors—they slid open with ease.

Before I could marvel at my great achievement, the elevator gears began to rotate, almost causing my eardrums to explode inside my head.

I risked a glance inside the shaft, and saw that the elevator was moving, climbing the cables up from the bottom floor.

I leaned in a little further and looked down. It was almost pitch black inside, but I saw that the elevator had stopped at the third floor, giving me a good view from the top.

I caught a glimpse of the service hatch—my point of entry to get inside the elevator.

"You'd better close those doors now, Kennedy," said Cosmo, peering down into the shaft. "If the elevator is on its way up here, we don't want to be caught in the act."

Taking Cosmo's advice, I stepped back and closed the elevator doors shut. Then, I pressed the up button.

"Where are we going now?" asked Cosmo.

"To the top floor. We need to see the elevator control room."

Within ten seconds the elevator arrived, and the doors sprang open once again—only this time, it was an automatic function. Cosmo and I stepped inside, rode the elevator to the top floor and began searching for the control room.

Luckily, we found it conveniently located right beside the elevator. I looked around. We were directly opposite the restaurant, but it still hadn't opened for the day and nobody was inside. Tomorrow lunchtime, it would be a different story. I didn't let that worry me for now, and began to direct my attention back to the control room. I extended my arm towards the door handle and tried to turn the knob. No go. It was locked.

"How do you suppose we get in there?" asked Cosmo, trying the door himself. "Find somebody to bribe so they'll open it for us?"

I studied the lock, and smiled. At last we had a bit of luck.

"The door isn't locked. It's just a spring bolt," I said.

Cosmo stared. I'd lost him.

"When a door is closed, the catch slides into place and keeps the door shut. Normally when you lock the door, the catch is locked into place too, but since we're not dealing with a dead lock—"

"—What the hell are you going on about, Kennedy?"

I sighed. Rather than trying to explain it, I showed Cosmo.

Just by chance I'd brought a pocket knife along with me. I pulled it out of my pocket, and jammed it into the space between the door. I slid it down to the catch and applied force. The catch retraced back into the door and it opened up.

"Get it now?" I asked, putting the knife away.

Cosmo didn't give me an answer. Instead, we quickly checked over our shoulders, and slipped through the door.

The elevator control room was massive and noisy, particularly as the elevator began to descend down to the bottom floors. I started to look around at my surroundings when I spotted surveillance screens for the main foyer. Brilliant. The cameras were so perfectly angled, that they focused in on the elevators in the background. Cosmo could easily watch the surveillance screens and notify me when Nathan Burwell entered the hotel.

Better yet, there were also surveillance cameras inside the elevator, so Cosmo could watch me from the inside.

I then turned my attention to the main controls. A day ago, they would have overwhelmed me, but thanks to my good friend Google, I'd learned how to operate a pulley-operated elevator. It was far from simple, but only one button mattered to me—the stop button. It was easy to pick out, considering it was big and red and had the words 'STOP/START' scribbled above it. I beckoned Cosmo over and showed him.

"This," I said, pointing to the stop button, "is all you need to press."

"And when exactly should I press it?" he asked.

"Just before the fifth floor. I'll be on my mobile, looking down into the shaft, and I'll let you know when to press it. That's all it is. When I've convinced Nathan to come with us, and I'm sure it won't take long, you hit the same button again and the elevator will restart. The second you've done that, you leave and meet Nathan and I back at the car. We'll drive straight to the bank and go from there."

He nodded, satisfied with the instructions, until a concern sprang to mind.

"Do you think the hotel staff come up here often?" asked Cosmo.

"I'm not sure," I began, speaking before thinking, "but hopefully not. I suspect the staff will only visit the control room for routine inspections or malfunctions."

"But we're going to stop the elevator tomorrow. Surely somebody will notice and come up here to check it out?"

Damn it. That was something I hadn't taken into consideration.

"Well," I said, still searching for an answer, "if that happens, I guess you'll have to make a run for it. I'm not sure what will happen if we get caught."

"Thanks, that's comforting."

"Just keep an ear out. You'll be fine."

Cosmo gave me an uncertain stare, but let it go. I think he knew we'd have to take some risks if we had any chance of success.

Without warning, the elevator started up again. The floor beneath us vibrated followed by a clicking noise. The cables began to rotate around the sheave, and I was positive the elevator was coming back up. Cosmo and I left immediately, and closed the control room door behind us. In good timing too, because not a moment later the elevator doors opened up and a woman stepped out, carrying two bags of vegetables. She eyed us as she walked by, heading towards the restaurant. I forced a smile. She didn't smile back.

Figuring it was better not to draw attention to myself, I quickly entered the elevator before the doors closed. Cosmo followed in behind me.

"What now?" he said, waiting for instructions.

"We go," I replied, hitting the ground floor button. "We've done all we can for now."

# 32

*August 13th*

Once again, I spent the night as an insomniac.

I was positive that I hadn't slept a wink, or if I had, I certainly didn't remember it. I lay on the bare ground in darkness, but the room was anything but silent. Even at night, the rehearsal warehouse was very much alive—the blown PA system humming continuously, the wooden boards beneath me creaking from the slightest movement, and I'd discovered Cosmo had a bad habit of sleep talking. Sometimes he'd mumble something completely inaudible, and other times he was like a Tourette's syndrome sufferer, yelling out single words uncontrollably.

But even if it had been silent, I don't think sleep would have come.

Eyes wide open, I lay flat on my back, staring into the darkness. I held the gun across my chest, feeling its weight burrowing into my lungs each time I inhaled. I kept going through the details in my head, visualising the inside of the elevator shaft.

But above all, my thoughts were with Rochelle. God, I missed her. I wondered if she was sleeping right now. Or maybe she was still awake, thinking about me? For only a brief moment, it crossed my mind that maybe she wasn't able to do either, but I pushed the concept from my mind, and buried the destructive idea.

Thoughts like that could kill a man.

For hours, I remained in the darkness, waiting for daylight. But the sun never showed up that day, instead, thick grey clouds clung to the sky. It was still incredibly dark inside the rehearsal room, so I flicked on the lights—only two out of five were functioning—and prepared myself for the day ahead. I was desperately craving a shower and a shave, but our accommodation did not provide such amenities. Instead, I threw on clean clothes and read the files inside the manila folder for the umpteenth time. Eventually, Cosmo awoke from his slumber.

"Shit," he said, only moments after opening up his eyes. "You're up already?"

"Yeah. Couldn't sleep," I replied.

"So, should we get going?"

"No point, Cosmo. Nathan won't be at the hotel until twelve thirty. Besides, we don't want to get there too early, because if the hotel staff catch us hanging around, they'll get suspicious."

"Good. Then let's get something to eat. I'm fuckin' starved."

I told Cosmo to leave without me. With so much on my mind, how could I possibly eat? I supposed that maybe I should—because, Jesus, I couldn't remember the last time I'd sat down and had a proper meal—but the very thought of food made my stomach churn.

During the time Cosmo was away, I read the documents, taking in the details I already knew too well. Today had to be faultless. Too much was at stake. As I read, I held the gun between both hands. It was then that I considered how I should take aim at Nathan. Should I raise it towards his head? Or maybe simply holding it would be enough? Then I figured I might as well cut through all the bullshit and dig the muzzle right under his chin. It would be the best way to get results, without question. But in the end, I decided to wait until I was there to pick my technique. No point in dwelling on it right now.

Just before eleven o'clock, Cosmo returned and he brought me back a can of lemonade and a cold meat pie. I was in no mood for eating, but I figured I needed the energy, so I thanked him and indulged gratefully. It wasn't long before it was time for us to depart. I tucked my weapon in the back of my trousers and hid it under my jacket. Next, Cosmo and I checked that we both had our new pre-paid mobile phones, and gave them a test run. No problems there. Figuring it would take us a good half an hour to get to the Harrison Inn, we left the rehearsal warehouse and went down to the car park. Cosmo demanded to drive. I allowed him.

On arrival, the hotel's car park was still completely full. Irritated, I told Cosmo to park as close to the hotel as possible. We were a little more fortunate today, and only had to park around the corner. Time was chasing us, so we walked back to the hotel as quickly as possible, and headed straight towards the elevator. I got out at the fifth floor, while Cosmo stayed behind.

"Give me a call when you're inside the control room," I told him, just before the elevator doors snapped shut.

Pulling a fresh bike spoke from the inside of my jacket, I decided to do another scope of the floor, to ensure I would not be seen entering the elevator shaft. No one was around. I hoped it would remain that way.

Just then, a call from Cosmo came through.

I pressed the answer button and put the mobile to my ear.

"I'm here," said Cosmo. "I'm in the control room."

"Did anybody see you?"

"Nah, man. I'm far too sleek for that."

"Are you watching the surveillance cameras?"

"Yeah. No sign of Nathan yet."

It was almost twelve thirty. It wouldn't be long.

"Just stay on the line, Cosmo. Let me know when you see him."

"What if he doesn't come?"

I scoffed at the question.

"Trust me," I said. "He'll come."

We waited in silence for a while. I figured I'd best use the time to prepare my gun. It was already loaded with a fresh magazine. Did I need it? Probably not. I was sure the very sight of the weapon would paralyse Nathan with fear, but just in case he doubted me, I would fire a stray bullet. Besides, in times like these, I felt safer knowing the gun was loaded.

I then pulled the bike spoke from my jacket and jammed it through the access hole. Today, I unlocked it with ease. I gently edged apart the elevator doors, but I would not open them fully until I knew for sure that my target was in position.

166

"He's here," said Cosmo, his voice cutting through my thoughts like the blade of a knife. "Nathan just walked through the main entrance."

Adrenaline pounded through my veins in an instant, but I was not nervous anymore, just focused.

"Get ready," I told Cosmo. "The moment I tell you to stop the elevator, you push the button. Is that perfectly clear?"

"Yep. No worries, man."

"And where is he now? Almost there?"

"Yeah. He's heading towards the elevator right now," said Cosmo, pausing as he watched the surveillance cameras. "He's got that briefcase attached around his wrist too. With the handcuffs locked on it and all."

That briefcase. Nathan seemed to take it everywhere with him, and it was always attached to his wrist—with those handcuffs. Why was it always with him? What did he keep inside it? Why did he need the excessive levels of security? But that wasn't important now. Unless he had fifty million dollars inside it, I couldn't have cared less.

"Is he alone?" I asked.

"Yep. I can't see any—no, wait. Fuck! Somebody else is walking behind him. Shit!"

"Who?" I asked, my world almost teetering off its axis.

"Dunno. Some guy. I don't think he's with Nathan, but he's heading towards the elevator too."

I kept the mobile to my ear and tried to keep calm. I knew, of course, an extra person inside the elevator was a huge problem. I couldn't risk another witness. However, I wasn't ready to call off the operation just yet.

"What's happening, Cosmo? What do you see?"

"The elevator doors on the bottom floor have just opened up. Nathan's getting in first and—yep, he's holding the doors open for the guy," said Cosmo. "Shit, are you still going to go through with this? Or do we abort?"

"We wait and see what happens," I said, my voice steady. "We wait until the very last minute."

He fell silent, and so did I. It wasn't long before I heard the elevator come to life, listening as it climbed the cable.

I then pulled the elevator doors open and gazed down into the shaft. It was getting closer, and I knew at any minute I would have to call off the plan.

Just then, the elevator stopped a few floors down.

"Cosmo?" I asked, waiting for an explanation.

"It's stopped," he replied. "I think—yes! That guy is getting off at the third floor."

"Nathan's alone?"

"Yeah! You're good to go, man."

I was overwhelmed by a sense of relief. For once, the odds were in my favour.

"Doors are shut," said Cosmo. "He's coming up."

"Wait for my signal."

I peered into the shaft again and watched as the elevator began to climb the cables once more. It was close now. Almost there.

"Now!" I shouted, perhaps too loudly.

Cosmo's reflexes were impeccably fast, and he'd stopped the elevator maybe a few milliseconds after I'd given the go ahead. I didn't wait to give praise or a thank you. I shoved my mobile into my jacket and climbed into the shaft.

The elevator had come to a halt barely three feet from the fifth floor.

In actual fact, I could have maybe waited another second or two before giving the signal, but none of that really mattered. The elevator had stopped and it was time to make my move.

I dropped my feet down onto the top of the elevator's roof and closed the floor's open doors behind me. I then stepped towards the service hatch and prepared to make my entry.

For a brief moment I wondered if the hatch would open cleanly, or would it be jammed shut? When was the last time this hatch had been used anyway? Enough. There was no point in worrying about it now.

Timing was essential and so was the element of surprise. I needed to make this one quick, smooth motion. Besides, the elevator had already been stopped for about fifteen seconds, and time was not on my side.

Hands shaking, I readied my gun. I then pulled open the hatch and jumped down inside. On my landing, I kept my knees tucked in, and planted my free hand on the ground. I did this to allow time to position myself so that I was facing Nathan, but there was no need— he was already standing right in front of me.

His face had drained to a faint pale colour, as if somebody had ripped off layers of his skin. I rose to my feet, and jammed the gun directly in between his eyes—not a movement I had planned—but it felt natural.

Without saying a single word, I was expecting Nathan to buckle down in front of me, begging for his life—but he didn't. Nathan stood perfectly still, and as the seconds ticked by, the colour returned to his face. He'd adjusted to the situation. Almost instantly.

"Well," he said, speaking before I had the chance, "I can't say I'm happy to see you."

I tried to jam the gun deeper into Nathan's flesh. He didn't even flinch.

"You're coming with me," I hissed.

"No, I'm not."

"I will shoot you if you don't comply."

"No, you won't."

His statement had a paralysing effect on me. This was not the situation I had first envisaged—Nathan was the one in control, not me.

My mind went blank. I was losing my focus. What now? The initial fear had disappeared, and Nathan was almost somewhat relived to see me. What the hell? I had executed my plan without the slightest mistake, so why was he not afraid? Was I not daunting enough? Did he sense the weakness within me? My head was overloading with questions, but I needed to concentrate.

As a final attempt to intimidate, I pulled down the hammer. The sound of the click was chilling, even to me. I had not planned to go this far, but I needed to prove that my threat was real. Nathan needed to believe his life was on the line.

"I will shoot you dead," I snarled, feeling aggression surface, "and I won't stop with you. Your family will be my next targets."

Jesus-fucking-Christ. Did I really just say that? Did I just threaten this man's innocent family? I was revolted with myself. Sure, it was an empty threat, but saying it—hell, even thinking it—was despicable. For a moment I considered apologising, but Nathan snapped back at me before I even had the chance.

"Don't ever say that to me," he hissed, each word falling hard.

I tried to justify myself.

"I haven't got anything against you or your family, but you're going to have to come with me."

"As I previously stated, no, I'm not."

A minute had passed. I'd completely lost my momentum.

"Fifty million, Nathan," I said. "That's all it takes and I'll be out of your life. For good."

He smiled. That son of a bitch smiled.

"You haven't thought this through very well, have you?" he began, his voice flawlessly steady. "What is the logic in threatening my life, when you need me alive to get what you want? If I'm dead, how do you plan on getting my money? Exactly. You can't."

The statement crushed me. It felt like the walls around me were closing in, narrowing by the second. No—I had to fight. I'd been through too much to let it all slip away now.

"If you refuse to come with me quietly, I will take you by force, even if that means putting a few bullets in your body first," I said, regaining my footing.

"I'd like you see you try," he said, the smile returning. "And just so you know, I will learn your name, and I will have you hunted and shot down like an animal."

I ignored the threat, even though I believed it was probably genuine.

170

"I don't know why, but I'm feeling charitable today," began Nathan, "so I will give you the chance to turn around and leave. If you stay, it will be at your peril."

I raised the gun so it was in the middle of his forehead.

"I'm not going anywhere, Nathan."

As each minute passed, he seemed to relax. Clearly he found comfort in my delay to react, but I knew I'd have to do something and it would have to be soon.

"This is not the first time I've had a gun pulled on me," said Nathan, his tone suddenly softening, "and on each occasion I've walked out of it without even a scratch. But I must say, you're not like the rest. You're different. Even as you hold this gun to my head, I know you won't hurt me."

Without even letting the words sink in, I retracted the gun away, before slicing it across his face. The muzzle broke through the skin on impact, and the blood began to reach the surface, slowly dripping down.

After the initial shock, Nathan laughed, pulling a handkerchief from his pocket. He dabbed it on his forehead, trying to clear up the blood. As I watched, something inside of me welled up and exploded into fragments. What had I become? This was not me. My desperation had changed me into someone I didn't want to be. It was then I questioned myself, how far would I go to ensure Rochelle's safety? Would I lie? Would I deceive? And would I kill? So far I'd done two out of three, and I was not proud of myself.

"If I hadn't said that," said Nathan, with a slight chuckle, "you wouldn't have struck me. Hit a nerve did I? Are you ashamed to admit you just don't have that killer instinct?"

Killer instinct? I was not that way inclined. I'd been dragged into a situation beyond my control, but I had been foolish enough to side with the enemy. For once, I needed to grow a goddamn backbone, and make the right choice.

"The money is not for me," I said, my voice sounding strangely distant. "My girlfriend is being held hostage by these men, and I need your money, otherwise they'll kill her."

Silence fell heavily, but the truth had never felt so good.

"And at last you make sense—" said Nathan.

My hopes soared so goddamn high, that for a brief moment I thought I'd finally reached the end, but Nathan brought me back down almost instantly.

"—But you're dragging me into your own battle," he continued. "I sympathise with you, I truly do, but this changes nothing."

If words could kill, that would have been the end of me. All the confidence I had built up over the last few days had washed away, and the familiar disappointment and anguish returned in a flood of emotions.

Before I could dwell in my own self-pity, my mobile phone sounded and vibrated in my jacket. I whipped it out—still holding the gun at Nathan—pressed the green button and put the phone to my ear.

"Get the fuck out of there!" yelled Cosmo, cutting to the chase. "Right now."

I registered the words, but I still pressed for answers.

"Why? What's wrong?"

"Burwell's bodyguards are climbing the stairwell. They're here!"

The fact pierced my brain like a searing hot bullet. I dropped the phone to the ground—not even caring to end the call—and looked at my exit. That was my first mistake. For maybe less than half a second, I turned my head and looked at the hatch, disregarding Nathan. That was my second mistake. In a panic, I tried to escape, but I was grabbed from behind.

Nathan had lunged out at me, placing a firm hand around my neck. He used his thumb and middle finger to apply pressure. The pain shot down my spine. As I dropped to my knees, I turned and faced my adversary, and it was only instinct to take aim at Nathan. If I'd had maybe a few more seconds, survival mode would have kicked in and I may have even taken the shot, but I left it too long. Nathan had the upper hand in this situation. His first attack had come as a surprise, but I never would have predicted his second attack. He raised his foot and stomped on my face. I bent back on my knees, but before I could retaliate, Nathan had my arm twisted around my back, and snatched the gun right from my hand. I felt the muzzle of my own gun pressing into my skull.

"Did you really think I was alone?" asked Nathan, his voice filled with hatred. "I'm wearing a wire. Everything that just transpired—my men heard it. No matter where I am, they can be there in less than five minutes."

A wire. Of course. How could I have not taken that into consideration?

"The last time you crossed me, I gave you a clear warning," he continued, "and I could have had my men kill you then and there, but I was compassionate, and I gave you another chance."

Nathan cracked the gun into the back of my head, splitting open an old wound. I howled in pain, collapsed forward, and fought to stay conscious. Somehow, I managed. Eyes closed, I heard a click, which I initially thought was the gun, but I was mistaken—it was the handcuffs. Nathan had unlocked them from his wrist and briefcase, and had attached them to my wrist and the elevator handrail. I was trapped. Nowhere to escape.

Dizzy and disoriented, I somehow managed to focus my eyes. Nathan stood over me, with the gun resting at his side. Without warning, the elevator jolted and started moving again, and since I hadn't given Cosmo the signal, I knew that he hadn't been the one to reactive it.

"You should have known better," said Nathan, tucking the gun into his jacket.

I said nothing. There was nothing left to say.

The elevator doors opened up at the fifth floor. Nathan stepped outside, his hand firmly gripped around his suitcase, staring down at me with the most unbearable smirk.

"My men will be waiting for you at the top floor," he said, without a trace of remorse, "and they'll make it quick. I promise."

I turned away just as the elevator doors shut again. The elevator began its journey upwards, and now I knew what would be waiting for me on the other side.

I closed my eyes and blocked out the world. If I was going to die, I wanted my last thoughts to be of Rochelle, and now that I'd let her down, her death was inevitable. I could only hope Rochelle's last thoughts would be of me too.

# 33

I wanted to be afraid, but there was barely enough time to process it.

Dying at the hands of Nathan Burwell's bodyguards was not the way I wanted to go, but I had no other choice. I'd had this coming right from the start. Would they simply shoot me, and dispose of my body in a ditch? Or would they make me suffer, breaking every bone in my body until I begged for death? Part of me knew I should block out the negative thoughts and not give up hope, but I had already endured so much.

I looked up at the flashing numbers at the top of the elevator, and they increased every couple of seconds as I moved by another level. I recalled that the hotel had a total of sixteen floors. When I reached sixteen, I would reach my fate. Eight, nine, ten. I only had a few moments to prepare myself for what was to come. Eleven, twelve, thirteen. Nearly there now.

I was so mentally prepared to make my final stand, that I was left stunned when the elevator stopped just before the fourteenth floor.

Everything came to a sudden halt. What the hell? I waited alone, but before long I heard footsteps on top of the elevator, followed by a familiar voice from above. Yes. Cosmo.

"Quick! Get up!" he shouted, his face peering down on me from the elevator hatch.

"How did you—?"

"Fuckin' hurry up!"

"Can't. I'm locked up," I said, raising my hand with the cuff attached.

He muttered something under his breath and dropped down into the elevator. He then pulled out a handgun—I had no idea where he got it from—and without hesitation, he took aim.

"Keep your head down, Kennedy."

I saw what he was doing.

"Cosmo! No!"

He fired. The bullet came close. Too close. But he was not aiming for the chain between each cuff; he had fired at the handrail, breaking it away from the elevator. Then it was only a matter of sliding the cuff off the broken end, and I was free to move.

I would have thanked Cosmo, but he had already jumped up and pulled himself through the hatch. He demanded for me to follow. Immediately, I tried to jump and reach the hatch. Missed it. Cosmo let out a string of insults, and dipped his arm—the one without the cast—back into the elevator. I quickly grabbed his hand, and he managed to pull me up. Jesus. His obsession with bodybuilding had finally paid off.

Finally out of the elevator, I turned my head to see a bright light just a few feet off the ground. Cosmo had opened the elevator doors by jimmying them open with his own bike spoke, and then he'd managed to manually override the system by obstructing the cables within the shaft—with a mop. The obstruction had forced the elevator into an emergency stop. Genius. His quick thinking had probably saved my life.

He hopped up and slid through the half open doors. I did too. Once we were both through, Cosmo yanked the mop free. The doors shut once again. It was only instinct to start running, but he stopped me in my tracks.

"Not that way," said Cosmo, jogging in the opposite direction. "Follow me."

I chased after him, having no idea where we were going. We didn't run too far, just up the corridor, and stopped in front of the ladies bathrooms. Cosmo pushed open the door a crack, and took a look inside.

"Cosmo, what are you—?"

"Get in," said Cosmo, holding the ladies room door open.

"We can't go in there!"

"Yes, we can, it's going to save our arses for another day. Now get in."

I hesitated, but I guessed it truly was our only option. I stepped inside, Cosmo right behind me. But there was a woman in the bathroom, resting up against the sinks, staring right at us. I panicked. I tried to back out, but Cosmo pushed me in.

"She's with us," hissed Cosmo, gripping the back of my jacket. "If Daphne wasn't here, we would be screwed, Kennedy."

Daphne. His girlfriend. She had posed with Nathan Burwell for the so-called affair photographs. I don't think I'd ever personally met any of Cosmo's girlfriends before, but she looked exactly as I'd pictured—bleached blonde hair, caked in make-up with an enormous chest. Daphne was not the kind of woman that I found attractive, but I knew plenty of men that would.

"Hi," I said to Daphne, but I was in no mood to fake a smile. "What are you doing here?"

She opened her mouth to give an answer, but Cosmo butted in.

"Because we needed a back-up plan," he explained. "It's not that I didn't have faith in you—but I knew there would be risks. So I called Daph and told her to meet us here."

"And I'm going to help you guys out," said Daphne, her voice so high-pitched it was like she had been sucking on a helium balloon.

"How exactly?" I asked.

Cosmo, still holding onto my jacket, pushed me towards the end cubicle and said,

"Burwell's security guards will search every inch of this hotel, including the ladies bathrooms, but do you think they'll come in this bathroom when there's a woman inside screaming at them to get out? Exactly. They'll turn around and leave."

Again, genius. Sometimes I was really sceptical of Cosmo's abilities, but he truly was on the ball. Without his assistance, I'd probably be dead by now.

Cosmo locked the cubicle door and told me to keep quiet. I obeyed. The two of us barely had room to stand, and we were stuck shoulder to shoulder—but I stayed completely still. It wouldn't be long before Burwell's guards would come for us. By now I predicted they'd already worked out I'd escaped, and they were probably searching each floor, and every room.

Only a few minutes had passed when I heard a door burst open.

I couldn't be sure if it was just another woman wanting to use the bathroom, or if it was one of Burwell's guards, but Daphne's screeches confirmed what I had suspected.

"Hey!" screamed Daphne, so beautifully rehearsed. "Get the hell out, pervert!"

"Uh, sorry," said the voice of a man, and then there was the sound of a door closing.

It had worked. I tried to relax a little, but I couldn't. We weren't in the clear yet. I knew that the security guards would be sweeping every inch of the hotel, and they would not rush the process. A minute or so passed, and Cosmo unlocked the cubicle door and cracked it open a few inches. Through the crack, I could see Daphne still standing at the sinks. Cosmo whispered out to her.

"I'm going to need you to stay another hour or so," he said, a voice so quiet it was almost inaudible, "when some time has passed, I'll get you to go out and inspect the hotel, and make sure they're not waiting for us on the outside."

Daphne nodded. Cosmo locked the cubicle again.

Suddenly, a dire thought crossed my mind.

"What about the surveillance cameras, Cosmo? Surely Burwell's guards will watch over them and they'll work out where we've gone and—"

Cosmo waved me off.

"I'm way ahead of you, man. I wiped all of the surveillance recordings from this morning until now, and then I shut them off. They won't have a damn clue where we've gone."

"So, how long do we have to stay here for?" I asked, arching an eyebrow.

"Honestly?" began Cosmo, leaning up against the cubicle wall. "We'll be lucky if we get out before sunset."

# 34

I had tried so hard.

I'd broken dozens of laws, bent the truth, deceived, betrayed and threatened a man with a loaded weapon—but it wasn't enough. Even though I had done all I could, once again I had not succeeded. I hadn't even come close.

It was a little after eight-thirty at night before Cosmo and I were able to step out of the end cubicle in the women's bathrooms—but we weren't safe just yet. We had asked Daphne to inspect every floor, and check outside the hotel just in case Burwell's guards were waiting for us—and they were. They had stayed behind for hours, adamant that we would emerge at some point. We had no choice but to wait it out.

We had grown tired and impatient, but at eight thirty Daphne confirmed that the guards had left. However, even though she had given us the all clear, there was a chance that Burwell's guards were still in the area, monitoring the hotel from nearby. We had to be cautious. We'd gone through too much to blow it all now.

Daphne escorted Cosmo and I down to the basement, and we waited in the shadows until she came and picked us up in her Ford Focus. We would have to leave our rented car on the streets for the night, otherwise we would risk being spotted, and our lives were at stake.

We stuck to the main roads. It was a lot safer than being sprung on a quiet street. The further we drove, the more I could relax. I watched out the rear window as the city faded into the distance. For the night I would have to return to my accommodation at the rehearsal warehouse—but I would stay there alone. Cosmo said he wanted to spend the evening with Daphne. Although I dreaded the thought of being on my own—I kept my mouth shut and let them drop me off outside the warehouse. They drove off shortly after.

I retreated inside the warehouse, taking the stairs over the elevator to the top floor, and walked to room 'B'. I opened up the doors and stepped inside, but I didn't turn on the lights.

I was exhausted—both mentally and physically. Over the last few days I had functioned on pure adrenaline, and now that it was gone, there was nothing left of me. Although I didn't want to, I found myself dropping to the ground below. My body curled into the foetal position, and my eyes began to close. I'd blacked out even before my head hit the floor.

# 35

*August 14th*

It was the beginning of the end, or at least it felt that way.

In the past, whenever the situation looked bleak, I would use my optimism to get through it—but not today. My optimism had worn thin.

I awoke just after nine-thirty in the morning. I'd had a solid twelve hours' sleep, but I still felt drained. I sat upright, my head spinning as if I'd been turning around in circles, so I closed my eyes and tried to fight through it. It didn't work. Sometimes dizziness was just a state of mind, so I tried to focus on something else—like calling Cosmo.

I checked my pockets and searched for my mobile. Couldn't find it. I pulled myself off the floor and frantically began looking for it in amongst my papers and in my backpack. No sign of it. I tried to remember where I'd last had it. Well, I'd had it yesterday. It didn't make any sense at first, but then something clicked. When Cosmo had called, telling me to get out of the elevator, I had dropped my mobile. I panicked. Had Nathan taken it? Did he have my mobile? I had taken great caution by buying a cheap prepaid one, and I also hadn't saved any contacts to the phone or sim card, but surely the call history would show up. Shit. I'd really screwed up. I'd have to tell Cosmo to dump his phone, because any link to him was a link to me. Nathan could never learn of our identities, because I knew what would happen if he did.

I left the rehearsal room and stepped out into the corridor. The warehouse was already goddamn noisy even during the early hours of the morning. I followed the corridor to the end, and spotted a counter on the other side of the room. There was a man standing behind the counter, tuning up a guitar, and he smiled when he saw me. Cosmo had already introduced me to him just a few days ago, but his name escaped me.

"Hey, Jord. How's it going?" he said, as I approached.

I forced a smile and searched for his name. He obviously knew I'd forgotten because he laughed and said his name was Alex.

"Sorry, Alex," I began, but the apology was empty, "but could I use your phone? I need to call Cosmo. Urgently."

"Sorry, mate. Our landline is busted, and it won't be working again until next week. I'd lend you my mobile, but there's no reception, and that's mainly because we're encased in about four different layers of cement," said Alex, with another hearty laugh.

I cursed under my breath, and rubbed my hand across my forehead.

"Hey, what's that?" asked Alex.

I'd heard what he said, but I wasn't sure what he was talking about—then I noticed the handcuffs. One was still attached to my wrist, and the other was dangling from the chain link.

I tried to think of a good excuse, or a decent explanation, but nothing came to mind. Besides, I had grown tired of lying to people.

"I had a rough day yesterday," I eventually replied.

"Rough as in...sexual?"

"What—? No."

Alex stared, with an eyebrow raised, but he didn't question me. Good. I wasn't in the mood for it.

"There's a payphone out front," he said, quick to change the subject. "Just take the elevator down, go out to the street, and you'll see it in front of the servo station."

I thanked him and left without delay. Once again, I picked the stairs over the elevator. After all I'd been through yesterday, the thought of stepping into a confined space made me nervous.

I walked out of the warehouse and into the daylight. At first, I was overcome by a sense of confusion. It was warm outside—which was definitely out of the ordinary for this time of year. It had been such a harsh winter that I had almost forgotten what warmth felt like, but it felt good. Immediately, I peeled off my jacket and carried on down the street.

I found the phone booth out the front of a dodgy-looking petrol station. I put in a two-dollar coin—I didn't have anything smaller—and called Cosmo's number. He answered.

"Hello?"

"Cosmo," I said, before he had the chance to say anymore. "Are you alright?"

"Kennedy? Yeah, man. Why? What's going on?"

I evaded the question.

"Where are you?"

"Just left Daphne's place, and now I'm heading into the city to pick up the car."

"Where can I meet you?"

"Uh, how about Pain Threshold? It's a tattoo parlour on George Street."

Not exactly what I had in mind, but I agreed.

"OK, I'll meet you there in an hour."

"Cool. See you then."

"And Cosmo?"

"Yeah?"

"The moment we hang up, you must throw your phone into the nearest bin."

Our call ended. He didn't even have to ask for an explanation.

\*\*\*

By the time I arrived at the tattoo parlour—Pain Threshold—Cosmo was already sitting backwards on a chair waiting to be inked.

I'd thought Cosmo had suggested the place because it was easy to find—I hadn't realised he'd booked in to get a new tattoo.

I had wandered inside the parlour that morning wearing my white polo shirt and my Calvin Klein jeans. I didn't fit in with the crowd at all. It was the equivalent of a teenage boyband fan girl attending a Metallica concert—I was very out of place. I ignored the stares though. I needed to talk with Cosmo.

I sat down in a chair against the wall, directly opposite Cosmo. However, before I had the chance to speak, he beat me to it.

"I dumped her," he said, so matter-of-factly.

"What?" I said, lost in his statement, but I quickly caught up to speed. "You mean, Daphne?"

"Yep. We'd been together for a few weeks now, and it felt right to end it last night."

Go figure.

"That's wrong, Cosmo," I scolded. "She did so much for us yesterday, and your timing was well off the mark. I mean, Daphne must have been really upset."

"Not really, she said I was a pain in the arse."

"Oh."

"But we still had a good night together. Lots of wild break-up sex. The very best kind."

I tried not to cringe, but the mental images were there.

"But anyway," I said, quick to change the topic, "I want to talk about yesterday."

Cosmo's eyes changed, and he turned his head away from me.

"I know I've underestimated Burwell's ability," I began, "and I know I screwed up, but we've only got a few days left before it's all over. And I just don't know what else I can do."

"And now it's up to me to save the day. Is that it, Kennedy?"

His hostility surprised me. He'd been so supportive up until now.

"No," I said, "but I value your input."

He scoffed at my statement. I knew I had worded it wrong, but it was too late to correct myself.

"I don't want to say it, but we're royally fucked," said Cosmo. "Maybe it's time you start negotiating with Mal, and offer him something else."

"But wasn't it you that told me not to give up?"

Cosmo fell silent. It was something I remembered clearly. I could tell he did too.

"You should get inked," he said, attempting to redirect the conversation. "It will relax you."

Relax? Tattooing was my depiction of hell.

"Sure," I replied, "because having a needle dug into my skin, only to painfully inject ink into my flesh, is exactly what will relax me right now."

At first, Cosmo missed the sarcasm. But only for a moment.

"Fuck you," he growled.

I gave a *'what did you expect me to say?'* shrug.

"Look, man," said Cosmo, pausing as he searched for an excuse, "I've been doing all I can and more to help you out, but it's starting to fuck with my head. I want to do something normal, like get a new tat, do a gig and then get shit-faced with the boys. I just need a couple of days to myself, you know."

Perhaps I had been asking too much of him. After all, I'd dragged Cosmo into a situation I should have dealt with alone. We'd officially lost our jobs, diced with death and matters weren't getting any easier. Although I'd run out of options, and of almost all hope— I knew I'd have to take the final road alone. It wasn't fair to bring Cosmo down with me.

I felt like apologising to him, because I'd derailed his life. He'd lost so much, and although it could be regained, it would take time.

Before I could tell him I was sorry, a tattoo artist approached Cosmo and started cleaning his shoulder blade. They discussed the design in a mock up drawing, then an outline was used, and before long the needle was switched on and it pierced through Cosmo's skin. Blood began to spill from the open wound. That was enough for me, so I figured it was best to leave him. I would find another opportunity to express my regret.

For now, I had work to do.

# 36

Moments after leaving the tattoo parlour, I found the nearest phone box and called Mal Lawson.

Although I knew my chances were slim to none, I called him and asked for a time extension. As predicted, he said no, and hung up on me. I knew the call had been risky—because Mal now knew I was without a plan—but it was the only hope I had left.

I had tried everything, and now perhaps I would have to look at things from a new angle. Mal Lawson wanted money. That was the bottom line. Did it really matter if it came from Nathan Burwell? Probably not. Fifty million was a sum I could barely wrap my head around, but I would have to think of another way to get it. Unfortunately for me, I was without a plan, and time was running out. I had less than three days, because I'd already wasted four.

My head began to throb. I was over thinking everything, and it couldn't have been good for my health. Although I should have been taking action, I took a leaf from Cosmo's book and decided to do something normal—so I grabbed a Samantha Myles coffee and sat down at a table outside in the sunshine.

It felt good to do the mundane. For a brief moment, it even made me happy. I recalled times when Rochelle and I had met up after work and had coffees together. Although our beverages were always way over priced, it was something we always looked forward to. She would tell me about her day, and I would tell her about mine. Rochelle would do most of the talking actually, but that was OK because I loved to listen. God, I missed it. A few months back I'd grown tired of my daily routine, but now it's all that I wanted.

Something deep inside of me imploded before bursting into fragments. I deserved to be punished. I'd been greedy. I'd wanted more, but at what cost? Now I'd lost everything. Only now I could see how good I'd had it. I had everything I'd ever need, but I was self-indulgent, and had been looking for something else to fulfil me.

My mistake would stay with me. I doubted normality would ever be restored.

Weakness surfaced once again. I felt close to breaking point, but then I felt a hand tap my shoulder.

In a burst of panic, I jerked my head around to see a familiar face.

At a first glance, I thought it was Nathan, but despite having the same build and an identical haircut, the facial structure was different. I'd seen this man before. He had dined with us on the night I'd drugged Nathan. It was his step-son, Brad Burwell.

Instantly, I tensed up. I should have known it was not safe to be out in the open, especially so close to the network building. Idiot. Everyone associated with Nathan was probably out in the city looking for me.

"Good morning, Mr..." began Brad, but he paused awkwardly, "—actually, I don't know your real name, and there's no point in calling you Mr. Zimmer, is there?"

He knew I was a fraud. Many more probably knew too. Instantly, I pushed back my chair and began walking without saying a word. Brad followed.

"My step-dad," said Brad, right behind me. "He's been obsessing over you lately."

"Well, he shouldn't. I'm out of his league," I replied, picking up the pace.

I then promptly turned a sharp corner, into a swarm of people walking in the opposite direction. I tried to lose him. No such luck. I wanted to run, but I didn't want to draw attention to myself. I had to get out of this situation as cleanly as possible.

"Wait!" called Brad, still following me. "We need to talk!"

I kept walking. If that was his best attempt to stop me, I was truly disappointed. I had expected more from a Burwell.

"I know what you're doing, but I can't help unless you listen to me!"

Out of all the things I'd expected Brad to say to me—that wasn't it. At last, I stopped. I should have kept on walking, but with all odds against me, I was willing to take the risk. I turned around and faced him. People shoved and barged into us, so Brad pointed to a pub a few metres behind me. I walked towards it. He trailed behind.

"Go inside," he said, "it'll be quiet in there."

The thought of entering a quiet pub with a member of Nathan Burwell's family raised a little red flag in my mind. What was waiting for me inside? It seemed clear that I was probably being set up, but running would get me nowhere. My best option would be to stay and fight.

I walked inside the pub. I expected to be pounced on, but nothing happened. The place was almost empty apart from an old man sitting at a table with a schooner of beer in his hand.

"I won't take much of your time, I promise," said Brad, pointing to a table in the corner.

I looked over my shoulder. Nobody was there. Maybe I wasn't being set up after all. I sat down at the table. Brad sat down opposite, and I waited for him to speak first.

"You're trying to blackmail, Nathan," said Brad, without any hesitation, "and I know you've had a lot of failed attempts, but you're getting close. You have to keep digging."

At first, the words didn't register. I understood what he was trying to tell me, but coming from his mouth, it just didn't compute. Thousands of questions surfaced.

"How did you—?" I began, but he cut me off mid-sentence.

"I saw you drop the pill into Nathan's drink."

"Then why didn't—?"

"—I stop you? I wanted you to succeed, so I played oblivious to the whole thing. Nathan doesn't know that of course."

Another thousand questions entered my head all at once, so I started with the first.

"But, you're Nathan Burwell's son. Why would you let me get away with something so disgraceful?"

"Step-son," he corrected, "and I know him well, probably better than anyone else. But he doesn't know that I'm aware of his demons."

188

My hopes soared, as if they'd been resurrected from the dead.

"What do you know about Nathan?" I asked, trying to keep my voice steady and calm.

"You threatened my step-father with a gun yesterday at the Harrison Inn, correct?"

Obviously, Nathan had informed the rest of his family of what had transpired at the hotel.

"Yeah, I did," I replied, a little uneasy.

"Every week my step-father meets with friends at the restaurant inside the hotel, but after what happened yesterday, they had to postpone their meeting until tomorrow night—"

"—Where are you going with this?" I asked, cutting Brad off.

"Just hear me out," he said, raising a hand. "Nathan and his friends have rearranged their meeting to Sunday sips at The Falcon's Claw. After drinks, his bodyguard, Dustin, will pick him up from there a little after eight o'clock. Follow them. You'll get what you're looking for."

"And what is it? Aren't you going to clue me in?"

Brad was silent for some time.

"If I told you," he began, searching for words, "you probably wouldn't believe me."

"So I'm going to have to take your word for it, and follow them tomorrow night?"

"Yeah, that's exactly what I'm telling you."

I tented my fingers together, as an attempt to look intimidating. I don't think it worked.

"And why should I trust you?" I asked. "How do I know this isn't just a set up?"

Brad leaned forward a little and lowered his voice.

"Sometimes," he began, "you need to take the gamble, and go against your better judgement. I've witnessed dozens of men trying to blackmail my step-dad, but they were criminals, only looking for self-gain. But you? You're not the enemy here. You're just a pawn in somebody else's game."

The kid was bang on. How he could tell? I'd never know.

"And don't get me wrong," continued Brad, "Nathan has been good to my mother, and the rest of the family too. That being said, it still doesn't make up for all he's done. He needs to be exposed by somebody like you, and maybe he'll change his ways."

Although I still felt a little unsettled by trusting a member of the Burwell family, it was my only option left. The chance was there and I had to take it.

Suddenly, Brad dug his hand into his pocket. For a moment he put me on edge, but he only pulled out a wallet. Before I could ask what he was doing, Brad opened up his wallet and slid out a small key, then handed it to me. I looked at it, blankly.

"What's this for?"

Brad gestured to my wrist, pointing to the handcuffs. I'd almost forgotten it was still there. I put the key into the hole, and they slid off my wrist in a loud thud. At last, I was a free man. I thanked Brad, and tried to give him the key back, but he refused.

"You'd better keep it," he said with a half smile. "Just in case you need it again."

I hoped I wouldn't, but nevertheless I put the cuffs and the key into my pocket. Without delay, Brad stood, wished me luck, and left. Once again I was alone.

I thought about calling Cosmo, but I knew he wanted some time to himself. Besides, this was not something I wanted him involved in. Tomorrow night, I would face Nathan Burwell on my own.

# 37

*August 15th*

Tonight, I was fearless.

There was nothing more to lose, which in some strange way was a comfort to me. I would give my all—but just this one last time. If I failed, I would gracefully accept it, and allow my enemies to end my life. No, death didn't scare me either. In my eyes, if I lost Rochelle, then I would go down with her. After all, without her I would not be able to continue on. The hole in my chest would never be filled. Simple as that.

I wasn't trying to be melodramatic, but I was beyond the point of caring. If the worst should happen, it would be on my shoulders. All that had transpired was my fault. Without a shadow of a doubt. I wouldn't be able to carry on with the burden, so I would do the honourable thing and sacrifice myself. Besides, the thought of resting my beaten body was heavenly.

As the day faded into night, and the warmth of the sun dispersed and vanished, I readied myself for what was to come. Just as Brad had advised me, I would face Nathan Burwell.

Although, I wouldn't risk following him directly, because I knew I'd probably be caught. I needed to be discrete. I needed to be vigilant. So I wouldn't trail—I would track.

Over the last twenty-four hours, I had researched vehicle tracking devices. After a quick Google search on the topic, bam, I had thousands of matches. It wasn't hard to find a website that stocked them either. Better yet, I even found a place in Sydney that sold them over the counter.

Installing tracking devices seemed pretty easy too. It was only a matter of reading the instructions in order to set it up, and then it would need to be planted on the car. The tracking device I had purchased had a strong magnetic case, so I was hoping I could quickly place it under a tyre rim without anybody noticing. When the device was in place, I could keep track of where the car was going via a laptop or smartphone, and I would be able to follow, while still maintaining a decent distance.

A little before seven o'clock, I walked to my destination—The Falcon's Claw. The streets were busy, with hundreds of people swarming the footpaths. I blended in, which was a good thing, because there was a lesser chance of being caught. I was without a weapon tonight, but instead I carried a backpack filled with useful devices—the tracker, a video camera, a new prepaid mobile and a laptop. To be honest, I wanted a gun—just for that little bit of extra comfort—but perhaps laying low was my best option.

Rather than standing right outside The Falcon's Claw, I stood on the opposite side of the road behind a row of parked cars. I remained there for almost forty minutes, waiting for something to happen. I hadn't seen Nathan, nor had I seen his bodyguard, Dustin. Although part of me considered the fact that Brad Burwell had deceived me, I tried to remain positive, and I continued to wait.

At a quarter to eight, I spotted a black Mazda pull up directly outside The Falcon's Claw. Although it was strictly a no-parking zone, the Mazda's engine died and flashed its hazard lights. Finally, a door opened up and Dustin stepped out from behind the wheel.

My heart soared. Maybe I shouldn't have put my hopes up so high, but tonight, I wanted to succeed. I had to take action.

The tracking device I had purchased earlier would need to be placed on the car—but how the hell was I meant to do it? Dustin wasn't moving away from the car, and surely I would be spotted if I got too close. Goddamn it. Even though I'd felt so well prepared, I truly hadn't thought everything through.

But now was not the time to give in. Someone else would have to plant the device for me.

I scanned my eyes around, searching for somebody to bribe. My options weren't looking too good. There were a lot of seedy looking people walking the streets tonight, and although it was wrong of me to judge them based on their appearance, in this situation I had to be picky. I looked further up the street, and I saw a young teen. Hell, he barely looked over the age of fourteen. Most people would question why some punk kid was standing outside a nightclub on a Sunday night, but I didn't, because I was hoping he'd be up for a bribe.

I began to approach. The teen took notice. I was looking directly at him, and he was looking straight back. I wasn't the intimidating one in this situation either—the kid was. He crossed his arms, and looked ready to snap at any given moment.

"Hey," I said, keeping my distance. "Could I ask you for a favour?"

"Fuck off," he snarled at me, flashing a silver grill worn across the bottom row of his teeth.

The younger generation. I would never understand them. But I didn't turn around and walk away. Instead, I gave him my offer.

"You could make some money," I said, pulling a fifty from my top pocket. "I just need you to stick a device on a car across the street."

The teen looked me up and down, his aggression expanding with each second.

"You a terrorist? I ain't gettin' involved in that shit."

"No," I said, perhaps a little too firmly. "The device is nothing but a tracker. I need to plant it on a car, but I need somebody else to help me with it."

"Fuck off," he said again, turning his head.

I was growing desperate, and pulled another fifty from my pocket.

"One hundred dollars for three seconds of work," I said. "Please, help me."

The teen looked at the cash, and then looked at me.

"Two hundred, and maybe I'll consider it," he said, almost smiling.

I had the money, but I didn't want to lose it. Then again, I really had no other choice. I agreed to pay him one hundred now, and the other hundred once he'd done the deed. I pulled out the tracking device from my backpack and explained that he needed to discreetly attach it underneath the tyre rim of the black Mazda outside The Falcon's Claw, without the bodyguard—Dustin—seeing him. The teen took the device and began walking across the street. I watched from afar, feeling the adrenaline surface.

I had nothing to worry about though—the kid was sleek. While Dustin was facing the opposite direction, the teen walked directly past the car, ducked down for a split second and placed the tracking device under the tyre rim. It took maybe two seconds, and without looking back, the teen crossed the road and walked towards me.

"Too easy," said the kid, flashing the grill again. "So pay up, and be on your way."

The teenager's attitude infuriated me, but he'd done what I'd asked, so I paid him the rest and thanked him for his help. I then walked further up the street and watched Dustin from the distance. Dead on eight o'clock, Nathan and several other men exited The Falcon's Claw. They spoke amongst themselves for a moment, but then the men dispersed in opposite directions, while Nathan slipped into the black Mazda. Dustin then slid behind the wheel, and the engine came to life. They were leaving.

I didn't waste a second. I stood at the curb and tried to flag down a taxi. By the time one pulled up, Nathan was gone. It didn't matter though. I wanted to keep my distance. I slid into the backseat of the taxi, and pulled out my laptop. From here, I would be able to monitor where Nathan was heading. Technology—it continued to amaze me.

"Where to?" asked the driver, looking in the rear-view mirror.

"I don't know yet," I replied, "but wherever we go, I'll make it worth your while."

"And what's that supposed to mean?"

"I'll pay you well," I said, bluntly. "I promise."

Another bribe, but it worked. The driver pulled away from the curb, as I gave directions from the backseat. To my surprise, Nathan was heading out of the city, and up north.

Where was he going? I didn't know. What was he doing? Well, I didn't know that either. Even though I had failed to bring Nathan down more times than I could count, tonight felt different. Call it intuition, but I had a feeling my luck was about to change.

# 38

The city was long gone, and so was any sign of civilisation.

I'd followed Nathan Burwell all the way from Sydney, onto the F3, and I had taken the exit to Popran National Park. Trees surrounded both sides of a dark, narrow road. I was well beyond my comfort zone, but there was little to be done about it.

I'd already run up a taxi bill well over two hundred and fifty dollars, and of course, that didn't include a tip. I continued to monitor the laptop, wondering how much longer this would last. Hell, it was almost nine thirty.

"How much further, bro?" said the driver, as if reading my mind. "Because I'll give you another half an hour, but then I've got to call it quits. Alright?"

I reluctantly agreed. I wasn't quite sure what I'd do if Nathan kept going when my mode of transport abandoned me, but just three minutes later, the car tracker indicated no more movement. Nathan's vehicle had stopped. At first, I thought maybe there was a mistake, because the tracker placed the car in the centre of the national park—in deep and dense bushland—but the road ahead was narrowing off. The tracker was accurate.

What the hell was this? Lots of possibilities entered my mind, but none seemed to fit the picture. What was about to transpire? I simply couldn't guess.

"Take me in as far west as possible," I instructed the driver. "Into the National Park."

Although I could sense some frustration, the driver followed instructions and pulled off the road. He drove slowly, trying to keep control of the wheel as he drove along the uneven landscape. He managed to drive for roughly thirty seconds, before the trees blocked a clear route. I quickly paid the taxi driver—with a very generous bonus—and slipped out of the car. I was left abandoned, in the middle of nowhere, seeing nothing but darkness. The only source of light was my laptop, so I held it close as I continued my journey on foot.

I followed the tracker, walking deeper into the bush. Nerves were there, but my focus was stronger. I must've walked for at least twenty minutes—if not more—through the unknown in minimal lighting. Just when my doubts began seeping through, I could see a faded light in the distance. I walked closer and the light became clearer. With every cautious step, I came closer to what I had been looking for—a black Mazda parked in the middle of a clearing. The car's headlights were still on. A dead giveaway. I crouched down, snapped shut the laptop and watched. Behind tinted glass, Dustin was sitting behind the wheel reading a magazine, and Nathan? I couldn't see him. Then it occurred to me he wasn't there. Nathan was gone—most likely somewhere out in the dense bushland. Doing what? God knows.

There was no point in waiting here, because I had to find Nathan. Maybe this is why I should have kept a closer track of him? Now I was without a trail to follow. Moving as stealthily as possible, I began to wander aimlessly in the darkness. Was I scared? Yep. This curve ball had thrown me way off track, and now I didn't know what to expect. I was in dangerous territory. For all I knew, somebody could be preying on me, watching and waiting for an opportune moment to strike. The very thought triggered a shockwave of panic. No, now was not the time to lose it. I would not die here. Not without a little bit of dignity.

I tried to move as silently as I could, but the ground beneath my feet was scattered with fallen branches and dry, decomposing gumtree leaves. With each step, my feet crunched down and disappeared into the debris. I was unable to move quietly, and somebody heard me.

"Who's there?"

The voice cut through the air like a freshly sharpened knife. I stopped, panicked, as my heartbeat inclined instantly.

Suddenly, a beam of light appeared from the distance. Somebody ahead was scanning a flashlight amongst the trees. They had heard me coming.

Shit. I'd given myself away. My body shut down and I lost the ability to move. I could not fight, and I could not flee. My demise seemed certain.

But then, a second voice pierced through the silence.

"That you, Nathan?"

Another beam of light shone through the darkness, maybe less than ten metres away from me.

"Rick?" said the voice that could only belong to Nathan Burwell. "Where are you?"

The two flashlights scanned across from one another, and I caught a brief glimpse of two faces; one was Nathan, the other was a man no more than a stranger to me. The two men closed the gap between them, while I took the opportunity to duck behind a fallen gumtree.

"Let's get this over and done with, Rick," said Nathan, clutching his briefcase in one hand, and the flashlight in the other. "This is far beyond my comfort zone."

"Jesus, Nathan, you sure are an edgy guy," said the stranger I now knew as Rick.

"Yes, well, when I asked to meet with you...this wasn't exactly what I had in mind."

"But it feels good to be out here. You know, back to nature and all that shit."

Rick smiled, Nathan did not.

"Let's cut to the chase, shall we?" began Nathan, dimming his flashlight. "I'm curious to know how the trade went."

"Flawlessly," said Rick. "All I need is a little faith, Nathan, and I get the job done."

"And money. You needed my money too."

"Well, yeah, that too."

I wasn't following their conversation. What the hell was going on?

"How much did we successfully transport?" asked Nathan, his voice growing a little louder with each word.

"Eighteen kilos. It was far from easy but, 'cause we had to make twenty-three separate shipments, just to get it all over here to Australia."

"What about the sales? I invested a lot of money into this project. You know that, don't you?"

"Yeah, 'course I do, and there's good news all around," replied Rick, bearing a sly grin. "The coke was quality shit. Really top notch stuff, so we upped the street price, and got a huge motherfuckin' profit."

The words registered, but my reaction was severely delayed. My blood in my veins turned cold. Pressure was building under my chest. Even though I understood now, the very realisation was almost too much to take. Twenty seconds ticked by. I had to capture this moment. I needed evidence, because without it, I had nothing.

After the initial shock, I unzipped my backpack, hands shaking, and pulled out the video camera. I switched it on and began to film from the darkness. The picture wasn't perfect, so I quickly flicked it to night mode as I listened in to their conversation.

"Did you sell it all?" questioned Nathan.

"Every single gram," replied Rick, still smiling. "We had no trouble getting it onto the streets. This batch of coke was phenomenal."

"And what were the profits?"

"Just over eight million in total, Nathan. Told you I wouldn't let you down."

At long last, I'd heard what I needed to know. It had been the most challenging few weeks of my life—and it still wasn't quite over yet—but now I had solid proof that Nathan Burwell was not perfect. He was not clean-cut. He was involved in a drug trafficking ring, reaping in on the profits. I wasn't powerless anymore. Finally, the upper hand was mine.

Even though I had what I needed, I continued to film. The more footage I had, the better.

"So where is my profit, Rick? I was promised sixty percent, plus expenses."

I watched as Rick pulled out what seemed to be a piece of paper from the top pocket of his coat, and handed it across to Nathan. Immediately, Nathan placed his briefcase on the ground beside him, and opened up the piece of paper. He held up his flashlight and began to read.

"It's all there," said Rick. "That's a cheque for the full amount."

Nathan's eyes were fixed on the cheque for the longest time, before he folded it back up, and slipped it into his pocket. He pointed the flashlight towards Rick again.

"Let me ask you one thing," began Nathan, "how do I know this cheque won't bounce, or that you won't cancel it from the moment we leave here tonight?"

Rick was silent, but only for a few seconds.

"I give you my word, Nathan."

"I'm sorry, but that means nothing to me."

He shrugged at Nathan.

"Well, I guess you're just going to have to trust me."

Again, the silence fell back in. I could sense the tension, and Rick didn't seem as confident as he did before. A moment passed, before Nathan crouched down and laid his briefcase flat across the ground. He opened it up, and began to make adjustments to something inside. What the hell? I continued to film.

"Trust," repeated Nathan, just seconds before pulling a gun out from his briefcase and taking aim at Rick. "It's not something I do much, and regrettably, you're no exception."

A shot was fired, and it was right on target. The bullet went straight into Rick's chest. He gasped once, before his eyes rolled back into his head, and collapsed on the ground below. Nathan stepped closer—with a smoking gun still raised—and looked down at Rick. He was already dead, but that didn't stop Nathan from firing a few more bullets into his body. At closer range, the bullets did more damage. I watched, paralysed with fear. The camera was still rolling, and I'd captured every second of it. I'd witnessed Nathan Burwell kill a man.

This was too much for me. Memories began to surface, and I felt my body surge with emotion. I was on the verge of a panic attack. I wanted to look away, but I couldn't. I was too petrified to even blink.

Nathan walked around the corpse a couple of times, looking quite satisfied with his work. He then put the gun away back into his briefcase and found his mobile phone. Nathan struggled to find reception at first, but the call went through. He put the phone to his ear and waited for somebody to answer.

"Hello, Dustin? I need you to get down here. Just leave the car where it is, and head west," said Nathan, his voice perfectly calm. "And bring the shovel."

The call ended. I was close to a breakdown.

Now that Nathan had called for backup, there was a risk I could be exposed. Crouching down behind a fallen tree was no longer a safe haven, and I needed to get out. But how? If I moved, Nathan would surely hear me. I had no choice—I would have to stay put.

But what about the footage? If I were found, they would kill me on the spot and erase the video from the camera. Finally, I stopped filming and carefully put the camera back in my bag. As quietly as possible, I concealed the bag inside a hollow log beside me. I had to protect the footage. If I were to die tonight, I would bring Nathan down with me.

Twenty minutes passed, but it wasn't long before I heard footsteps. They were coming closer too, growing louder with each second. My breathing constricted instantly. The adrenaline in my veins hit a new high. I kept my head down, closed my eyes and pressed my body against the fallen gumtree, praying I wouldn't be spotted.

The footsteps were close now, perhaps just metres away.

For a moment, I couldn't even breathe. It was like an invisible rope was being tightened around my neck. I was frozen, still too terrified to move.

A light beamed from behind me. I closed my eyes. The footsteps moved closer, and by luck, they moved past me. I was overcome by a sense of relief, and I gratefully took a breath. Opening my eyes once more, I peered over the tree and spotted Dustin ahead of me, walking closer to the clearing. He had brought the shovel along with him too.

Nathan heard Dustin's footsteps, and pointed the flashlight in his direction.

"What took you so long?" asked Nathan. "It's been twenty minutes since I called."

"Couldn't find you, Nathan. You should have provided better directions."

Nathan said nothing. He pointed his torch at the bloodied body. Dustin walked closer and surveyed the corpse.

"I thought you said you weren't going to take the kill shots anymore," said Dustin, with a slight tone of frustration in his voice. "You said you'd leave it up to me and my boys."

"It would have taken you too long to get here. I had to do it myself."

He had confirmed what I had suspected—Nathan had killed before. How many people? I'd never know, but Nathan was far too calm in this situation, and he seemed quite practised at using a handgun.

"So I guess we'd better get digging," said Dustin.

"No, not *we*. *You* dig," corrected Nathan.

Dustin gripped the shovel a little tighter, let out a sigh and said, "You always give me the dirty work."

"Well, that's what I pay you for, don't I?"

"Yeah but, I deserve a raise after this."

Nathan didn't answer him. He crossed his arms and watched as Dustin kicked away the leaf litter. Once the ground was clear, he

202

began digging. The soil below was tough, and after minimal rain through a long drought, it was not easy to dig.

It took close to an hour before Dustin dug a deep enough hole. Nathan did not help whatsoever. He stood and watched, and occasionally asked his bodyguard to hurry up. Finally, Dustin placed down the shovel and stepped back to admire his work. The hole was small and cramped, but deep. However, Nathan wasn't satisfied with it.

"You'll need to dig the hole wider," he said. "Rick's not going to fit in there."

"Sure he will. I'll just shove him in until he does."

Nathan frowned.

"What?" hissed Dustin. "It's not like he's going to be uncomfortable, is he?"

He didn't answer the question. Nathan's patience had worn thin.

Dustin began dragging the body closer to the hole, leaving a trail of blood. I couldn't watch anymore. I'd always been squeamish and today was no exception. I closed my eyes and waited it out. By the sounds of it, Dustin had some difficulty at first, but then I heard him begin shovelling soil back into the hole. I opened my eyes again to take one last look. They were burying the body, and once the hole was filled, Dustin covered it up by scattering leaves across the top. At last, they were finished.

"Good enough," said Nathan, picking up his briefcase. "Let's go."

Immediately, I ducked down again and waited. The flashlight shone in my direction, but luckily for me Nathan and Dustin walked right past me. I'd survived the ordeal, and although I desperately wanted to leave, I decided to play it safe and wait in the darkness a little longer.

So many thoughts were swimming through my head. Had it really been that easy? Over the last few weeks Cosmo had been putting our lives on the line to get the dirt on Nathan Burwell, and he had been clean until now. But Nathan was far more corrupted than what I initially thought. I had expected a secret debt or an affair, but nothing of this scale. The cocaine trafficking had come as a shock, but the murder? I could barely understand it.

However, at last Nathan's behaviour and routine was beginning to make sense. Why else would he invest so much money into his personal security? Why else would he need surveillance cameras and bodyguards? Evidently, he was a man with a secret.

It also explained why Nathan would meet with his friends at a restaurant without any of his bodyguards. Clearly, he had conspired with hardened criminals and his guards would only seem intimidating to his alliances—which is why Nathan opted to wear a concealed wire. Finally, the pieces were beginning to connect.

But one question still lingered; how had one man managed to play the entire country as fools? What had driven the well-respected owner and CEO of Channel 5 to kill? Was it because of greed? Or power? I guess I'd never really know, but now that I had solid evidence, I would bring Burwell down.

At long last, I grabbed my backpack out from inside the log and stood up. I began to venture out of the bush and back to civilisation. Earlier today, I had felt vulnerable and powerless—that wasn't the case anymore. My newfound confidence reassured me that I could get the job done. I would not fail again, and that was a certainty.

# 39

It was almost one-thirty in the morning by the time I found my way back to the road.

My GPS proved to be useless, as the towering trees blocked out all hope of finding a satellite to guide me home. I was exhausted, and desperately craving some shut-eye, but there was too much to do now—I'd just witnessed Nathan Burwell murder a man, and then bury his bloodied body in the middle of a national park.

Just thinking about it made me light-headed.

I would have to quickly make plans to blackmail him again, and I would rob that son of a bitch for all he was worth. Unfortunately, a detail I missed earlier had finally surfaced. I had come to the realisation that I couldn't have it both ways—if I blackmailed Nathan, I would have to erase the video in exchange for money. I would let Nathan, the drug trafficking murderer, stay in society and turn a blind eye to all his crimes. The very thought didn't sit too well with me, but what option did I have left? If I leaked the footage to the media I'd have no chance of getting the money and no chance of seeing Rochelle again. I considered making extra copies of the video, but if I ever released it, Nathan would know I'd betrayed him.

My head was spinning. I wanted to see Nathan locked up in a filthy prison cell, but more than anything I wanted Rochelle safe and in my arms. It seemed impossible to have both, so I decided to disregard my morals and focus on my new blackmailing attempt.

After finding my way back to the freeway, I crossed six lanes and stood on the opposite side of the road, with the cars headed towards Sydney. I tried hitching a lift, and as predicted, it wasn't easy.

However, after standing around for half an hour and frantically waving at every vehicle that went by, I finally hitched a ride with a truckie. He was kind enough to take me all the way in to Pennant Hills, and from there I called a taxi to take me out to Alexandria. It was now close to 4am, and I was so tired I could barely believe I was still standing.

I had returned to my safe haven—the rehearsal warehouse. Delirious and sleep deprived, I was ready to drop to the ground and sleep until daylight, but first I had to make a phone call to Cosmo. I slipped my backpack off my shoulder, zipped it open and fished out my new mobile. I tried to call his mobile number. No answer. Then I remembered I'd told him to throw out his prepaid phone. I tried his home phone, and luckily he picked up after a few rings.

"Hmm...hello?" he asked, blearily.

"Hey, it's Jordan."

"What the fuck, Kennedy?" asked Cosmo, clearly not happy to have been woken up in the early hours of the morning. "Isn't it past your bedtime?"

"Cosmo, I need you to come down to the warehouse. As soon as possible."

"Well, I can't right now. I'm busy."

It was then I heard voices in the background. Female voices. I put two and two together, and realised I was probably ruining his evening alone with his, uh, lady friends.

"Sorry," I said, feeling slightly awkward, "then how about we meet up first thing tomorrow morning? It's very important."

"How important, Kennedy?"

I was silent, even though I desperately wanted to tell Cosmo what I had seen tonight, I knew I couldn't just yet. I had decided to take every precaution and would not risk telling him over the phone. I wanted to tell Cosmo in person, but how could I explain to him just how important the situation was? However, my long pause seemed to be a good enough response anyway.

"Look, I'll get there about nine o'clock," he said, after some time. "Alright?"

"OK. Thanks, Cosmo."

He hung up the phone. So did I. Feeling fatigued and weary, I headed towards the warehouse roller door. I pushed the intercom button, waiting for somebody to answer. Nobody opened the door for me. It was then I remembered the time, and that the warehouse would have been shut up for the night hours ago.

Knowing I would have to wait until daylight, I dropped down to the cold gravel ground beneath me, curled up and crashed out.

# 40

*August 16th*

"Jesus, mate, have you been out here all night?"

A sudden, gruff voice interrupted my sleep. My eyes flashed open and I shot upright. Still a little dazed, I prepared myself for an impending attack, but there was none. The rehearsal warehouse owner, Alex—I remembered his name today—was standing above me, with an arm wrapped around a bag of shopping.

"What the hell happened to you?" asked Alex, pressing for answers.

"I got, uh," I said, climbing to my feet and picking up my backpack, "I had a bit of a late night."

"I can tell," he replied, bluntly. "You look like shit."

"I was out until four in the morning, and I had nowhere else to go."

Alex shrugged his shoulders at me and opened up the roller door. He entered first, and I trailed behind him. We took the elevator up to the rehearsal space, and for the first time, it was silent. The screeching guitars, booming bass and pounding drums were gone, but in only a few hours time, they would be back. It was still only a quarter past eight and I'd had a little over four hours sleep, however, it would have to do.

I watched sheepishly as Alex switched on the lights inside the rehearsal space and unpacked his shopping—which was nothing but cans of soft drink and chocolate bars. I decided I'd wait around until Cosmo showed up.

"So, what were you doing out so late?" asked Alex, looking at me uneasily.

"I was just..." I began, searching for an excuse, "I had a big night. That's all."

He stared. I'm not sure if Alex believed me, but did it really matter if he didn't? I felt a tad uncomfortable with him staring at me, so I slipped away and found room B. Cosmo and I were paying a hundred bucks a day for this room, so I figured I might as well use it.

I switched the lights on and sat down on a milk crate. I was so exhausted I thought about curling up on the floor and sleeping the day away—but there was too much to do.

I spent some time hooking up the camera to my laptop, and I uploaded the footage. I then made numerous files of the same video saved under different names, and then saved them onto a USB. I had three copies of the video now, and when I had the chance I would email the footage to myself—call it paranoia, but I had to ensure that I would not lose the footage.

For the first time in my life, I understood what it was like to have power, and it felt good. With a few clicks, I could sabotage a man's life. I could drag his name through the mud and sentence that bastard to life in prison. And then, the power frightened me. I just wanted this to be over and done with, so I could get back to living the mundane.

I had time to kill, but what was I meant to do? I decided to watch the footage. Again. It sickened and enraged me—but I still barely comprehended the situation. I thought I understood the clockwork of Nathan's mind, but no, not quite. Had he always been a killer? Even before he became the CEO of Channel 5? I also questioned how he'd been getting away with it for so long. Why had nobody picked up on it yet? Or did Nathan simply pay-off or kill those who tried? I then wondered why his step-son, Brad, had tipped me off. Why hadn't he told the police if he knew about it? How could he have let Nathan live a double-life? The situation was too confusing, so I forced myself to stop thinking about it.

Unfortunately, it didn't last long, because Cosmo arrived shortly after.

"So," he said, stepping through the rehearsal room door. "What was so important that it couldn't wait, Kennedy?"

I didn't even know how to begin explaining it, so instead I handed him the video camera. Cosmo took it, and then looked at me blankly.

"What the fuck—?" he asked, obviously needing further instruction.

"Look at the saved recordings, Cosmo. There's a video there. Watch it."

He nodded and began to play the footage. Cosmo seemed lost in the dialogue between Nathan and Rick at first, but then the pieces came together.

"Shit," he said. "Is Burwell part of a drug ring?"

"Keep watching."

He obeyed. I watched him. Cosmo's reaction said it all. Like me, he couldn't believe what he had just witnessed, and he understood the power we had over Nathan.

For the first time, maybe ever, Cosmo was lost for words. He opened his mouth to speak, and then closed it. So I took the liberty to fill in the blanks.

"Nathan's a murderer, and we have the proof," I explained.

"But, how did you—?"

"—I followed them last night."

"Shit," said Cosmo, not knowing what else to say.

He watched the video again. Same reaction. I wasn't sure what Cosmo found harder to believe—the fact that Nathan Burwell was a killer, or the fact I'd managed to get the footage without his assistance.

"We're blackmailing him," I said, cutting to the chase. "Today."

"But how? The last time we tried, we got our arses kicked," replied Cosmo.

"We underestimated him last time, so we'll take a new approach. I'll call Burwell today from a payphone, and it's Monday so he'll be at work. I'll then tell him what I witnessed and that I've made copies. And unless I have fifty million by the end of the day, I'll leak the footage."

"But we're still going to have to meet with them. How else will we get the cash?"

Luckily, I'd already thought it through.

210

"We're the ones that will be calling the shots, so they'll meet either you or me outside Pain Threshold at six o'clock this evening. If they try to pull anything suspicious or don't pay up, then one of us will have that video on YouTube before the day is out—but it won't come to that. Nathan will do everything to preserve his reputation."

Cosmo nodded, but then fell silent for a moment.

"I'll do the meet-up with Nathan," said Cosmo after some time. "You can lie low until we've got the money, and then we'll do the exchange with Mal later tonight."

Truthfully, I wanted it that way. Cosmo was better at keeping his nerve than me. I think he knew it too. With no time to waste, I took the camera back off Cosmo, threw it into my backpack and headed towards the door.

"Wait, where are you going?" he asked.

"I'm going to call Nathan," I said, just before walking out. "No point in stalling now."

# 41

I found a phone box outside a small shopping centre in a suburb called North Rocks.

I'd chosen this particular phone box because it was far away from everywhere. If Nathan and his men tried to track me down, I'd already be gone. Better yet, the trail would lead them nowhere, as it provided no clues to where I was hiding out.

This was the safest place too. I wouldn't need to show Nathan the evidence, because just telling him would be enough. I felt prepared today. Now that I was almost at the end of this ordeal, I wouldn't let it all slip through the cracks.

I fed a few coins into the phone booth. Just hearing the dial tone made the adrenaline pulse through my veins. I punched in the number, and a receptionist named Susan answered my call within two rings. I requested to speak with Nathan Burwell, but then Susan asked me what it was regarding, and if I was a client of his. I didn't have the time for her bullshit.

"Just tell Mr. Burwell that Milo Zimmer is on the line, and wants to talk with him."

"One moment, please," said Susan, and I was put on hold.

As predicted, in under a minute my call was put through, and Nathan picked up.

"Well, my friend," began Nathan, choosing not to call me by my false name. "I was wondering when I'd hear from you again."

"Yeah, I figured I'd call rather than seeing you in person."

"And that," said Nathan, his voice unnaturally upbeat, "was a wise decision."

"It certainly was. In fact, that's why I chose to keep my distance last night."

Silence.

"What?" asked Nathan, his tone changing in an instant.

"Caught you off guard, didn't I? You had no idea that I was right there, watching you."

More silence. As I had said it, my hand had been shaking as I held the receiver tightly. I had rattled Nathan's cage in the past, but what I had just said would have put his world into a spin.

"What the hell is that supposed to mean?" he hissed, losing his nerve.

"I was there, Nathan. I had a tracker device placed on your car—"

"—Impossible," he snapped. "My car is searched daily for tracking devices."

"I had it planted under a tyre rim right before you left The Falcon's Claw. I guess your car hasn't been searched today, otherwise I'm sure you would have found it by now."

Once again, silence. It was clear to me that Nathan had done everything to keep his private life private, but he'd let his guard down. Did I feel sympathy for him? No, not in the slightest. It was almost ironic thinking back to how guilty I'd felt when I'd drugged and betrayed Nathan—but now I just didn't care. I would ruin his life with no regrets, but it was clear Nathan wasn't handling the situation at all.

"There's just no way..." he eventually replied, his voice a weak whisper.

Without a single trace of empathy, I continued to destroy his life.

"I followed you up the F3 and to your destination. I witnessed your discussion with a drug trafficker and then filmed you murdering him. I have it all on camera."

"—Jesus Christ..."

"I've already made several copies of the video. And I will leak this footage to every network, every media outlet and every goddamn newspaper."

Nathan exploded into panic.

"No! Please! You and I, we can make a deal."

"So are you willing to negotiate with me now? Or will you go to prison before you decide?"

"We'll talk! Please, I'm not a bad person."

"Yes, Nathan, you are."

I think he started crying at the other end of the phone. Good. At long last I was the one in control, and he was defenceless, with no choice but to listen to me.

"You want money, that's it? Right?" he asked, his voice weak and frail.

"Fifty million," I said. "And I need it today."

"No, that can't happen. I could only pay you gradually, not all of it at once."

"Then you need to make it happen," I said firmly, growing with power every second.

Nathan started sobbing at the other end of the phone. He had taken a man's life without remorse less than twenty-four hours ago, but now that he had been caught out for it, he couldn't take it. Nathan Burwell was a far more complex man than what I'd first thought.

"I can get you two million," replied Nathan after some time, "and I'll pay it up today as a sign of good faith, but I won't be able to get the rest to you until the end of the week."

"Two million today, the rest tomorrow morning. I will not wait any longer."

"But it can't be done!"

"You're worth billions, Nathan. Don't fuck around with me. It can be done."

"Not true—why do you think I'm involved in a drug ring? The taxman is not kind to me, I assure you. I have a lifestyle that I need to maintain, and I'm still paying out millions in bullshit lawsuits, including one from my ex-wife. I have money, yes, but not nearly as much as you think. The drug money is a necessity in my survival. It's not a choice."

"And killing a man? That was a necessity too?"

"Of course! I can't afford any loose ends. I have to cover my tracks. Always."

In that moment, I wanted to ask Nathan how many more people he had killed, but I knew I'd never get a straight answer.

214

"Nathan? Spare me the sob story," I hissed. "Just get me the cash."

"OK! I'll find a way! Just please, have some compassion."

"Compassion? That's a little hypocritical, don't you think? After what you did last night?"

He started crying again. I let him be for a moment, and then I went through the details.

"This is what's going to happen, Nathan," I began. "At six o'clock this evening a friend of mine will be waiting outside a tattoo parlour on George Street called Pain Threshold. He will be easy to recognise because he'll be talking on his mobile phone, and carrying a green backpack. You will pay up the two million today, and tomorrow morning at eleven o'clock will we go through the same process—for the rest of the money. Is that understood?"

"Yes," said Nathan, finally calm.

"And another thing, if anything happens to my friend, I will leak the footage. We're not playing games anymore, Nathan. Is that clear?"

"Six o'clock, George Street. I understand."

I'd done it. I'd successfully blackmailed Nathan Burwell. And I was not ashamed to admit that I felt good about it. Sure, he deserved to be locked up in a prison cell, but at least now I could secure Rochelle's safety. Finally, my next step was to call Mal Lawson and inform him of my triumph, but I had to finish up the call with Nathan first.

"I'm glad you understand, Mr. Burwell. We'll speak again tomorrow."

"But wait!" he croaked, desperation seeping through his voice. "If I give you the money, how can I know for sure that you won't go ahead and leak the footage anyway?"

"Well, Nathan," I said, seconds before hanging up the phone, "I guess you're just going to have to trust me."

# 42

Now that I had almost accomplished the task assigned to me, there was one last thing to do—inform my enemies of my success.

And even though I was still standing in front of the phone booth, I would not place the call here. I was positive Nathan would attempt to trace my call, and probably other calls I may have made, and I did not want to risk Nathan tracing my call to Mal Lawson, and linking the association.

I caught a bus from North Rocks to another suburb called Blacktown. There was a line of payphones right outside the shopping centre. The first phone booth had no receiver, and the second booth had buttons covered in god-knows-what. I picked the third phone booth and fed some coins into the machine. I called Mal, feeling unusually calm. He picked up after just one ring.

"Mr. Kennedy," began Mal, knowing it was me even before I even had the chance to say a word. "I was wondering when I'd hear from you again."

"I've blackmailed Nathan," I said, cutting to the chase, "and he's going to pay up."

Out of all the things Mal expected me to say—that wasn't it. I wasn't surprised though, because I had failed him on countless times before, so I guess he'd lost faith in me completely. Hell, up until yesterday I'd lost faith in myself too.

I could hear Mal at the other end of the phone, but he wouldn't talk. I guess he was still a little sceptical, but he would have to take my word for it.

"Let's talk exchange, Mal. I've held up my end of the bargain, so let's talk about yours."

"So do you have the fifty mil yet?" he asked, his voice cutting through like a knife.

"Not yet. He's paying me two million today, and the rest to-morrow morning."

"As I recall, I gave you a deadline of one week. The deadline ends today, Mr. Kennedy."

"No, I still have just over twenty-four hours."

"But I've waited long enough. I want the money today."

I'd had enough of his bullshit games.

"If you want the money, Mal, cut the crap. You'll wait until tomorrow morning."

He chuckled, and his laughter was genuine.

"I'm impressed, Mr. Kennedy. You've finally grown yourself a backbone."

"The exchange," I said again. "We'll meet in a public place tomorrow afternoon."

"Not possible. I'll give you the address for my current location once you have the money. Call me again at midday tomorrow, and then we'll talk some more."

"The fuck we will! You listen to me now."

But my effort was wasted, because Mal had already hung up on me. I bashed the receiver on the back wall of the phone booth—several times—and then slammed it back into its cradle.

I wanted to have power over Mal, but while he still had my girlfriend, I would have to buckle down to his demands. Meeting in a public place had been ideal, but I should have known it wasn't going to be that simple.

I checked the time and came to realise it was almost a quarter to three already. Somebody would be meeting with Cosmo shortly to make the first payment, so I had to ensure I'd be back in time for it. I called myself a taxi and told the driver I needed a ride into the city. At long last, the lack of sleep had caught up with me. Only a few minutes after slipping into the taxi, I rewarded myself with a well-deserved nap.

# 43

I sat in the corner booth of a little coffee shop in Annandale.

The place was a dump, but it was full of people. After a long day at work, I guess it was appealing to unwind by catching up with friends with an almost decent cup of coffee. All around me, people smiled and laughed. But I wasn't. I had a laptop in front of me, and a mobile to my ear. I had chosen this spot because I was invisible. People in coffee shops usually kept to themselves, and I highly doubted anybody would disturb me. Besides, if anybody looked in my direction, I had a stare so cold they'd look the other way in an instant.

To the side of me, there was a window. On the horizon I could see the sun setting behind the city, with the last of its rays casting an orange haze across the skyline. It didn't last long though—within a few minutes it was gone, leaving nothing but darkness. It was close to six o'clock now, and shortly somebody would be meeting with Cosmo.

I was already on a call with him; waiting for an update, but neither of us had anything to say. We knew what we were doing, and our focus was solid.

On the wall in front of me, there was a clock hanging above the door. With each second, my heart raced and my fingers trembled. I tried to keep calm. I did not want to draw attention to myself. However, my heart was racing so fast it almost seemed unnatural—but then Cosmo spoke. It almost made my heart stop.

"Somebody's coming," he said, his voice flawlessly steady. "It's not Nathan—but he's got two briefcases."

"Who is it then? Dustin Pinfold or one of the other guards?"

"Nah, I think it's the kid. Nathan's step-son."

"Brad Burwell?" I questioned, trying to keep my voice down.

"Yeah, think so."

I panicked. Was Brad in on this? Had I been set up all along? Or was this a sheer coincidence?

218

"What's happening, Cosmo?"

He didn't answer. Cosmo had refocused as he waited for Brad to approach. Within a minute, I heard them exchange greetings, before getting right down to business. I heard Cosmo ask if it was all there, and then I heard a second voice, but it was inaudible. I couldn't stand it. I had to be a part of it.

"Cosmo, let me talk to him."

He ignored me at first. He was still asking Brad questions.

"Please, Cosmo! I need to talk with him right now."

At last, he listened to me.

"My mate wants to talk to you," said Cosmo as he handed the phone to Brad.

I think I heard Brad ask for a name, but Cosmo didn't give him one. After a moment or two, Brad tried to talk, but I spoke over the top of him.

"I took your advice, Brad," I said. "Just like you asked me to."

"Mr. Zimmer? Is that who I'm talking to?"

"Of course, who else would it be? Or have you told others what you told me?"

"No, you're the only one," he said, then added, "but I have to ask, just how much is my step-father paying you?"

"That's probably a question you should have asked me before you tipped me off."

Brad laughed. I didn't.

"Yes, you're right. I guess I should have."

"But let me ask you a question now, Brad. How could you keep your step-father's secret to yourself for all this time?"

"Wasn't easy," he replied, "but I didn't know how else to deal with it."

"But blood has been spilled, and it's going to be on your hands too."

He fell silent. Perhaps it was not my place to expose Brad's mistake, but I wanted him to feel the guilt. How many more had fallen under Nathan's gun? I was positive Rick was not Nathan's first victim.

"Why is it on my hands? I did nothing wrong," said Brad.

"Yes, you have. You should have spoken up earlier, because you could have prevented a death, and perhaps several more."

"Death? What are you going on about?"

The question was genuine, and the realisation collided into me like a runaway train. I kept the phone to my ear, while Brad repeated the question. It took me a while to answer.

"Shit," I heard myself say. "You don't know, do you?"

"Know what?" said Brad, irritably. "He's in with a drug trade. He funds money for the drugs to be concealed and shipped over here. That's all I know."

"Jesus," I said, "I thought you knew..."

"What happened last night? He met with a drug client, didn't he?"

"He did more than that, Brad."

I didn't need to go into the details. Brad had already worked it out.

He went quiet for a moment. I wasn't sure what haunted him more, the fact that his step-father was a killer, or the fact he could have put an end to it sooner. If I'd been in Brad's shoes, I would have done the right thing—but maybe that's easier said than done in hindsight.

"I didn't know! I swear!" said Brad, losing what was left of his calm. "I know that maybe I should have spoken up sooner about the drug funding, because yeah, it's bad, but I didn't know about anything else. Otherwise I would have done something."

"I'll be honest with you," I began, "I don't feel comfortable taking Nathan's money, and I'd much rather see him rot in prison, but I have no choice. I've got too much at stake."

"Look, I've got to go," said Brad and he ended the call.

I wasn't finished with him yet though, so I tried calling back. Cosmo answered.

"Put me back on the phone to Brad," I said.

"Can't," replied Cosmo. "He's already gone."

Damn it, but I guess it didn't matter though. Once again my morals were getting in the way of business, so I let it go and focused on the central issue.

"Have you got the money?" I asked.

"Yeah, he handed me the two briefcases. I haven't checked them yet, but when I get a moment to myself I will."

"Ditch the briefcases. They could be bugged," I said. "Just take the money, put it in another bag and then meet me back at the warehouse."

"No worries, see you then."

End call.

# 44

I'd never seen so much money in my life.

Cosmo and I had followed through with our arrangement, and now we were back at the warehouse, sitting on milk crates while staring at two million dollars in cash.

"Hey, if we took a couple of grand for ourselves," began Cosmo, "do you think Mal would notice?"

Already, Cosmo's greed was seeping through. It was not hard to understand how money changed people, but I was not even slightly tempted to help myself—to me, this money was just Rochelle's ticket to freedom.

"I reckon we could easily take five grand each. Mal would never know the difference."

"No," I said, firmly. "We're not taking any of it."

"Fuck Kennedy, I was only kidding around."

I didn't believe him. I could see the hunger in his eyes. Cosmo was staring at the money like a wild animal, just waiting to pounce on his prey at any given moment. Suddenly, I questioned my friend's loyalty. Had he helped himself to a few grand before handing the cash over to me? Was all the money really there? It wasn't something I would dare ask my friend, because showing my scepticism would only damage our friendship—and let's face it, in times like these, I needed friends.

"It's fuckin' stupid that we don't get a share for all we've done," began Cosmo, continuing on with his endless rant. "I mean, you and I did all the hard work..."

I tried to talk, but Cosmo wouldn't let me get a word in.

"Fuck, we should have upped our price when we blackmailed Nathan. You know, like sixty mil? Then we could have spilt ten between us—"

I cut him off.

"Don't lose sight of why we did this," I said, my words falling hard. "We are not criminals—just Mal's puppets on strings."

"Yeah, I guess," said Cosmo, bitterly. "But it still sucks that we've come out of this with nothing."

"I'll have Rochelle, safe and unharmed. That's enough for me."

"Yeah, *you* get something, but I don't."

He hit a nerve, but I gave myself a moment before responding.

"So you only assisted me for self gain? Didn't think you were that kind of person, Cosmo."

He clenched his teeth, said nothing. Sometimes I think Cosmo forgot just what was at stake. I know Rochelle didn't matter to him—why would she? But having her back was all that mattered to me. After a few awkward moments of silence, Cosmo apologised to me—something I don't think he did very often.

"So what are we going to do from here?" asked Cosmo, his voice low.

"Well, I don't think I'll last another night in this place, so I'm going to stay in a hotel nearby."

"Mal will find you."

"No, he won't. As long as I don't use my credit card, I'll be fine. Besides, Mal wouldn't dare do anything stupid while I have what he wants."

"Yeah, alright," replied Cosmo. "I might see Daph then and spend the night at her place."

"I thought you broke up with her?"

"Oh, I did. But Daph still loves having me as a casual fuck buddy."

"Charming," I said, but I only meant to think it.

Cosmo didn't hang around, we made plans to call and meet up tomorrow morning, and he left without delay. Once alone, I stuffed the cash into a sports bag and made my departure. For the first time in almost a month, I felt like I was in control. In the beginning I'd barely been able to keep it together, but I was stronger now. The last few weeks had challenged me, both physically and mentally, but now that I had survived, and the ending was in sight—I was positive that nothing would ever seem as hard.

***

Getting a hotel in Sydney without a reservation was not easy—at least, all the reasonably priced hotels that is.

All I wanted was a decent bed and a hot shower, but the first hotels I tried to check into were all full, so I decided to go all out and checked into one of the most prestigious Sydney hotels—The Harbour View Hotel. Luckily for me, they had a room—a deluxe executive suite.

I requested to pay with cash rather than my credit card—because I still didn't want Mal Lawson tracking me down—and they were happy for me to do so, just as long as I made a six hundred dollar deposit first. I reluctantly accepted, using the last bit of cash on me—excluding the two million of course, but I wouldn't dare touch that.

At long last, I took the elevator up to the sixth floor and found room 603. I had trouble with my key card at first, but then I realised the arrow on the card was pointing towards me, meaning I was inserting the card in the wrong way.

I blamed it on my tiredness.

Finally, I entered my room. The place was a masterpiece. The paintings on the wall were huge oil portraits of important-looking people from—at my guess—the eighteen hundreds. These portraits were equally spaced apart and no matter where I stood, they seemed to be staring at me. Maybe I was just losing my goddamn mind, but still, I would have preferred a nice scenery painting instead.

Staring at the bed and the rest of the furniture, I could tell they were expensive antiques. The duvet cover was maroon with gold stitching, and by first glance, it looked hand-sewn. There was not one single fold or crease either, which was just a little too eerily perfect for my taste.

It was damn obvious the hotel had gone for an old timey theme, but the flat screen TV embedded into the wall seemed to spoil it, but hey, I wasn't complaining.

224

I tossed my belongings down on the bed, and headed straight for the bathroom. All I wanted was a hot shower—because I couldn't even remember the last time I'd had one—and it was heavenly. After towelling off, I picked up a razor, but then stopped. I remembered that Rochelle liked me with a bit of stubble, so I figured I'd give shaving a miss for today.

Deciding to indulge in luxury while I had it, I slipped into a hotel robe and ordered up room service—pan-fried Atlantic salmon, and a nice cold beer. Dinner arrived within ten minutes, so I flicked on the TV. A movie was on—some kind of hostage thriller—and I found myself enthralled in the plotline. And yes, I certainly could relate to it.

As the film progressed, I helped myself to more beers from the mini bar. I decided to stop drinking for the night after the walls around me started spinning. And no, I was not comfort drinking, but I needed to relax. It had been a tense few weeks, so I didn't see the harm in unwinding.

I watched the film in its entirety, and as predicted, it was a happy ending. I liked it, and it reinforced my belief that no matter how bleak things seem, you could still overcome it. Sure, maybe I was only thinking this way because I was partially drunk and had succeeded in completing my objective—because I certainly didn't feel this way just two days ago.

It was almost midnight, and I could barely keep my eyes open. I had a big day ahead of me tomorrow and I was craving a decent night's sleep. I switched off the TV, ripped back the duvet, closed my eyes and allowed my mind to shut down.

At last, I would sleep well tonight.

# 45

*August 17th*

I awoke a little after eight-thirty that morning.

At last, I'd had a solid eight hours sleep. Although I had awoken with the expectation of feeling shady after so many drinks late last night—I felt fine. Better yet, I felt focused. Today Nathan would pay up the rest of what he owed me, and I'd made it perfectly clear that I would not allow any more extensions.

I kicked back the duvet and rose for the day. My mobile phone was resting on the end of the bed—just where I'd left it last night—and I switched it on. Just as I was getting dressed, seven missed call messages came through. Odd. I picked up my phone and checked it out. All the calls had been made from 3AM to 8AM this morning. I recognised the number too—Cosmo.

I rang him back, but before I could even greet him, Cosmo's mouth fired off like a torpedo,

"Why the fuck did you switch your phone off, Kennedy? I've been trying to call you all fuckin' night!"

Stunned by his hostility, I simply replied,

"I didn't want to be disturbed."

"Didn't want to be disturbed?" repeated Cosmo, his tone thick with aggression. "Well, we're royalty fucked now, aren't we? There's nowhere to go from here."

"Huh? What the hell are you talking about?"

"Jesus fuckin' Christ. Turn on the news, Kennedy."

Instantly, I felt something crawl up into my throat, and seconds after switching on the TV, I was sure I was going to be sick.

The news bar at the bottom of the screen read just three words—NATHAN BURWELL DEAD.

I stared. Said nothing. A hot shockwave pulsed through my veins, instantly weakening me. While I could comprehend what had happened, I refused to believe it. Something inside my chest had

226

imploded, and every fear and anxiety I'd tried to keep locked away had been released. Unknowingly, I'd sat down on the end of my bed and pulled the phone away from my ear. I wanted to switch off the TV, but I couldn't look away. The news anchor on the screen stood right outside the Channel 5 building, and he spoke into the camera showing no emotion whatsoever, while the mourners in the background fell to pieces.

I could faintly hear Cosmo's voice, continuing to shout at me from the mobile I held loosely in the palm of my hand, but I wouldn't even know what to say to him right now. In the past, a situation like this would usually trigger a breakdown, but today there was nothing—just an unbearable emptiness.

After a few minutes, I put the phone back to my ear, and found the strength to ask,

"Who killed him?"

"There's been no official word on it yet," replied Cosmo. "But from what's been said this morning, it's been alleged that he probably committed suicide."

The raw fact pierced me like a spear through the chest.

"How?" I asked, hands shaking, but I fought to keep them steady.

"Don't know yet," replied Cosmo. "But my guess is that he made a noose."

I quickly picked up the remote and switched it onto Channel 5—they were playing a memorial video for Nathan, no mention of a suicide. I flicked back to another channel and turned up the volume. I had to wait a few minutes, but soon enough, I got the answer I was looking for.

A red bar flashed across the screen reading; BREAKING NEWS. A female news anchor stood directly outside the Channel 5 headquarters door, microphone at the ready, and began to read off the auto-prompt,

"We can now confirm Mr. Burwell died inside his Sydney home by a self-inflicted gunshot to the head. It is understood that family members found him, and paramedics were called in at approximately two o'clock this morning. However, Mr. Burwell was pronounced dead at the scene. We will continue to follow this story and give you updates throughout the morning..."

I felt another implosion in my chest. Sheer panic ripped through my insides, and then the devastating realisation sank in—with Nathan Burwell dead, I would never get his money.

I spoke into my mobile once more, my voice thick with emotion.

"Where are you, Cosmo?"

"Parramatta," he replied. "I'll be in the city in a little over an hour."

"Call me when you get here," I said, and I ended the call.

I placed my mobile beside me, and focused my attention back to the TV. Within a matter of just three minutes, another breaking news bulletin came through.

"We have just heard from a reliable source that Mr. Burwell left a suicide message before taking his own life," said the news anchor. "Sources say Mr. Burwell typed a few short sentences on his computer, it allegedly read, 'You will never get my money. See you in hell, bastards.' This message will be investigated over the coming weeks."

I switched off the TV, because I couldn't take another second of it. The emptiness I'd felt was gone, and now I was filled with desperation, frustration, and the understanding that the life I once had was gone for good.

If Nathan Burwell did in fact leave that exact suicide message, then he'd hardly left it open for interpretation. People would rule out depression and insanity, and they would begin to speculate and assume Nathan was being blackmailed, and rather than paying up, he chose to end his life instead.

I had driven a man to kill himself—and that fact caused destruction in my mind.

I could not find the logic in Nathan's decision, or maybe it was because I just couldn't understand it. He was a highly paranoid man constantly surrounded by security—but what for? His security wasn't

228

enough to keep him from putting a bullet in his skull. And what about his family? Did protecting his reputation and fortune mean more to him?

My head began to throb. Why was I trying to justify the reasons for Nathan's suicide when I had so much more to worry about? I was supposed to be making an exchange with Mal Lawson today, but I didn't have the full sum of money. Would two million be enough? The possibility that it wouldn't be made my world stand still.

All my hard work, all the risks I had taken—they seemed like nothing now.

My mind flashed back to last night. I'd been so relaxed, so at ease—and now I felt guilty. I thought about the hostage film I'd watched last night. Nine out of ten times, Hollywood films had a happy ending, but I was living in reality, and not everything works out how it should.

I picked up my mobile again. Soon, I would have to call Mal Lawson and make a negotiation. I guessed it was my only option left, but I wouldn't call him yet. I would wait until Cosmo arrived, and delay the inevitable—even if it was only for an hour or so.

I stood from the bed, knees shaking, and tried to continue my morning routine as if nothing had happened, and I was able to pretend for about two minutes until the world caved in around me. I slipped down to the bathroom tiles, dug my fingernails into my forehead as my body convulsed with emotion. I prayed for divine intervention, although I knew it would never come.

# 46

I felt hollow.

I'd experienced a lot of pain in my twenty-seven years on earth, but today the pain felt different. I could remember when I first thought my younger sister Amy had died in the London Bombings—it was excruciating, all consuming and I was sure nothing would ever match up to that moment, but now I couldn't be sure. Maybe because it was such a long time ago now—and the memory had faded—or perhaps the anguish seemed less because Amy had survived the blast. Either way, it didn't really matter, because I was sure today's grief would conquer above all the other sorrows I'd experienced in my life.

After half an hour, I found my feet and stood up. I approached the bathroom sink, turned on the taps, and splashed water on my face. Did it make me feel better? Not really. For a moment I considered doing something to keep my mind occupied—like having breakfast—but the very thought of food was enough to make me gag.

I splashed water on my face again, and then studied my reflection in the mirror. I looked unwell, but it was to be expected. My eyes were dark, my complexion was pale and I was evidently exhausted. I then began to study my scars—the one above my eyebrow was a result of the London Bombings. Something had struck me in the explosion, leaving me with a deep gash. The scar had faded considerably compared to what it once was, but the mark was still there. I then removed my shirt, curious to study the rest of my past injuries. On my shoulder blade, there was a stab wound—a result of an illicit drug trade gone wrong. The scar was, for lack of better words, revolting. I had been stubborn and I'd refused to see a professional, so Rochelle had mended the wound herself. I then put a hand over my shoulder and felt a second scar, a consequence of a bar brawl early last year. And finally, I turned around and faced my back to the mirror, looking over my shoulder I gazed upon the bullet wound, courtesy of a man named Beau O' Riley. He'd shot me in the back—nearly killed me—yet I was still standing.

My body had been through a lot, but every man had a limit, and soon I would reach mine. In fact, I'd come so close to death in the past that I felt like I was already on borrowed time. Did I deserve to be here? Or should I have fallen long ago? On reflection, my survival had been pure luck, and like every gambler on a winning streak, soon it could all come to an end.

I heard my mobile ring. Fear hit me like a punch to the gut, but I composed myself, exited the bathroom and answered the call.

"Kennedy, where are you?" asked Cosmo, skipping the pleasantries.

I told him the hotel name, the street it was on and my room number.

"I'll be there in ten."

End call. I tossed the phone back down, put my shirt back on and waited. Once again I found myself in deep thought, wishing I could turn back time. What if I had told the police of my predicament? What if I had asked others to help? Would I be in this situation right now? Enough. There was no point pondering what could have been. I would have to accept reality, regardless of how unbearable it was.

There was a knock on the door, and I was thankful it interrupted my train of thought. I quickly crossed the room, opened up the door and let Cosmo in. Unlike me, Cosmo looked calm and focused. He had recovered from the initial shock, and goddamn it I wished I could too.

"Called Mal yet?" he asked.

"Just about to," I said, picking up my mobile once again.

I sat down on the bed, while Cosmo stood by the door, arms crossed. I began dialling in Mal's number. Yesterday I'd felt so much power, so much control—but once again he had the authority above me. I hated being in this position, but there was nothing left for me to do.

I put the phone to my ear, and listened to the phone ring. Eventually, somebody picked up, but no words were spoken.

"Hello, Mal?" I said, my voice almost sounding like a desperate plea. "It's Jordan Kennedy."

Still no answer.

"I want to negotiate with you. Just as we discussed yesterday."

"As we discussed yesterday," hissed Mal, his voice cutting through like a sword, "you said you would be meeting up with Nathan Burwell today. Do you recall that, Mr. Kennedy?"

"Yes—"

"—But I'm curious, Mr. Kennedy. How do you plan to meet with Nathan Burwell when he's dead?"

My composure collapsed. I had tried to maintain my façade, but my weakness seeped through.

"I didn't know it was going to happen!" I gasped. "I did all I could!"

"And yet you were still unsuccessful in getting me what I wanted."

"I have two million," I said, trying to bargain with him. "I've got it in cash, and I've got it right here. We can still meet up today and make an exchange."

"Two? Just two, Mr. Kennedy? What was the agreed amount?"

"I know, but—"

"Do you really think it's enough? It doesn't even come close," he snarled. "Twelve men invested five hundred thousand *each* into this project. Do the math, and that's six million. Some of it went towards technology, weapons, ammo, accommodation and a car. The rest of the money went to Bruno Samuel, the man who originally signed on to complete the project, and he requested to be paid in advance. I'm at a loss, Mr. Kennedy."

"But surely you'd rather have something than nothing at all. We can still make an exchange."

"No, we can't. Two million isn't going to cover it."

My hands were shaking. My mind was racing.

"I did everything you told me," I said, adrenaline pulsing through my veins. "I tried my hardest, and worked myself down to the bone—"

"—No, Mr. Kennedy. You cannot justify your failure," he barked, and then he said the only two words I didn't want to hear. "She dies."

The statement made my blood run cold, but anger quickly surfaced.

"Don't you dare threaten Rochelle!" I shouted, fury pulsing through me. "This shit is between you and me now. You will let my girlfriend go free."

"Do you think I feel any remorse for you? Any sympathy? Of course not."

And then I said something foolish. Something I shouldn't have said, because I planted a seed in Mal's mind, and that seed grew into something sinister.

"You will not harm her," I hissed, without giving it a second thought. "If you dare touch Rochelle, then trust me, you will regret it."

Mal was silent for a long time, and then I heard his voice again—but he wasn't talking to me. Somebody else was with him, listening in to our conversation.

"Did you fucking hear me?" I shouted, unable to control my rage.

"Mr. Kennedy, do you think she's still alive? After all this time?" asked Mal, and as he said it, I could picture a smile on his filthy face. "Do you truly believe I've kept up my end of the bargain?"

I fell silent for a moment. I had not seen nor spoken to Rochelle in over three weeks, and while the thought had entered my mind a few times, I had refused to believe it. My whole body now trembling, I made a demand.

"Just let me talk to Rochelle," I said, as calmly as possible. "Right now."

He laughed. I felt a chill across the back of my neck. I heard Mal talk to the voice in the background again, and then there was a click noise—a sound I was now very familiar with. I repeated my demand, my voice cracking.

"I'm sorry. Rochelle is not able to talk to you at the moment," said Mal, matter-of-factly. "At the present time she has a gun barrel down her throat."

"No!" I screamed. "Please! Don't!"

He laughed. Panic seized me. I begged for mercy.

"I truly wish you could be here to witness this, Mr. Kennedy. It just doesn't have the same effect over the phone."

"Please!" I shouted, barely able to get the word out.

There was silence for a second, followed by a gunshot. And then I heard a scream. Her scream.

"No! Stop!"

Mal erupted into laughter, and every time he tried to talk, he laughed again. I continued to scream at him. Whatever pain I'd felt in the past was nothing compared to this.

"Mr. Kennedy," said Mal, after almost a minute. "There's no need to be alarmed. It was a stray bullet. I pulled the gun from her mouth and fired a bullet just above her head, but she certainly is easy to frighten."

The relief swept over me like a tidal wave, but it quickly vanished and all that was left was a storm of utter animosity.

"I'm going to kill you!" I shouted.

He laughed again. It infuriated me knowing that I was entertaining him, so I clasped my mouth shut, and tried to think of a new way to make a negotiation. However, Mal was not interested in striking a deal, his plans were set in stone.

"She'll live for the time being," said Mal, "but Rochelle will continue to suffer, until she finally begs for death. However, I will happily make it quick and as painless as possible, but first you'll have to give yourself up. I'll give you a few days to think about it."

"You can have me right now," I said, with no hesitation, "but Rochelle must go free."

234

"Not going to work like that, Mr. Kennedy."

"She's done nothing wrong! Jesus Christ, why punish her too?"

Mal evaded my question.

"Three days, that's all you have. If I don't hear from you, she'll die, and the pain will be severe. Then again even if you choose to hide, rest assured I will find you. It might take me months, even years, but I will find you. Just know that, Mr. Kennedy."

Before I could reply, he hung up. The line died. My hopes did too.

My face found the palms of my hands, and I felt my head fall forward. I gritted my teeth, feeling a sensation of agony tear inside my chest and through the chambers of my heart. A firm hand was placed on my shoulder. Cosmo. I'd almost forgotten he was with me.

"Hey, what the hell happened?" he asked, but I suspected he had an idea.

I had no words. I almost felt like I was choking on them.

"Look, just stay here for a bit," said Cosmo, removing his grip and taking a step back. "I'm going to go out and see what I can do."

"Can't stay here," I said, not caring to look up. "Check out is at eleven."

Cosmo pulled a set of keys out from his pocket, and dangled them in front of me.

"Then go to my apartment. You'll be safe there for a few hours, and then we'll find another place to stay."

At last, I looked up.

"Never been to your apartment. I don't know where it is," I said, my voice hoarse.

"401 Kendall Road, Parramatta," replied Cosmo. "You'll see a coffee shop out the front, and there's a staircase on the right hand side of the building. My apartment is at the top of the staircase. Can't miss it."

I hesitated, but eventually I took the keys. Cosmo departed without another word to say and I was left on my own. I slid to the floor, feeling my face fall into my hands. I so desperately wanted to stand up, but the fight in me was gone—something I was ashamed to admit. Rochelle's terrified scream was still ringing in my ears. I tried to drown it out with other thoughts, but it was impossible. I knew that scream would stay with me forever.

# 47

I checked out of the hotel a little after ten o'clock.

In the lobby, the television was playing in the background, and all I could hear was Nathan Burwell's name. I had to get out of here. I couldn't tolerate another second of it.

I paid for my overnight stay, reclaimed what was left of my deposit and headed to the exit. As I walked out of the hotel, I spotted two police officers standing out the front. I panicked. Why were they here?

I kept my head down and walked in the opposite direction, feeling an instant adrenaline hit. Did these coppers suspect me? Had they been tipped off? Then I remembered about the money. The sports bag in my right hand had two million dollars inside—and if these police officers stopped me and asked to inspect my belongings, then I'd be in deep shit.

I had to get out of here. Quickly. I picked up the pace and almost ran to the taxi bay. A taxi was waiting there. I slipped into the backseat.

"Where to?" asked the driver.

I gave him the address—Cosmo's apartment. By luck, the driver didn't hang about. He pulled away from the curb and we drove off. As the city faded in the distance, I felt more at ease, but I couldn't relax just yet. Why had there been police right outside my hotel? Had it been a coincidence, or had somebody heard me screaming at Mal Lawson over the phone? I couldn't be sure. Nathan Burwell's suicide had come as a shock—especially to me—but nobody could ever know I'd been the one to rattle his cage. My actions had been enough to tip him over the edge, and that was a secret I would take to the grave.

Soon enough, I arrived at my destination. I had never been to Cosmo's apartment before, but then again, he'd never invited me over anyway. I paid the driver with my credit card—yeah, I didn't give a damn if Mal tracked me down anymore. Besides, I'd rather confront him, and my anger was so raw that I felt like I'd be able to match up to him anyway.

I pushed open the taxi door, climbed out and followed Cosmo's instructions—up the staircase and to the door at the very top. I tried the keys that Cosmo had given to me and unlocked the door. As I stepped inside, I had expected a mess, but it was far beyond that.

Cosmo had an apartment so compact and cluttered that I could barely even move without bumping into something. I guess that was to be expected considering it was a studio apartment located above a coffee shop, but the space had not been utilised to its potential at all. There was—for lack of better words—shit everywhere. A dirty, dark green sofa almost blocked the door, and there was a table right in front of the sofa, completely covered in junk. On closer inspection, the junk consisted of a collection of novelty shaped bongs, and piles of hardcore porno magazines. To the left of me, was a double bed, unmade of course, and it looked like the sheets hadn't been changed in—years. Did Cosmo bring his girlfriends here? I hoped not. I felt filthy just standing in the goddamn room.

For a moment I thought about sitting down—but where? And through my vexation, I fought back the urge to breakdown. I shouldn't be here. I should be meeting with Mal Lawson, accepting my fate, but instead I was hiding alone in a cramped apartment. The weight on my shoulders was crushing me—how much more could one man take? I needed help. I needed advice. In a moment of utter weakness, I pulled out my mobile phone and began dialling. It took a while for the call to go through, but eventually, somebody picked up—my dad.

"Hello?" said the voice of my father, Harry Kennedy.

Right then, I wanted to crack, but for the sake of my sanity, I held myself together.

"Hey dad," I said, forcing the words through.

"Jordan? What's wrong?"

He could already tell, and my disguise of equanimity was immediately torn away, just like a superhero that had finally been unmasked. Goddamn it, I thought I was past this. I thought I could control my emotions—but I guess not. I cried. Hard. Harry kept trying to calm me down, pressing for an explanation, but how could I tell him? Where would I even begin? In a moment of absolute clarity, I recognised that very few people could ever be fully trusted—but I could always trust my own father.

So I told him. Everything. And the moment I did, it felt like the pressure across my chest had finally been released. I told him of my current situation, and all I'd done to get here. I told him of my despicable behaviour and my law-breaking antics. I'd become so deeply involved that I'd almost lost myself, and now I felt as if I'd fallen back to square one. Why hadn't I been better? Why hadn't I tried harder? Again, this was easy to say in hindsight, but it didn't relieve the pain.

And when I'd finished telling him of my predicament, Harry didn't say anything for a while. That didn't matter to me though, because I'd only wanted him to listen. My father was good like that. He understood that sometimes people just needed to talk out their problems, and best of all he always tried to offer his advice—but today, I doubted his advice would help.

"Call the police," said Harry, his tone firm, but fair.

"Can't do that, dad. These men will kill Rochelle on the spot."

"By the sounds of things, these men plan to kill her anyway."

I didn't want him to say it, but I knew he was right. This was not a win-win situation. No matter what I did, it seemed as if Rochelle's death warrant had already been signed. However, regardless of that fact, I would continue to deny it for as long as I could.

"You need to hang up the phone right now, and call the police," said Harry.

In due time, I would, but right now I didn't want to end the call. I was sure this was the last conversation I'd ever have with my father. Unfortunately, fate cut my time short. The landline phone rang, and in between the clutter, I spotted a portable phone lying on the coffee table. At first, I let it ring—figuring it would be for

Cosmo—but in a split second decision, I said goodbye to my dad and answered the other call.

"Hello?" I said, bringing the phone to my ear.

"Kennedy, meet me at 17 Westwood Way, Bankstown," said Cosmo, his tone sounding solid and heavy. "I'll be waiting for you at the basement level car park at eight o'clock tonight."

"Why? What's happened?"

"Don't ask questions," he said, just before hanging up. "I'll explain why once you get here."

*\*\**

*Earlier that afternoon...*

He arrived unannounced, but Cosmo was not afraid.

With no hesitations, he had driven out to Arcadia to meet with Mal Lawson in his current hideaway, hoping to reach some kind of agreement.

Cosmo kicked open the driver's side door, jumped out of the car and headed to the front door. He was without his weapon—perhaps not the wisest move—but Cosmo knew Mal wouldn't kill him. After everything that had transpired, they had built up mutual respect for one another.

But even if Mal did point a gun at Cosmo, would it really matter? Cosmo figured he had nothing to lose—except maybe his friendship with Jordan Kennedy—but he was replaceable. People come and go. Very few friends stick around for the long haul.

Despite that fact, Cosmo wasn't ready to dust his hands yet.

Just metres away from the house, the front door opened up and a familiar face appeared—Isaac Fuller.

"You must have some nerve to turn up here without an invitation," said Isaac, his mouth barely moving as he spoke.

"Where's Mal?" asked Cosmo, cutting to the chase. "We need to sort some shit out."

Isaac turned around, walked back inside, but left the door open. Cosmo followed. He was led down a hallway and to the closed door at the end of the room. Isaac knocked twice, pushed open the door, and stepped inside.

"Mal, you have a visitor," said Isaac, staring into the darkened room.

Cosmo didn't wait for a formal invitation; instead he pushed past Isaac and stepped inside to find Mal Lawson sitting at the end of a table, working on a laptop.

"Well, this certainly is a surprise," said Mal, not looking up from his laptop. "What brings you here, Mr. Rowland?"

"Thought maybe we could start the negotiations," said Cosmo, crossing his arms. "How about you leave Kennedy's girlfriend out of this and let her go? I know you've been making threats and shit, but you don't want her blood on your hands. Trust me."

At last, Mal looked up.

"Isaac, you can go now," said Mal after some time. "I wish to talk with Mr. Rowland alone."

Isaac nodded, and stepped out of the room without delay. Mal closed the laptop down, pushed it aside, gained eye contact with Cosmo and simply said,

"Mr. Rowland, I expected better of you."

"What the fuck do you mean?"

"You arrived here just moments ago, unannounced, and then you use coercive tactics to pressure me into making a move that is completely illogical."

"Bullshit," hissed Cosmo, risking a few steps closer. "As far as I'm concerned, it makes no sense to kill the innocent."

"Nobody's ever truly innocent. We all have demons."

Cosmo knew he was in an argument he couldn't possibly win. Mal had made up his mind, forcing Cosmo into a stalemate. This was Cosmo's opportunity to turn around and leave, but to save face, he would stay and fight until the end.

"I must ask you," began Mal, leaning forward in his chair. "If Jordan had succeeded in paying up the full amount, did you think I'd follow through with my part of the deal and reunite Jordan with his girlfriend? Did you really think I'd let them walk free?"

Cosmo stared.

"Think about it. Regardless of the outcome, their fate was set in stone—they would be killed."

The thought had entered Cosmo's mind a few times, but he'd never admit it.

"You're not a very honest bloke, Mal."

"And neither are you."

Cosmo smirked and thought about debating it, but again, he would lose.

"I'm glad you're here though," continued Mal, tenting his fingers together. "Please, take a seat. I have a proposition for you, Mr. Rowland."

"Yeah? Like what?"

Mal gestured for Cosmo to take a seat. He remained standing. Mal just maintained his smile, leaned back in his chair and said,

"I'd like to offer you a job, Mr. Rowland."

"What? Working for you? Not likely, mate."

"Just hear me out. I think you'll find the salary quite generous."

Cosmo should have left when he had the chance. Better yet, maybe he shouldn't have come at all. What else could he do? He was powerless.

"My situation has changed," began Mal, losing eye contact momentarily. "Now that Jordan Kennedy has failed to pay up the agreed sum, I too, have failed. I am a target now. The men I used to do business with want nothing more than to spill my blood."

"So what, you want me to be your bodyguard?"

"No, that's Isaac's duty," replied Mal, smiling again. "What I need, is for somebody to help me eliminate the enemy."

"When you say eliminate, do you mean—?"

"Kill them? Yes."

Cosmo laughed, but he was not amused.

"You're asking me to be your hit-man?"

"Yes, I am," replied Mal. "I have seen your potential."

Again, Cosmo laughed.

"Well, I'd love to help you, Mal, but then I remembered you're a fuckin' douchebag."

Mal wasn't going to take no for an answer. He knew Cosmo was perfect for the job, and more so, he was easily persuaded by money. Mal would mould him into his weapon.

"Mr. Rowland, I am a very wealthy man. I own an apartment overlooking Bondi beach, and another two properties up in Cairns—so why do you think I'm renting out this isolated, run-down house in the middle of Arcadia? For the views? For the location? No. I am being hunted, and I don't want to spend the rest of my days in hiding."

"Yeah, I sympathise, but I've already told you I'm not interested."

"Don't say no just yet," said Mal, rising from his seat. "You haven't heard what I'm willing to offer you."

Money. His weakness. Cosmo was always out of pocket, and whenever he had money, his sex and drug addictions proved to be quite costly. Besides, now that Cosmo was without a job, with rent and debt to pay, money was almost impossible to pass up.

His words feeling like razor wire as he said them, Cosmo forced himself to ask,

"How much money are we talking here, Mal?"

"Ten thousand for each hit," he replied, and added, "and rest assured there are a lot of people out there needing bullets through the skull."

"Yeah? Like who?"

"Well, at the present time Jordan Kennedy is at the top of my list," said Mal, grinning ear to ear. "I need somebody to bring him down. Somebody that knows where to find him."

Cosmo stared. Unable to talk.

"Do you think you're capable of such a task, Mr. Rowland?"

"Fuck you," snarled Cosmo, unable to disguise his disgust.

"The job offer is there, but first we need to establish loyalty. Take out Jordan Kennedy first, and then we'll talk business."

His head was spinning. For reasons he could not fathom, Cosmo was second guessing himself. He had come here in the hopes of reasoning with the enemy, and yet the situation had changed. Cosmo wanted to walk away, forget what he had been offered, but it wasn't possible anymore.

"Why the apprehension, Mr. Rowland?" asked Mal, now circling him.

"Are you fuckin' serious? You ask a man to knock off his mate, and you expect him to do it without a second thought? Don't be fuckin' ridiculous."

"It's actually very simple. You take the shot, and you'll be rewarded. If you don't, then you're at a loss no matter which way you look at it."

"Look, I'll rough somebody up without any regrets, but I don't kill."

"Lies," hissed Mal. "I know your history, Mr. Rowland. Or have you forgotten about Ian Strafford?"

The name. The name Cosmo thought was dead and buried, but alas, it had resurfaced.

"What the fuck did you just say?"

"Ian Strafford," said Mal, almost smiling.

"How the hell did you know—?"

"We've already been through this, Mr. Rowland. I have resources. I have connections. That's all I need to learn everything about you."

Ian Strafford. Cosmo's first and last encounter with him had happened a little over eight years ago. Being seventeen at the time, Cosmo had a tendency to act first, think later—which usually landed him in hot water. Thinking back to the moment, Cosmo recalled the day he and his friends had spent a hot summer's day at the beach—surfing, hitting on bikini-clad chicks, the usual—but the day was ruined when they crossed Ian Strafford. He had been a local kid, but Cosmo didn't know that at the time, hell, he didn't even know his name. Ian was a stranger, and perhaps that's the way it should have stayed, but every action has a consequence.

Ian was a few years older than Cosmo, built like a tank, and guarded his territory like a bloody Rottweiler. Ian was convinced the beach was his terrain, and was constantly causing minor turf wars. Unfortunately, Ian had seen Cosmo and his friends as outsiders, and wanted them gone.

Cosmo reminisced and remembered the moment when Ian had first approached Cosmo and his group of friends. They had been sitting on a sand dune, watching the sun set over the headland, keeping to themselves until Ian intervened. First it started with talking shit, Ian demanding they leave and 'fuck off home to the suburbs.' As the minutes passed, the argument intensified. In the beginning Cosmo had been a spectator. He had wanted to take action, stand his ground, but there was still an element of fear. Ian was bigger and probably stronger, so who in their right mind would dare take him on? Jimmy Richmond—Cosmo's friend—decided he would.

Jimmy had stood up, beckoned Ian closer, trying to intimidate. As predicted, Ian snapped and let his fury break loose. He and Jimmy began to brawl. The rest of Cosmo's friends backed away, preparing to run—which would have been the wise thing to do—but Cosmo stepped forward and decided to help out his friend. Was it honourable? Yes. Was it smart? No. Cosmo had wanted to take a hit at Ian, but before he had the chance, Jimmy had pulled out a knife. He'd tried to take a stab, but Ian had clasped his hands around Jimmy's wrist, forcing the knife back. The weapon was then dropped onto the sand. Jimmy and Ian wrestled for a moment, but Cosmo took the opportunity to grab the knife. That was his first mistake. Within seconds, Ian had successfully knocked Jimmy to the ground, leaving Cosmo as the next target.

Ian ran at Cosmo. He was charging at him with no signs of stopping, and well, survival mode kicked in. Cosmo was about to be attacked, and he was the one with the weapon. Without a second thought, Cosmo jabbed the knife right through Ian Strafford's chest.

At first, there was nothing. It took a while for Cosmo to realise what he had done.

Cosmo only comprehended the gravity of his actions as Ian Strafford's blood began to ooze over his hands. He had stabbed a guy, through the chest, and he was dying. Some of his friends fled, only a few stayed behind. Somebody called an ambulance, but they didn't get there in time, and Ian was pronounced dead at the scene.

At the age of only seventeen, Cosmo had taken a life.

He carried many regrets, but Cosmo regarded Ian Strafford's fate as his biggest regret. The ghosts of the past still haunted him, and he'd tried to drown them out with alcohol, drugs and women, but the memory had forever been imprinted on his conscience.

And what was the consequence of Cosmo's actions? Well, nothing really. When the police questioned Jimmy Richmond, he had lied and twisted the story. He claimed Ian had pulled out the knife, and that Cosmo had only stabbed him in self-defence. Cosmo had then run with Jimmy's versions of events, his friends likewise. There were lengthy court proceedings and police interviews to follow, but Cosmo had gotten off scot-free, and that bothered him. On reflection, Cosmo wished he'd been locked up for that crime, because from that point on his life was a landslide. He got involved with the wrong crowds and pushed the boundaries—just to see how far they could be pushed. Eventually, Cosmo had landed himself jail time for assisting a robbery and carrying an unlicensed weapon—but a couple of years in prison seemed like nothing in the grand scheme of things. Maybe if he'd been put in his place at a younger age, things would have been different.

Cosmo wished he could take it back, but the past stays with you forever.

"You killed him," continued Mal, each word like a dagger. "So don't tell me that you don't have what it takes, because you do, Mr. Rowland. This is nothing new."

Cosmo said nothing. Old wounds had been ripped open, and the memories were agonising.

"Still unsure, Mr. Rowland? Then how about I sweeten the deal?" said Mal, now just inches away from Cosmo. "Fifty thousand for Jordan Kennedy. That's more than he's worth."

"He's been a friend to me," said Cosmo, mentally weighing up the pros and cons.

"A friend? Hardly. Jordan pulled you into this."

"No, he didn't. You did."

"Nonsense. You wouldn't have ever met me if it weren't for Jordan. He told you about me. He told you what I'd done, and then he begged you to help him."

Cosmo considered that, and it was true.

"Meet with him. Tonight," urged Mal.

"Can't do it. Not a mate. Regardless of all the shit he dragged me in, I won't knock him off."

"He has taken you for granted, Mr. Rowland. He's a liability. Dispose of him."

Cosmo could barely think straight.

"You need to make a decision right now," hissed Mal, placing a hard hand on Cosmo's shoulder. "Otherwise, forget the job offer."

The very thought of passing up the offer was enough to make Cosmo change his mind. He needed money more than he needed a friendship. Screw Kennedy. For once, Cosmo would watch his own back.

"Then I want to be paid in advance," said Cosmo. "You need to prove your loyalty to me too, and only then will I kill Kennedy."

"Of course. I can have the cash ready for you within the hour," replied Mal, smiling.

Something deep within burned through Cosmo's chest. Was it guilt? Or regret? Either way it didn't matter, because Cosmo would disregard his trepidation and focus on his reward. Money. That's all that mattered right now.

"17 Westwood Way, Bankstown," said Mal, grabbing Cosmo's attention once more. "Call Jordan and tell him to meet you there at the basement level car park at eight o'clock tonight. Take the shot, then leave. Don't worry about the clean up duty. I'll make it somebody else's concern."

Cosmo nodded, and not a moment later, Mal pulled a gun from his jacket and placed it on the table. He slid it towards Cosmo. He picked it up and studied the weapon's features. It appeared to be a semi-automatic handgun, with an easy-load magazine chamber. It would do its job.

"If I can be honest," said Mal, "I must confess I don't use guns much, but this one is a favourite of mine."

Cosmo nodded, and asked for a new gun magazine. Mal provided him with one, and then began to explain some of the gun's characteristics, but Cosmo cut him off.

"I don't need a lesson," said Cosmo, loading in the fresh magazine. "I already know how to use it."

# 48

Just before eight o'clock, I arrived at the agreed meeting point.

Rather than wasting another small fortune catching a taxi, I caught a bus into Bankstown. Luckily for me, my stop was close to my destination. I found 17 Westwood Way, Bankstown with no trouble—but why had Cosmo asked me to meet him here? Perhaps there was a valid reason, but for now, I couldn't see it.

I strolled up to the unit, noticing all the lights were off, and even the car park looked closed up for the night. So how was I supposed to meet Cosmo at the basement level? Then I noticed the fire exit—it had been pried open a little bit.

I investigated, pulling the door ajar and peeking inside. There was a dim light and a staircase leading down. Figuring it must've been the way into the car park, I tugged open the door a little more and slipped inside. I stepped down the staircase, following it to the very bottom.

There, in the darkened distance, I saw Cosmo.

He was standing alone in the abandoned car park, head hung lowly, not caring to acknowledge me, although he was aware of my presence. Something was not right. I began to walk over to him. Still no reaction.

The air seemed colder tonight, but I guess considering we were standing on the basement level, it was to be expected. Finally, I had crossed the car park and was now standing a few metres away. At last, Cosmo looked up.

He reeked of alcohol—probably drunk. His eyes were blood-shot—probably stoned. I didn't like dealing with Cosmo when he was in this state, but it seemed like this meeting had been urgent, so I looked beyond it and asked,

"What's happened, Cosmo?"

"It's not good news, Kennedy," he replied, putting my world in a stand still. "I thought you should see it for yourself."

My immediate thought—Rochelle. Maybe I was too late. Maybe I should've given myself up when I'd had the chance. I waited for Cosmo to say more, but he had fallen silent. What the hell was going on? I demanded answers.

"What is it?" I asked, the desperation cracking through my voice.

Cosmo raised his arm and pointed in the distance to the left. I turned my head. It was too dark to see anything.

"Over there," said Cosmo, still staring off into the distance. "She's over there."

She. That one word made the world collapse around me. I didn't need to hear anymore—I just began to run. Cosmo too. I could hear his footsteps behind me.

Earlier this morning, I felt like every scrap of energy had been torn out of me, but now I was running so hard my feet barely touched the floor. And then, I came to a sudden stop. I'd reached the other end of the car park, and there was nothing.

I no longer heard Cosmo's footsteps behind me. He had stopped too. Before I had the chance to turn around, I heard a click—a sound I was all too familiar with.

I turned my head over my shoulder, and confirmed what I had feared—Cosmo had pulled out a gun, and he was aiming it directly at me.

At first, confusion dominated above all other emotions.

"Cosmo," I said, struggling to put words together. "What are—?"

"Turn around," he snapped, both hands now clasped around his weapon.

The realisation came quickly—once again I had been played as a fool.

His shady behaviour had been far from normal, but at least now I knew why. Cosmo had deliberately made it seem as if something had happened to my girlfriend, and he'd played on my emotions for his own advantage. However, there was still something I failed to understand. I completely comprehended the fact that I was being held at gunpoint, but I couldn't work out why Cosmo was the one aiming the weapon.

Over the last few weeks, I had depended on him. Without Cosmo's assistance, I may not have made it this far. I'd called him a friend—so why the hell was he doing this? I should have been afraid. I should have tried to run, or at least, tried to negotiate with him, but instead, I just wanted answers.

"What's brought this on?" I asked, while gazing down the barrel of the gun.

Cosmo said nothing, and took a step closer, closing the gap between us.

He wasn't backing down. Even with drugs and booze swarming his system—Cosmo was focused. He would shoot me dead, with no remorse. I quickly began to make assumptions, and put the pieces together—somebody had manipulated his mind, and had successfully persuaded him to kill. Who had put him up to it? I still wasn't sure. I had more enemies than I cared to keep track of, but I knew Cosmo was not acting on his own instinct. By my guess, he had probably been bribed. When money came into the equation, he was easy to corrupt.

Suddenly, I had an impulsive urge to put my hands out in front of me. I raised my palms. As long as I seemed non-threatening, maybe Cosmo would lower his weapon. For a moment I considered running, but any sudden movements could set him off—it was just like the animal kingdom. Humans are no different.

I felt more in control of the situation by every minute. Considering Cosmo had not taken a shot yet, I figured he was still a little apprehensive. Good. I could work with it.

"How long have you been planning to betray me?" I asked, my voice steady and concise.

"I never fuckin' wanted any of this," he barked. "You dragged me into this shit."

"Then I'm sorry," I said, my confidence building with every second, "but as I recall, you agreed to help me."

"Yeah, and do you know what happened? Fuckin' Mal and Isaac tracked me down and held a gun to my head, and that's all because of you."

Mal. More pieces came together. I hadn't realised it until now, but Mal had used Cosmo as his puppet. I should have noticed it earlier, but I was so focused on what I wanted to achieve, that I had been led blindly.

"I had to watch over you," continued Cosmo. "They gave me no choice."

"And this?" I said, gesturing towards the gun. "Do you really have no choice?"

He smirked, took another step closer. I took a step back.

"This is how it's going down, Kennedy," he hissed, aiming the gun a little higher.

"But you're not like them." I said. "You're better than this."

"Just turn the fuck around! Now!"

I knew why he wanted me to turn my back. It was easier on him, because that way, he wouldn't have to watch my face as I died. I wasn't going to give him the courtesy.

"No. If you're going to pull the trigger, then I want you to witness my death," I said sternly. "I want you to remember it for the rest of your life."

"Jesus Christ," he said, his voice cracking slightly. "Turn around!"

"I don't know what they've said to you," I began, daring to take a step closer, "but they've planted a seed."

"You don't know shit."

"I know you're my friend, and up until now, I trusted you with my life."

Without warning, his fuse snapped. Cosmo advanced towards me. He kept the gun steady. My confidence crumbled as fear consumed me.

There was no space between us anymore. Cosmo was right in front of me. With no place to run, I dropped to my knees. It seemed like instinct, but now I felt like I was pleading for my life—and maybe I was. I kept my hands in front of my head, trying to protect myself as Cosmo stood over me, his gun still aimed at me.

Just moments ago I'd felt like I had the upper hand, but my ignorance had once again led me into a false sense of security—and now I would pay for it with my life.

There was only one option left, but before I had the chance to beg for mercy, Cosmo shot out his arm and jammed the gun on top of my head. The action had been so quick, and so fierce; the gun muzzle had broken through my skin. I felt blood ooze from the wound, trickling down my scalp. In a matter of seconds, my head began to spin and I fought to stay conscious.

"Please! Stop!" I heard myself say, but my voice sounded distant.

Cosmo kept the gun in place, but he was hesitating.

"Cosmo! Don't!"

My valiant attempt to survive had been wasted, as my words had no impact. Cosmo had made his decision. He would not let me live. I felt the gun slowly slide down my head, until the muzzle was nearly between my eyes.

And then he pulled the trigger.

When you weigh up the probability, there was no way the shot would miss. He was in close range, the gun barrel practically embedded into my forehead. The bullet would go through my skull and pierce my brain, or maybe my head would just explode into masses of blood and flesh. Either way, I wouldn't survive. The shot would kill me instantly.

But Cosmo had pulled the trigger, and I was still breathing.

I risked a glance up. His face confirmed it—the magazine had jammed. Something neither of us had expected. After the initial moment of shock, Cosmo pulled the gun away from my head and didn't care to correct the problem—instead he threw the gun across the car park as his composure crumbled.

Cosmo turned away from me, dug his fingernails into his skull and screamed out a string of profanities. I remained where I was, still on my knees, unsure if I should take the opportunity to run. I made a split second decision and stayed. Cosmo was without his gun and no longer posed as a threat. It would have taken Cosmo only a few seconds to correct the magazine jam, but he'd chosen to disarm himself.

For a moment, I continued to watch Cosmo, and it was like he had lost his mind. At first he'd stomped around the car park like a two-year-old having a tantrum, but now he was punching a cement pillar. Hard. Cosmo was on the verge of self-destruction, but after what had just happened, I wasn't sure I could help him.

The perplexity of the situation had faded, and now all that was left was sheer anger. I wanted so much to even the score—hurt that bastard, and then I'd call it even—but I figured we'd both suffered enough, and as the time passed, Cosmo was able to regain control of his rage.

Cautious with each step, Cosmo walked back to where I was. Both hands were shaking by his sides as he approached, but I was not afraid. He stood now just inches from me, and he extended his hand. I grabbed it, and he pulled me up from the ground. Now that I was on my feet, my head spun and the world rotated around me. I managed to stay standing.

At first he was reluctant, but Cosmo found the strength to make eye contact with me. For a brief second I thought Cosmo was going to apologise, but then he stopped himself, because we both knew it would never be enough.

Disgraced with what he had done, Cosmo moved away, finding comfort in the darkness. I started to walk away. Cosmo started talking.

"121 Banksia Road, Arcadia," he said, his voice barely audible. "Rochelle's there. They've got her locked up in the second last room along the main corridor."

My heart stopped momentarily, feeling an adrenaline hit rise from within.

"Have you seen her?" I asked, with all urgency. "Is she alright?"

"Don't know," replied Cosmo, turning his back on me. "But you'd better go."

I'd already started running. I was without a plan, but I guess it really didn't matter anyway.

# 49

Cloaked in darkness, I broke into a sprint.

I ran as fast as I could manage, down the dim streets of Banks-town.

Catching a bus or a train wasn't an option, because it wouldn't take me to where I needed to be, and I wasn't prepared to wait for a taxi. I was without a car, but I needed one. In desperation, I would do something I would always deeply regret—steal a car.

At first, I wasn't sure how to do it. Besides, if I was going to sink so low and go through with such a despicable act, I didn't want to get caught. I wanted a disguise, or at least something to hide my facial features. Acting quickly, I ducked into the closest service station and purchased a dark pair of sunglasses—hardly a disguise, but it'd have to make do. While paying for them at the cash register, the young clerk behind the counter said,

"Sir, your head is bleeding."

I looked up, acknowledged him, but didn't care to give an an-swer. I handed over the money and left as promptly as possible. Already, I was starting to draw suspicion. I had to get out of this suburb and closer to where I needed to be. Time was slipping away, and each second was proving to be crucial.

I started to run again, practically sprinting down the sidewalk. If I was going to steal a car, I had to get off the main roads and find quiet streets. From there, I would pick my target.

I continued to run for at least another ten minutes, feeling the blood on my scalp dry and crust over. I wasn't sure where I was anymore. I tried reading the street signs, but they provided no clues. Struggling to catch my breath and close to passing out, I stopped for a moment under a street light. In the distance, I could see a quiet intersection with a pair of traffic lights. Perfect. This is where I would make my attack. I moved closer towards the intersection, as I put on my disguise for the first time that night. I snapped the sunglasses over my eyes, and pulled the hood on my jacket over my head. I stood a few metres away from the traffic lights, feeling sick and desperate but damn well focused. I waited impatiently for a car to pull up and stop right in front of me.

Luckily, within a few minutes, a Holden Ute pulled up.

Better yet, it was the only car at the intersection, and it had been stopped by a red light. I could faintly see the driver behind the wheel, bopping their head up and down as they waited for the light to go green.

I sprung out from the darkness and prepared to make my move.

I walked behind the car, noticing it was covered in freshly displayed red provisional plates, so I assumed the driver was probably a kid, barely old enough to be on the road. I quickly dug one hand into my jacket pocket and extended my index finger, poking it against the material. Yes, it was a pathetic attempt at imitating a weapon, but I hoped it would do its job.

My feet pounding on the paved road, I knew I had only seconds left before the light turned green. As I approached the driver's side, I looked at my victim through the window. He was a young, buffed-up male. Shit. I hoped that he wouldn't retaliate, but I had nothing to worry about—the kid practically crapped himself as I yanked open the driver's side door.

"Get out of the car," I said, putting on an Australian accent.

The kid panicked and noticed that I had one hand in my pocket. He snapped off his seatbelt and complied with my demand. The poor guy was shaking, and held his hands in the air.

"Don't kill me," he stammered.

Instantly, my conscience was plagued with regret.

"Sorry," I said, sliding behind the wheel, "but I'll take good care of your car. Promise."

The fear stained eyes vanished, and he was overcome with a sense of confusion. I shook the guilt from my mind and reminded myself that I was doing this for Rochelle. She was all that mattered right now.

I slammed the driver's side door shut. The light had gone green some time ago. I put my foot on the accelerator and drove off, leaving the kid standing on the side of the curb.

*** 

I'd almost reached my destination, and most likely my resting place.

I'd parked the stolen car a little further up the road, a few metres away from the house—perhaps I should have dumped the car elsewhere, but I wasn't expecting to return, so I guess it didn't really matter.

In the darkness, I killed the car engine and shut off the headlights. I stepped out of the vehicle, locked the car and took the keys with me, as I edged closer to the house.

According to Cosmo, this is where I would find Rochelle.

I studied the house from across the road. The lights were on. Shit. I was hoping that maybe there was a chance Mal or Isaac wouldn't be home, but now it seemed unlikely. Once I stepped inside, I doubted I'd ever make it out alive.

Dying no longer scared me, but the thought of never seeing her again did. I tried to remember the last time I'd seen her face, and at first the memory struggled to reach the surface—but it was still there, although somewhat hazy. Rochelle and I were staying in a bed & breakfast—mainly to seek refuge from the rain—in a place called Hardy's Bay. I could remember what she looked like the last time I'd seen her. Rochelle had been lying between the bed sheets, naked, smiling at me from across the room. Her blonde hair was untamed, and she wore no make-up—but goddamn it she was beautiful. I wished I'd told her that. I don't think I'd told her enough.

The memory comforted me for a moment, but as the winter night's chill seeped through my skin and down to my bones—reality was restored, and I was alone.

Tonight, I would sacrifice myself. I began to approach the house from the left hand side. My teeth began to chatter, so I bit down hard to make them stop. As I circled the perimeter, I was overcome by a sense of déjà vu. Just a week ago, I had been in the very same situation, but now I had no gun.

For lack of better words, I had fucked up my first opportunity to save Rochelle, so tonight I would do things differently. To begin with, I would make my attack from the back of the house instead of the front. Keeping my hands in my pockets and moving quickly, I began to examine the best point of entry. The windows at the back of the house had all been locked up—although that was to be expected—but one of the windows ignited my curiosity. Thick bolts had been fitted around the frame of the window, and the curtains had been pinned up against the glass by several wooden boards. My heart soared. I was convinced Rochelle was just metres away from me.

I had to be quick. The last time I had done this, I had been far too cautious and slow. Tonight I would quicken the pace, hoping that I might at least gain the element of surprise by making a move they didn't see coming.

Although I was sure Rochelle was behind the boarded up window, I knew I'd waste too much time trying to get inside. I had to be sleek, so I turned my attention to a second window just a few metres away. No bolts. No wooden boards. I found a decent-sized stone beside my foot. I picked it up and hurled it through a window. It smashed and shattered into tiny pieces and the glass had barely hit the ground before I began to climb inside. Tiny shards pierced my skin as I clambered through, but I was so focused that it muted my pain.

I viewed my surroundings. I was in a lounge room, but I could see an open door in front of me. I sprinted towards it, stumbled out into a corridor and already I could hear feet moving rapidly from upstairs. Somebody had heard me. Somebody was coming.

Knowing I had only seconds to live, I ran.

I sought refuge in a cupboard under a staircase. I held the door closed, and only seconds passed before I heard footsteps stomping down each step, inches above my head. I held my breath and lis-

258

tened. The footsteps appeared to be moving further away from me, but I could clearly hear the voices of Mal Lawson and Isaac Fuller. A hot shockwave tingled down my spine.

As predicted, they found the broken window. Either Mal or Isaac raised their voice, and I was sure I heard my name mentioned. Two pairs of footsteps quickly scattered away in different directions. I heard doors open and close, and then an unbearable silence settled in. They knew I was here. They were hunting me.

I had two options now—I could either remain in the darkness and wait to be found and killed, or make a final stand and die with a little bit of dignity.

In the past, I would rather hide than fight, but I had nothing more to lose, so I pushed open the cupboard door and walked out into the corridor.

I was alone, but I was sure I was being watched. For a moment I stood still, waiting for somebody to step forward and aim a gun at my head—but nothing happened. I continued to wait. Still nothing.

I risked a step forward, my heart violently hammering against my chest. Cold sweat drenched my shirt. Where the hell were those sons of bitches? Had they run from me? Or were they merely leading me into a false sense of security? I was wasting time by standing and waiting, so I began to walk to the second last room at the end of the corridor, just as Cosmo had instructed me to.

I reached inside my jacket pocket, frantically trying to find my gun, but then I remembered—I was unarmed.

Over the last few weeks I'd become accustomed to carrying a weapon, but now that I was without it, I felt more defenceless than ever. Death was inevitable, and I was the target tonight.

Or perhaps more accurately, I was like a sitting duck in an open field, just waiting for somebody to take the first shot. The odds were against me, but I would stand and fight regardless of the risks. Truthfully, I no longer cared if I lived or died, just as long as the woman I loved was safe. She was the one in the line of fire. She was the one in danger, and I was the one who put her in that position.

As I walked down the corridor, towards the room where Rochelle was being held captive, I thought about all that I could have done to avoid this situation. There had been many opportunities to survive this ordeal, but because of me, the chances were long gone.

The blood in my veins turned to ice as I reached for the door handle. I mentally tried to plan an escape route, but the chances of escaping unscathed seemed slim to none. I pulled the door handle down, but before I'd even opened the door an inch, somebody else grabbed me from behind, snaked an arm around my neck, and held me in a headlock.

I tried to scream, but the air could not reach my lungs. I tried to struggle free but my body was already too weak. I'd already accepted this is how I would die, but I wanted to see Rochelle just one last time. It'd been so long since I'd gazed upon her hazel eyes.

I kept hoping that maybe my last wishes would be respected, but I think my life ended the second I heard a gun shot echo from inside the room, followed by her excruciating screams.

And then I went limp. My body, my fight—all gone.

Her scream was like poison. I could feel it running through my veins, slowly shutting down every vital organ in its path. I was just moments away from death. Facing defeat, I closed my eyes. I'd taken my last breath.

However, just as I prepared to accept my fate, I was hit by a second wave of animosity. Her scream. Her pain. Those bastards.

And then, my last bout of energy burst through the surface as I kicked my feet up and planted them on the wall. I quickly sprung back, using what was left of my strength, and forced the son of a bitch that was strangling me up against the wall. For a moment, he loosened his grip—but that's all it took. I pulled his hands away from my neck and slipped through.

I turned around just in time to see Isaac take another swing at me, but I blocked him with my elbow, and shoved him back against the wall. He hit his head on a picture frame, and smashed the glass. For a brief moment, the blow left him disorientated, so I took the opportunity to lunge out in an attempt to open the door again.

I grabbed the door handle, pulled it down and pushed. The door flung open. Mal was there, holding a smoking gun by his side. It was only natural instinct to charge at him, but Isaac grabbed me by the shirt and dragged me to the floor. He held me down. I couldn't move. Mal crouched down beside me and began to shout words of sheer hatred, but I ignored him and looked ahead into the darkened room. I had heard Rochelle. She had screamed from behind the door just moments ago.

And then I saw her. On the floor. Eyes shut.

"Rochelle!" I screamed, frantically trying to free my body.

Just as she began to open her eyes, Mal stomped down on my skull, forcing me to close mine.

# 50

There was darkness.

Nothing but pitch black, and at first, I thought I had descended into death.

Even though I held no religious beliefs, right now I was waiting for something—a bright light, a heavenly choir, or maybe even fire and brimstone—but there was nothing. Just darkness.

However, as the minutes passed, I came to the realisation that I wasn't dead. No, because I could feel pain. The pain was real. I lay on the wooden floorboards, flat on my back, and my head was throbbing each time I blinked. I tried to reach out and feel my surroundings, but my hands were bound. My feet too. Instantly, I tried to scream, but my words couldn't reach the surface. My mouth was gagged.

Panic rose from within, and I frantically began to thrash about, trying to free my hands. The rope wrapped around my wrists had been tied so tightly, that it was practically burrowing into my skin.

I managed to roll over to my side. Using the last bit of power left in me, I managed to sit upright. For a moment, I tried to stand, but the rope around my ankles made it quite impossible. Where the hell was I? Why was it so dark?

And then I thought about Rochelle.

I had seen her. She had been lying on the ground, and the very thought ignited another wave of panic. I wasn't sure how long I'd been unconscious for—maybe minutes or maybe hours—I had no record of time. In fact, my memories were beginning to blur into one, and I couldn't recall when one day ended and a new one began.

Where was Rochelle now? What had happened to her?

And then there was a noise. A knock on the wall beside me. I managed to lift both hands and I tapped them against the wall a couple of times. I waited. Nothing. I knocked again, this time harder—and somebody knocked back. Rochelle. It had to be.

She was just inches away from me. It was the closest we'd been in weeks. I closed my eyes and tried to visualise her lying next to me, but the fantasy was ruined because I could picture her being in the same situation—bound by the hands and feet, unable to move. True, I wasn't much of an optimist anymore, but at least Rochelle and I were together—regardless of a wall acting as a barrier between us.

For a moment, I rested my head on the ground, continuing to tap my hands against the wall every few minutes. For a moment, I enjoyed the solitude—well, as much as one could in this predicament—but I figured this was as close as I would ever get to Rochelle, so I would make the most of it while I could. Mal would kill us both. I didn't know when, but it was a certainty.

I closed my eyes and waited for death to consume me—but the moment of serenity was interrupted by shots of gunfire, echoing out into the night.

***

Betrayed.

That good-for-nothing bastard had betrayed him, and Mal did not take betrayal lightly. He had trusted Cosmo Rowland, paid him thousands of dollars to follow through with one simple task—but instead Cosmo had stabbed him in the back. Several times.

Not only had he failed to kill Kennedy, but he'd given away Mal's location. Bastard.

Sitting in the darkness, behind an old timber desk, Mal reminisced. This was not the first time he had been stabbed in the back. Throughout his entire career he had been the victim of betrayal. Mal often contemplated leaving his field of expertise, but once you were in the game, it was almost impossible to escape it. He was trapped in a vicious cycle, unable to breakaway. Each day a new client requested him to track down another individual—a few years ago he had liked being in the game, but not anymore.

A little over two years ago Mal had grown tired of being a professional tracker, so he had made the decision to branch out, in order to add to his credentials. Mal wanted to begin blackmailing, and why not start with the biggest prize of all? Nathan Burwell. He was the target.

Mal had advertised his plan to many loyal clients and they had wanted a piece of the action. Next he'd signed on Bruno Samuel, knowing he would get the job done. And then what happened? He was murdered.

As predicted, Mal's clients fumed. Something had to be done. Mal was at a loss and to ease the pain he had sought revenge. Then, he'd been led to believe a false promise. He was told that maybe Nathan Burwell could still be blackmailed by forcing Jordan Kennedy into the position, but it had fallen through for a second time.

So this is where it would end. Mal had pissed off too many clients to live a normal life, so he would have to hide forever. How many times can one man screw up before accepting failure? The number is finite.

Mal had made the decision that he would move on tonight. His ex-business partners were now closing in on him, and in due time, he would be found. Mal wasn't going to risk it.

As for Jordan Kennedy and his girlfriend, they would be eliminated from the picture, but Mal wasn't quite sure how to do it.

He could hear them upstairs, tapping against the walls.

They had to be disposed of without delay.

Mal rose from behind his desk. As he began to walk, each step was arduous. It felt like his feet were being anchored down. Defeated. Mal's intensity had been crushed, and all that remained was a broken man.

Mal exited the room and stepped out into the main corridor. He found Isaac standing by the staircase, listening to the subtle noises from upstairs. Hand on his gun, Isaac was ready to silence them.

"I need you to do me a favour," said Mal, grabbing Isaac's attention. "Wait outside by the car, and keep an eye out for anything suspicious. I'll be out in a few minutes."

"What? But what are we going to do with Kennedy and the girl?"

"We douse the place in petrol and strike a match."

Isaac's gaze fell hard. He did not approve.

"But Mal, wouldn't it be easier to just shoot them? Get it over and done with?"

"No. I don't want to leave behind a single trace."

"Jesus, you think that will be enough to erase what we've done? Forensic science is better than what it used to be, Mal. Everyone will know we've done this."

Mal knew it, but that was the least of his concerns. There were already too many people that wanted him dead.

"Just wait out the front," said Mal, after some time. "I'll be out shortly."

264

Isaac stood his ground, defiantly, but then let it go and followed orders. Mal heard the front door close behind him. Rather than wallowing in his own self-pity, Mal sprung into action. He collected a box of matches and a few petrol drums from the garage, and one by one, he began to pour it out over the floorboards. Mal decided he would leave almost everything behind, taking only a single briefcase with him. The rest would burn, along with the life he once had.

Just as Mal prepared to pour out the last of the petrol drums, there was a sound. A bang. A noise he was very accustomed to—a gunshot, ringing out, followed by unreserved silence.

Mal dropped the petrol drum, allowing it to gush out across the floor. He ran. The shot had come from outside, and although he was sure he knew what had happened, Mal refused to believe it. Not now. Not today. What else could go wrong?

Stepping out into an icy winter's night, Mal saw the twisted body lying on the grass beside the car. Mal ran closer, holding onto denial, but reality bit back hard.

The only person Mal had trusted, the only person he could depend on, was now lying in a pool of blood, with a bullet wound through his skull. Dead. Isaac Fuller had been killed.

Mal heard another noise—a smash. He jerked his head around, glancing back towards the house.

For the second time tonight, Mal had been betrayed.

\*\*\*

There was silence, but the gunshot was still ringing in my ears.

There had been some kind of altercation outside. What had happened? Why had a shot been fired? My train of thought was interrupted as I heard a window smash. I froze, and kept my ear to the floor. What the hell was going on?

Footsteps thundered up the stairs, now just metres away. Without warning, a door in front of me was forced open, and a burst of light poured into the room. I saw a figure standing outside, with a gun. The figure approached, and as my eyes adjusted, I realised the figure had once been a friend—Cosmo Rowland.

I tried to speak, but alas, I couldn't.

Cosmo crouched down beside me and pulled a flick knife out of his pocket. He cut the rope around my hands and ankles.

"Up," he said, his voice raspy. "We need to move."

I ripped off the gag that had been taped around my mouth, and exhaled. I tried to talk, and at first I struggled, but one of my words managed to escape,

"Rochelle!" I screamed.

Cosmo was already searching for her. Somehow, I managed to pull myself onto my feet and I scrambled outside the door, following Cosmo. He had broken into a second room, and was kneeling down on the floor, beside my girlfriend.

Just the briefest glimpse of Rochelle ignited a hit of adrenaline. I dashed over to her, dropped down to my knees and scooped her up into my arms. Tears surfaced. I couldn't hold them back. I held her tight, not willing to let her go. I felt her fingertips hover over my shoulder. If she had the strength, Rochelle would have held me too.

"Move!" shouted Cosmo. "Get her up. Let's go."

I looked down at Rochelle. Her head lulled forward into my chest and she lost consciousness in my arms. That's when I saw the wounds—on her arms, on her neck, the bloodstains on the checked shirt she wore. One wound was fresh, a bullet graze across her collarbone. The realisation struck hard as panic seized me, but she regained consciousness again.

"Jordan," she whispered gently, her eyes flickering as she looked up at me.

"Get up!" screamed Cosmo, bashing a fist against the door.

We couldn't stay here any longer. We were still in the line of fire. A new wave of energy pulsed through my veins and I managed to pick Rochelle up as I rose to my feet.

Cosmo guided us down the corridor, holding the gun out in front of him, leading us to safety. Just as we reached the staircase, there was an explosion from downstairs. An ominous orange glow appeared from the darkness. Flames quickly followed.

Through the rising smoke, I caught a glimpse of Mal Lawson staring up at us from the bottom of the stairs. Cosmo aimed his gun and prepared to fire, but he wasn't quick enough—Mal Lawson had already jammed the gun barrel under his own chin and fired.

***

Minutes before his own death, Mal Lawson had gazed down at his dead friend, knowing he could not leave him like this.

By tomorrow morning, police would be swarming around the area. A crime scene would be established. Isaac's body would be subjected to a post-mortem examination and the police would try to piece together what had happened. No, Mal wouldn't allow it. There would be no autopsy if there wasn't a body—so Mal grabbed Isaac under the arms, and began to drag him back inside.

Mal heard footsteps and shouting from upstairs. He ignored it. The final thread had already snapped, the levee had broken—Mal had nothing more to lose.

Mal dragged his fallen associate into the petrol drenched room. The fumes were intoxicating, but Mal's mind was clear. Tonight, he would fall too.

Adrenaline raging, Mal pulled out the box of matches, finding solitude in his final moments.

He had not planned for this, but what other choice did he have? It was either hiding in the darkness for the rest of his days, or taking his own life. Neither option is what Mal wanted, but the life he once had was gone. A string of errors and bad choices had led to his peril.

Mal struck the match and threw it. The second the flame hit the petrol, there was an explosion of light. The flames engulfed Isaac's body, and fire came hurtling towards Mal. He stepped backwards, his gun by his side, and he stood in front of the stairs. Then he saw them. Those betraying bastards. Just as Cosmo began to take aim, Mal discharged his gun and beat him to it. Pain only lasted a second, and then there was nothing. Nothing at all.

***

The moment he took the shot, I was overcome by the greatest sense of relief.

Mal Lawson had ended his own life, and for all he had put me through, I felt no remorse. However, a greater concern surfaced—we were trapped inside a burning house, with the fire growing stronger with every second.

I looked down the stairs just one last time. A wall of fire began to build as the flames engulfed Mal's torso, and smoke bellowed higher in thick black clouds. While I was ready to accept my time was up, Cosmo was not.

"Come on!" he shouted, tucking his gun away as he raced back down the corridor.

My knees almost giving way, I followed, carrying Rochelle in my arms. The fire raged from below, and the intense heat could be felt through the floorboards.

We ran to the end of the corridor, seeing a window. Cosmo stuck his elbow through the glass, shattering it instantly. I looked out below, seeing nothing but blackness.

"Jump out!" shouted Cosmo, grabbing Rochelle from my arms. "It's only a short drop."

"What about Rochelle?" I screamed.

She was still out cold, unresponsive and barely alive.

"I'll bring her down with me," reassured Cosmo. "Promise."

He was not the kind of man that used that word often, so I knew it was genuine.

The orange haze was now right behind us, so I jumped. As I descended into darkness I tucked my knees in, preparing for the impact. I didn't land on my feet, but on my side. Pain ripped through my muscles and cut into the bone, but somehow I summoned the strength to get back up. Disoriented and dizzy, I gazed up at the broken window. I caught a brief glimpse of Cosmo jumping down beside me, cradling Rochelle close to his chest.

Without warning, the smoke inhalation hit me, and a coughing fit ravaged my body. Cosmo was already running. I tried to catch up.

As I ran, I dared to look over my shoulder. Fire had consumed the entire house, and the structure was beginning to fall apart. Ahead, Cosmo had made it back to the street. I managed to shout out to him, and told him I had a car parked a little further up the street. We advanced towards it, and I unlocked the car—although I wasn't sure why I had bothered to lock a stolen car. I stood back as Cosmo spread Rochelle out across the backseat. Cosmo slid behind the wheel. I joined Rochelle in the back, and supported her head in my lap. She was still out, but breathing. The car started and we raced off, hearing police and fire sirens echo in the near distance.

# 51

Fighting to stay conscious was no longer a physical, but a mental barrier.

Screeching wheels. Rough terrain. Flashing lights. My mind desperately wanted to shut off, but not now. I had to hold on. I had to stay focused.

As Cosmo drove, I clutched onto Rochelle's hand and monitored her breathing patterns. In the state we'd found her in, she had been clinging onto life. I'd nearly lost the one thing I truly cared about. I gazed down at her, catching glimpses of her battered face. The scars would heal, but the memories would remain forever. Death didn't seem good enough for those that had done this to her. The anger was still fresh, but I knew I'd have to let it go. Nothing more could be done.

We could hear the sirens in close proximity, but we stuck to the back roads.

"I'm taking you both home," said Cosmo, his voice cutting through the silence. "You'll be safe there."

I wanted to negotiate with Cosmo, and convince him to take us to the hospital, but it was too risky. If he took us there in the condition we were in, we'd instantly be pinned to what had just transpired with Mal Lawson. I knew I could care for Rochelle at home, and I guess that's all that really mattered.

The police and fire sirens had now faded in the distance. No doubt the news would spread fast, and by tomorrow morning the deaths of Mal and Isaac would be splashed over the front page of every goddamn paper. Would they see the link to Nathan Burwell? It was possible. Perhaps there would be no clear link, but the media would probably make one anyway. I just hoped I'd broken my connections with all of them.

Suddenly, Rochelle's eyes started to flicker. She was beginning to regain consciousness. I whispered her name. She tried to acknowledge me. I took her by the hand, uttered words of reassurance, but I'm sure it meant nothing to Rochelle right now.

I gazed down at her again, realising the red checked shirt she was wearing belonged to me. I had worn it on the last day we'd been together. I hadn't even noticed the shirt had been missing, but it wasn't in the same condition I'd last seen it in. Rips and tears decorated the shirt, while dried blood had permanently soaked into the fabric. Feeling my heart sink, I gently lifted the shirt up, exposing the beaten body beneath.

Raw emotion surfaced. What had they done to her? How could they? I wanted answers. Better yet, I wanted vengeance. Irrational thoughts rotated around my head, but I exhaled and tried to block them out. It was over. Nothing more could be done. I had to mentally repeat those words on a loop, and as the minutes passed, the aggression faded.

Familiar buildings and roads surrounded us. Cosmo drove peacefully through the neighbourhood I knew so well. It felt surreal to me. I had envisaged this moment for so long, it barely seemed like reality.

Soon enough, Cosmo drove down a narrow dirt road, lined by towering gumtrees on both sides. Our house was still there. Just the way I'd left it.

Cosmo stopped the car, and pulled up the handbrake. I looked down once again to see Rochelle had fully opened her eyes, and she was looking right back at me.

"Where are we?" she asked, her voice a frail whisper.

"Home," I said, fighting to keep my composure. "We're home, babe."

# 52

Using what was left of my strength; I pushed open the passenger's side door and stepped out.

Cosmo told me to open the front door. I took a moment to find the spare key while he helped Rochelle out of the car. Still too weak to walk, Cosmo carried her inside. I flicked on the lights, and cleared the sofa so that Rochelle could lie down. As Cosmo placed her across the cushions, she closed her eyes again. I crouched down beside her and took Rochelle by the hand. She slept. Peacefully.

"I'm leaving now," said Cosmo, feeling out of place. "I'm going to dump the car further out west and then I'll burn it up."

"Don't," I said. "I want it left in a decent condition."

"Not happening, Kennedy. The car needs to be destroyed, otherwise it's just another link back to us," replied Cosmo.

I wanted to argue, remembering the promise I'd made to the teenager I'd stolen it from. I didn't want to go back on my word, but I didn't want to be caught either. I wanted to believe I'd stolen a car for all the right reasons, but I could never justify it in court. I nodded my head, and Cosmo departed without delay.

I heard the car back up the driveway and drive off into the night. At last, Rochelle and I were alone. I had surpassed the point of tiredness, and now all I wanted was to be there for Rochelle. For a while, I just remained beside her, wanting to be there for her when she woke up. Twenty minutes may have passed, and she opened her eyes again.

Still disorientated, she tried to say my name.

"I'm here," I whispered, tucking a piece of her golden hair behind an ear.

"I feel," said Rochelle, struggling to get the words out, "like death."

"You're alright," I reassured.

"My shoulder. Hurts. Like it's on fire."

The graze was still fresh, but no longer bleeding. Luckily, it wouldn't require stitches, but it did need a patch up. I let go of Rochelle's hand, told her I'd be back, and fetched the first-aid kit from the bathroom.

I found a few sterilize gauzes, and prepared to stick it over the wound. Rochelle stopped me.

"Antiseptic first," she said, breathing heavily.

I raided the first-aid kit, and found nothing.

"Use alcohol," said Rochelle. "Vodka."

I nodded, and quickly looked through the liquor cabinet. I found an almost empty bottle of Vodka at the very back of the cabinet, but I figured it would do. As I unscrewed the cap on the Vodka bottle, I was suddenly overcome by the greatest sense of déjà vu. I had been in this position before. It was more than a year ago now, but I could recall when Rochelle tended to a stab wound I had sustained in a knife brawl. I could remember the pain; especially the moment Rochelle poured alcohol into my open wound. A stinging sensation had burned through my entire body. I didn't want to put Rochelle through the agonising pain, but she left me no choice.

"Pour it," she said. "I'll be fine."

I obeyed, and as predicted, she gritted her teeth and squirmed the moment the alcohol hit her flesh. I pressed a gauze over the wound and waited as the pain subsided. The ordeal had left Rochelle drained, and had lost the strength to talk or even look at me. I gently tended to the wound by bandaging it up. Once finished, I crouched down beside her again in silence, just grateful we were both home together at last.

I let Rochelle rest for a while, but I could tell she was still uncomfortable. Now that she was under harsh light, I could see just how damaged she was. Her skin was dry and cracked, and scars littered every inch of her body. I also noticed Rochelle's right ankle had swollen up and I doubted she'd even be able to walk on it.

And then the guilt hit me. I was responsible for her pain. There was nothing I could do to erase the past, but I would make it up to her.

"Is there anything I can get you?" I whispered gently. "Something to eat maybe?"

She shook her head once.

"Or do you want me to run you a bath?"

She forced a smile and said,

"I'd like that."

I promptly stood up and entered the bathroom. I ran a bath, lukewarm temperature. While the water was running, I did a quick tidy up of the bedroom and laid out fresh sheets on the bed. I was trying to make it more comfortable for Rochelle, but right now I doubted she'd even notice. Once the bath had filled up, I assisted undressing Rochelle and helped her into the tub. Her body was fragile, so delicate. As I bathed her, Rochelle kept falling in and out of consciousness, and I had to support her head because she struggled to keep it up from the water.

Rochelle had succumbed to exhaustion, so I carried her out of the tub, towelled her off and dressed her into something warm. Rochelle woke up just as I laid her down on the bed.

"Jordan," she said, but I hushed her.

"Sleep now," I said, pulling the blankets over her. "You can tell me in the morning."

# 53

*August 18th*

First light was visible on the horizon, as the sun prepared to rise for another day.

For the first time in weeks, I was not waking up in a strange or unusual place. I woke up in my own bed, safe and secure. I rolled over, expecting to see the woman I loved—but she was not there. The sheets had been pulled back and there was an empty space where Rochelle should have been.

Immediately, I sprung from the bed. I called out her name. I heard a reply.

"Jordan, I'm in the bathroom," she called out from behind a closed door. "I'll be out in a minute."

I'd worked myself up into a frenzy of panic for no reason. I slumped back down in the bed, and waited for Rochelle. From now on I knew I would always be a little more cautious and protective of her. I would never let anybody hurt her again. After some time, I heard the bathroom door unlock and Rochelle opened up. She was limping on her bad foot. I sprung to my feet.

"Don't walk on that ankle, babe," I said, probably too firmly. "You'll hurt yourself."

Rochelle put her hand up.

"Jordan. I've been walking on it for weeks. I'll get by just fine."

I wanted to argue, but already I was getting the impression it would be a battle I just wouldn't win. I bit my tongue, and watched helplessly as Rochelle limped back to the bed and crawled back under the covers. It was clear she was trying to disguise the pain.

I knew very well that Rochelle didn't like a fuss. She liked to be independent, so the coming weeks would be difficult on both of us. I wasn't prepared to stand back and let Rochelle bury her own demons. I was going to be there for her—whether she liked it or not.

"I'll be back in a minute," I explained, heading towards the bedroom door. "I'll get you something to eat. What do you feel like?"

"Nothing for the moment."

"You haven't eaten since we got back. You need to eat."

"Toast then," she replied, her frustration seeping through.

"OK," I said, with firmness thick in my voice, and I exited the bedroom.

In a matter of minutes I'd brewed Rochelle a tea and prepared a slice of Vegemite toast. I knew I should've fixed something for myself too, but I still didn't have the stomach to eat. On my return to the bedroom, I placed the breakfast by the bedside table. After a minute or two, Rochelle found the strength to sit upright and began to pick at her breakfast.

I stood and watched anxiously as she pulled the toast into tiny pieces to nibble on. This was not the same woman I had previously shared a bed with. She had changed. Rochelle had been weakened, not just physically, but emotionally too. There was harshness in her eyes now. The hazel eyes I once knew no longer comforted me, because I could see the damaged woman within. Instead of warmth, there was judgement. Instead of trust, there was uncertainty. Although it was probably too soon, I knew I would have to press for answers. I wasn't sure what had happened to Rochelle over the past few weeks, but I needed to know.

I sat down at the end of the bed, feeling my heart almost in my throat. Rochelle had her eyes down, looking at her toast, almost pretending I wasn't there. I waited for her to speak, but alas, no words were exchanged. I knew I'd have to fire the cannon.

"Rochelle," I said, forcing her to look at me. "What happened while you were in that house?"

Immediately, she looked down again. At first, she said nothing. My heart dropped back down into my lungs. Eventually, she began to speak.

"I hardly ever saw Mal," she said, "but Isaac—he was always there."

"Then did he—? Did Isaac hurt you?"

Rochelle didn't lie or sugar-coat it.

"Yes," she said. "He did."

A swarm of hatred pulsed through my body, but as the aggression died down, I was left weakened. Isaac was dead. Nothing I could do. I had to keep reminding myself of that fact—but it still didn't seem good enough for that son of a bitch. Guilt began to surface, but I knew I would have to press for more answers.

"What did Isaac do?" I asked, struggling to keep my tone steady.

"He was rough with me," she said, finally looking up.

I closed my eyes, the pain feeling like an icy blade slicing into my body.

"Did he..." I tried, finding it hard to put words together. "Did he abuse you?"

"Sexually? No. But physically? Yes. Everyday."

"How?"

"He liked to push the boundaries. He liked to see how far he could push me until I cracked. He would stir me up, and when I tried to defend myself, well, that just made it worse."

"You're not being direct with me," I said, perhaps a little too firmly. "Tell me exactly what he did to you. I can handle it."

"I know," replied Rochelle, her voice now a whisper, "but you have to understand I don't really want to talk about it."

Again, the guilt hit me.

"Sorry," I said, not knowing what else to say.

"Besides," said Rochelle, "you haven't told me what happened with you."

"To be fair, I don't really want to talk about it either. Maybe someday, but not now."

She stared for a moment, trying to read me, but I was a closed book on the topic. Rochelle and I had been through a battle, and we had both felt pain—so now was not the time to compare notes. Today was a fresh start. We would turn the page and start again.

Rochelle finished her breakfast in silence. I wasn't sure what else to do. In my head, I had dreamed about reuniting with Rochelle after such a lengthy ordeal—but this is not at all how I had envisaged it. I had imagined that normality would have been restored, but I was wrong. We were broken souls, spiritless beings, with the life sucked out of us. I wasn't sure how long this would last, but I would do all I could to make it right again.

"There's something else I wanted to talk to you about," began Rochelle, propping herself up a little more.

"It can wait," I said. "You need your rest."

"No, I'd like to talk about it now. If that's OK?"

I recognised the urgency, and a nervous feeling burrowed deep within. I nodded, waited for her to continue.

"It's about what happened during our last night together. You know—before we were separated? Do you remember?"

I could recall. It was—how many weeks ago? I'd lost count. Rochelle and I had made love on the beach. Shortly after, we found somewhere to stay—a little bed & breakfast over the hill—and we had continued our love making session.

I wanted to smile at the memory, but under the circumstances, I couldn't.

"Yeah, I remember. What about it?"

Her gaze met mine. I could almost feel it.

"We weren't very careful," said Rochelle, lowering her voice, "with precautions."

Shit. Already, I knew where this was heading, but in a moment of panic—I played dumb.

"What are you getting at?"

She stared back at me, painfully. I took her by the hand, knowing she was hesitating.

"I think I was pregnant."

The statement had been almost what I had expected, but one particular word threw me off. Was? Past tense? What the hell was that supposed to mean? I pushed for an answer.

"What do you mean *was?*" I asked, perhaps a little too firmly. "Are you, or are you not?"

"I'm not. I took the test this morning—just a minute ago. But I'm almost positive I was."

"But—? How do you know?"

"I know you don't believe in that woman's intuition bullshit, but I felt like I was pregnant. I guess, I just felt different. That's all. Plus I had all the classic signs. But then, well, I think I lost it. But I guess that's to be expected after everything I've been through."

"So why are you telling me if it's gone?"

"I needed to know," she said, pausing for a moment, "would you have stayed? You know—if I was still pregnant with your child?"

The question caught me off guard. For a while, I said nothing. I'm not the kind of guy that was keen on parenthood. I didn't ever want children of my own. Of course, I was capable of holding a relationship together, but a family? I wasn't sure what to say. But fortunately for me, I looked into her hazel eyes before answering— and the harshness was gone, and the warmth had returned. After all we'd been through, the answer seemed clear.

"Of course, I would."

She smiled—the first one I had seen in weeks. I moved closer towards Rochelle, and she snuggled into my chest. I held her there, never daring to let her go again.

# 54

I heard a car pull up outside my house a little after two in the afternoon.

Permanently on alert, I sprung to my feet and took a peek outside the window. A rusted dark green Volvo was parked out the front. Behind the wheel, I saw the man almost responsible for my death, but also the man accountable for saving my life—Cosmo Rowland.

I waited for him to step out of the car, but he didn't. Instead he remained in the driver's seat, hands on the wheel, looking through the window, staring at me. I was unsure if I wanted to go outside to greet him, but I put aside my childishness and headed to the front door.

Rochelle was resting in the bedroom, so I called out to her, telling her to stay put. When she asked why, I evaded the question and told her I'd be back in a moment.

Just as I walked out the front door, Cosmo stepped out of his car. He had his shades on, using them as a barrier against eye contact. I stood in the doorframe, crossed my arms and waited for Cosmo to talk. I waited a long time.

"Hey," said Cosmo, finally.

"Hi," I replied, but I could not disguise my discomfort.

We fell into silence. There was so much I could say, but I chose not to.

"How's Rochelle?" asked Cosmo, after sometime.

"Good," I said. "She's resting at the moment."

"That's—that's good to hear."

I didn't have the time for his small talk bullshit. I knew the reason Cosmo had come here today. He wanted to be forgiven, but I knew I wasn't ready yet. What had transpired between Cosmo and I yesterday evening in the car park was not something to be dismissed so easily. He may have done the right thing—eventually—but I kept recalling the moment of his disloyalty. I could still hear the sound of

Cosmo forcing back the trigger. If the magazine hadn't jammed, I would have been dead already. A minor mishap had saved me. Regardless, I couldn't forget Cosmo's intention.

I remember how I felt—the anger and confusion dominating my thoughts. I could almost feel the gun barrel resting against my head. It was true that I had almost given up hope, but the betrayal left me with a scar that may never heal. I had grown dependent on Cosmo through the trying days, but the confidence and faith I'd once seen in my friend had been destroyed. Sometimes, what is destroyed cannot be rebuilt.

Half a minute passed. I began to walk back inside the house.

"Jordan," he said, failing to conceal the disgrace in his voice. "I know that I royally fucked up yesterday. You know—with all that shit that went on."

I turned around and listened.

"You have to understand that I never meant for any of it," said Cosmo, risking a step closer, "but I'm hoping I might have redeemed myself by coming to rescue you guys last night, but I know it might be hard to forgive me for my actions earlier in the evening."

"I might forgive you in time," I said, "but I'm not sure if I'll ever be able to trust you again."

That hurt Cosmo. I could tell.

"Yeah, I know," he said, bitterly.

Cosmo looked down. Knowing that he had let me down was worse than any injury he had sustained over the entire ordeal, and he was struggling to justify his actions. Once again, I tried to walk away. Cosmo pulled off his sunglasses.

"Hey, I did put my arse on the line for you and Rochelle though," said Cosmo, trying to defend himself. "Like, I could've left you guys to die there. But I didn't."

I considered that. It was true he had risked his own life in order to rescue us, but that didn't cancel out his disloyalty to me.

"I want to thank you for saving Rochelle and I, because no doubt without your help we would've been dead by now," I said, finally stepping out of the door frame, "but you have to realise that you deceived me, and were ready and willing to take my life in exchange for money. Once I had real admiration for you Cosmo, but not anymore."

Cosmo pressed his lips together, and took a moment to collect his thoughts.

"Did—did you tell Rochelle?" asked Cosmo, sheepishly. "About what I did?"

"No," I said, "and I'm not going to tell her either."

He exhaled. Although Cosmo had never met Rochelle until last night, clearly he wanted to conceal a certain reputation he may have earned. I had considered telling Rochelle what had happened— but what was the point? Undoubtedly, she wouldn't want to associate with him.

"But I'm trying to be better than all that shit," said Cosmo. "And I've started today."

I believed it, but it meant nothing to me. Building a trusting friendship takes time, but demolishing it only takes seconds. Unfortunately for Cosmo, building a trusting friendship for a second time takes even longer, and there's no guarantee the foundation will ever be as strong.

"Look, I have something for you," said Cosmo, turning around and walking back to his car.

He opened the passenger's side door and pulled out a bag that had been lying across the back seat. I recognised the bag. I had left it at Cosmo's apartment yesterday afternoon. Although it was just a worn down sports bag, I knew what was inside—two million dollars. In cash.

"This is all Nathan's money, plus the money Mal gave me," said Cosmo, placing the bag down at me feet. "I haven't touched any of it. You can count it if you like, but I haven't taken a cent."

Already, I could see that gaining back my trust meant a lot to him—because if it wasn't for the fact he'd betrayed me, there was no doubt Cosmo would've kept the money for himself. This truly was a milestone, and I was grateful for it.

"Thanks for bringing it to me," I said, with a nod of approval.

I could see the pain in Cosmo's eyes, but I wasn't sure if it was from the guilt, or the fact he'd given up over two million dollars in exchange for my faith in him.

"And now you can use the money for your own good," said Cosmo. "Buy a house or something."

My gaze met his.

"This is not my money, Cosmo." I said, picking up the bag. "It needs to be returned to its rightful owner."

Cosmo stared, barely comprehending my words.

"What? Nathan Burwell is dead," pressed Cosmo. "You are the rightful owner now, man."

"No, I'm not. The new CEO of Channel 5 is the rightful owner. I'm going to call him this afternoon, and I will return the money to him as soon as I can."

Cosmo winced, clearly frustrated and angry with me. Handing over the money was no easy task, but knowing that I would give it back—after we almost died in order to gain it in the first place—would have been brutal for Cosmo to witness.

"Don't return it," he said, desperation seeping through. "Just use it."

I didn't listen. I'd already pulled out my mobile and I began to make the call.

# 55

*August 20ᵗʰ*

"Another short black, my dear?" asked the waitress as she picked up my empty coffee cup.

"Please," I said with a smile, using the 'ol Kennedy charm.

She returned the smile, and sauntered back behind the bench and readied the espresso machine. I was sitting alone in the second last booth against the wall in a little café I had grown to love. It was hidden behind a chain of high-fashion clothing shops, in a small locality called Round Corner. Rochelle and I came here quite frequently. The place was usually busy during lunchtime, but in the afternoon in was almost deserted. I liked coming here, mainly because it was private and secluded. Naturally, I had suggested this meeting location to the new CEO of Channel 5, and he had accepted the invitation. We would be able to talk freely inside the café, without being disturbed. However, he was late. We had settled on a four o'clock meeting, but already it was quarter to five.

Five minutes passed, and the waitress brought over my second coffee. As I indulged, Brad Burwell walked through the front door of the café a little before five o'clock. Brad spotted me, sitting in the second last booth against the wall. He offered a half smile and approached.

Knowing the sense of occasion, I stood and shook Brad's hand.

"Sorry for my tardiness," said Brad. "I was caught up in a meeting."

"I can imagine you have lots of meetings now you're the CEO of Channel 5," I said, taking my seat.

Brad sat down opposite me.

"That's very true. My schedule has changed quite dramatically this week."

284

"Well, I appreciate you driving out here to meet with me, Mr. Burwell."

"Just call me Brad," he said. "No need for formalities here."

I nodded and picked up the sports bag that had been resting on the seat beside me. I slid it across the table to Brad. He picked it up and placed it on the seat next to him, thanking me.

"I have to say, I am surprised you were so willing to return it to me," said Brad, gazing down at the bag.

"It was the right thing to do," I said, plainly. "Otherwise it would've weighed down on my conscience."

He smiled and folded his hands on the table.

"You're a unique individual," said Brad. "People should be more like you."

The waitress approached the table once again and asked Brad if he wanted a coffee. Brad politely declined, watched as the waitress walked away, and turned to me.

"If I may ask," said Brad, now lowering his voice, "what exactly was your situation? I mean, what was your motive behind your actions?"

Brad wasn't being direct, but I knew what he meant. Brad had figured out some time ago that I was blackmailing his step-father under someone else's influence.

"It's complicated," I said, choosing to cut the conversation short.

Brad stared, waiting for more information, but I wasn't going to take it any further. What had transpired over the last few weeks was now in the past, and I wanted to keep it in the past.

"However," I said, pulling a USB from my pocket. "I want you to have this."

I handed Brad the USB. He studied it for a moment, but then looked up, uncomprehending.

"The footage," I said. "What you have in your hand is the only surviving copy of the recording I obtained a few days ago."

Instantly, Brad knew what it was. I had handed over the video of Nathan's crimes. I could have uploaded the footage to the Internet—anonymously—without any trouble at all, but my battle with Nathan Burwell was over. It was true that I still didn't like the fact Nathan had not been exposed for all his wrong-doings, but it was not my place to decide whether to release the footage or not, so I had given it to Brad. He was in control now.

Brad clutched the USB in his hand, with his eyes down.

"I destroyed all the other copies, but I kept that one," I explained. "The power I had was too great for me, so I'm leaving it up to you to decide what you want to do with it."

"My step-father is dead," said Brad, after some time, "so there is no point in dragging his name through the mud now that he is gone. Besides, it's my reputation I have to worry about now. I have to do what is right for my family."

"So you'll destroy it?"

"Yes," replied Brad.

I had expected his response. Besides, if the footage had been released, it would have opened more questions into Nathan's suicide. Overall, it was probably best to move on. However, Nathan hadn't acted alone when carrying out his crimes. He'd had an accomplice— namely, Dustin Pinfold, his bodyguard. Although it was probably not my place, I asked Brad what would become of Dustin and the rest of Nathan's bodyguards.

"It's been taken care of," said Brad with a half smile. "They're no longer working for my family or the network. Let's just say, they've been exposed for all their sins."

I nodded, satisfied with the answer.

"Well, thanks again for coming out here to meet with me," I said, knowing that it was time to part ways.

Brad stood. I did likewise, and we shook hands. Brad then picked up the sports bag and slung it over his shoulder.

"Thank you, Mr. Kennedy," said Brad, and he turned around to leave.

And for maybe a second, I let him go, but his final statement buzzed in my brain. It took maybe another second to put two and two together, but at last I worked out that something was amiss.

286

"Brad," I called out, feeling adrenaline rise from within. "What did you call me?"

"What?"

"Just now—you called me by my surname."

Brad's eyes changed. He stared back at me, opened his mouth to talk, but failed to find the words. In a moment of panic, Brad pushed open the café door and walked out.

I probably should have let him go, but goddamn it, I wanted an answer.

I slipped a ten-dollar note under my empty coffee cup, and dashed out of the café. I saw Brad walking briskly to his car. I followed.

"Brad!" I called out. "Wait up a sec."

He ignored me. He just kept on walking.

"I never told you my name," I said, walking faster and faster. "How is it that you somehow know?"

Brad unlocked his car, his hand shaking as he turned the key, and put the sports bag inside the car. He then slipped behind the wheel. I grabbed the driver's side door before Brad had the chance to close it.

"I used a false identity when dealing with you and Nathan," I hissed, staring down at him, "but you know my surname is Kennedy. How can that be?"

Brad didn't look at me. He stared out the windscreen, wishing he could disappear, but I wasn't going to go until I was given an explanation. I needed an answer.

Eventually, knowing there was nothing else to do, Brad caved in.

"Get in," said Brad, hands clasped over the wheel, "and I'll tell you."

I complied and walked around the car to the passenger's side. I opened the door and slid inside. Just as I closed my door, Brad closed his.

"My step-father," began Brad, still not looking at me. "He learned of your name the night he died."

At first, the fact did not sink in. I had been so vigilant when concealing my identity, so I couldn't understand how it was possible. But then another thought struck me, and something did not quite add up.

"That doesn't make the slightest bit of sense," I said, defensively. "If Nathan figured out who I was, then why did he commit suicide? Surely he would have sent his men out to hunt me down."

"Yes, he would have," said Brad, "but I stopped him."

"What?"

Brad closed his eyes painfully, as his composure began to crumble.

"My step-father did not commit suicide..." said Brad, his voice fading. "I killed him."

A million different thoughts and questions pierced through my brain, and temporarily jammed, leaving me with the inability to speak. I waited for Brad to talk, but he couldn't. For a while I sat still, completely dumbfounded, but eventually I found my voice.

"Why—?" I said.

"It was more an act of self defence," replied Brad, his voice still frail. "You see, never once did I have a gun in my hand. No. Nathan had the gun. The gun was aimed at me—"

"Back up a second. Why did he have a gun pointed at you?"

Brad exhaled a few times, and forced himself to regain his tranquillity.

"In the hours before his death," he began, "Nathan had been behaving erratically, but of course, I knew why. You had out-smarted my step-father, and he refused to let it go. So, that evening Nathan had been working in the study, and he had a laptop in front of him. It was your laptop."

At first, I couldn't work out how Nathan had my laptop—but I scanned my brain for an explanation, and I found one. After failing to blackmail Nathan for the first time, his security guards had attacked us, taking the items we had, including a laptop.

"Nathan was losing his mind," continued Brad. "He kept looking through every file on that laptop, and eventually he found

288

something. I'm not sure exactly what it was, but a file you had saved on your laptop had your name on it. I was with Nathan when he found it. I had been standing in front of his desk, asking him to retire for the night. But then he found it—and he said your name out loud—Jordan Kennedy."

For a moment the air could not reach my lungs. Just thinking about what may have happened was enough to constrict my breathing.

"Nathan kept saying the name. Over and over," continued Brad. "He then picked up the phone to make the call—you know, for his men to begin the hunt and kill. I slammed my hand down on the phone hook, and refused to let him do it."

"Why—? Why would you do that?"

"I told him I knew about the murders. I told him that he had gone too far, and that the power had gone to his head. Nathan didn't like that. Nathan would silence those with a voice, and he wanted to silence me too."

"And then he tried to kill you," I said, filling in the gaps.

"It happened so quickly," began Brad, still gazing out the windscreen. "In a matter of seconds, Nathan had opened a draw and pulled out a gun. Fearing that his reputation and the foundation he'd built was in jeopardy—he aimed the gun right at me. It was only instinct to go into survival mode. I didn't run, because I knew there was nowhere to go, so I leaned over the table and forced his arm back. I forced it all the way back until it was under his chin. Nathan's finger was already on the trigger, and I may have forced his finger down."

Brad fell silent. I had no words either. I tried to collect my thoughts, but knowing how differently things might have ended was causing destruction in my mind. If Nathan had ordered his guards to find me, I would've been dead. Mal and Isaac would probably still be alive, and they would have killed Rochelle.

I had come so close to losing it all, but Brad's actions had spared us.

"The gun was in Nathan's hand when he died, and I didn't touch it once," said Brad. "It looked like he'd killed himself, so I used a pencil to key in a brief message on his computer, kind of like a suicide note. I wanted to set up the scene to eliminate any possibility of getting caught."

"But—surely there was an investigation into his death? Forensics would have proven you had been with Nathan before he died."

"Of course, but it was my home too. I used the study just as much as Nathan, and besides, I was the one who called the ambulance. When they arrived, they found me on the study floor trying to resuscitate him."

A chill ran across my shoulders, and down my spine.

"You tried to save him?" I asked.

"To be perfectly honest, no. That was not my intent. I tried to resuscitate Nathan as an attempt to tamper with the evidence. Otherwise, they may have found my prints on Nathan's hand and suit as I forced his arm back, but since I had moved Nathan onto the ground, they weren't able to prove that I had been the reason for his death."

"Then what did you tell the police?"

"I made up a whole story about how I was with Nathan when he tried to commit suicide, and how I heroically tried to pull the gun away to stop him from killing himself. I pretended to try and save Nathan before the paramedics arrived at the scene. I was questioned by detectives, but the evidence that Nathan had taken his own life stacked up."

When I first heard Nathan had committed suicide, I simply didn't believe it. It didn't make sense to me, because why would Nathan end his own life when he went to extreme measures to ensure his safety? At least now I knew the truth. I was probably the only other person that would ever know the truth too.

Already, I had decided I would not speak of what I had learned to anybody—not even Rochelle. Besides, at the end of the day, it really didn't matter if Nathan Burwell committed suicide or if he was murdered—because he was dead. It was in the past, and that's where it should be left.

"Where is my laptop now?" I asked.

"I destroyed it," replied Brad, "otherwise somebody else could have found your name and tracked you down."

"Thank you," I said, "and thank you for being honest with me."

At last, Brad looked at me, and managed a half smile. Now that I had been told what I wanted to know, I said goodbye and pushed open the passenger's side door.

"Jordan, wait."

I turned back around to see that Brad had stepped out of his car, holding the sports bag in one hand. He extended his arm out, and tried to give me the bag. I stood still, uncomprehending.

"Keep it," said Brad. "Think of it as hush money."

I stepped back and put my palms up.

"No. Brad—I can't. It's wrong."

"You know my secret, and I need to know you'll keep it to yourself."

"You have my word," I said. "But I don't want your money."

Brad stepped forward and dumped the sports bag by my feet, then made his way back to the car.

"It's yours," he called, just before climbing back into his car. "It's up to you what you do with it."

Before I could protest, Brad had turned on the engine and he drove away. Now I was standing alone in an empty car park, with more than two million dollars at my feet.

I wanted to walk away. I wanted to leave it there, but there was a chance that somebody undeserving would find it, and use it for no good. I put my hands on top of my head and inhaled deeply. I stared at the bag, and after a minute or two, I picked it up.

I couldn't risk letting the money fall into the wrong hands.

***

The last light of the sun vanished behind the skyline and night had fallen.

Winter's icy chill clung to the air, and now I just wanted to be home with Rochelle. My hand was clasped around the bag tightly as I made my way back to my rented car. I fumbled around with the keys and unlocked the driver's side door. I slid into the car, tossed the sports bag on the backseat and locked the doors. For a while, I didn't do anything. I sat alone in the car, taking it all in.

I still had a few unanswered questions, but I guess now was the time to drop it and let it go.

I knew tonight everything would change. After all, money changes everything. What would Rochelle say? At the present time we were both unemployed, paying ridiculously high rent for almost nothing at all—but now we had money. Now we could afford a place of our own, now we could get by as we looked for work. Without a doubt, having money was a blessing. Hell, we could even plan a holiday. Somewhere far away.

I figured that after all Rochelle and I had been through, we were more than deserving of this money. We had faced our toughest battle yet, but now it was time to lick our wounds and get on with life.

I brought the engine to life and pulled off the curb.

Tonight, we would start again.

# 56

*October 13ᵗʰ*

Gazing out into the ocean, I found myself lost in the tranquillity.

The warmth of the midday sun beamed down on me, and the smell of spring wattle trees clung to the air. I was standing barefoot on the deck of my new home. Rochelle and I had moved in just one week ago, but already it felt like home.

We bought ourselves a house beside the beach, in a little place called Killcare. Rochelle and I had been here many times before, and we loved it. It was peaceful and quiet—far from the city and the lives we once had. Our house was small, but it overlooked the entire beach. It was a two-bedroom place with an open-plan setting, but it was enough for us.

I heard Rochelle's footsteps behind me as she padded across the deck. She placed two cups of tea on the deck railing, and put an arm around me. We stood, side-by-side and stared out into the ocean. For a while we said nothing. Instead, we enjoyed a peaceful moment together in the sunshine.

Rochelle and I had changed, but at least we had changed together. We were more aware of our surroundings, and now we did check over our shoulders. After almost losing our lives on countless occasions, we were more sceptical of the people around us.

After what we had endured, you see the world through different eyes.

People say that life is short, but when you're young and naïve, you still take it for granted. I was smart enough to know that I was not indestructible, but I was oblivious to just how dark the real world could truly be. I had survived the London Bombings of 2005, and I could have died. I figured that I'd never be that close to death again, but I was wrong.

In life, death is the only certainty. Eventually, no matter what, we will all die. However, before I take my last breath, I will question myself and wonder—was my time well spent? Some people waste their lives and in their dying days, when they reflect on what they have done during their time on earth, they realise that they have accomplished nothing. I would not do the same. I would use my time wisely and at the end of it, I would make sure it was all worth it. Rochelle vowed to do the same.

"What are you thinking about?" asked Rochelle, nestling her head into my chest.

"Nothing really," I replied, although Rochelle knew it wasn't the truth.

It had been almost two months since the death of Nathan Burwell, but I still think about what happened. It had almost become an obsession—analysing every moment, the memories practically plaguing my conscience. In time, I was sure I would think about it less. However, I had found ways to drown out the distracting thoughts. I kept myself busy. Some days, there was barely a chance to breathe, let alone think.

Moving up the coast had taken a fair chunk of time, as well as picking new furniture with Rochelle. We had also started renovating the backyard—and I had never been much of a handy man or a green thumb, but suddenly I had become one. And yes, we finally had a family dog. We had spent weeks discussing which breed and gender we would buy, and it was therapeutic to do something normal. Truthfully, I wasn't at all fussed about having a dog, but I knew Rochelle wanted one. We had picked up a female German shorthaired pointer from a shelter, and Rochelle had chosen to name her Sassy. We'd only had her for one week, and already I had grown a liking to the dog. Rochelle, of course, adored her.

I'd kept myself busy with my own projects too. Rochelle had put her plans to be a personal trainer on hold, and was keen to get her own small business started. There was a space available at the local surf club and Rochelle had the idea to use the space and turn it into a café. I was there to support her. I was in the process of getting together a small business of my own too. There was a shop space available at Erina Fair Shopping Centre, and I was confident I could open a music store. Of course, I wouldn't be able to do it alone, so Cosmo had volunteered to be my business partner.

Cosmo and I were still on speaking terms, and slowly we were beginning to hang out like we used to. No, I didn't entirely feel comfortable around him, but I would not let it show. As for the attempted assassination, Cosmo and I had never spoken about it again. I wanted to bury it in the past, and clearly, he did too.

In just two months, everything had changed. Having money made all the difference, but so did my perspective of the world. I was more cautious than ever, but I knew I couldn't keep living behind closed doors. So, what could I do to ensure that Rochelle and I would always be protected? I had now armed myself with a gun.

I hadn't told Rochelle I had acquired a gun, because I knew she wouldn't approve. However, I would only use it for self-defence. I might never encounter a trying situation again, but I would keep the gun for peace of mind. Whenever I was out, I kept it on me at all times—somewhere easy for me to reach if I needed to. While I was at home, I kept the gun and a bit of ammo in a shoebox in the back of the wardrobe. I was fairly certain Rochelle would never find it.

For a few minutes longer, Rochelle and I stood on the deck, soaking up the sun and enjoying the view. We finished our cups of tea, and tried to find things to do to keep ourselves occupied.

I followed Rochelle inside, and watched her empty the washing basket in the bedroom.

"What are you doing now?" I asked, sheepishly.

"I've got to get a load of washing on while the weather is good, but I'll need to pick up some groceries later too."

"I'll get the groceries," I said. "I'll just walk over to the bay side and pick some up now."

"Sure you don't mind?"

"Of course not," I said, but truthfully I only wanted to do it to keep myself busy.

"OK, well I'll give you a list of things I need. You can take Sassy for a walk while you're at it."

I was grateful to have something to do, regardless of how little the task was. I picked up my wallet and sunglasses, and quietly walked into the bedroom and pulled out my gun from its hiding place. I tucked it into the back of my shorts and pulled my shirt over the top of it. Sure, I was only walking to the bay side and back, but I never left home without my gun.

As I emerged from the bedroom, Rochelle was waiting for me. She handed me a dog leash and a shopping list, planted a kiss on my cheek and told me not to be too long. I snapped on my sunglasses, slipped on my shoes and stepped outside.

I walked to the back of the house where I was greeted by a dog. Sassy was excitedly waiting by the back gate, and she jumped and chased her tail at the very sight of the leash. I opened up the gate, snapped on the leash before she could run past me, and began my journey to the bay side. Within twenty minutes, I'd walked to the shops. I tied Sassy out the front, walked inside, and read the shopping list as I went.

I scanned my eyes over each item on the list—bread, milk, fruit, vegetables and to my surprise Rochelle had written 'Bath salts and massage oils—for later tonight' and she had drawn a winking smiley face. I grinned.

I grabbed a basket by the door and quickly filled it. I even picked up a bouquet of fresh flowers—beautiful white roses. After all we'd been through, Rochelle and I had never been closer. We finally understood each other on a deeper level, and I couldn't possibly imagine life without her. Rochelle, I was sure, felt the same way about me.

I arrived at the counter and paid for my items. The young girl behind the counter put my shopping into plastic bags and wished me a good day. I thanked her and wished her the same.

I turned around, with my groceries in one hand, and headed towards the exit. On my way out, I took a glance at the customers waiting in line. There was a mother and her newborn baby, a young surfer covered in tattoos, and a man wearing dark shades—and at a first glance, this man seemed all too familiar to me.

As I passed by the man, I found myself double-taking. I'd glanced once, but it was only instinct to turn around again. The man finally turned his head and stared at me. I stared back. I knew him, and I was sure of it. I found myself struggling to put a name to a face, but as he removed his shades—his eyes confirmed his identity.

My body seized up and my blood turned stone cold. It was like my one true enemy had been resurrected from the grave. I failed to comprehend it.

"Hey," said Eamon Bronson, staring right at me. "What the hell are you doing here?"

# 57

He waited for me to answer, but I could not find my voice.

This situation was impossible. Other customers were starting to turn around to see what was happening, and I had drawn the attention of others. Was this a case of mistaken identity? Doubtful. He had spoken to me first, and even questioned what *I* was doing here. He had visibly aged since the last time we'd met, but I was not wrong—the man standing in front of me was indeed Eamon Bronson.

And he was alive—which was a fact I simply could not comprehend.

Without warning, Eamon snapped his shades back on and briskly walked towards the exit. I followed. As I dashed outside, Eamon was already running up a hill, trying to get as far away from me as he could. I wasn't going to let that son of a bitch get away so easily. I had questions, and I needed answers.

I dumped the shopping bags on the ground and ran like hell. Up ahead, Eamon turned his head around to see if I was following, and when he realised I was, he darted off the pathway and ran in between two shop buildings. I'd caught up to him, and without even a second thought, I pulled out my gun.

Eamon looked over his shoulder again and saw the gun. Immediately, he stopped. He raised two hands, begged me not to come any closer, but I grabbed him by the throat, pinned him against a brick wall, and jammed the gun directly under his chin.

"Please," cried Eamon, barely able to get the words out, "don't kill me."

My hand was shaking as I held the gun in place. Eamon had asked me not to kill him, but I could not fathom how he was still alive. He had died. I had seen footage of his death. Mal Lawson and Isaac Fuller had murdered him while he was in prison. I tried to talk, but a combination of hatred and confusion had forced my jaw shut.

"Take it easy, Jordan," he croaked. "Just put the gun away."

At last, my animosity broke through the surface.

"You have exactly three seconds to explain how the hell this is possible!" I screamed, digging the gun further under his chin.

Eamon gasped and choked, so I loosened my grip around his throat, but only slightly.

"I'm not saying anything while you have a gun pointed at me."

"Answer me!" I barked. "How can you be alive?"

"Well, I'm breathing, aren't I?"

I quickly retracted the gun away and sliced the nozzle across his face. The force had been strong enough to break through the skin. Blood began to trickle from the wound, but I didn't care. I wanted answers. I needed closure.

"I saw you die," I said, trying to control the tone of my voice. "Mal Lawson taunted you, before Isaac Fuller finished you off. I've seen the video, Eamon."

"And yet here I am," he said, a twisted smile appearing on his face.

I kept the gun steady, and slowly pulled down the hammer. The moment Eamon heard that sound, he tried to squirm free, but I kept him pinned against the wall. Would I fire the gun? No, I wouldn't. Eamon was not the threat in this situation—I was. So why pull down the hammer? Eamon needed to know that I was serious.

"The video," I said, the words falling hard. "A few months ago Mal sent me a video of a man being murdered. Somebody died, so if it wasn't you, then who did?"

"Nobody died," replied Eamon, gasping for air. "The footage was a setup."

"Don't play games with me."

"I'm not! It's the truth, I swear."

"But in the video, there was a body. Somebody got shot. There was screaming and blood, and Mal told me it was you."

"Rest assured that was me in the video, but it was staged," said Eamon, making every word perfectly clear. "Mal, Isaac and I were all in on it, and we created a video just for you. We didn't use real bullets. I was being hit by rubber bullets, and I had blood packs concealed under my clothing. We tried to make it as legit as possible, and sure, it wasn't perfect, but it obviously had you convinced."

I shook my head, still not believing what I was hearing.

"But Mal showed me a photograph of your dead body," I snapped. "Your face was practically blown off."

"It was photo shopped, Jordan. I edited the photo myself."

Thousands of questions churned around my mind. My head was spinning. I had to focus, but I began to think back to the day I first saw the footage. I thought it was the real deal. I even showed the footage to both Rochelle and Cosmo—but they were convinced it was fake. They had both dismissed the footage without a second thought. Why couldn't I see what they had seen? How had I been fooled?

Maybe I was always going to believe what I wanted to believe.

"None of this makes any sense," I said, my head pounding. "How did you know Mal and Isaac? Why would they help you fake your death?"

"Just over three months ago, Mal and Isaac visited me in prison," said Eamon, no longer struggling. "When they came during visiting hours, I didn't even know who they were, but I learned quickly. They had come to provoke me, and they wanted me dead for what I did to their friends. I didn't want to die. So, I bargained with them. I did have something I could offer them."

"And what was that?"

Eamon smiled and simply said, "You."

I stared, uncomprehending.

"You see," began Eamon, "I was in quite the predicament, and I needed to get out of that situation. Mal was pissed, and he told me about the Nathan Burwell assignment. He said I had killed the only man who could've finished the job. I said he was wrong. So that's when I told them about you. I said that you had potential, and that you were capable of filling some big shoes. I said that you would be able to pull off the Nathan Burwell assignment."

I felt something twist and knot deep within my chest. At last, it made sense. Mal had continuously told me that somebody had recommended me for the assignment, and now I knew who had. Eamon. That son of a bitch put me in the line of fire to save his own skin—and I'd almost lost Rochelle for good.

Fury engulfed my body. The reaction made me clasp my hand tighter around his neck. For a moment, I deprived him of air. Eamon panicked and furiously tried to pull my hand away, but he couldn't. I had him pinned against the wall, still with the gun under his chin. His face turned many different shades of colour. Just before Eamon could pass out, I loosened my grip.

He coughed and spluttered, and I enjoyed watching him suffer. Yet still, my integration was not over.

"You've made it clear you bargained with Mal to ensure your own safety, but that doesn't explain how you managed to get out of prison."

"Mal and I had an agreement," heaved Eamon, still struggling to breathe. "He said he would get me out of prison under one condition—I would have to monitor you. He wanted me to watch over you to ensure you wouldn't fail. But I guess Mal trusted me too much, because I slipped under the radar and broke away."

Eamon had betrayed Mal, but I guess that was to be expected. And since Eamon had not monitored me like he was supposed to, Cosmo had been forced to fill his place.

"Eamon Bronson is dead," he continued. "To the rest of the world, I don't exist anymore, and that's because my record in prison says I was beaten to death by other inmates."

"How is that possible?"

"Mal had connections. Once I said yes to the agreement, he organised to have me smuggled out of jail, and he had paperwork altered to make it seem like I'd been killed whist serving out my sentence. You underestimated just how much power he did have."

"But if records say you died in prison, surely there would have been an investigation, and a coroner's report to prove your identification. I mean, wasn't there a body?"

"Once again, Mal had connections," explained Eamon. "Paperwork was tampered with. There are documents of my detailed post-mortem examination—but it was not my body. Mal pulled a lot of strings to have me walk free."

"...but Mal hated you," I said, my voice sounded distant to me.

"That's right. Mal loathed me, and I'm sure if I'd stuck around to monitor you like I was supposed to—he would have killed me in the end. I was sure of it. So that's why I vanished. As soon as he got me out of prison, I was gone, and I've been in hiding ever since."

"But the video," I said again, still hovering in and out of disbelief. "Why would you go through so much effort to fake your death?"

"The video was my idea—not Mal's. He and Isaac only went along with it because they thought it was a necessity. I told them that it would be impossible for me to monitor you in close range, especially when I was supposed to be in prison, so I told them I'd watch you from a distance under a new identity. Besides, I knew footage of my death would rattle you. I wanted you to think I was dead."

"But why?"

"Why do you think? How else could I start a new life? I was serving a thirty year sentence in prison. So when I saw an opportunity to get out? You bet I took it."

I fell into silence, and tried to gather my thoughts. Eamon Bronson was the reason for all my pain. I had always loathed Eamon, but now my hatred of him was far deeper—right down to the bone. He was scum. Just like vermin, he did not deserve to live. And Eamon was right—I was a lot happier thinking he was dead. I knew I could not pretend this encounter had never occurred, so I had two options; let this son of a bitch go, or take vengeance and put Eamon in his grave—where he belonged.

As I contemplated the options, there was clarity. A memory I had long forgotten suddenly surfaced in my mind.

"I saved your life once," I hissed.

Thinking back to the moment, I recalled how close Eamon had come to death. Beau O'Riley had aimed a gun at him and prepared to fire, but I had intervened in the last second. I had stepped forward and risked my life, rescuing Eamon from death's grip. Now I was wishing I'd let Beau take the shot. If I'd let Eamon die, then the ordeal I had recently endured would have never happened.

I wanted revenge. I rested my finger on the trigger and wanted to fire. Words could not describe how much I wanted to discharge my weapon. For a moment, I closed my eyes and tried to imagine how good it would feel to take away his life. I almost wanted to smile, but alas, I knew my conscience would not let me take the shot. I had purchased the gun for protection, not for vengeance.

I thought about turning him into the police—I could ruin his life in an instant. However, I feared the repercussions. There would be questions, an investigation and in turn, I could potentially put my own welfare in jeopardy.

With no options left, I would be forced to turn a blind eye.

At last, I let go of Eamon and lowered my weapon. I stood back, gun by my side, and stared. Eamon stared right back at me, smiled and said,

"Still don't have that killer instinct, huh?"

I raised the gun once more.

"Don't tempt me," I snarled. "If it were a different time or place I wouldn't hesitate, but not here. Not now. I've finally got things going right and I'm not going to ruin it now."

Eamon maintained a crooked smile.

"But if you cross my path again," I said, "trust I will not give a second thought before I shoot you dead. So you'd better leave right now."

The smile faded.

"For the time being, Killcare is my home," said Eamon, stepping forward. "I've been keeping a low profile here for months. I'm waiting for a new passport under a new identity, and once I have it, I'll be leaving this country. However, it's a slow process so I'm not leaving Killcare anytime soon. Besides, if it hadn't been for me, you wouldn't know this place even existed."

"You're not staying here," I hissed. "Rochelle and I live here now. You need to find somewhere else to go."

Eamon opened his mouth to argue, but now staring down the barrel of the gun, he knew the fight was lost. For a moment, we stood still. I kept the gun steady.

"Just remember what you promised me the last time we met," said Eamon, now lowering his voice.

"What the hell are you talking about?" I barked.

"You promised to keep Amy and Millie safe. Not a day goes by when I don't think about them, but we can never be together again. I asked you to protect them from harm. Have you held up your end of the bargain?"

I vaguely remembered making the promise to always look out for my sister and niece——but it was a given. Why did he still care? Eamon was no longer married to Amy, and he was never Millie's biological father, so why bring it up now?

"Well? Have you?" asked Eamon, waiting for my answer.

"Of course," I said, as I gripped my gun a little tighter. "I'm doing a better job than you ever did."

He frowned. I guess nobody liked hearing the truth. Without another word to say, Eamon lowered his head and turned his back. With heavy steps, Eamon walked away, vanishing into the world once more.

Finally, he was gone. I was hoping that it would be the last I'd ever see of him—but there would always be an uncertainty. I waited a minute or two, just to make sure he didn't return, and then I allowed the world to crumble down on me. I tucked my gun away, placed both hands behind my head and exhaled. I was still in disbelief, still shaking from an impossible encounter. I fought to keep my composure, and after everything I had been through, it was no easy task.

Minutes passed. Rochelle was probably at home wondering what was taking me so long, so I made my way back to the footpath and tried to press on. I picked up the groceries I had dumped beside the footpath, and untied Sassy from the front of the shop. I walked home, pretending that everything was still the same, but inside, I knew everything had changed.

When I arrived home, Rochelle was sprawled across the leather sofa, reading a book.

I walked through the front door, but she did not even acknowledge me. Rochelle had the ability to engage herself so deeply into literature that she was able to block out the world. I wasn't as fortunate, and even when I tried to read I was constantly distracted by my own thoughts.

Right now, my thoughts were consuming me.

I unpacked the shopping, not saying a word. The encounter with my enemy was still playing on my mind and it had ripped open old wounds. It was then I remembered about the gun. After putting the milk away in the fridge, I quietly entered the bedroom and put my weapon away. I took a great comfort in knowing the gun had already proved to be useful.

Returning from the bedroom, I stood in the living area and watched Rochelle read. What could I say to her? Would she even believe me? I exhaled deeply.

"What's wrong?" she asked, finally looking up at me.

I locked eyes with Rochelle. I had the intent to tell her, but now gazing into those hazel eyes, I knew I didn't have it in me.

"It's nothing," I said, choosing to protect her from the truth.

Rochelle put down her book and moved over and made some room for me. I sat down beside her and found her hand. I held it for a moment, and she leaned closer and kissed me. I felt my body relax. Her love was enough to heal any wound.

Rochelle rested her head on my lap, while I gently stroked her hair. We listened to the waves crashing in the not so far distance, as the crickets in the backyard started with their song.

All my life, I had always wanted more, but I had been blind to what I already had. I was healthy, I was happy, I owned a beautiful home by the sea and I shared it with the most amazing woman in the world—and for once in my life, that was good enough for me.

# Loved this book?

Jordan Kennedy will be returning in the next exciting thriller **Cigarette Burns**.

Coming soon.

# Acknowledgments

As always, here's a big thank you to my loving family. You guys are the best.

To all my friends, old & the new, thank you for encouraging me. I appreciate every single one of you. I've been chasing this dream of mine for over fifteen years now, and some of you are still here, supporting me every step of the way. Cheers!

JH—I've changed the CD for good. Thank you.

A huge thanks to Lauren for editing the manuscript, and many thanks to my proof readers—Sara and Tez (or Tezza, if you like...)

Lastly, thank you, dear reader, for taking this journey with me.

- Jen Dennis

# About the Author

Jen Dennis was born and raised in Sydney, Australia. At the age of just thirteen, Jen discovered a love for storytelling, and wrote prolifically in the years that followed. In 2013, Jen published her first work, a children's picture book *Snoozy Sam*. Jen also writes for adults and teens, in a range of different genres.

For news and updates, you can find Jen Dennis on Facebook & Twitter.